USA TODAY bestse[...]
London, England. S[...]
sons—which gives [...]
insight into the male [...]
film journalist. She [...] her job, which involves
getting swept up in a world of high emotion, sensual
excitement, funny and feisty women, sexy and
tortured men and glamorous locations where laundry
doesn't exist. Once she turns off her computer she
often does chores—usually involving laundry!

Canadian **Dani Collins** knew in high school that she
wanted to write romance for a living. Twenty-five
years later, after marrying her high school sweetheart,
having two kids with him, working at several generic
office jobs and submitting countless manuscripts,
she got The Call. Her first Mills & Boon novel won
the Reviewers' Choice Award for Best First in Series
from *RT Book Reviews*. She now works in her own
office, writing romance.

CONTRACTED AS HIS CINDERELLA BRIDE

HEIDI RICE

THE MAID'S SPANISH SECRET

DANI COLLINS

MILLS & BOON

First Published in Great Britain 2019
by Mills & Boon, an imprint of HarperCollins*Publishers*
1 London Bridge Street, London, SE1 9GF

Contracted as His Cinderella Bride © 2019 by Heidi Rice

The Maid's Spanish Secret © 2019 by Dani Collins

ISBN: 978-0-263-27353-3

MIX
Paper from
responsible sources
FSC™ C007454

This book is produced from independently certified FSC™ paper
to ensure responsible forest management.
For more information visit www.harpercollins.co.uk/green.

Printed and bound in Spain
by CPI, Barcelona

CONTRACTED AS HIS CINDERELLA BRIDE

HEIDI RICE

To my editor Bryony—I couldn't do this without you!

CHAPTER ONE

'CALLING RIDERS IN the vicinity of the Strand. Got a pick-up at the jeweller's Mallow and Sons. Drop-off in Bloomsbury.'

Alison Jones skidded to a stop at the amber light on Waterloo Bridge to decipher the crackle of the dispatcher's voice on her radio through the driving rain.

Cold water had seeped through her waterproof hours ago as the rush hour had slowed to a crawl in London's West End. She'd been ready to crash head-first into a bubble bath since six o'clock and lick her wounds from another evening pedalling the mean streets of Soho. But once she'd registered the instruction, she clicked on the call button and shouted into her receiver. 'Rider 524. Got it!'

She still had several instalments to pay on the debt she'd racked up four years ago for her mum's funeral—and next month's rent on her room in the house she shared with a group of other fashion students in Whitechapel wasn't going to pay itself. Plus she'd already reached peak misery for the evening. She certainly couldn't get any wetter.

The dispatcher confirmed her pick-up as she tried to focus through her exhaustion.

'Delivery's a wedding ring,' he shouted. 'Client's name for drop-off is Dominic LeGrand, address is...'

A shiver wracked Ally's body, the address barely registering as the name scraped across her consciousness, triggering a wealth of disturbing memories from the summer she had turned thirteen.

The heady scent of wild grass and roses. The baking heat of the Provence sun warming her skin. Pierre Le-Grand's face—so handsome, so charming—his voice deep and paternalistic.

'Call me Papa, Alison.'

Her mother's smile, so untroubled and full of hope.

'Pierre is definitely the one, Ally. He loves me. He'll take care of us now.'

And then the pulse of heat settled low in her abdomen as she pictured Dominic. The memory of Pierre's sixteen-year-old son was as vivid and disturbing as if she'd seen him yesterday, not twelve years ago.

Those sensual lips always quirked in an insolent, *don't-give-a-damn* smile; those chocolate eyes full of resentment and secrets; the mysterious crescent-shaped scar that hooked his left eyebrow; the brutally short dark blond hair that had lightened in the sun and given his brooding beauty a golden glow.

Dominic, who had been beautiful and bad and fascinating, and landed like a fallen angel into that perfect summer bringing with him danger and excitement.

'I can't take the job,' Ally croaked into the receiver, as the memory of her final night in Provence returned, too.

Her mother's face—so sad, so fragile—a purpling bruise marring her cheekbone. The cloying scent of lavender and gin. Her mother's voice—frantic and fearful and slightly slurred.

'Something terrible's happened, baby. Pierre's very angry with me and Dominic. We have to leave.'

A bus horn blared beside her, jerking Ally out of her trance. She shoved the distressing, confusing memories back where they belonged. When she'd buried her mother four years ago, she'd finally stopped reliving the horror of that night as she stood over the grave and felt nothing but relief that Monica Jones was finally at peace.

She couldn't take this job. She didn't want to see Dominic LeGrand again. Especially as Dominic wasn't the reckless, delinquent boy who had starred in all those innocent adolescent fantasies a lifetime ago, but a billionaire property developer now. Hadn't the tabloids dubbed him 'Love-Rat LeGrand' a year ago after one of his supermodel girlfriends had sold her story of their affair for a six-figure sum? The wedding ring had to be for the fairytale romance with Mira Somebody Ally had read about a month ago.

'What do you mean you're not taking the job? I just put it through the system.' The dispatcher's voice sliced into Ally's misery. 'Either you do it or I'm pulling you from the roster. Make up your mind.'

Ally breathed in and breathed out, trying to control the panic making the air clog in her lungs.

She *had* to take this job. She didn't have a choice. She couldn't afford to lose the work. Pressing her freezing finger on the radio, she spoke into the receiver. 'Okay, I'll take it. Give me that address again.'

'The wedding's off, Mira. Your hook-up with Andre the ski instructor has seen to that.' Dominic LeGrand kept his voice even; he wasn't sad or upset, he was furious. They'd had a deal. And his so-called fiancée had broken it.

'But I… I told you it was nothing, Dominic.' Tears sheened Mira's eyes, her voice breaking with emotion. Dominic's impatience sharpened his fury. The woman had the emotional maturity of a two-year-old.

'I thought I made it plain before we entered into this

arrangement I expected exclusivity. I'm not marrying a woman I can't trust.'

'But I didn't sleep with Andre… I swear,' Mira said. 'I was a little drunk and flirtatious, that was all.' She leaned across his desk, her breasts pressing provocatively against her low-cut gown, her lips pursed into the pout he'd found hot two months ago, when they'd first met. 'I'm not going to lie—I quite like that you're a little jealous,' she added.

The coy flirtatious look on her face was probably supposed to be enticing. It wasn't.

'I'm not jealous, Mira. I'm angry. It's a breach of our agreement. It could jeopardise the Waterfront deal.' Which was the only reason he'd asked her to marry him in the first place.

The Jedah Consortium, who owned the tract of real estate in Brooklyn he wanted to develop, was made up of conservative businessmen from a string of oil-rich Middle Eastern countries. They'd been wary of doing business with him after Catherine Zalinski's kiss-and-tell article last year had made him look like a man who couldn't control his own libido, let alone the women in his life.

This marriage was supposed to fix that, until pictures of his fiancée kissing her ski instructor had hit the tabloids this afternoon.

'The whole purpose of this marriage was to stop any more unsavoury gossip about my private life,' he added, in case she didn't get it.

'But you left me alone for a whole month.' The pout became more pronounced. 'I waited for you to come to Klosters but you didn't. We haven't slept together in even longer. What did you expect me to do?'

He hadn't had time to go all the way to Klosters to visit her. The fact he hadn't been particularly desperate to ease the sexual drought confirmed something else—

this agreement had been ill-advised from the start. He'd grown bored of Mira even sooner than he'd expected, in bed as well as out of it.

'I expected you to keep your mouth off other men. And your legs closed.'

'Dominic, don't say things like that.' The shocked hurt in her eyes looked genuine. Almost. 'It makes me feel cheap.'

He let his gaze coast down the designer dress he'd paid for.

'Mira, the one thing you're not is cheap,' he said wryly.

She stiffened at the insult.

'Find your own way out,' he said. 'We're done here.'

'You… You heartless bastard.'

Mira's hand whipped out so fast, he heard the crack before the pain blazed across his cheekbone.

He leapt out of his chair, holding her wrist before she could strike him again. But the smarting pain where she'd struck him had a bitter memory spinning back of another slap, from the summer he'd finally been invited into his father's world—only to be kicked out again a month later—and the voice of the girl who had defended him.

'You mustn't hit Dominic, you'll hurt him, Papa.'

'Some people deserve to be hurt, ma petite.'

'You're right, Mira, I *am* heartless. I'm also a bastard.' He ground out the words, the hollow ache in his chest at the memory of that slap an emotion he'd thought he'd cauterised long ago. How infuriating to find he hadn't…quite. 'I consider that a strength,' he added, releasing Mira's wrist. 'Now get out. Before I have you arrested for assault.'

Mira's face collapsed, her lips trembling. 'I hate you.'

So what? he thought dispassionately, as she swung round and rushed out of his study.

Hearing the front door slam, he walked to the drinks

cabinet, swiped the trickle of blood at the corner of his mouth, then poured himself a glass of single malt Scotch.

He only had a week to find himself another wife to secure the deal he needed to take his business to the next level. The business he'd built from nothing after crawling off his father's estate that summer, his ribs feeling as if they were being crushed in a vice, the welts on his back burning.

He'd flagged down a truck, and the driver had taken pity on him, giving him a ride all the way to Paris. As he'd sunk in and out of consciousness on that endless, agonising journey, he had promised himself he would never see or speak to his father again. And that he would build something to prove to his father, and everyone else who had rejected him, had belittled or dismissed him, that they were wrong.

He welcomed the sting as the liquor hit his split lip.

He would find another wife. Preferably one who did exactly what he told her and knew how to keep her legs closed. But tonight he planned to celebrate a lucky escape.

CHAPTER TWO

'GET OUT OF my way, you filthy...' The woman's voice trailed off into a sneer as she shoved Ally and her bike out of the way.

Ally stumbled, rammed into the gatepost, the bike's pedal scraping against her calf as the woman marched past her and got into a sleek red sports car.

Ally hauled the bike up. She would have shouted after the woman, but she was too tired and too anxious to bother—and anyway the woman wouldn't have heard her in the rain.

The car peeled away from the kerb in a squeal of rubber.

Ally watched the red tail lights disappear round the corner of the Georgian garden square.

Hadn't that been Mira Whatshername? The woman the wedding ring she had in her pack was for?

The woman had looked furious. Maybe there was trouble in paradise? Ally pushed the thought to one side.

So not your business.

She wheeled the bike to the back of the mansion house, which stood at the end of the square in its own grounds. Taking a fortifying breath, she propped the bike against the back wall and pressed her freezing finger into the brass bell at the trade entrance.

He won't answer the door. He'll have staff to do it. Stop freaking out.

The rain had reached monsoon levels as she'd left Mallow and Sons. It beat down on her now, drenching her. The tiny package she'd collected weighed several tons in the bike bag hooked over her back.

Unfortunately the freezing March rain, and the numbness in all her extremities, not to mention the now throbbing ache in her calf muscle, felt like the least of her worries as the harsh memories continued to mess with her head.

Stepping back from the door, she peered up at the house. Every window was dark, bar one on the floor above. Swallowing heavily, she pressed the bell again, with a bit more conviction. A figure appeared at the window. Tall and broad and indistinct through the deluge. Her heartbeat clattered into her throat.

It's not him, it's not him, it's not him.

The pep talk became a frantic prayer as she detected the sound of footsteps inside the house.

She jerked her bag to her front. She should get the wedding ring out so she could hand it over as soon as the door opened.

She fumbled with the wet fastenings, her heartbeat getting so loud it drowned out the sound of the storm.

A light in the hallway snapped on, casting a yellow glow over the rain-slicked panels, then a large silhouette filled the bevelled glass.

Ally barely had a chance to brace herself before the door swung wide. A tall man filled the space, his face thrown into shadow by the light from the hallway. But Ally's numbed fingers seized on the bike bag when he spoke—his deep, even voice thrusting a knife into the memories lurking in her belly like malevolent beasts.

'Bonsoir.'

The French accent rippled over her skin, sending sickening shivers of heat through her chilled body—and making the ball of shame wedged in her solar plexus swell.

How could he still have the power to do that? When she was a grown woman now, not an impressionable teenager in the throes of puberty?

'You'd better come inside before you drown,' he murmured, standing aside to hold the door open.

The manoeuvre lit the harsh planes and angles of his face. Ally stood locked in place absorbing the face she had once spent hours fantasising about.

Dominic had always been striking, but maturity had turned his boyish masculine beauty into something so intense it was devastating.

The blond buzz cut had darkened into a tawny brown streaked with gold, and was long enough now to curl around the collar of his shirt. Those dark chocolate eyes had no laughter lines yet, but then that would have been a contradiction in terms—because the Dominic she remembered had never laughed. A new bump on the bridge of his nose joined the old scar on his brow, while the shadow of stubble marked him out as a man now instead of a boy.

As Ally's gaze devoured the changes, she registered how much more jaded the too-old look in his eyes had become, and how much more ruthless the cynical curve of those sensual lips.

The inappropriate shivers turned into seismic waves.

'*Vite, garçon,* before we *both* drown.' The snapped command made her realise she'd been staring.

She forced herself to walk past him into the hallway.

Just give him the ring, then this nightmare will be over.

She bent to fumble with her bike bag, wishing she

hadn't removed her helmet, but luckily he didn't seem to be looking at her. He had called her a boy, after all.

The drip, drip, drip of the rain coming off her waterproof seemed deafening in the silent hallway as he closed the door.

'You're a girl,' he murmured.

She made the mistake of looking round.

His scarred brow lifted as the chocolate gaze glided over her figure, making the growled acknowledgement disturbingly intimate.

'I'm a woman,' she said. 'Is that a problem?'

'Non.' His lips lifted on one side. The cynical half-smile reminded her so forcefully of the boy, she had to stifle a gasp. 'Do I know you?' he asked. 'You look familiar.'

'No,' she said, but the denial came out on a rasp of panic as her hand closed over the jeweller's bag.

Please don't let him recognise me—it will only make this worse.

She yanked the bag out and thrust it towards him. 'Your delivery, Mr LeGrand.'

She kept her head bent as he took the package, snatching her hand away as warm fingertips brushed her palm and the buzz of reaction zipped up her arm.

'You're shivering. Stay and dry off.' It sounded more like a demand than a suggestion, but she shook her head.

'I'm fine,' she said, drawing out her data console. 'Sign in the box,' she added, trying for efficient and impersonal, and getting breathless instead.

He tucked the jeweller's bag under his arm and took the data-recording device, brushing her hand again.

'You're freezing,' he said, sounding now and impatient. 'You should stay until the storm passes.' He signed his name and handed the device back. 'It's the least

I can do after dragging you out in this weather on a fool's errand.'

'A fool's errand? How?' she asked, then wanted to bite off her tongue.

Shut up, Ally, why did you ask him that?

Starting a conversation was the last thing she needed to do. Her heart thumped her chest wall so hard she was amazed she didn't pass out. To her surprise, though, he answered her.

'A fool's errand because I broke off the engagement approximately ten minutes ago...' The cynical tone reminded her again of the boy.

No wonder Mira Something had been furious. She'd just been dumped.

He ripped open the package and drew out the velvet jeweller's box, then flipped it open.

Ally's heart stuttered. The ring was exquisite—a platinum and gold band.

The irony washed through her, as she thought of another ring.

The ring her mother had said his father had offered her all through the summer. A dream that had died that terrible night when Pierre LeGrand had kicked them out, but the loss of which had tortured her mother for the rest of her life.

'Pierre was the only man who ever really loved me and I ruined it all, baby.'

Her mother had blamed herself, but what had she done to make Pierre so angry?

Dominic snapped the ring box closed, dragging Ally back to the present. 'Which makes this a rather expensive waste of money.'

'I'm sorry,' she mumbled, trying to swallow down the

volatile emotions starting to choke her. Emotions she didn't want to examine too closely.

'Don't be,' he said. 'The engagement was a mistake. The eighty grand I spent on this ring is collateral damage.'

The offhand remark had the shame and guilt twisting in her gut.

She shoved her data device back into the pocket on her bike bag, her fingers trembling with the effort it was taking to hold back the raw emotions.

What was happening to her? Why was she making this into a big thing, when it really wasn't? Not any more. Her mother was dead, and so was Pierre. It was all ancient history now.

'I should go. I've got other jobs to get to,' she said. She just wanted to leave. To forget again. It was too painful to go over all those memories. To remember how bright and vivacious her mother had been that summer, and the hollow shell she had become after it.

'Come in and have a drink, warm up,' he said, or rather demanded.

Was he coming on to her? The thought wasn't as horrific as it should have been, which had the knot of shame in her stomach tightening. But then the clammy feel of the soaked and grubby fabric sticking to her skin made her aware of how much like a drowned rat she must look.

This man dated supermodels and heiresses—women with style and grace and effortless sex appeal. Something she had never possessed, even when she hadn't spent the last six hours cycling around London's West End in a monsoon.

'And we can deal with your leg,' he added.

'What?' she mumbled.

'Your leg.' The chocolate gaze dipped. 'It's bleeding.'

She glanced down to see blood seeping out of a gash

on her calf, exposed by a rip in her leggings. It must have been caused by her altercation with his fiancée—or rather his ex-fiancée—and she'd been too cold to feel it.

'It's nothing,' she said. 'I have to go.'

But as she turned to leave, he spoke again.

'*Arrêtes.* It's *not* nothing. It's bleeding. It could get infected. You're not going out there until it has been cleaned.'

The emotion started to choke her. She couldn't stay, couldn't accept his kindness—however brusque and domineering.

'I've got work, another job,' she added, frantically. 'I can't stay.'

'I'll pay for your time, damn it, if the problem is money. I don't want an injured cycle messenger on my conscience as well as an eighty-grand ring.'

He was too close, surrounding her in a cloud of spicy cologne and the sweet subtle whiff of whisky. Her pulse points buzzed and throbbed in an erratic rhythm.

But then he hooked a knuckle under her chin, and nudged her chin up.

'Wait a minute. I *do* know you.' His eyes narrowed as he studied her face. For the first time, he was actually seeing her. The intensity of his gaze set off bonfires of sensation all over her chilled skin. She fumbled with the helmet she had hooked over her other arm, desperate to put it on, to stop him recognising her.

But it was too late as the swift spike of memory crossed his face.

'*Monique?*' he murmured.

Tears stung her eyes. 'I'm not Monica. Monica's dead. I'm her daughter.'

'Allycat?' he said, looking as stunned as she felt.

Allycat.

The nickname reverberated in her head, the one he'd

given her all those years ago. The name she had been so proud of. Once.

As if he'd flipped a switch, the adrenaline she'd been running on ever since she'd got the commission drained away, until all that was left was the shame, and anxiety. And the inappropriate heat.

She dragged in tortured breaths, struggling to contain the choking sob rising up her torso. She didn't have the strength to resist him any more. And what would be the point, anyway?

'Breathe, Allycat,' he murmured.

She gulped in air, trying to steady herself, and got a lungful of his scent—spiced with pine and soap.

'Bad night?'

'The worst.' She bit back the harsh laugh at his sanguine tone. And shuddered, the pain in her ribs excruciating as she struggled to hold the sobs at bay.

What exactly are you so upset about? Having Dominic LeGrand pity you isn't the worst thing that's ever happened to you.

'I know the feeling,' he said, the wry smile only making him look more handsome—and more utterly unattainable.

She forced a smile to her lips as she shifted away from him, and scooped up the helmet that had clattered to the floor.

'It was nice seeing you again, Dominic,' she said, although nothing could have been further from the truth. *Nice* had never been a word to describe Dominic LeGrand. 'I really do have to go now, though.'

But as she headed for the door, he stepped in front of her. 'Don't go, Allycat. Come in and dry off and clean up your leg. My offer still stands.'

She lifted her head, forced herself to meet his gaze. But where she'd expected pity, or impatience, all she saw was a pragmatic intensity—as if he were trying to see into her soul. And something else, something she didn't recognise or understand—because it almost looked like desire. But that couldn't be true.

'I can't stay,' she said, hating the tremble in her voice.

She didn't want to feel this weak, this fragile. She hated showing him even an ounce of her vulnerability, because it made her feel even more pathetic.

'Yes, you can.' He didn't budge. 'As I said, I will pay for your time,' he added, the tone rigid with purpose.

'I don't need you to do that. I'm shattered anyway. I'm just going to cycle home.' She needed to leave, before the foolish yearning to stay, and have him care for her, got the better of her.

Mon Dieu, who would have thought that Monique's shy and sheltered daughter would grow into a woman as striking and valiant as Jeanne D'Arc?

'So there are no more jobs tonight?' Dominic asked.

The girl frowned, but, even caught in the lie, her gaze remained direct. 'No, there aren't,' she said, the unapologetic tone equally captivating. 'I lied.'

He let out a rough chuckle. '*Touché,* Allycat.'

He let his gaze wander over the slim coltish figure, vibrating with tension. Her high firm breasts, outlined by her damp cycle gear, rose and fell with her staggered breaths. With her wet hair tied back in a short ponytail, damp chestnut curls clinging to the pale, almost translucent skin of her cheeks, blue-tinged shadows under her eyes, and an oil mark on her chin, she should have looked a mess. But instead she looked like the Maid of Orleans—passionate and determined.

And all the more beautiful for it.

Not unlike her mother. Or what he could remember of her mother.

Monica Jones had been his father's mistress, during that brief summer when his father had acknowledged him. But the truth was it was her daughter, the girl who stood before him now, her wide guileless eyes direct and unbowed despite her obvious misery, whom he remembered with a great deal more clarity.

She'd been a child that summer, ten or eleven maybe, but he still remembered how she had followed him around like a doting puppy. And defended him against his father's abuse. She had stood up to that bastard on his behalf, and because of that he'd felt a strange connection with her. And it seemed that connection hadn't died. Not completely.

Although it had morphed into something a great deal more potent—if the sensation that had zapped up his arm when he had touched her was anything to go by.

She was quite stunning, pure and unsullied—despite her bedraggled appearance. The compulsion to capture her cold cheeks in his palms and warm her unpainted lips with a kiss surprised him, though.

Why should he want her, when she was so unsophisticated? *Un garçon manqué.* A tomboy without an ounce of glamour or allure. Why should he care if she was cold, or wet, or injured? She wasn't his responsibility.

Perhaps it was simply the shock of seeing her again, and the memories she evoked? Maybe it was the compelling contrast she made with the woman he'd just kicked out of his life? Not spoilt, entitled and indulged but fierce and fearless and proud. The most likely explanation, though, for his attraction was that erotic spark that had arched between them the minute she'd stepped into the house.

After all, it had been over a month since he'd made love to a woman, and considerably longer since he'd felt that visceral tug of desire this woman seemed to evoke simply by breathing.

'Then I will order a car to take you and the bike home in due course,' he answered, because he was damned if he'd let her leave before he had at least had a chance to explore why she intrigued him so much. And no way was he letting her cycle home tonight. It was practically a hurricane out there.

A shiver ran through her and he noticed the small puddle forming at her feet.

'There's a bathroom on the first floor. Dry off and help yourself to the clothes in the dresser,' he said. 'I will meet you up there once I have found some medical supplies for that leg.'

The flush on her face brightened. She looked wary and tense, like a feral kitten scared to trust a helping hand.

'You don't have to do that,' she said.

'I know,' he replied. 'Now go. *Vite.*' He shooed her upstairs. 'Before you flood my hallway.'

CHAPTER THREE

'I DISCOVERED WHERE my housekeeper hides the medical supplies,' Ally's host announced as he strolled into the large study on the first floor and placed a red box on the mahogany desk.

Ally swallowed down the lump of anxiety in her throat. She wrapped her arms around her midriff, but remained rooted to her spot by the room's large mullioned windows.

How did Dominic have the ability to suck all the oxygen out of the room simply by walking into it?

At least she was warm and clean and dry now. Unfortunately, the oversized sweatpants and top that smelled of him, which she'd found in the guest bedroom next door—after taking the world's fastest shower in the en-suite wet room—still put her at a huge disadvantage.

In her bare feet, he towered over her, his suit trousers and white shirt perfectly tailored to accentuate his lean, well-muscled body.

'I see you found some dry clothes.' He studied her makeshift outfit in a way that made her feel like a street urchin playing dress-up before a king.

The intense look had her heart thundering harder against her ribs.

'Yes, thank you,' she said.

'Is the leg still bleeding?' The gruff question had goosebumps springing up all over her skin, despite the cosy cotton sweats.

'I don't think so,' she said. 'I took a shower to clean it. I'm sure it's fine.'

'We'll see,' he said, sounding doubtful. He beckoned her with one finger and indicated a large armchair in the corner of the room. 'Sit down so I can inspect it.'

She debated arguing with him again, because goose-bumps were rising on the goosebumps now at the thought of getting any closer to him. But she could see by the muscle twitching in his jaw he wasn't going to take no for an answer.

She crossed the room, trying not to limp, and sat in the chair. The sooner they got this over with, the sooner she could start breathing freely again.

To her astonishment he knelt down in front of her. She braced her hands on the arms of the chair as he opened the box, and began to rummage through the array of medi-cal supplies.

How had this happened? How had she ended up play-ing doctor with Dominic LeGrand? In his billion-pound house? In the intimacy of his study? While wearing his sweats with virtually nothing under them?

The traitorous heat—which had been lodged in her belly ever since the dispatcher had said his name—throbbed and glowed at her core.

But this time, she replayed the pep talk she'd given her-self in the shower.

Why should she feel ashamed of her reaction to him? They were both consenting adults. Dominic had always captivated her, even as a delinquent boy, and he was a world-renowned womaniser now. So she was bound to find him a little overwhelming—especially as she was so pathetically inexperienced with men.

Looking after her mother and keeping food on the table and a roof over both their heads hadn't left her any time to date while she was at school. And after her mother died, trying to realise her dream of becoming a fashion designer and stop her finances from slipping into a black hole hadn't increased her opportunities much. In fact, despite a few fumbling encounters, she was still a virgin. Which explained why she had such a violent reaction to someone as overwhelming as Dominic LeGrand.

Having rationalised her attraction, she watched him unobserved as he arranged a bandage and a packet of antiseptic wipes on the side table.

Even when he was on his knees, his head was almost level with hers. The light from the lamp behind her caught the streaks of gold in his tawny hair. She could make out the scar on his brow, the one she'd wondered about often when they were children. How had he got it?

His shoulders flexed, stretching the seams of his shirt, as he reached down to cradle her heel in his palm.

She jumped, sensation sprinting up her leg and sinking deep into her sex as callused fingers gripped her ankle.

'Does that hurt?' he asked, his chocolate gaze locking on her face.

'No, it's just…' *No man has ever touched me there before.* 'I was just surprised.' *Who knew my ankle was an erogenous zone?*

'Okay.' He frowned, but seemed to take the explanation at face value. 'Let me know if it does hurt.'

She nodded, her whole foot humming as he gripped her heel and used his other hand to lift the leg of her sweatpants past her knee.

He hissed as the gash was revealed. It wasn't too deep, more like a bad scrape where the pedal had dug into the skin, but it was still bleeding a little and there was some bruising visible around the wound.

'Nasty,' he murmured as he grabbed one of the antiseptic wipes with his free hand.

He ripped the small packet open with his teeth.

'Do you know how you did it?' he asked, dabbing at the wound.

'I got in the way of your fiancée while she was leaving,' she said.

His fingers tensed on her heel. 'Mira did this?' he said and she could hear the fury in his voice.

She nodded, wishing she could take the words back.

Why did you bring up his broken engagement?

He'd seemed pragmatic about it downstairs, but how did she know that wasn't all an act? Like the act he had put on as a boy, when his father had referred to him as 'my bastard son' at the supper table, or the *don't-give-a-damn* smile he'd sent her when she had witnessed Pierre backhand him across the face—and she'd tried to defend him.

'*Some people deserve to be hurt,* ma petite.'

His father's answer still haunted her.

No one deserved to be hurt, least of all Dominic, who had seemed to her back then—despite that *don't-give-a-damn* bravado—like a lost boy, jealously guarding secrets he refused to share.

What if he was just as hurt about his broken engagement? And his anger now was only there to disguise that hurt?

'I'm sorry,' she said. 'I didn't mean to upset you.'

'Upset me?' The flash of anger was replaced by an incredulous look. 'What could you have done to upset me?'

'By bringing up the end of your engagement. I didn't mean to remind you of it. I'm sure it must be awful for you. The break-up?'

She was babbling, but she couldn't help it, because he had settled back onto his heels and was staring at her as if she'd lost her mind.

'Alison,' he said and she could hear the hint of condescension. 'In the first place, *you* haven't upset me. *She* has, by her spoilt, unpleasant behaviour. She made you bleed…'

'I'm sure it was an accident,' she said, despite the warm glow at his concern.

'Knowing Mira and her selfish, capricious temperament, I doubt that,' he said. 'And in the second place, the break-up has not upset me. The engagement was a mistake and the marriage would have been an even bigger one.'

'But you must have loved her once?' she said, then felt like a fool, when the rueful smile widened.

'Must I?' he said. 'Why must I?'

'Because… Because you were going to marry her?' *Wasn't it obvious?*

He tilted his head, and studied her. 'I see you're still as much of a romantic as you were at ten,' he said, with much more than just a hint of condescension.

'I wasn't ten that summer, I was thirteen,' she countered.

'Really?' he said, mocking her now. 'So grown up.'

She shifted in her seat, supremely uncomfortable. It was as if he could see right past the bravado, the pretence of maturity, to the girl she'd been all those years ago when she'd idolised him. But she wasn't that teenager any more, she was twenty-five years old. And maybe she didn't have much relationship experience, but she had enough life experience to make up for it.

'If I was a romantic then,' she said, because maybe she had been, 'I'm certainly not one now.'

'Then why would you believe I was in love with Mira?' he said, as if it were the most ridiculous thing in the world.

'Maybe because you were planning to spend the rest of your life with her.' She wanted to add a 'Duh' but managed to control it. The room was already full to bursting with sarcasm.

'It wasn't a love match,' he said, the pragmatic tone disconcerting as he bent his head and continued tending her leg as he spoke. 'I needed a wife to secure an important business deal and Mira fit the bill. Or so I thought. But even if I hadn't discovered my mistake in time, the marriage was only supposed to last for a few months.'

'Your marriage had a sell-by date?' she asked, shocked by the depth of his cynicism.

'I might have been misguided enough to propose to Mira,' he said, smiling at her as he grabbed the bandage on the side table. 'But I would never be foolish enough to shackle myself to her, or any woman, for life.'

'I see,' she said, although she really didn't.

He'd always been guarded, and wary, even at sixteen. But had he always been this jaded?

One encounter blasted into her brain, when she'd caught him sitting in one of the chateau's walled gardens, inhaling deeply on a cigarette after his father had goaded him at the lunch table, calling him a name in French she hadn't really understood but had known was bad.

'You shouldn't smoke. It's bad for you. Papa will be angry.'

'Go ahead and tell him if you want, Allycat. He won't care.'

He'd had the same mocking smile on his face then as he had now, but she'd seen the sadness in his eyes—and had known his father's insult had hurt him much more than he'd been letting on. There was no sadness in his eyes now, though, just a sort of rueful amusement at her naiveté.

He finished bandaging her leg.

'All done.' He ran his thumbs along her calf, and she shivered as a trail of fire was left by the light caress. 'How does it feel?'

'Good,' she said and then flushed at his husky chuckle.

Had he sensed it wasn't only her leg she was talking about?

A sensual smile curved his lips and her breath clogged in her lungs.

Yes, he did know.

'Bien,' he murmured, then grabbed the arms of the chair, caging her in for a moment as he levered himself to his feet.

Her heartbeat thundered into her throat and some other key parts of her anatomy as he offered her his hand.

'Let's try walking on it,' he said.

She placed her fingers in his palm, but as she got to her feet the warm grip had the sweet spot between her thighs becoming heavy and hot.

She tested her leg as he led her across the room.

'Still good?' he asked, still smiling that knowing smile.

'Yes,' she said. 'Still good.' And couldn't resist smiling back at him.

Maybe it was dangerous to flirt with him—if that was what they were doing. But she'd never had much of a chance to flirt with anyone before. And certainly not someone as gorgeous as he was.

And let's not forget the massive crush you had on him once upon a time, her subconscious added, helpfully.

'How about that drink?' he asked as he let her hand go, to walk to the liquor cabinet in the bookshelves.

She ought to say no. But she was feeling languid and a little giddy. Maybe it was the fire crackling in the hearth, or the sound of the rain still beating down outside, or the cosy feel of the sweats she'd borrowed, or the glimmer of appreciation in his hot chocolate eyes—which was probably all in her imagination. Or maybe it was the fact he had tended her leg.

When was the last time anyone had taken care of her?

Whatever the reason, she couldn't seem to conjure the ability to be careful or cautious for once. She'd denied herself so many things in the last twelve years—why should she deny herself a chance to have a drink with a man who had always fascinated her?

'Were you serious about ordering me a cab home?' she asked. Because she couldn't drink if she was going to have to cycle all the way to East London.

'Of course,' he said.

'Then thank you, I'd love a drink.'

'What would you like? I have whisky. Gin. Brandy.' He opened the drinks cabinet and bent to look inside, giving her a far too tempting view of tight male buns confined in designer trousers. 'A spicy Merlot? A refreshing Chablis?'

'Spoken like a true Frenchman,' she teased.

'*C'est vrai.* I am French. I take my wine seriously,' he said, laying on his accent extra thick and making her grin.

'The Merlot sounds good,' she said.

He poured the red wine into a crystal tumbler, his fingers brushing hers as he passed her the glass. The prickle of reaction sprinted up her arm, but it didn't scare her or shame her this time. It excited her.

She took a sip of the wine, and the rich fruity flavours burst on her tongue.

'*Bon?*' he asked.

'Very.'

He leaned his hips against the cabinet and crossed his arms over his chest, making his pectoral muscles flex distractingly against the white linen.

'You're not drinking?' she asked.

'I have already had one whisky tonight. And I want to keep a clear head.'

'Oh?' she said. She wanted to ask why he needed to keep a clear head, but it seemed like a loaded question—especially when he smiled that sensual smile again, as if they were sharing an intimate secret.

She got a little distracted by the astonishing beauty of his face—rugged and masculine—dappled by firelight and the ridged contours of his chest visible through the tailored shirt.

She took another sip of the wine, let the warmth of it spread through her torso. This was definitely better than having to cycle back to Whitechapel in the pouring rain.

Mira Whatsherface's loss was Ally Jones's gain.

'Are you enjoying the view?' The deep mocking voice had her gaze jerking back to his face.

She blinked, blinded by the heat of his smile. Momentarily.

Her cheeks heated.

For goodness' sake, Ally, stop staring at his exceptional chest and make some small talk.

'What's the deal?' she asked.

His scarred eyebrow arched. 'Deal?'

'The deal you were prepared to enter into a loveless short-term marriage for,' she elaborated.

'An extremely important one for my business,' he said, without an ounce of embarrassment or remorse. 'There is a large tract of undeveloped land on the Brooklyn waterfront. It is the only undeveloped parcel of that size in the five boroughs. I intend to reclaim it, and build on it. Homes mostly. Unfortunately it is owned by a group of men who refuse to invest with someone they regard as—how did they put it? "Morally suspect."' He used finger quotes while sending her a wry smile. 'My private life needs to be stable and settled without a whiff of scandal while the project is in its early stages. As soon as I was in a position to engineer a board takeover and buy them out, I planned to end the marriage.'

'So it's all about money?' she said.

His smile quirked as if she had said something particularly amusing. 'Money is important. You of all people should understand that,' he said, and she felt her blush heat. 'But no, it's not all about money. This is about taking my business to the next level. This project will put LeGrand Nationale in a position to dominate the regeneration market in the United States.'

So it wasn't just about money, it was also about legacy and prestige. Was it any surprise that would be so important to him? When he had been forced to prove himself from a young age, the illegitimate son who had been called a 'bastard' by his own father. She couldn't blame him for his drive and ambition, even though his cynicism made her feel sad.

'But let's not talk about business,' he murmured as he released his arms and walked towards her. His thumb glided down her cheek and her breath caught in her throat, the sizzle of heat darting into her sex. 'Tell me about you. How did you come to be a bike messenger? Has your life been hard, since that summer, Allycat?'

His voice caressed the childhood nickname in a way that inflamed her senses—but his attention was even more potent. She needed to be careful; this was a casual conversation, nothing more.

'Not that hard,' she lied. 'I became a bike courier because it's good money. And I can fit it around my classes. I'm… I'm in college at the moment,' she added, as she found herself staring into his eyes, spotting the strands of gold in the chocolate brown.

'So you are smart as well as beautiful.' His thumb glided across her lips and her mouth opened instinctively on a sigh, the blood rushing in her ears.

'If I asked to kiss you, Alison,' he said, the rasp of need in his voice both raw and sublime, 'what would you say?'

She nodded without thinking.

Kissing Dominic probably wasn't a good idea, but she was incapable of controlling the euphoria rioting in her blood. The knowledge he wanted her was even more intoxicating than his fresh woodsy scent and the feel of his thumb tracing over the pulse in her neck.

'You must say the word,' he coaxed as he stroked the well of her collarbone.

'Yes.' *Please.*

'Merci.'

The hoarse thank-you was as tortured as the need twisting her belly into tight knots.

Her bottom bumped the wall as he pressed her against it, found the hem of her sweatshirt and slid his hands under it to hold her steady.

Then his lips were on hers, hot and firm and seeking. A groan escaped from her constricted throat and his tongue plunged deep into her mouth.

He explored in masterful, demanding strokes as his fingers dipped beneath the waistband of her sweatpants and cupped her naked bottom.

He ripped his mouth away. 'No panties?' he said, the pupils so dilated his chocolate brown eyes had become black.

'They… They were wet,' she choked out.

'I may have to punish you for that, Alison,' he murmured, the mocking tone so fierce it was only half joking.

Raw need careered through her.

'I want to see more of you,' he said. *'D'accord?'*

She nodded again, having lost the power of speech.

Lifting the hem of her sweatshirt, he tugged it over her head. She shuddered as his gaze glided over the damp sports bra she had donned after her shower.

Could she have been wearing anything less alluring?

But his gaze when it met hers still blazed with arousal. *'Trés belle.'*

Capturing both her wrists in one hand, he lifted her arms above her head, until she was pinned against the wall, her breasts thrust out, begging for attention, her breathing so ragged it sounded deafening.

He covered one straining breast with his free hand and scooped it free of her bra. Exposing her to his gaze.

'Magnifique...' he murmured, then lowered his head and licked across the swollen tip.

She bucked against his hold, shocked by the sensations firing down to her core as he teased and tortured the over-sensitive peak with his tongue, his teeth.

She couldn't stop shaking, sobbing. Until he covered the erect nipple with his mouth and suckled.

It was too much and yet not nearly enough. The jut of his erection, so hard and large confined in the suit trousers, pressed against her belly. She wanted to feel it inside her, to take the ache away.

Her breathing guttered out when at last he released her engorged nipple. But the relief was short-lived, as he un-hooked the bra and freed her other breast to begin again. Torturing, teasing, tormenting.

She was begging, bucking against his hold when he finally returned his mouth to hers. He held her captive, both wrists shackled above her head. The huge erection notched between her thighs, her bare breasts crushed against his chest. The hard shaft found that sweet spot through their clothing, rubbing, rocking, the waves of sensation building from her core.

The orgasm built so swiftly, she couldn't control it, the shattering wave crashing over her with staggering intensity. Her body arched as the bright light fired from her core and shattered into a million glittering shards.

She was struggling to breathe, her body slumped against his, when his voice rasped against her ear.

'*Dieu*, did you just climax, Alison?'

Her eyelids fluttered open, to find him staring at her with a need so fierce it was terrifying and liberating all at once.

Her thundering heart began to slow. He did not look happy. In fact, he looked stunned. Had she done something wrong?

'Yes…' she said. 'I'm… I'm sorry, I couldn't stop it. Was I supposed to?'

His lips quirked and then, to her astonishment, he dropped his head back and laughed.

She tugged on her arms, tried to wrestle herself free of his hold, humiliation engulfing her.

He was still fully dressed. With her bra hanging from one arm and her nipples raw and swollen where he'd played with them she'd never felt more exposed.

'I should go,' she murmured.

But he didn't release her, as the rough chuckles died. His thumbs pressed into the rampaging pulse at her wrists.

'No way. We're not finished yet. Even if you jumped the gun.'

'I said I was sorry about…' She tried to protest, but he silenced her, the swift kiss both demanding and possessive.

'There was no need to apologise,' he said, his gaze compelling—the humour replaced with something much more potent. 'Do you have any idea how adorable you are?'

The gruff words were quietly spoken, but so achingly sincere her heart punched her ribs.

Cupping her cheek, he swept his gaze over her, the approval she saw making her heartbeat thunder in her ears.

What was happening? Because this felt *too* intimate, *too* emotional. More than sex.

'Please, I…' she began.

'Shh…' He stroked his hand down to her collarbone, the ripple of sensation making her shiver. 'I wish to take you to bed, Alison. How do you feel about that?'

'I… I want you too.' *Very much.*

'Bien.'

He sent her a devilish grin, full of wickedness and intent. Letting her arms drop, he dragged the bra away, leaving her standing before him in only the baggy sweatpants.

'Très, très belle,' he murmured again, his voice thick with arousal. 'My gym pants have never looked so good.'

She crossed her arms over her breasts, brutally aware of how naked she was, compared to him.

But then he scooped her into his arms.

She grasped his neck as he marched her into the spare bedroom. The room was luxuriously furnished with a large tester bed complemented by an array of antique pieces. He closed the door to the study, so the only light in the room came from the bathroom and the bay window that looked out onto the house's grounds. The low lighting had a little of her anxiety retreating as he laid her on the bed.

Her pulse sped up again though as he unbuttoned his shirt, then stripped it off.

Moonlight flickered over the tanned skin, putting the bunched muscles of his torso into stark relief. He was magnificent. Tall, muscular, lean and powerful. The dark hair that defined flat brown nipples and arrowed down into his trousers through his abs had her lungs seizing. Her throat dried as he released the hook on his suit trousers and kicked off his shoes.

The rigid erection sprang up as he lowered his boxers.

Her gaze met his, her breathing so shallow now it was a miracle she didn't faint as he climbed onto the bed.

'Lose the pants, *ma belle*,' he said.

She wriggled out of the sweatpants and flung them away. He climbed on top of her. His skin felt hot and firm as he pressed her into the mattress and a rough palm coasted up her bare thigh. A hoarse cry escaped her throat.

Their skin touched everywhere. His fingertips electrified her nerve endings as they found the sensitive seam of skin at the top of her thigh, then located the slick heat at her core.

'So wet for me, *ma belle*.' She could hear the hunger in his voice. 'Tell me what you like.'

I don't know.

She trapped the answer in her throat. And flattened her palms against the ridged muscles, stalling for time. She didn't know how to answer that question; no man had ever seen her naked before, let alone touched her, stroked her.

His thumb found the bundle of nerves again and she moaned, jerking her hips towards the intimate torture.

'You like that?' he asked as his thumb circled, not quite touching her again where she needed.

'Yes, yes, please do it again.' She didn't care any more about the naked need in her voice, the raw desperation. She wanted to feel that glorious release once more.

'Can I touch you, too?' she asked.

The deep groan against her neck felt like a benediction. *'Oui.'*

She slid her hand down his chest, feeling the muscles quiver. His whole body shook as she wrapped her fingers around the stiff column of flesh. She had a moment of panic as she gauged his size, his girth and the steely strength beneath the velvet-soft skin. How would anything that large and hard ever fit inside her?

But then his thumb found that devastating spot between her thighs and every thought flew out of her head.

She stroked him as he stroked her. But where his caresses were firm and assured, her movements were jerky and uncertain. Still she took pleasure in his shudder when her thumb found the bead of moisture at the head of his erection. She could feel his passion building as the coil at her core twisted and tightened. Her knees fell open, her hips angling forward, in a wanton display of need she couldn't control. Her fingers gripped his rigid flesh as one blunt finger entered her, sinking into the tight flesh, his thumb still working her into a frenzy.

'You are very tight. It has been a while, yes?' he asked.

She nodded. Because what else could she say? It was a lifetime since she'd felt this good.

He swore softly in French, his hips driving into her hand, the hard flesh getting longer, thicker.

'Come for me again, *ma chérie*,' he demanded, and just like that the wave slammed into her, flinging her over that final peak.

She let out a hoarse moan as she fell to earth, sinking into the glorious oblivion. But as the afterglow settled over her like a glittering cloud, her fingers flexed on the erection. He was still rigid, still huge.

Leaning over her, he fumbled in the bedside drawer, the rip of foil was loud enough to be heard over her staggered breathing.

Lifting her hand from his erection, he kissed the knuckles. 'I cannot wait any longer,' he murmured, the urgency sending new ripples of longing through her exhausted flesh.

He rolled on the condom, then grasped her hips.

She felt the head of his erection probe, before he thrust deep.

Rending pain seared through her and she choked off a sob.

'Merde!' He reared back.

She bit into her lip to stop the cry of pain. Intense pleasure had turned to shock and discomfort, but far worse than the soreness where his erection was lodged deep inside her was the look of pure horror that shadowed Dominic's face.

He knew.

The thought doused the heat, until all that was left was the chill of his disapproval.

Of course, he knew. Why had she thought he wouldn't notice? A man with his experience, who had probably slept with dozens of women.

She shifted, trying to adjust to the thick length inside her, hoping to regain the desire that had disappeared in a rush. But his fingers flexed on her hips, and he flinched.

'Don't move,' he groaned. 'I don't want to hurt you more.'

'It's okay, it doesn't hurt.'

'Don't lie,' he said, his gaze shadowed now, the horror replaced with surprise and something that looked like guilt. 'I am your first. Is this not the case?'

She wanted to lie, to take the guilt out of his expression. But how could she, when it was clearly obvious?

'Yes, but it's not a big deal,' she murmured, because it really wasn't. Or at least it shouldn't have been. Up until the moment he had entered her, she'd been delirious with pleasure. He'd brought her to orgasm. Twice. And more than anything she wanted to do the same for him. To see him shatter the way he had made her shatter.

'I must withdraw,' he said.

'No, don't.' She clasped his shoulders. 'Don't stop. I don't want you to stop.' The tearing pain had already lessened, the tendrils of heat building again at her core, the pulsing ache becoming sharp and insistent.

'Damn it, Alison, you don't know what you ask of me. I am not sure I can be gentle.'

The growled admission, grudging and yet gruff with desperation, had her heart contracting.

'I don't need you to be gentle, Dominic. I just need you to treat me like a woman.'

To treat me like your *woman.*

The foolishly romantic thought echoed in her head.

She buried it deep. She hadn't lied when she'd told him her virginity was not a big deal to her. She was twenty-five years old. It was ridiculous she'd waited this long. And yes, it had hurt. But already the full stretched feeling had changed into something closer to pleasure than pain. He filled her up in a way that made her breath hitch, and her clitoris throb with renewed yearning.

'I'm not fragile,' she added, because he was still braced above her, not moving, his face strained with the effort it was taking him to hold still. 'Really I'm not. I know what I want.' *And what I want is you.*

She threaded her fingers into his hair, coaxing him to do what they both needed. He swore softly, but then placed a hand at her cheek, brushing his thumb across her lips.

'D'accord, ma belle,' he murmured, his gaze becoming dark and intense as he glided out of her, then thrust back in, slowly, carefully, sinking in to the hilt.

The head of his penis massaged a spot deep inside her and she gasped, the delicious shudder adding to the heat at her core.

'C'est bien?' he asked, his perfect English having deserted him.

'Yes,' she moaned. 'It's good.'

He established a rhythm—slow at first, and then building—digging at that spot ruthlessly, relentlessly as heat fired over her skin.

The waves of pleasure gathered again with each new thrust of his hips, each new jolt of desire. She clung to him, the only solid object in the storm engulfing her. Every pulse and heartbeat became attuned to the ravages of pleasure he was waging on her body. The steady rhythm became harder, faster, overwhelming, unstoppable.

She couldn't think any more, couldn't make sense of the sounds and sights around her, all she could do was feel…

Her moans became pants, her sex contracting, massaging the hard length. The brutal pleasure coiled tighter at her core. The edge of desire so sharp she felt buffeted, burned, undone.

Then his thumb found the swollen folds where their bodies joined, triggering a conflagration so fierce and all-consuming she cried out.

Her body arched into his, the shattering orgasm exploding along her nerve-endings, like a shimmering light, splintering and then retreating to splinter again.

She could hear her own sobs, her fingers fisting in his hair, as he finally let her tumble to earth—his shout of fulfilment following her over that high wide edge.

His big body collapsed on top of her, his raw pants matched hers, the musty scent of sex and sweat mingling with the shiver of surrender.

She hugged him, exhausted, spent. Her sex sore, her body limp. She caressed the silky strands at his nape now damp with sweat, and tried not to acknowledge the debilitating wave of emotion threatening to engulf her.

It's just sex. Just for one night. It doesn't mean anything.
But still she couldn't quite ignore the faltering beat of her heart at the realisation that, after twelve years, all her foolish teenage fantasises had finally come true. And it had definitely been worth the wait.

CHAPTER FOUR

BREATHE, DAMN IT. Breathe.

Dominic's hands slipped from Alison's hips as he withdrew. She flinched and the dart of shame stabbed at his chest.

His fingers shook as he imagined the bruising imprint of his thumbs on the soft skin where he'd gripped her as he'd pumped into her.

What the hell had just happened? Because what should have been a smooth, subtle seduction had become something frenzied and frantic.

He'd planned to make love to her tonight as soon as they had been alone together in the study—and he'd seen the arousal in her eyes.

She was beautiful, captivating, she wanted him. And she could solve all his problems.

Figuring out where his housekeeper had hidden the first-aid box downstairs had given him more than enough time to consider the tempting possibilities Alison Jones's reappearance in his life tonight might mean.

He needed a wife and she could be perfect for the role.

Not only did she turn him on to the point of madness, something Mira had never done, but he could offer her a home, and financial security. The fact she was completely unknown to the press with no scandal attached to her was another huge point in her favour. It would be a relatively simple job to set up a new PR narrative to explain their whirlwind romance and wedding. Mira had been out of the country for over a month, he and Alison had known each other as children, they'd met again when she'd delivered something to his home and one thing had led to another.

The only question had been whether she desired him, too. Had he imagined that spark? Because it suited his own ends so perfectly?

But as soon as he'd walked into the study and seen her face flush and her breathing accelerate, he'd known he hadn't imagined anything. And when he had touched her bare foot, and she'd nearly jumped out of the chair, he'd had to swallow a harsh laugh.

Game on.

But why hadn't he questioned her artless responses, the beguiling blush that had spread across her collarbone as soon as he'd started flirting with her?

She'd been as eager as him, that was why. He'd assumed the blush, the innocence were all an accomplished act, an act to disguise the fact she was more than ready to take Mira's place—especially when she had questioned him about the business deal.

He'd been in her situation himself, years ago when he'd been destitute after arriving in Paris with three broken ribs and not a penny to his name, so why would he judge her for taking the easy option? Of snagging a rich man? Hadn't his own mother—and hers—tried to do the same?

But once he'd tasted her, the sophisticated seduction he'd planned had changed into something elemental.

She had tasted like she smelled. Strawberries and chocolate. Sweet and decadent. But more than that, she had tasted of summer, and sunshine, and joy and surrender.

The fanciful thoughts had scattered, becoming dark and earthy and driven as she'd squirmed against his hardening erection, like a cat desperate to be stroked.

Bon Dieu, but he hadn't been able to get enough of her, exploring the recesses of her mouth like a man possessed.

And once he'd freed her breasts, felt her nipples harden and swell against his tongue, he'd been lost in a passion so intense it had been a major battle not to take her right there against the wall of his study.

When his hands had cupped her naked bottom, sensation had hurtled beneath his belt with the speed and accuracy of a heat-seeking missile.

Suddenly, he'd become the desperate boy again, instead of the experienced lover.

He'd had to force himself to slow down, to carry her to the bedroom and strip off his clothes, to draw forth another orgasm—simply to prove he could wait to have her, that he was still the one in control—before he'd plunged into her.

But when she had gasped and stiffened in pain, he'd known instantly—this was no act.

She had been a virgin, for God's sake.

He should have stopped then, but, even while he was frantically trying to assess the repercussions of her innocence, his body had refused to obey him once she'd given him permission to continue—so he'd taken what she'd offered, because he'd been unable to do otherwise.

And now here he was, lying in bed beside her, not knowing what the hell to say to her.

Should he apologise? Explain? She'd said it wasn't a big deal, but somehow it was to him. He'd never been a woman's first lover. Had deliberately avoided that sort of intimacy. And what did he do now about his plan to suggest they marry? Because this could complicate things in ways he did not want, and had not anticipated.

His gut twisted as he felt her shift on the bed beside him. She hadn't spoken, probably because she was as shocked by the intensity of their lovemaking as he was. And appalled by his lack of sophistication.

Or was she? How would she know the power of their connection—or how catastrophically he had lost control—if she had never slept with another man?

She sat up with her back to him, but as she went to stand he flung his arm out and caught her hip. 'Where are you going?' he asked, pleased when the words came out reasonably smoothly despite the rawness in his throat.

She glanced over her shoulder. 'I hope you don't mind if I borrow your sweats? I'll return them tomorrow.'

What?

It took a moment for him to register what she was asking him and why as she bent down to scoop the sweatpants off the floor. But when she tried to stand, he at least had the presence of mind to keep his hand anchored on her hip.

'You're not going anywhere tonight, Allycat,' he said, moving across the bed to band an arm around her waist.

She twisted round again, her face so close he could see the confusion in her eyes. 'Why...why not?' she asked.

Mon Dieu, she was even more innocent than he had assumed.

He kissed her shoulder blade. 'Because I have exhausted you. And it is still raining.' They weren't the main reasons, not even close, but he didn't want to talk about anything else until he had calmed down enough to figure out all the angles.

Perhaps her virginity didn't have to be a bad thing. At least it seemed unlikely that as his wife she would be photographed kissing other men. And perhaps his spectacular loss of control was a one-off. She'd unsettled him the minute she had arrived. They had a history; she knew more about his background than any of the other women he had slept with. And he hadn't been with a woman in six weeks. Maybe he'd had longer dry spells before while he was building his business, but perhaps this need, this desperation, the intensity of their connection were nothing more than chemistry and opportunity.

'I thought I'd just get a cab, like you suggested,' she said.

Why had he suggested the damn cab?

'Alison.' He pulled himself up on the bed, and sat behind her, his legs straddling hers. He wrapped his arms around her waist, and dropped his chin on her shoulder. 'There is no need to leave. I want you to stay.'

The heat surged back into his groin—making the erection swell against her bottom.

She stiffened slightly. 'I don't... I'm a bit sore, I don't think I want to do it again tonight,' she said. And he was caught between a laugh and a groan.

'Ignore that, I have no control over my body's reaction to you.' Wasn't that the truth? 'I have no intention of touching you again tonight,' he said. He lifted the sweatpants out of her hands and then manoeuvred himself off the bed so he could stand and put them on. Grabbing the bathrobe that hung on the back of the bedroom door, he passed it to her.

She scrambled into it. He couldn't make out her expression in the half-light, but he could sense her embarrassment and uncertainty. And suddenly the pulse of reaction in his crotch wasn't nearly as disturbing as the pulse of something around his heart.

She was sweet and adorable and genuine, not something he usually looked for in a hook-up. But then she wasn't a hook-up; he was hoping she would agree to become much more than that, tomorrow. And for what he had in mind, perhaps her innocence could be a huge advantage.

But until he'd had a chance to consider his plan carefully in light of this new information, he didn't intend to let her out of his house.

For tonight, though, it would be best if he kept her out of his bed. Or he would find it very hard to keep his promise—not to touch her again.

'Are you hungry?' he asked.

She shook her head. 'Just tired.'

'Then come with me,' he said, ignoring the renewed pulse of emotion as she hesitated before taking his hand.

He guided her out of the bedroom and into the study.

'There is another bedroom with an en suite on this floor.' He led her down the darkened hallway and across the landing to open the door to another of the house's six bedrooms. He leant against the doorframe as she stepped into the room.

'Get some sleep. I will see you in the morning.' Once he'd worked out exactly how to proceed.

She stood in the room, looking a little lost. 'But I left my bike outside,' she said.

He huffed out a strained laugh. 'I'll bring it in out of the cold.'

'Okay, thanks,' she murmured. 'For everything.' Then flushed, obviously realising the double meaning.

He had to hold back another harsh laugh.

Damn, but she really was utterly adorable. He grasped the lapels of her robe and tugged her close, but restricted the goodnight kiss to a chaste peck on her forehead. '*Bonne nuit*, Allycat.'

Tomorrow they would talk. But for tonight he needed space and distance; they both did. Their spectacular chemistry did not have to be a bad thing, in fact it could be a very fortuitous thing, and not just for his business.

But first he needed to ensure her innocence hadn't created complications he couldn't control.

CHAPTER FIVE

IT TOOK ALLY a moment to adjust to the dawn light shining through the open shutters of the big bay window when she woke the next day. She pushed herself up on her elbows, the sheet sliding over sensitive skin. It took her a moment more to figure out where she was.

Then the memories came flooding back in a dizzying kaleidoscope of scents and sights and sounds and sensations.

The crackle of the dispatcher's voice shouting out Dominic's name through the rain, the aroma of pine soap and whisky, the rich fruity taste of the Merlot, the flicker of moonlight caressing the muscular planes of Dominic's chest, the rending pain and then the shocking pleasure as he filled her to bursting.

And the confusing thoughts as she'd drifted into sleep afterwards.

She swung her feet to the floor and wrapped the sheet around her naked body, aware of all the places Dominic had caressed with such skill and efficiency the night before. Her breasts, her lips, her sex.

What she'd experienced had been so much more than she had been prepared for. She hadn't expected that level of pleasure, or that level of intimacy. How had he known exactly how and where to touch her? Was this what her mother had always craved, that pure physical connection? Was that why she'd exposed herself so easily? To so many men? After Pierre had discarded her?

A chill rippled over Ally's skin, even though the house's heating was set at the perfect ambient temperature.

Another thought intruded, of how Dominic had kept his composure last night, and she'd lost all of hers.

She walked across the room on unsteady legs and shrugged on the bathrobe he'd given her the night before, inhaling the scent of him, which still clung to the material. Then felt foolish.

She needed to leave. She should have left last night. Seeing him this morning would be awkward and uncomfortable for both of them—the fact of her virginity, and the lies she'd told to conceal it from him, not just an elephant in the room but a ten-ton pachyderm.

It was still early, she thought, assessing the light through the window. Probably only six, if that. She had time to take a quick shower, then hunt up her clothing, find her bike and get out.

But when she dashed into the bathroom, she spotted her reflection in the mirrored wall opposite the shower cubicle.

The sight stole her breath. She hadn't expected to look different, to feel different, had assumed that was a myth women told each other to make their first time have meaning.

But she did look different. Her hair was rumpled, her skin pink in places where his stubble had rubbed against it.

The stupid wave of emotion took her unawares.

Not a big deal. Not a big deal. Don't make too much of it.

A heavy weight sank into the pit of her stomach.

Don't you dare cry.

After a quick shower, she ran her fingers through her

hair and stared at herself in the bathroom mirror, pressing her thumb against the skin of her cheek—tender from beard burn.

Last night had been an experience, an experience she refused to regret. But it was a new day now, the harsh light of the March dawn after the storm signalling a return to real life.

Tiptoeing down the hall, she slipped into the study, cold now with the fire burnt out. She found her bra on the floor where Dominic had discarded it.

Now all she needed was the wet cycling gear she'd left in the bedroom where they had made love. The door was ajar. She huffed out a shaky breath when she peered into the room to discover it empty, the large bed still rumpled from the night before.

A vision of Dominic's magnificent chest limed by moonlight blasted into her brain. The heavy sensation at her core throbbed.

She shook her head, trying to expel the dazed feeling. *So,* so *not the point.*

She found her cycling gear where she'd left it, hanging over the heated towel rail in the bathroom. Dropping the robe, she slipped on the now dry clothing, easing the torn cycling pants over the bandage on her leg.

The memory of his fingers, gentle and efficient as he bandaged her calf, had the heat eddying back through her body. And the emotion squeezing her ribs. She breathed. In, out. And waited for the wave to pass.

But as she left the bathroom, she stumbled to a stop as her gaze connected with the unmade bed—and the pulse of guilt and yearning wrapped around her heart like a vice, the bloodstains on the bedsheet like a banner ad to her naiveté.

Had she really believed she could sleep with Dominic,

have him be her first lover and suffer no emotional fall-out whatsoever?

But even as she acknowledged the foolishness of that assessment, she refused to regret her decision. How many women could say they had been initiated into sex by their childhood crush—and got three amazing orgasms into the bargain?

Dominic and last night had been a gift. A gift she had deserved after the harsh realities of her life ever since that summer in Provence. Through the many dark days spent watching her mother become addicted to prescription pain-killers, and throw herself at men who didn't treat her with respect, or kindness. Seeing her become a shadow of the beautiful woman she'd been that summer when Pierre Le-Grand had loved her.

Perhaps it was ironic it was Pierre's son who had given Ally this boon, but why did it have to be significant?

She already knew the gift of great sex wasn't something that could last.

It was the one thing she had discovered while watching her mother sink into despair. That it was far too easy to mistake sex for love—and love, even when it was genuine, was totally unreliable.

It required you to allow your life, your happiness, to be dependent on the whims of others. She'd learned a valuable lesson in the last twelve years: not just that love could destroy you if you let it, but that survival meant relying on yourself and no one else.

The yearning she felt, the sadness that last night was never going to be repeated, was purely physical.

Dominic was a handsome, powerful and overwhelming man—and an experienced lover. And they had a past dating back to the days when she'd still believed in love and romance. Of course she'd been captivated by him.

But she could not allow what had happened last night to have any lasting significance in her life.

Plus she was never going to see him again—if she got a move on.

Once she was back on her bike, delivering pizzas and urgent documents and maybe even someone else's wedding ring—last night would all be a wonderful dream, which she'd be able to pull out of her subconscious and enjoy whenever she needed a pick-me-up or an incentive to get through another day.

She flung the sheets over the bloodstains, and sat down to wrestle her still-damp cycling shoes back on. Then walked back out of the room.

There was no sound coming from the floor below.

Thank God, she hadn't sabotaged her getaway with loads of pointless soul-searching.

She rushed down the wide sweeping staircase, then headed along the hallway towards the back of the house, retracing the steps she'd taken the night before; the cleats of her cycle shoes clattered on the polished wood flooring. She spotted her bike, parked inside the back door, and felt the tight feeling in her chest release—and her lungs deflate a little.

It's all good. A quick getaway is for the best, to save the discomfort of the morning after.

A rueful smile tugged at her lips. Never having had sex before, she didn't know the etiquette for a one-night stand, but even *she* knew the morning after was something best avoided. Especially if you'd effectively tricked your lover into taking your virginity.

But as she stepped past the door to the kitchen, a wry voice rang out.

'Alison, you're awake. I hope you slept well?'

Crap! She was totally busted.

Dominic sat on one of the stools next to a large breakfast bar. The doorway she was now standing in like a dummy led into a huge open-plan kitchen—its state-of-the art appliances and stark metal and glass design in striking contrast to the Georgian majesty of the rest of the house.

But it wasn't the kitchen design that had all her attention.

Her lover looked every inch the master of industry in a sharp two-piece business suit, polished loafers and a starched white shirt. Gold cufflinks peeked out from the sleeves of his jacket and she could spot a dimple in his chin she hadn't noticed the night before thanks to his now clean-shaven jaw.

Apart from the fluorescent lighting shining on his slicked-back hair, which suggested he'd showered fairly recently, too—probably while she was wasting time with all her pointless soul-searching over a couple of bloodstains—he couldn't have looked any more indomitable.

Her lover.

The words reverberated in her chest. Novel and delicious—and also ludicrous. Dominic wasn't her lover. He was a man she'd had one glorious night with.

As usual it was impossible to read his expression. The tenderness from the night before, when he had kissed her goodnight, was gone, replaced by a sensuous but oddly impersonal smile. He'd been in control last night, but he was even more so now.

She wrapped her arms around her waist, feeling naked beneath that searing gaze, despite her muddy cycling gear.

'How are you?' he enquired, his gruff French accent rumbling through the already far too sensitive parts of Ally's anatomy.

'I'm good, thank you,' her reply came out on an unconvincing croak.

Fabulous, Ally—can this actually get any more awkward?

She forced herself to release her arms and jerk a thumb over her shoulder. 'I was just heading off.'

'So I saw,' he said, the wry amusement not helping with her breathing difficulties. He beckoned her towards him. 'Come here. We need to talk.'

Her breathing accelerated.

What about?

She walked into the kitchen, her cleats clinking against the room's expensive slate flooring, her heartbeat gagging her.

He patted the stool next to him. 'Sit down.'

She did as she was told, aware of his gaze gliding over her bandaged leg. The rush of adrenaline, the shot of heat melting her panties, only made her more self-conscious.

'How's the leg?' he asked.

'Great. Listen, I really don't have time to—'

'I have a proposition for you,' he interrupted her, then placed his palm on a sheaf of papers on the breakfast bar next to his mug of coffee, and slid them towards her. 'It should be more than worth your time to hear me out.'

'A proposition?' She glanced at the papers, confused. They looked like legal documents. Was he going to sue her or something? What for?

'Yes, a proposition.' He tucked a knuckle under her chin and forced her gaze back to his. 'Don't look so scared, Allycat. This isn't bad, it's good.'

The amused, assured tone hadn't faltered.

'What's the proposition?' she asked.

'You haven't guessed it already?' he asked, and alongside the amusement she could hear the cynicism, which had made her sad for him the night before. It wasn't making her sad for *him* now, it was making her sad for herself. Had she ever been more clueless and out of her depth?

'No,' she said, because she had no idea what he was talking about and there wasn't much point in trying to disguise it, however much she wished she could.

'I need a wife. And you would be perfect.'

'A…what?' she said, her mouth going slack with shock. But the way her heart was pinging around her chest cavity like a ball trapped in a pinball machine told a different story. 'Did you say a *wife*?'

Because she couldn't possibly have heard *that* right.

'Yes, as I told you yesterday. I have an important deal in Brooklyn that's about to go up in smoke if I don't find a way to persuade the conservative consortium who own the land that my private life is…' he shrugged '…stable. And not about to attract any unwanted scandal. I proposed to Mira to solve the problem, but marriage to someone like her would have created other problems. Trying to persuade anyone I was madly in love with her when I could hardly stand the sight of her would have required a level of acting talent I simply do not possess. You, on the other hand…' His gaze darkened as it drifted over her. The tug of desire became a sharp yank in the hot sweet spot between her thighs.

'I… I don't know what to say,' she said, because she really didn't.

She was still processing her shock. In truth, she ought to be horrified. He was proposing marriage as if it were a business transaction.

She wasn't a romantic, and she'd known he was a deeply cynical man, from the way he'd spoken about his broken engagement with Mira yesterday… And maybe even before that, all those years ago, when he'd seemed so much older than his sixteen years.

But if she was so shocked and horrified by the ruthlessness of his proposal, how exactly did she account for her pinballing heartbeat?

'I guess I'd need more details,' she said, to buy time, until her ricocheting heartbeat wasn't threatening to ping right out of her chest.

'Smart girl,' he said, his gaze still dark with desire, but his tone stark with pragmatism. 'I'd need you to sign a non-disclosure agreement and a pre-nup, on the understanding the marriage will only last as long as I need it to. And then we would divorce. It shouldn't tie up your private life for more than three or four months, six at the most. And I'm willing to offer you a generous settlement if you help me.'

'I don't want your money,' she said, her pride kicking in at last.

'Why not?' he said. 'When you can clearly use it.'

'Because it would make me feel compromised,' she said, finally finding the horror she'd been looking for.

Hadn't his father bought her mother for that one summer? Monica Jones had been Pierre LeGrand's mistress. Maybe Ally would never be gullible enough to misconstrue such an arrangement for love, but she wasn't about to offer herself for sale either. Not after she'd seen what it had done to her mother.

'How would you be compromised?' he asked, sounding genuinely confused.

'Well, because we'd be sleeping together, wouldn't we?' she asked.

He chuckled, and lifted his hand to run his thumb down the side of her face. The flare of desire in his dark chocolate gaze was intense and searing. 'I certainly hope so. Yes.'

She captured his finger, and dragged it away from her face, resisting the urge to give into the fierce rush of need dampening her panties.

'Then, that's why,' she said, not sure where the prickle of disappointment was coming from. 'I refuse to become any man's mistress, the way my mother was. Your father bought and paid for her that summer. I know it was her fault she allowed herself to believe he felt more for her than he did, and that's why it broke her when he kicked us both out. I'd never make a mistake like that. But I still don't want to put myself in that position. With you or anyone else. It's demeaning.'

Dominic stared at the flushed and wary expression of the woman in front of him, which only made her face—the soft skin of her jaw rouged in places by the ferocity of his kisses the night before—more beautiful.

And wanted to punch a wall.

How could he have screwed up this negotiation, so fundamentally? He was an expert in the art of the deal; he knew how to get exactly what he wanted when hashing out a contract.

But as soon as he'd got everything straight in his head last night, then put in a call to his legal team, his emotions had been more engaged in this process than he would have liked—which was probably why he had made so many fundamental errors.

He couldn't risk Alison walking away from this proposal. He was running out of time and she was the perfect candidate to be his wife. She was smart and sensible and a realist. She'd had to live in the real world, unlike Mira, and, as she'd just stated, despite her inexperience she was not a romantic. And he still wanted her, even dressed in the muddy torn clothing; he would have quite happily lifted her up onto the countertop and started up where they had left off last night. In fact, as soon as he'd spotted her making a beeline for the back door, he had briefly considered trying to seduce her into agreeing to this marriage. The only reason he hadn't was that he knew she had to still be recovering from last night's excesses and he couldn't guarantee he could be gentle with her now any more than he had been able to last night.

And then there was the fact of her virginity. The more he'd thought about that last night, the more it had come to seem like a massive benefit instead of a complication.

One of the biggest problems with marrying Mira had been the thought of how hard it was going to be to persuade anyone he was in love with her. Helping Ally discover the limits of her own pleasure, showing her how much she had been missing, was a project he could get behind one hundred and one per cent—making it a great deal easier to pretend he loved her. Passion was often confused for love, after all.

He'd never slept with a virgin before, because he didn't want the responsibility, but he had never considered what it might be like to initiate a woman as innately passionate and responsive as Ally.

She had no idea how much fun they could have together. Hell, fun was too tame a word for what they could do together. On the basis of what they had shared last night, fun didn't even begin to cover it.

But he couldn't seduce her again until he'd got her to accept this deal. And he could see that what had happened between his pig of a father and her sweet, gentle, hopelessly vulnerable mother was going to be a major stumbling block. He should have figured that out sooner.

Luckily, he was good at thinking on his feet.

'To be clear, Alison,' he said, 'I won't be paying you for the sex. And you're certainly under no obligation to sleep with me. My hope was that you would want to. Last night demonstrated we have a rare chemistry…' Being a virgin, she probably didn't realise that. 'I'd love to explore that in the months ahead, making this a business arrangement with considerable benefits for both of us. But if that makes you feel demeaned, I won't press the point.'

He smiled, determined to put her at ease if it killed him.

'I certainly wouldn't expect you to sleep with me against your will.' That much at least he could be very clear on. 'And the divorce settlement I'm offering...' he placed his palm on the sheaf of papers he'd had his legal team and his accountants up all night preparing '...which includes a generous allowance and all your other expenses during the marriage plus a one-off alimony payment of a million pounds sterling when we part, is compensation for your time and your agreement to act as my devoted wife. But only in public. What we do in private is entirely up to you.'

'A m-million pounds!' she stuttered, her pale skin flushing a deep dark pink. 'Seriously?'

She looked so shell-shocked, he found his lips quirking, despite all the missteps he'd made.

He still had the upper hand in this negotiation. Of course he did. Alison was an innocent. She'd never had another lover, and from the peaks of her nipples thrusting provocatively through the soft cotton of her cycling shirt it was clear she was no more immune to him than he was to her. Plus she could definitely use the money.

'I want you to marry me, Alison,' he said, while she struggled to close her mouth again. 'It would be a mutually beneficial agreement. I travel quite a lot and if the Waterfront deal goes ahead...' which it would as soon as he had this woman on his arm, because her integrity and honesty were as visible and beguiling as those thrusting nipples '... I'll be living in Manhattan, mostly,' he added. 'While I assume you'd want to continue attending college here? So I wouldn't require too much of your time once we have established the narrative. I would just require you to be available for events my wife would be expected to attend with me.'

He'd thought it all through. This relationship would be run on his terms and his timetable. Them having mostly separate living arrangements made sense. He *would* need to spend the majority of his time in Manhattan once this deal got the green light. And she could continue attending college in London. He didn't want this marriage to impact her life too much as it would only complicate things when they parted. And, in the unlikely event he did get bored with her, he would be able to control the amount of time they spent together.

'The narrative?' she asked. 'What narrative?'

'The narrative of our relationship,' he said. 'It is best to stick as close to the truth as possible. My publicist will work out a press release—but it will be along the lines that we knew each other years ago, got reacquainted when you made a delivery here while Mira was in Klosters and I broke off my engagement with her once I realised I was in love with you.'

'Do you think the press will buy that?' she asked. 'You only broke up with her yesterday.'

'I don't really care if they do or not. The important thing is that the Jedah Consortium believes our marriage is real—which they will once they see us together, all loved up for a few key events a week from now in New York.'

If she agreed to his proposal.

He didn't like that *if*. He wanted this settled. Now.

But she hadn't said a word. She still looked dumbfounded. He forced himself to take a breath. And back off a little, before he spooked her altogether.

Unfortunately, he didn't have the luxury of time. He had a Eurostar to catch in two hours for a meeting in Paris this afternoon, then he was travelling to Rome tomorrow for several days—and from there he would fly to New York to finish the final negotiations on the Waterfront deal. By which time, if he wanted the negotiations to go smoothly, his marriage needed to be finalised.

He waited for her to say something, but she simply stared at him.

'Do you have any questions?' he prompted as he glanced at his watch, unable to hide his impatience.

She nodded, and the tension in his chest eased.

'Could I have time to think about it?'

He had to bite his lip to stop the husky, self-satisfied laugh from bursting out of his mouth. This negotiation was already in the bag. Of course it was; he didn't even know why he had been concerned about it. If the price was right, anyone could be bought. Even a woman as artless and forthright as Alison Jones.

He didn't think less of her for it. Money was important. Something he had learned at an early age—while he and his mother had struggled to survive in the slums of Saint Denis on the outskirts of Paris, on the tiny amount she'd been able to scratch together working two jobs—after having been refused child support from the wealthy man who had discarded her as soon as she'd fallen pregnant.

Alison and her mother had struggled in a similar way after that summer thanks to their association with his father, by the sound of it. He had no idea how bad it had become, but he didn't doubt she had to be fairly desperate to be risking her life each night as a cycle courier simply to pay her rent. Alison, unlike the spoilt debutantes and career women he had dated in the past, had to know what real poverty looked like; he was offering her a route out of that.

'Unfortunately, I need a verbal commitment from you this morning,' he said. 'As I have to catch a train to Paris in…' he checked his watch '…one hour and forty-eight minutes. You can take your time to read through the paperwork and negotiate any changes with my personal assistant, Selene, before you sign. If you want to renegotiate the alimony payment I can be flexi…'

'I don't want any *more* money,' she said, sounding horrified. 'Are you nuts?'

He barked out a laugh, unable to stop his amusement at the absolute horror on her face.

'I'm not a complete mercenary,' she added forcefully.

'Noted,' he said, thinking she didn't seem that mercenary to him at all. If she'd pressed he would easily have been persuaded to up the lump sum to two million pounds.

Getting the Waterfront deal was worth a great deal more than that to him.

The pulse of arousal struck him unawares. And he was forced to admit it wasn't just the thought of signing that deal that was driving his enthusiasm. She really did look good enough to eat—her eyes wide with confusion and uncertainty. The desire to capture her strawberry and chocolate taste on his tongue was all but overwhelming.

A week-long cooling-off period wouldn't be a bad thing at all. He needed to get a choke hold on his hunger before he made love to her again. Or things had the potential to get out of control, the way they had the first time. He wanted to show her he could savour her, that she was worth savouring.

'Come here, *ma belle.*' Before he could second-guess himself, he snagged her wrist and tugged her into the space between his knees.

Inhaling her scent—strawberries and sin—he unfurled her fingers, which had tightened into a fist. Lifting her palm to his mouth, he bit into the soft flesh beneath her thumb. Her shudder of reaction had the heat swelling in his groin. He lifted his gaze to hers, and smiled at the shocked arousal on her face.

'I want very much to make you my wife, Alison. And I'm willing to admit my reasons for suggesting it are not all about business—nor are they entirely honourable.' In fact, if the ache in his crotch was anything to go by, he wasn't sure any of them were at the moment. 'I think the months ahead will be beneficial to both of us, in a financial sense. You'd be doing me a big favour and I'm willing to pay handsomely for your time, it's as simple as that. But this marriage could also be very entertaining for both of us, on the evidence of last night.'

He dropped her hand, and got down off the breakfast stool. Capturing her shoulders, he pressed a kiss to her forehead, forcing himself not to press, not to push, not to take what he so desperately wanted. If she agreed to his proposition, there would be more than enough time to enjoy their chemistry to his heart's content in the months to come.

'You have twenty-four hours to read over the paperwork but I need your answer now,' he said. 'What do you say, Alison? Will you marry me?'

It was wrong. She knew that. Wrong to marry for convenience, for a business deal and definitely wrong to marry him for money. Whatever he said, whatever qualifications he put on what he was offering her, a part of her knew she was basically selling herself.

Maybe she wasn't selling her body; that much was true. She believed he wouldn't press her if she told him she didn't want a sexual relationship with him, but they both knew the chances of that were precisely zilch now she'd experienced how wonderful he could make her feel.

She also knew he was right about the comparison to

his father and her mother's relationship. It wasn't the same thing at all; she could see that now. In fact, it was exactly the opposite—Dominic was offering her marriage and security with no pretence of love, while his father had offered her mother nothing *but* the pretence of love.

And that was the real temptation, she realised. The offer not of marriage, but of security. She didn't want his one-million-pound divorce settlement and she'd tell his PA as much when they ironed out the details of the contract. Whatever he said, she knew her time wasn't worth that much money; it was absurd. But the chance to live in this beautiful house, to have her expenses paid for the next few months, not to have to worry about the rent or the bills or her college fees. To be able to devote her time and energies exclusively to her studies, to designing the collection she wanted to design, maybe even get some of her designs seen while she was playing his devoted wife at the high-profile events he'd talked about. And to travel to places like New York and Paris, places she'd never seen but always wanted to see. That was another major temptation.

And then there was the fairy tale of being with him at those events. That was a powerful temptation too. Because he fascinated her. He always had. She wanted to find out how he'd become so successful, what had driven him, what drove him still.

And let's not forget the sex.

Six months of sex with Dominic LeGrand was not to be sniffed at. After waiting for twenty-five years to discover what all the fuss was about, last night she'd found out. Big time. She wanted to know more. To know everything. And she couldn't think of a better tutor than a man who could make her spontaneously combust simply by crooking his finger at her and directing her to 'come here' in that demanding tone of voice.

Was it really so wrong to say yes to all of that?

As long as she kept her wits about her, and remembered that this was a temporary arrangement, which had a hard and fast sell-by date.

He was offering her a chance to change her life. Why shouldn't she take it?

Didn't she deserve this chance? After everything she'd been through? And she could help him too, to get his business to the next level.

She wanted to do that. If for no other reason than to say thank you to that rebellious boy who had made her feel special and important, once upon a time.

The buzz of the doorbell made her jump, jerking her out of her thoughts, and the frantic reasoning as she tried to make a decision.

'That will be the car to take me to St Pancras International,' he said. 'I'm sorry to rush you, but I need your answer, Allycat?' The request sounded casual, indifferent even, but she could see the muscle in his jaw flexing and the hooded look in his eyes.

He wanted her to say yes as much as she wanted to say it, she realised. Even though he was trying hard not to show it.

That tiny glimpse of the boy she'd once known, who guarded his emotions, his needs and desires with the same ferocity she had learned to guard hers, was enough to release the dam forming in her throat.

'Okay, I'm in. Let's get married.'

Relief crossed his face first, almost as if he'd actually been in doubt about her answer.

'*Fantastique,*' he murmured.

A wide smile spread across his far too handsome features. And it occurred to her it was probably the first genuine smile she'd ever seen on his face.

The inappropriate joy exploded in her chest.

This isn't a real marriage, Ally. It's a fake one. For goodness' sake, get a grip.

Tugging a pen out of his jacket pocket, he scribbled something down on the legal papers on the breakfast bar. 'This is Selene's number. She is my personal assistant. She can arrange to have your belongings moved into this house while I am away. I want you to resign immediately from your job as a courier.'

'Resign?' she asked dumbly.

The smile widened as he gripped her chin between his thumb and forefinger and pressed a kiss to her mouth. 'Yes, my little daredevil. I don't want my wife's life put at risk before I have a chance to consummate our marriage.'

My wife? Consummate? Goodness.

She didn't have a chance to process the information—or the heat flooding through her system as his kiss became carnal—before he had torn his mouth away again.

'Hold that thought,' he said. 'Selene will liaise with my legal team once you sign the pre-nup, and the publicist about a press release. We will be married as soon as you land in New York.' His gaze raked over her figure, making her even more aware of her grubby, torn cycling gear. 'Selene can also arrange someone to buy you the right clothes. As irresistible as I find your current attire, I'm afraid it's not going to work at the sort of events you will have to attend as my wife.'

She didn't need a stylist. She could design and make her own clothes—she wanted to be a fashion designer, after all. But before she could point any of that out, he pulled the jewellery box out of his trouser pocket and flipped it open, to reveal the exquisite ring she'd delivered the night before. Her breathing stopped.

The doorbell buzzed again.

'Arrêtes!' he shouted, loud enough to be heard by his driver, and make her jump.

'As I have no engagement ring I would like you to wear this, to seal our promise.'

She nodded.

Lifting her hand, he threaded the ring onto her finger. It felt heavy, but not as heavy as the weight in her chest when he stroked the knuckle and smiled.

'It fits? *Oui?*' He sounded excited. But not as excited as she suddenly felt.

Excited and a bit dazed if she was honest—because the whole situation felt completely surreal.

Her gaze fixed on his. 'Yes, thank you. It's exquisite,' she said.

The quick grin dazzled her.

'Not as exquisite as you, *ma belle*,' he murmured. The doorbell rang again and he swore softly. 'I will see you in New York in a week's time.' Grasping her trembling fingers, he lifted her hand to his lips and pressed a kiss into her palm. 'Until then *au revoir*, Madame LeGrand.'

A startled breath expelled from her lungs as she watched him stride out of the kitchen to the waiting car.

CHAPTER SIX

I'M GOING TO be married. To Dominic LeGrand.

Ally repeated the information in her head as she stared at the woven strands of platinum and gold that Dominic had slid on her ring finger a week ago. She was still finding it difficult to grasp the reality of her situation though, the events of the past seven days whirring through her head.

She glanced out of the private jet's window as it banked into a turn over Brooklyn, ready for its descent into JFK.

Unfortunately, the sight of a city she had always wanted to explore did nothing to slow down the fleet of butterflies in her belly. That would be the same fleet of butterflies that had been going nuts in her belly ever since she'd agreed to Dominic LeGrand's proposal.

The butterflies whose wings had only got bigger and more manic when she'd moved into his town house later on that first day, her meagre stack of belongings looking overwhelmed by the expensive surroundings. Not unlike their owner, she thought with a huff of breath.

She'd signed the marriage contract the next day after a negotiation with his efficient and ridiculously friendly and accommodating UK assistant, Selene Hartley—who had been more than willing to have the one-million-pound alimony payment cut from the settlement. Given that the first payment of the allowance Dominic had stipulated in the contract had wiped out all her outstanding debts and paid the rest of her college fees, she felt that was more than fair.

The week that followed had been spent getting used to her new surroundings—not easy when there were six bedrooms and an espresso machine that could dumbfound a NASA technician—and designing and making a wardrobe fit for a queen, or rather Dominic LeGrand's high-society wife, which was a lot more exclusive. With her college closed for the Easter break, she'd used the full seven days to work on her collection. She'd set up a workshop in one of the mansion's spare bedrooms with the help of Dominic's housekeeper, Charlotte, and, after sourcing some stunning materials from a series of exclusive fabric retailers with the rest of that first allowance payment, she'd spent most days and every evening sketching and pinning and sewing. Working on the designs had helped to ground her, in between the daunting tasks of attending a doctor's appointment to get a prescription for the pill and being ferried in a limousine to a series of exclusive beauty salons and spas arranged by Selene.

In the last seven days she'd been buffed and plucked and moisturised in places she hadn't even known existed.

The plane descended, dropping through the late afternoon sunshine, the green and gold LeGrand Nationale logo glinting on its wing.

Her newly trimmed and painted fingernails grasped the padded leather of the seat in a death grip as her stomach plunged.

Instead of parking at the passenger terminals, the jet rumbled towards a private hangar at the end of the runway, not unlike the one she had been driven to—in a limousine, of course—that morning in Heathrow.

She ran her palms down the tailored jacket of the silk

trouser suit she'd finished the night before as she tried to stay focussed on her ring and her new job.

Of being Dominic LeGrand's wife.

Because this was a job, a job she was being well paid for, and she needed to remember that.

But as she waited for the jet's crew to finish the landing procedure—the butterflies began having a fit.

What on earth was she doing here? In this rarefied world. For goodness' sake, she'd never been on a budget airline before now—let alone a private jet.

The butterflies dive-bombed into her belly as she examined her suit for the five billionth time. Had she made a major error designing and making her own wardrobe for this trip? She had her own unique style, one she'd developed and explored during her two years of fashion college, and had enjoyed turning into reality during the long hours spent working at her sewing machine in the last week to help calm her nerves. But what if the clothes she'd designed were all wrong? She might have her own style, but it was an urban, edgy, East London style. How would it be received in the kind of circles Dominic moved in—circles she knew nothing about? What would he do if he found out she'd pocketed the money he'd given her to buy an exclusive wardrobe and made her own clothes? Especially if her designs made him a laughing stock? Would he be angry with her? Furious? Could he sue? Had she already screwed up the biggest opportunity of her life?

The increasingly frantic thoughts clashed with the dive-bombing mutant butterflies in her belly.

'Madame LeGrand?' The hostess smiled down at her, using the name on the travel manifest.

'Yes?' Ally croaked.

'Are you ready to disembark?' the hostess asked in her heavily accented English, the beatific smile not faltering.

Not at all.

As panic closed her throat she forced her fingernails to release their grip on the seat.

'The immigration officials have checked your documents and Monsieur LeGrand waits for you,' the hostess added, sweeping her arm towards the door of the aircraft in a polite indication for Ally to get a move on.

Ally understood; the poor woman had been on her feet for seven hours.

'Right, sorry,' she said, unlocking the seat belt and standing.

She brushed her trembling palms down the sheer blue silk. And made her way to the front of the plane.

As she stepped out onto the outer stairs, she spotted Dominic standing at the bottom busy tapping out a message on his phone with both thumbs. A man with a briefcase stood beside him who had to be the marriage officiant Selene had told her would be there to issue their marriage licence as soon as she arrived. Apparently the marriage itself would be performed tomorrow, as the law in New York required a twenty-four hour wait after the licence was issued. But it wasn't the thought of the formalities that had the dive-bombing butterflies going up in flames.

Even with his head bent, Dominic looked more gorgeous and overwhelming than he had a week ago. She couldn't help noticing how the seams of his shirt stretched over his biceps as she made her way down the gangway on unsteady legs. How could he seem part savage, even in a business suit?

He's going to be your husband. Seriously?

Her heels clicked on the tarmac and Dominic stopped typing.

His dark chocolate gaze coasted over her figure, burning right through the silk. His eyes flared as his gaze finally met hers, and her ribs tightened around her lungs like a vice.

'*Bonjour*, Alison.' The husky accent rippled through her, setting off bursts of sensation—and making her far too aware of the hours spent tenderising her skin in the spas and salons he'd paid for over the last week.

Was that why every inch of her body felt as if it were about to burst into flames too, along with the dive-bombing butterflies?

'How was your flight?' he asked.

'Great,' she rasped as he approached, and she became aware again of exactly how tall he was.

He had to be at least six foot three.

Thank goodness she'd used some of the money he'd given her to purchase a range of high heels. She was hardly a small woman, having reached her full height of five foot seven at the age of fifteen, but he dwarfed her, just as he had when they were kids. She'd been considerably shorter as a thirteen-year-old. But had he been this tall as a teenager? He certainly hadn't been this broad. Maybe it was the way he'd filled out that made him so much more intimidating.

Stop staring at his muscles.

She forced herself not to step back, but she couldn't hide the shudder of reaction when he took her hand and brushed a kiss across the knuckles.

'You look exquisite,' he said, the approval heating his dark gaze almost as disconcerting as the sensation now shooting up her arm and reigniting those flaming mutant dive-bombing butterflies in her belly.

'Thank you,' she said, but the praise hadn't helped to mitigate her nerves one bit.

He introduced her to the man standing beside him. The balding young man who had been especially hired from the New York City Clerks' Office verified her identity. After they had signed the forms, he issued their licence and explained he would return to perform the ceremony at Dominic's apartment tomorrow, at which point the marriage certificate could be issued.

'*Bon,*' Dominic murmured, after the clerk had smiled and left. 'Only one more day and we can get all the paperwork out the way.'

Ally shivered, knowing that, whatever the officiant said, this marriage was already binding, at least for her, because she'd made a promise seven days ago. A promise she had no desire to renege on.

She felt suddenly naked beneath Dominic's gaze, and the truth was she almost was. What had possessed her to wear nothing but a bra under the jacket?

You idiot! Ruining the jacket's line is not going to matter if you pass out at his feet before you even get a chance to say I do.

Dominic's lips quirked—the way they had when he'd proposed a week ago, as if he were sharing a private joke with her.

'Why do you look so terrified, my darling almost wife?' His gruff accent lingered on the word 'wife'—both provocative and possessive. 'I promise not to seal our bargain until we are somewhere private.'

The laugh she managed to huff out past her constricted lungs didn't sound as confident as she'd hoped.

'That's good,' she said, tugging her tingling fingers out of his grasp—the thought of him sealing the bargain they'd made a week ago sending a battalion of pheromones hurtling to every one of her erogenous zones along with those blasted butterflies. 'I wouldn't want to get arrested my first ten seconds on US soil.'

He laughed, the rough sound raw enough to stimulate her nerve-endings even more.

'*Touché*, Alison,' he murmured, the admiration in his dark hooded eyes so compelling she found herself basking in his approval. Even though she knew she shouldn't.

It's a job. It's a job. It's a job.

But the reminder couldn't stop the flaming mutant butterflies in her belly from going berserk as his warm arm banded around her waist and he led her across the tarmac to a waiting car—which was a huge black limousine. Of course.

Dominic clicked his seat belt into place, thankful for the physical restraint as the jacket Alison was wearing opened to reveal a seductive hint of purple lace while she strapped herself into the car next to him.

She looked absolutely exquisite, her willowy frame displayed to perfection in the striking blue suit, the shadow of cleavage making it hard for him to concentrate on anything other than the desire to get her back to his apartment as soon as physically possible.

He'd prepared for her arrival today by convincing himself his physical reaction to her a week ago had been exaggerated thanks to his long sexual drought, and the expediency of ensuring she agree to become his wife.

But as soon as he'd heard her heels on the tarmac, and looked up from his smartphone, he'd known he'd been kidding himself.

Dressed in grubby Lycra or oversized sweats, Alison Jones had been subtly sexy. Now she was stunning.

Long, slim, and stylish, her figure in the tailored suit looked both toned and athletic while at the same time being supremely feminine. And her striking bone structure, the translucent skin and those bottomless eyes the colour of a fine whisky, only enhanced by the hint of eyeliner and the lush sparkle of lip gloss, made her irresistible.

He wanted to undo the one button holding her jacket together, capture her full breasts in his palms and fasten his lips on the rampaging pulse fluttering in the delicate well of her collarbone.

The driving need to take her to bed as soon as was humanly possible was so strong, in fact, it had the potential to be problematic.

He didn't like being ruled by his desires—as much as he enjoyed sex, he had never had a problem controlling his hunger before now—and becoming addicted to Alison was not supposed to be part of this arrangement.

So stop leering at her and start talking.

He dragged his gaze away from her cleavage as the car left the airport and headed onto the expressway. She had her nose pressed against the window, obviously absorbing every new sight and sound, like a child outside a candy store.

'So you've never been to the States before?' he asked.

Her head swung round. 'I've never been anywhere before,' she said with an unabashed smile. 'Apart from Provence. But I've always wanted to come here. It's so exciting. Like being in a movie.' Her unguarded enthusiasm, like everything else about her, was utterly beguiling.

Her expression sobered suddenly, so much so he could see the nerves. He wondered what on earth she had to be nervous about.

'By the way, could I ask you something about the events we'll be attending while I'm here…?' she asked.

'What about them?'

'Do you think…?' She paused and bit into her lip, sending another shaft of heat straight to his groin.

'What is it?' he demanded, more curtly than he had intended as the lip bite tortured him. Was she doing it deliberately? If only she were, he thought, feeling less and less in control of the situation. But somehow he doubted it. Because... She had been a virgin.

What had seemed like such a boon before he'd married her—PR wise—seemed less so as the hot blood surged to his crotch with very little provocation. Why did the fact of her inexperience make him all the more eager to explore every aspect of her pleasure?

'I just wondered, do you think this outfit will be suitable?' she finally blurted out.

'*Excusez-moi?*' he asked, because it sounded as if she'd just asked him to give her fashion advice.

'This outfit?' She spread her arms wide, making the button strain even more.

He stifled a groan.

'Do you think it would work? For the kinds of events you were talking about...'

Mon Dieu, she *was* asking him for fashion advice.

'Selene gave me an itinerary,' she continued, the words pouring out as her nerves got the better of her. 'So I know what we're doing. But I've never been to the theatre before. Or the opening of an art gallery... So I had to wing it, and rely on some Internet research to figure out what to...' A guilty flush flowed into her cheeks. 'What to bring with me.'

He sat for a moment, trying to wrestle his libido under control and come up with a credible answer. Because it seemed to be important to her. And silently cursed his personal assistant. Why hadn't Selene employed an expert to help Alison with her wardrobe? Surely there were people who could advise you on your clothing? He was fairly sure he'd shelled out a small fortune for such a person for Mira.

But it was too late to suggest that now. He didn't want to make her more nervous or unsure of herself.

'Alison, your outfit is stunning,' he said with feeling, giving the flowing lines of the suit another once-over. That at least was certainly not a lie. 'It will do perfectly.'

Who the hell cared if what she was wearing was the norm, or suitable? he decided. She looked incredible in the suit—enough to tie his libido into knots in sixty seconds or less.

'You really think so? You like the suit?' she asked, and he could hear her insecurity again. 'It's what you had in mind?'

'I *love* the suit. And I didn't have anything particular in mind,' he said, because the truth was what she would be wearing had not featured at all in any of the many, many erotic fantasies he'd entertained about her in the last week. 'Women's fashions are not my forte,' he added, just in case that wasn't entirely obvious. 'But on the basis of this outfit, I'm looking forward to seeing whatever else you've selected for this trip.' Which wasn't truth either, because he'd been looking forward to stripping her out of her new wardrobe a great deal more. But the tentative smile that curved her lips made him glad he'd lied. 'Does that set your mind at rest?' he finished, trying to keep his mind at least nominally out of his pants and on the main reason why she was with him in New York.

Good to know at least one of us is able to do that.

The sheen of pleasure made the amber of her eyes twinkle in the sinking sunlight streaming through the car window, the distinctive hue becoming all the more captivating.

His pulse bumped his own collarbone as the irony of the situation occurred to him.

How exactly had he ended up having to persuade his own fiancée how attractive he found her?

'I'm so glad you like it,' she said, emotion thickening her voice. 'It means a lot to me.'

He steeled himself against the visceral tug of heat in his groin and the unsettling realisation she was genuinely moved by his compliment.

He'd never had a problem complimenting women on their appearance, especially when they looked as exquisite as Alison did in that moment, but there was something about her gratitude that reminded him of the little girl who had followed him around that summer, and how he'd clung to the open adoration in her eyes.

He cut off the thought, determined to forget the lost children they'd been that summer.

He wasn't that reckless, unhappy boy any more, desperate for any sign of approval. And she wasn't that little girl who had showered him with such unguarded affection.

He'd needed her to like him all those years ago—because under the veneer of teenage hostility and indifference, he'd been scared and confused, unable to understand why his father hated him so.

But he certainly did not need Alison—or anyone else—to like him now.

His phone vibrated, breaking the strange spell. He pulled it out of his pocket. And read the text from his business manager.

We have a problem with the Consortium. Mira Kensington just sold her story to the London Post.

He swore viciously under his breath and clicked on the call button.

Stop being a damn sap, LeGrand. Time to focus on what this marriage is actually supposed to achieve, instead of what it isn't.

* * *

'Dominic, is everything okay?' Ally asked as her fiancé swore in French.

'Yes, but I need to take this call,' he said, his tone curt and dismissive.

Everything didn't sound okay as he spoke in hushed tones to whoever was on the other end of the line in a stream of furious French.

After picking up that the conversation had something to do with Mira, she turned back to the window and tried not to listen.

Because thinking about his ex-fiancée would destroy the happy buzz his compliments had triggered.

A happy buzz that had gone some way to controlling her nerves—and all the feelings of inadequacy that had hijacked her during the flight.

Maybe it was pathetic how much she had enjoyed hearing him say he loved her outfit. And she probably ought to be shot for fishing for a compliment so shamelessly, but still his hot, unguarded approval had meant something.

She'd always believed that fanciful little girl had died after the summer in Provence. Because ever since that night she'd been forced to grow up, be a realist, not dream too big or too passionately, because she hadn't wanted to risk having her spirit crushed again. But that little girl hadn't died, she'd just been waiting for an opportunity like this.

Hearing Dominic's praise for her work, and knowing it was genuine, even if their marriage would be fake, had made her feel as if that child was able to believe in herself again… At least a little bit. And that felt liberating and empowering in a way she hadn't felt in a long time.

The car crossed the Brooklyn Bridge into Manhattan. The legendary skyline rose on the other side of the

East River, the skyscrapers like silent sentries to the city's wealth and prominence.

As they drove through downtown she gazed in awe at the canyons of steel and glass and the bustle of traffic and people at street level—like London but so much more urgent, and manic, and less restrained. But as she heard Dominic finish his call it was hard for her to stay focussed on the excitement of being in a new city for the first time in her life.

His tension was palpable as he shoved his phone back into his pocket.

She had caught snippets of the conversation. Her French certainly wasn't fluent, but as well as Mira's name being mentioned several times she'd heard the word *'vierge'*.

Virgin.

Had Dominic been talking about her virginity to someone? Because she didn't even know how to feel about that. Embarrassed mostly, but also confused. Why would that be relevant, to anything at all? The only way to find out what was going on, though, was to ask.

The muscle in his cheek was flexing as he stared out of the window, obviously thinking something through.

'Is there a problem?' she asked.

His head turned. He looked as if he was angry, but trying not to show it.

'No,' he said, too dogmatically to be entirely believable. She might know nothing about his business, but she knew when she was being hoodwinked.

'If there's a problem, I might be able to help,' she said.

The hard line of his lips quirked in a reluctant smile. 'Are you serious?'

She nodded. 'Yes, I am.' She had no idea why he found that amusing, but she decided him being amused was better than him being furious. 'The only reason I'm here is to help you get this deal sorted out.' She coughed slightly, as the blush burned in her cheeks. Okay, that was a blatant lie. 'Well, the *main* reason I'm here is to help you get this deal sorted out.'

'Is that so?' he asked, his eyebrows launching up his forehead as he choked out a laugh.

'Well, yes,' she said.

'*Dieu*, Alison. Have I told you yet how damn adorable you are?'

'Maybe,' she said, glad to see him smile. But even gladder she'd caused that smile.

Especially when he picked up her hand, opened her fingers and pressed his lips into her palm.

Her fingers curled around his cheek, heat shooting into her abdomen.

'Damn but I want you so much,' he said. The admission sounded a little tortured—which made her smile even more.

'Well, good,' she said. 'Because so do I.'

'*Bien,*' he murmured, with that hot possessive look in his gaze that was guaranteed to get the mutant butterflies partying in her pants.

He clasped her hand, and squeezed it. 'Okay, if I tell you what the call was about, will you promise not to be offended?'

'Of course,' she said. Confused now. Because he looked pained. And the slash of regret wasn't his usual default. He struck her as a man who made a point of regretting nothing.

'That was my business manager, Etienne Franco, on the phone. The consortium are questioning the validity of our love match because my former fiancée decided to give an exclusive interview to a British tabloid newspaper, which implied you're...' He paused, the muscle in his cheek flexing again. 'How did she put it in the article? "Being paid to service my sexual appetites while posing as my wife."'

Ally cleared her throat, not sure what to say, because although she knew she *should* be offended by Mira's comments, the fact he seemed to be offended enough for both of them had a bubble of pleasure forming in her throat.

'That's a bit unfair,' she said, trying to sound stern while the bubble of pleasure burst, creating a warm glow through her entire body. 'Seeing as she's never even met me—well, not properly,' she corrected, remembering the altercation on the street.

Damn it, why isn't she furious?

'Alison, it's not just unfair of her. It's libellous. She's basically suggesting you're a prostitute in a national newspaper.' Dominic ground out the words, still so furious with Mira he could barely speak. But the truth was he was just as disgusted with himself. He should have guessed his ex would pull a stunt like this. And he hadn't done a damn thing to prevent it, or protect Alison.

In fact he'd basically set her up for exactly this kind of attack.

An attack that she was uniquely vulnerable to, not just because she appeared to have no sense of guile whatsoever, but because, as he had just discovered, she had been in much harsher financial straits than he had assumed.

As well as Mira's bitchy comments, the *Post* article had included a detailed description of the harsh realities of Alison's life before he had 'plucked her from obscurity'— and it had turned his stomach. The struggles she'd faced in the last twelve years had been a great deal harder than he had imagined. It seemed she and her mother had been living in abject poverty through her teens—ever since the night his father had thrown them off the estate. Alison had been supporting them both since the age of fifteen with a series of part-time jobs. And her debts had only increased after her mother's death from an overdose of prescription painkillers four years ago.

He'd exploited her destitution to feed the rags-to-riches Cinderella narrative his publicist had used to explain their 'fairy-tale romance' but now it had backfired on him spectacularly. Because he'd had no idea how close it was to the truth.

His father had destroyed her life that night... But his father hadn't been the only one responsible for what had happened to Monica and by extension her daughter.

He pushed the bitter memories to one side.

Do not go there. You can't go back and solve what you did.

But, unfortunately, telling himself that didn't make him feel any less responsible. Not just for what had happened that night, but for the trashing of Alison's reputation now.

'I'm going to sue her and the newspaper. I refuse to have you slandered in that way,' he said, because that at least was explainable.

Maybe his marriage to Alison was essentially a business arrangement, but by this time tomorrow she would finally be his wife, so of course he would have to protect her reputation.

'Wouldn't it be better just to ignore it?' Alison asked, her teeth tugging on her bottom lip again, and sending a now incendiary shot of heat to his groin.

'No, it would not.'

'But, Dominic, what about the Waterfront deal?' she said as his furious thoughts galloped ahead of him.

'What about it?' he barked. Why was she being so damn reasonable and accommodating about this outrage?

'Surely getting embroiled in a legal battle with a British tabloid isn't going to be good for that? Especially if they find out our marriage *is* essentially a business arrangement after all.'

I don't care about the damn deal.

He opened his mouth, to say the words that ricocheted through his consciousness. Then closed it again. As his fury and indignation slammed into a brick wall.

What the hell had he just thought? Hell, what had he almost said? Out loud?

He *did* care about the deal. The deal was everything. The deal was why Alison was here. Why *he* was here. The only reason this marriage was happening. And she was right: if he sued Mira and the *London Post* the real reason behind their marriage would come to light.

'The deal will be fine,' he said, even though he wasn't entirely sure.

Calm the hell down and think.

'I told the business manager to point out to the consortium you were a virgin. That you have never slept with another man before you slept with me. Making you the furthest thing from a prostitute.'

The foolish spurt of pride hit him unawares—the way it had when he had told Etienne.

What the heck was that about, too?

Alison's lack of experience was something he could use, to help make their marriage seem more authentic and to help him secure this deal. That was the only reason it was relevant. Why should he care if he was her first?

'Oh,' she said as a delectable blush rioted across her cheeks. And he almost laughed at the irony.

She was embarrassed about her virginity, but not about being dubbed a prostitute in a British tabloid.

'Did you *have* to tell him that?' she said. 'It's so personal.'

'I know, and I apologise, but I wanted to refute Mira's claims in the strongest possible terms.'

To secure this damn deal, which I completely forgot about a minute ago. Mon Dieu, *LeGrand, get a grip.*

'They're not going to put *that* in the papers, are they?' she asked, sounding horrified.

The rough chuckle burst out without warning. After all the fury and recriminations, the agony of knowing he'd failed her—and jeopardised the deal, which was of course much more important—her reaction seemed hopelessly naïve, but also ridiculously endearing. So endearing it managed to achieve several things at once—defuse his temper, restore his sense of humour and, most importantly of all, restore his sense of perspective.

He'd overreacted, not just to Mira's attack, but also to the disturbing news about Alison's circumstances in the last twelve years. That much was obvious.

What had happened on that night twelve years ago had no bearing on their circumstances now. And yes, maybe he was using Alison, but he had been upfront about that and she had made an informed decision to sign the contract. She was on board with all of this. And he was paying her a million pounds for her pains. He hadn't deceived her or seduced her into this situation. She had come of her own free will.

Alison was also correct. Ignoring Mira's attack made sense—the story would die a death more quickly that way. He'd already told Etienne about Alison's unsullied state to refute the claims made in the article with the consortium. And displaying their happy marriage for all to see over the next few days by escorting his new wife to a few high-profile events would hardly be a chore given that he was struggling to keep his hands off her.

The reason he had lost perspective about Mira's article and its fallout was even easier to explain.

An idiotic part of him had panicked that Alison might back out of their arrangement at the eleventh hour—thanks to the frustrating extra twenty-four hours the officiant had insisted they would have to wait before dotting the last of the *i*'s on their deal. Plus he'd waited seven whole days to consummate this damn deal already—while enduring the sort of sweaty erotic dreams every night that hadn't plagued him since he was a boy.

But Alison wasn't going to back out of this deal. And he didn't need to wait any longer to seal their deal, in the only way that mattered.

'No, they won't put it in the papers,' he said. But couldn't resist the urge to run a thumb over her lips. The sooner he fed this hunger, the sooner it would stop messing with his head. 'But why are you embarrassed about it?'

'Probably because I'm twenty-five years old and being a virgin at that age makes me seem sad and like a bit of a freak!'

'Firstly, you're not a virgin any more,' he said, unable to keep the smugness out of his voice. 'And secondly, I don't think it makes you a freak. It simply makes you discerning. You waited, until a man came along who was a good enough lover to give you the spectacular experience you deserved for your first time,' he added, teasing her now—and going the full smug in the process. 'Which isn't sad, it's smart.'

She huffed out a laugh, but the sparkle of amusement in her eyes was like a drug. When, exactly, had making her smile become so addictive?

'Spoken like a guy with an ego the size of Manhattan,' she said, but the embarrassed flush had begun to fade, so he considered her mockery well earned.

'*Touché*, again, Alison,' he said, grinning back at her as the car stopped in front of the loft apartment building he owned in Nolita.

Nolita, short for North of Little Italy, was the thriving neighbourhood that had been up-and-coming in the nineties but had now firmly arrived, with a young, trendy, arthouse crowd moving in to the turn-of-the-century brownstones and rehabbed tenement blocks.

'What a beautiful building—is this where you live?' Alison asked, her enthusiasm making his ribs feel suspiciously tight.

He'd bought the condemned brick and cast-iron building on the corner of Lafayette five years ago for a steal, then proceeded to work a miracle—gutting and then refurbishing the structure to preserve its historic integrity in the elegant arched windows and cast-iron balconies, while at the same time giving it a luxury, high-spec interior. The ten-storey block now housed the offices of LN's US-based operation, and a four-bed, four-bath penthouse loft apartment where he stayed when he was in the city.

'Yes, I own the building. LN's offices take up the first nine floors and then my apartment's on the top,' he said, then realised he was boasting and didn't know why. He'd never felt the need to impress a woman before.

'It's gorgeous,' she said. 'I love the art deco details.'

He got out of the car, not sure why his chest tightened even more at her praise. 'I'm glad you approve.'

He offered his hand and she took it.

The lapels of her suit jacket—the jacket that had been driving him wild as soon as she'd stepped onto American soil—spread as she stepped out of the car, giving him another provocative glimpse of pale flesh and purple lace.

The familiar shot of adrenaline pounded back into his crotch.

The chauffeur stepped to the back of the vehicle to help the doorman with their luggage, leaving them cocooned on the sidewalk, the car door shielding them from passers-by. He couldn't see any photographers, even though Etienne had suggested they might be besieged for the next few days as a result of Mira's story.

But he found himself tugging her into his arms regardless.

He'd waited seven days to get his mouth on Alison again. And now she was as good as his wife, what better way to finally put his idiotic overreaction to bed and get this agreement back where it was always supposed to be?

He placed his hands on her hips, until she stood flush against his body.

'Madame LeGrand,' he murmured. 'Time to start practising your act as the dutiful wife.'

Although it didn't feel like just an act any more.

But then, it wasn't an act, entirely. This was always supposed to be a business arrangement with benefits. So why not start claiming the benefits?

She looked up through long lashes, her amber eyes like those of a doe who had spotted the huntsman taking aim. And it occurred to him how inexperienced she still was. The punch of lust at the thought that she had only ever been his was visceral and basic and impossible to deny— so he didn't even try.

Her virginity had clearly turned him into a caveman. But he could do nothing but run with it now.

She lifted her arms and flattened her palms on his chest—the movement as brave as it was arousing.

'*Es-tu prêtes?*' he whispered against her neck, his ability to speak English deserting him momentarily as he inhaled the rich, fresh scent of her, that glorious combination of strawberries and chocolate that had driven him wild in London—far too long ago.

Are you ready?

'Very,' she whispered back, her body shivering with reaction as he pressed his lips to the flutter of her pulse beneath her ear.

Plunging his fingers into her hair, he felt her soft sob against his lips before he angled her head and plundered. But as soon as his tongue tangled with hers, the surge of adrenaline became an unstoppable force.

He thrust deep, setting up an erotic rhythm spurred on by the grinding hunger beneath his belt.

She responded instinctively, her body surrendering to his will, her soft curves yielding to the hard contours as he pressed her back against the car's paintwork.

Had he ever been this desperate before, the need to rip off her clothes and plunge into the tight wet heart of her all but overwhelming? His hand slipped inside the open lapel of her jacket beneath the lacy bra until he was cupping the soft flesh of her breast, rejoicing in the feel of her nipple swelling against his palm.

'Mr LeGrand, do you have anything to say about Mira Kensington's piece in the London papers?'

The shouted question had him rearing back just as a camera flashed in his face.

Alison gasped and stiffened. The shocked arousal in her eyes turning the hot blood now running through his veins to wild fire.

The reporter stepped closer to shove a microphone between them as she scrambled to right her clothing.

The son of a...

'Get away from my fiancée,' he shouted in English, then repeated the command in French with a great deal more emphasis. The man seemed to get the message because he scurried away with his photographer.

Dominic grabbed Alison's hand.

'Let's finish this in private,' he said, realising the mistake of kissing her in public. He wanted to convince the consortium this relationship was real—but having a photograph of him baring her breast on the sidewalk emblazoned on the celebrity blogs would be counterproductive.

An older woman winked at him as he marched past. And a couple of teenage boys whistled from their spot on a nearby wall.

Dieu, forget the paparazzi—he'd just put on a show for the whole damn neighbourhood.

Leading Alison to the elevator at the back of the lobby, he stabbed the button. Damn it, he'd been about to take her right there on a public street.

He hadn't been aware of anything, not of the reporter or the photographer, who'd probably taken more than a few pictures, or the people watching, all he'd been aware of was her—the feel of her soft flesh cradling his erection, her fingers massaging his scalp, the drugging taste of her invading his nostrils and overwhelming his senses, the feel of her nipple hardening in his hand.

The elevator arrived quickly and whisked them to the top floor.

As they walked into the apartment her hand flexed in his and he heard her breath catch.

'Wow, what an incredible view,' she said.

He let go of her, and tried to focus. To give her a moment. To give them both a moment—before he dragged her straight from the street into the bedroom.

Iron colonnades broke up the penthouse's vast open-plan living space. The designer had insisted on lots of rugs and some bespoke pieces of furniture to warm the harsh concrete floors. Several stories higher than the surrounding buildings, the penthouse's leaded glass walls afforded incredible one-hundred-and-eighty-degree views of the neighbourhoods of SoHo and Little Italy. The Empire State stood proud to the north and the new World Trade Center rose like a phoenix from the ashes of Ground Zero to the south.

The breathtaking view was the apartment's signature feature, but he couldn't even see it because all he could focus on was Alison as she spun round in a circle to capture it all, her cheeks reddened from his kisses. He rubbed his chin and encountered the beard scruff he hadn't shaved since that morning—he needed to slow the hell down. Give her some time to adjust.

But as his erection pounded in his pants, the way it had done every night he'd spent in his bed here alone, the only way he could think of to handle the hunger was to feed it.

'Alison, do you want a tour of the apartment or to finish what we just started on the street outside?' he managed.

Maybe his voice sounded rough and raw, and demanding, but he was giving her a choice, damn it.

She blushed deliciously, her gaze settling on the prodigious erection tenting his pants. 'I'm sorry,' she said.

'Don't be sorry.' He took her hand, squeezed it to reassure her. 'Just tell me you want this as much as me.'

'I do.'

It was all the permission he needed.

Tightening his grip, he led her across the living space towards the master bedroom.

As soon as they were inside, he slammed the door, and unhooked the button on her jacket that had been tormenting him since she'd stepped off the plane. He slid the jacket off her shoulders. The soft flesh of her breasts was pushed up like an offering in the purple lace. He slid his thumbs into the waistband of the suit's trousers, but couldn't seem to find the fastening.

'Take them off. I need you naked,' he demanded, deciding he couldn't waste time searching for it. His hands were starting to shake.

She quivered, and drew a zip down at the side of the trousers. He was glad to see her fingers were as shaky as his.

'Lose the bra, too,' he said, and watched as she freed her breasts from the lacy confinement.

But as he hooked his fingers in the elastic of her panties, ready to drag them off, she pressed a trembling hand to his shirt. 'Please, I need you naked too.'

The surge of desire at the urgency in her voice had his groin throbbing so hard he was scared he might explode too soon.

Don't be insane, you have never done that. Not even as an untried kid.

He shucked his own clothes in record time, then tumbled her onto the bed. The bed he'd dreamed about having her in far too often in the last week.

But instead of climbing up there with her—and ending this even sooner—he grasped her hips, tugged her closer until she was sitting on the edge and knelt down, his knees sinking into the rug.

The sharp gasp as he hooked one of her legs over his shoulder, exposing her completely to him, only increased the surge of desire.

He pressed his face into her sex, inhaling her intoxicating scent. *Dieu*, but she smelt delicious—not just of strawberries and chocolate, but of heat and desire. He blew against the trimmed triangle of chestnut curls and licked the slick seam.

She moaned, her fingers plunging in his hair. He tasted

her, circling, tantalising, listening to her throaty sobs, learning her contours, finding what she liked, and what she loved. Holding her open with his thumbs, he found the hard, swollen nub with his lips and suckled hard.

She cried out, jerking as the spontaneous orgasm ripped through her. His erection hardened to iron. Her juices soaked his tongue as he lapped up the last of her pleasure.

He rose over her.

With her skin flushed, her nipples begging for his attention, her body sated, and her eyes dazed, she was like a banquet laid out before him. The vague thought occurred to him that he might never get enough of her.

But then the need to feast on her overwhelmed him.

Ally's breath clogged, her sex already tender from Dominic's mouth as he notched the huge head of his erection at her core. And thrust deep.

The tight sheath stretched to receive him this time, the pleasure becoming so intense as he filled her, it was almost pain.

He rocked out, thrust back, ruthlessly stroking the spot he had found a week ago, working her into a frenzy of need. The orgasm exploded from her core this time, in shattering waves of sensation.

The desperate pants, the moaning sobs turned to hoarse cries of agony and then ecstasy as the wave crashed over her.

He grunted, and hot seed exploded inside her.

He groaned and collapsed on top of her.

She held him, her fingers shaking. Her body drifting in afterglow as her lungs seemed to collapse in her chest.

Why was she struggling to breathe? She'd climaxed. The sex was as good if not better than their first time.

He groaned and rolled off her, easing the still large erection out of her with some difficulty.

'I forgot to ask,' he said. 'Are you on the pill?'

The tightness in his voice made the breath thicken in her lungs.

'Yes.'

'Dieu merci,' he whispered, his relief palpable.

Thank God.

It was one of the stipulations in the contract she'd signed. He'd provided a detailed medical report to prove it would be safe for them to have unprotected sex, but had requested that if she agreed to a sexual relationship with him, she would also arrange oral contraception.

The clause had made sense to her at the time she'd signed it. Neither of them wanted an accident. Risking bringing a child into a situation like theirs would be disastrous—but as she lay beside him, the scent of sex and sweat surrounding them, his question had an odd shaft of melancholy rippling through her tired body.

Because it reinforced the limits of this relationship.

Not that she needed to have them reinforced.

She looked away from him, towards the wall of windows that looked out onto the famous skyline. The sun had started to set, adding a romantic glow to the silhouettes of the Empire State and the Chrysler Building and the cluster of other skyscrapers to the north she couldn't identify.

Get it together, Alison. It's not cynical to be on the pill—it's smart.

She listened to him get off the bed and disappear into the bathroom; the lock clicked.

When he returned a few minutes later, she had managed to drag her exhausted body under the sheets.

He wore a robe, but still the glimpse of washboard abs

had the traitorous pheromones skittering back into her tender sex.

But she yawned, as the exhaustion of the flight, and everything that had happened since she had arrived, began to claim her.

'You should get some sleep,' he said, but the suggestion seemed strangely impersonal. 'You can stay in here and I'll pick one of the other bedrooms.'

What? They weren't going to share a bedroom?

A silly wobble of emotion tightened around her throat, but she didn't protest as she watched him gather a few pieces of clothing from the dresser drawers.

'I'll get the staff to reorganise our belongings tomorrow,' he said.

'You don't have to give up your bedroom,' she said, feeling stupidly bereft.

'Not a problem,' he said. Then strode back to the bed, leant down and kissed her forehead. The wobble intensified. 'Make yourself at home,' he added. 'Manny the doorman can order you in any food you want—just dial zero on the interlink. He can also arrange a car and driver if you want to go sightseeing or shopping tomorrow.'

'You won't be here?' she asked, then wanted to bite back the suggestion because it made her sound needy, and clingy. And she'd never been either.

'I'm going to be busy with the deal negotiations until tomorrow night… I'll see you back here at seven when the clerk is due and then to escort you to…' he paused '… whatever event we're supposed to be seen at.'

'The opening of the Claxton Gallery?' she said, because she'd memorised the schedule Selene had given her.

Stupidly she'd been looking forward to spending the next twenty-four hours with him, getting to know him a little better, because there had been nothing on the schedule.

She realised the foolishness of that supposition, though. He was a busy man, and his business came first. He was certainly under no obligation to entertain her while she was here.

'On the Upper East Side? At eight?' she added, because his face had gone blank, his gaze dipping down to the place where her fingers clutched the sheet over her breasts.

His head lifted. '*Oui*—that.' His smile seemed tight and a little strained, and she wasn't sure he had even heard her, but still the wry tilt of his lips helped the breath to release from her lungs. 'Will you be okay on your own?' he asked.

'Yes, of course,' she said. 'Terrific.'

But as he left the room, the wobble became a wave.

CHAPTER SEVEN

'HI. IT'S ALISON, isn't it?'

Ally swung round from the lavish buffet laid out against the raw redbrick wall of the stark modernist art gallery to find a beautiful and heavily pregnant woman—her plate already laden with delicacies—smiling at her.

'Yes, it's Alison, although everyone calls me Ally,' she said.

'Everyone except your new husband.' The woman's smile became sweetly conspiratorial. 'It's very hot the way Dominic calls you Alison in that French accent. Sorry, I should introduce myself. My name's Megan De Rossi—I'm Dario De Rossi's wife. De Rossi Corp were one of Dominic's early investors when he moved LN's main offices to New York a few years ago.' She offered her hand. 'Which means I've basically been abandoned too—because my husband and your husband have been talking shop ever since we arrived.'

Ally took Megan's hand, feeling hideously exposed by the woman's relaxed, friendly manner. She'd never felt less like Dominic's wife. Other than their marriage ceremony—which had been dealt with in a few short sentences—they had hardly spoken to each other since yesterday evening.

Not since their mind-blowing session to seal their marriage bargain. When he'd treated her as if she were a particularly sumptuous treat that deserved to be savoured and devoured at the same time—then abandoned her.

The memory of their lovemaking and his abrupt departure had kept her awake in the huge king-size bed most of the night. And she'd been obsessing about it most of the day while she took the car and driver Dominic had insisted she use to do some window-shopping in the fashion boutiques of the East Village.

Dominic had appeared at the same time as the clerk to complete the marraige and escort her to this event as scheduled an hour ago, but since the perfunctory ceremony, he'd barely spoken to her—far too busy typing on his phone.

She'd felt his eyes on her when she'd stood beside him in front of the clerk, but no compliment on her outfit had been forthcoming like the last time. And her enquiries during their ride over about how the deal negotiations were going had elicited one-syllable replies.

During the silent, tense ride in the limo, a thousand and one questions had spun through her mind—had she done something wrong, messed up somehow? But she'd forced herself to bury her insecurities deep.

This deal was important and he was obviously preoccupied. Not everything was about her.

So she'd remained silent during the ride. And when they'd arrived, she'd been far too affected by his nearness, warm and solid and overwhelming when he had taken her arm and held her close—as any besotted newly-wed would—as they'd run the gauntlet of reporters and press photographers outside the event, to breathe let alone speak.

As soon as they were safely inside, he'd introduced her to a couple of the consortium members who were attending the event—but once the conversation had moved on to the intricacies of the deal, which was clearly still being negotiated, she had known she was surplus to requirements and had excused herself by explaining she was keen to look at the art.

She'd been miserable ever since—feeling like the class geek who had been invited to the birthday party of the most popular girl in school by mistake. Everyone else here seemed to know each other, drinking and chatting and laughing and mingling to their hearts' content. Ally had stood in the corner, and watched them, trying not to go over and over in her head all the things she hadn't had the guts to ask Dominic in the car.

Being a trophy wife was so much tougher than it looked.

'I thought I'd come and join you,' Megan added. 'I hope you don't mind.'

'Not at all,' Ally said, stifling her discomfort. She knew of Megan De Rossi—she was an important influencer on the New York social scene, not just because her husband was a billionaire but because she ran a ground-breaking charity to help women trapped in abusive relationships and she was the daughter of Alexis Whittaker, a famous British It-Girl of yesteryear. What Ally hadn't expected was the other woman's thoughtfulness—having spotted Ally looking like a lost cat, she had come over to rescue her.

'When is your baby due?' Ally asked, hoping to direct the conversation away from the subject of their 'husbands'.

Megan smiled as she stroked a hand over the prodigious baby bump. An odd shaft of envy pierced Ally's chest.

'Not baby, as it turns out, but *babies*.' Megan laughed. 'Dario and I got the shock news four months ago and we're still adjusting to it. I'm actually only six months, even though I'm the size of an elephant. The two of them, both boys, are not due until June.'

'Twin boys!' Ally grinned, she couldn't help it, impressed by the other woman's *sangfroid*. 'Wow, that... That must be exciting...and terrifying.'

'Right on both counts.' Megan grinned back. 'Although the most terrifying thing so far has been explaining to our daughter Issy she's going to have two more younger brothers when she's not that impressed with the one she's got. Our only consolation is that my sister Katie, who is also due in June, discovered she's having a girl.'

'I'm sure your daughter will get over it,' Ally said, feeling stupidly envious now. 'It's so much better to have siblings than not, even if they are brothers!'

'Precisely, although Issy's not convinced.' Megan popped a delicate mini quiche into her mouth and swallowed. 'But enough about me. I wanted to come over and congratulate you on your marriage. I always knew Dominic would eventually find a woman worth keeping. He certainly seemed to be looking hard enough,' she added with a laugh.

'Thank you, I think.' Ally's heart wrestled with her tonsils at Megan's smile—if she could joke about Dominic like this they must be good friends, although he hadn't mentioned Megan, or anyone else. Embarrassed colour rushed into her cheeks as she realised how little she knew about her brand-new husband's private life.

'And I also wanted to discover where you bought that dress.' Megan's gaze slid over the cocktail dress Ally had spent the afternoon finishing while she'd waited for Dominic to arrive.

An above-the-knee design of aquamarine silk, inspired by a waterfall she'd seen once in a magazine, the dress was all flowing lines and quiet power. The gold band round her biceps had seemed like the perfect finishing touch. But Ally had been second-guessing her decision to wear it as soon as she'd arrived. Was it too revealing? Too funky? Not formal enough?

'It's so original and stylish,' Megan said. 'You look incredible in it.'

The flush of pleasure at Megan De Rossi's heartfelt praise had Ally's ribs contracting. This was exactly the kind of feedback she had hoped for.

'Actually I made it myself,' she said.

Megan's eyes widened, but then she whistled. 'That's even more amazing. You're really talented. I've never seen anything so cool and distinctive.'

Ally's heart squeezed. She'd hoped for a reaction like this, but she hadn't expected it.

'You're nothing like Dominic's other girlfriends—no wonder he decided to marry you,' Megan added, making the blush fire across Ally's chest. 'And that's without even factoring in that super-hot kiss,' Megan finished, her grin becoming decidedly wicked.

Ally's blush went ballistic.

Photos of their kiss on the sidewalk had hit the Internet yesterday. Ally knew because she'd been inundated with messages from her friends in London asking to know what the heck was going on. But she hadn't replied and she'd studiously avoided social media all day.

'I'm sorry,' Megan said, immediately looking contrite. 'I didn't mean to embarrass you. But, honestly, you two looked amazing together. So hot and so much in love, if anyone thought he shouldn't have ditched Mira they certainly won't after seeing that photo. Was that amazing blue suit one of your designs, too?'

'Yes,' Ally croaked, quietly dying inside.

She'd known she would have to lie, but she hadn't realised it would be quite this hard.

She already liked Megan De Rossi. The woman was smart, and witty, and sweet and surprisingly down to earth. And she clearly had exceptional taste. Megan and she might have become friends, if her marriage to Dominic had been real, instead of a subterfuge to secure a property deal.

'Um...' Ally began, not sure what to say, when she was rescued by a tall man in a dark grey designer suit, who swooped down on them like an avenging angel.

'Damn it, what are you doing on your feet? And holding something so heavy, *piccola*.' He whisked the laden plate Megan had been nibbling on out of her hand.

This was Dario De Rossi, Ally realised, in the flesh. She'd seen his picture in magazines, but it didn't do him justice. He was a strikingly handsome man, his Italian heritage evident in the black hair, olive skin, phenomenal bone structure—and his wildly overprotective manner.

'You are carrying two babies. *My* babies. You need to sit down, *piccola*,' he said, cradling his wife's elbow to lead her to a chair.

'And *you* need to stop calling me *piccola* now I'm the size of a house.' Megan rolled her eyes comically but allowed herself to be led. 'Ally, meet Dario—my very own papa bear. Dario, this is Ally, Dominic's new wife.'

Having deposited Megan on one of the white leather couches that lined the stark walls of the art gallery, and handed the plate back to her, Dario offered Ally his hand.

'Ally, it is good to meet you. I have heard much about you from Dominic.'

You have?

Ally shook his hand, wondering what on earth Dominic could have found to say about her, seeing as he hardly knew her. The firm handshake settled her nerves a fraction, until Dario shouted at someone.

'Dominic, over here.' He beckoned over Ally's shoulder, then smiled down at her. 'Your husband has been searching for you, like a besotted newly-wed.'

He has? But he isn't a besotted newly-wed.

Before Ally had a chance to process why Dominic might *really* have been searching for her, a large hand settled on the small of her back, burning the sensitive skin through the silk. She tried not to jump, not to overreact to the sensuous caress as Dominic's palm coasted to her hip and dragged her to his side.

'There you are, Alison,' he murmured in her ear, very much like an attentive lover but she could hear the edge in his voice. Something wasn't right.

'Megan, Dario, this is my *wife*, Alison,' he said, the possessive tone sending an inappropriate shaft of heat to her sex.

Fabulous, Ally, even his temper has the ability to turn you on.

'We've met,' Megan chipped in after swallowing another mouthful from her plate. 'And for once I approve, Dominic. Your bride is amazing,' she added, sending Ally a conspiratorial wink.

'*Merci beaucoup,*' Dominic murmured, dryly.

'Although I'm not sure you deserve her,' Megan added.

'I'm sure I do not,' Dominic replied, the tone deliberately self-deprecating but Ally could still hear that edge, even if Megan couldn't.

She had definitely screwed up somehow. Not acted quite dutiful or besotted enough, maybe?

'I can't believe you didn't at least mention in your press release about the marriage that Ally is a talented fashion designer,' Megan said.

Ally tensed at the innocuous comment as Dominic's hand jerked on her hip. Oh, crap. She hadn't expected Megan to blurt that out.

'By the way, I forgot to ask where your designs retail,' Megan asked her, caressing her baby bump. 'I can't wait to check them out, as soon as I get rid of these two and loose the five hundred extra pounds I've managed to put on.'

'Stop.' Dario cupped her cheek. 'You are not fat. You are pregnant and beautiful.'

'Spoken like a man who isn't carrying around five hundred extra pounds,' Megan said, but covered his hand with hers in a gesture that made Ally's heart leap into her throat.

What must that be like? To have a man be devoted to you? Exciting? Scary? She had no idea.

Dominic's hand had tightened on her waist. Whatever had annoyed him already, he was clearly a lot more annoyed now.

Why hadn't she told him she was making her own wardrobe for this trip?

'What designs?' he said.

His jaw had hardened. Okay, he wasn't just annoyed, he was *really* annoyed. And no wonder—she'd just potentially exposed what a sham their marriage was to two of his friends. She should have kept her mouth shut about the dress to Megan until she'd had the guts to admit she'd made it herself to Dominic.

'I need to go to the ladies' room,' she said, hoping to escape and defuse the situation. But he held her in place.

'What designs is Megan talking about?' The sharp frown made heat prickle over her skin.

She could feel Megan's and Dario's gazes on the two of them.

'Can we talk about this later?' she whispered. Surely he wasn't going to flip out in front of his friends—wouldn't that blow their cover completely? But he seemed unconcerned by their audience when he placed his free hand on her other hip and tugged her to face him.

'*What* designs, Alison?' he repeated, the tone broaching no more argument or prevarication.

'I… I made some of my own clothes for this trip,' she said.

'You didn't know?' She heard Megan's gasped question, but all Ally's focus was on Dominic now. On his reaction. Because his brows had lowered ominously.

I'm so sorry, I should have told you, but don't make a big deal of it or we'll both be totally busted.

She tried to communicate the desperate plea to him telepathically.

'Which clothes?' he said, not picking up on her frantic telecommunications.

'Well…' Colour burned her cheeks as his gaze roamed over the dress—in much the same way as it had when he'd recited his vows earlier.

'Tell me,' he said, stroking her hips now, making the soft silk feel like sandpaper as it rasped over her skin.

'All of them.'

He swore softly, let go of her hips and grasped her hand. 'We're leaving.'

Panic assailed her as she heard Megan's shouted comment. 'Where are you going?'

'I have to *talk* to my wife.' Dominic threw the comment over his shoulder.

Ally attempted to wave her new friend goodbye, but she was already being whisked through the crowd. People turned to watch as she was marched out of the gallery. Some of the women giggled behind their hands, a few of the men laughed, others simply stared at the spectacle they were making or lifted their phones to record her humiliation.

Ally allowed herself to be led; trying to resist would only make the situation worse. He was furious, obviously. It was the only explanation for the sparkle of heat in his eyes, the tight line of his jaw, the way his hand clasped hers in a firm, unyielding grip.

She should never have designed and made her own clothes, instead of buying them from somewhere expensive and exclusive the way he'd expected her to. He was a proud man and this marriage was all about appearances. She had miscalculated badly. Very badly.

Stopping on the sidewalk outside the gallery, he whistled through his fingers. The limousine they'd arrived in appeared out of the snarl of traffic like a magic carpet.

'I'm sorry, Dominic, I should have told you, about the clothes,' she whispered, trying to placate him. 'I realise you're probably annoyed that I didn't buy something from a named designer, but I've been studying design for two years and I—'

'Get in.' Dominic opened the door and held it for her.

She hesitated.

'Alison. Get. In. The. Damn. Car.' The tone was low, more firm than threatening, but still she felt it ripple down her spine. *'Now.'*

She jumped at the barked command, and slid into the seat. Moments later she was cocooned in the back of the car with him as it peeled away from the kerb. The scent of leather and man, spicy cologne and pine soap invaded her senses; the blare of car horns, the cacophony of sound from the street as New York woke up to the night buzzed in her brain, combining with the sensation careering over her skin.

Why was he so mad at her? And why did it still turn her on?

'Listen, I'm really sorry I wasn't honest with you about my wardrobe. But Megan liked this dress, really, it isn't all bad—'

'Stop apologising about the damn dress. The dress is

not the problem. It's stunning, and it's been driving me to distraction ever since I saw you in it. So I'd say Megan's opinion is correct.' The searing confession surprised her so much, the bottom dropped out of her stomach.

'Then… What is the problem?' Because there was clearly a problem and she still had no idea what it was.

He turned to her then, the naked hunger on his face so shocking the heat fired up her torso. 'The problem is, for this to work there has to be trust. You chose not to tell me about the clothes, and in some ways I understand that— you're obviously not as confident about your abilities as you should be.' His hand touched her thigh and she shivered, the sensation both brutal and yet delicious as the calluses trailed up her leg. 'Which is ironic, because the minute I saw you in this outfit tonight, all I wanted to do was rip it off you.'

'I'm not sure that's relevant,' she managed because she'd already started to lose the thread of this conversation, and she was still none the wiser as to why he looked so furious.

He swore suddenly and let her go, to lean back in his seat. 'Then it should be,' he said, staring out of the window.

She wondered if she should apologise again, for not telling him about the clothes, because it had upset him in ways she hadn't thought she could upset him, but she didn't want to keep apologising.

The ride through Manhattan seemed to take an eternity as she waited for him to say something, anything. Her thigh quivered where the imprint of his brief caress still lingered—making her brutally aware of exactly how tangled this situation had become. Because she still wanted him so desperately, even though on several levels he was completely infuriating.

Her need and her anxiety had reached fever pitch when he finally turned back to her.

'Why did you have Selene cut the one-million-pound payment from the divorce settlement?' he said tightly, the searing heat in his eyes accompanied by an emotion that made no sense whatsoever.

Guilt.

That was the problem? She opened her mouth to reply, but then closed it again, because she still didn't understand what she'd done that was so wrong.

'Answer me,' Dominic demanded. He was so angry and frustrated he was finding it hard to speak. He'd trusted her and she'd tricked him.

Hold it together. And don't touch her, damn it, because then you'll never be able to get an answer.

Her eyes had gone wide with confusion. Making the fury boiling under his breastbone threaten to ignite.

He'd only found out about the contract change a half-hour ago, when he'd been scanning an email from Selene while waiting to pick up a glass of champagne for Alison at the event's crowded bar.

He'd been planning to celebrate. And he'd wanted to celebrate with her. The consortium members had been completely charmed by her, as he'd known they would be. She'd put on a convincing show, not least by excusing herself when his introductions had led on to a discussion about zoning issues on the project. One of the business-men had laughed and congratulated him on his marriage and his beautiful wife, pointing out, 'Only a real wife would feel comfortable making it abundantly clear she found her husband's talk of business boring. My wife is exactly the same.'

The consortium members had agreed to sign the first phase of the deal tomorrow morning. His decision to marry Alison had been the right move.

But then he'd read Selene's outline of the marriage-contract negotiations, and the excitement had died. His assistant hadn't bothered to mention the change Alison had requested before now, because he'd given Selene *carte blanche* to negotiate the terms, telling her to refer anything problematic to his legal and financial teams. He hadn't wanted to be too closely involved. He'd been having enough trouble forgetting about Alison while he'd waited for her to arrive in New York. And, of course, his legal and financial teams had been more than happy to strike the lump-sum payment at the end of the marriage from the contract, because it would save LN a million pounds.

But he wasn't happy. He was furious about the unnecessary change.

The whole purpose of the payment was to keep his conscience clear. To pay off his responsibility after the marriage ended, not just towards the woman whose virginity he had taken, however unintentionally, and then exploited, but also towards the little girl who had been left destitute after that summer.

By refusing that payment, she had turned the tables on him. Made him responsible again. And guilt was not an emotion he enjoyed.

'I just… I didn't want the money,' she said. 'It was too much. You're already giving me so much.'

It was exactly the sort of naïve, artless statement he should have expected. He tried to bank his fury. But he could do nothing to hide his frustration.

'We agreed on the money the morning you agreed to this marriage. And then you deliberately reneged on that understanding. And you chose not to mention it before we actually went through with the ceremony. Why?'

'I didn't think you'd mind,' she said, still confused, which only spurred his temper more.

'Of course I mind,' he said. 'I always pay my debts. It's an important principle of the way I do business.' And something he'd stuck to throughout his career, even when it had meant going hungry. Because he had promised himself the night he had crawled off his father's estate he would never, ever be beholden to anyone again. That no one would ever have the power to control him in that way. And now this woman had managed to undermine that essential tenet to the way he lived his life—without even trying.

'Why did you even wish to change that part of the agreement?' he said. He had offered her a million pounds; why hadn't she taken it? Because he knew exactly how much she could use the money.

Her blush was visible even in the dark interior of the car.

'It's too much, Dominic.'

'No. It. Isn't.' He spat the words out. 'You're going to live as my wife for the next six months—do you really think I want to leave you destitute again when we divorce?' And why was it already so damn hard to say that word?

She looked shocked, which only infuriated him more. He couldn't let this pass.

The car drew up at the Lafayette apartment. He unbuckled them both and hauled Alison out of the car. She still hadn't said anything, but it was probably better they had this discussion in private. He didn't want to risk another display for the paparazzi out on the sidewalk.

He marched into the lobby, ignored Manny the doorman's jaunty evening greeting and stabbed the elevator button.

Unfortunately a couple of his staff arrived behind them, and joined them in the lift.

Her fingers flexed on his, but he didn't release his grip as he replied to his staff members' innocuous comments about the weather—even as the adrenaline raced through his bloodstream. How could he still be so aroused, when he was almost choking on his indignation?

At last the two employees stepped out of the lift and they arrived a few moments later at the penthouse apartment. He dragged her through the doors as soon as they swished open. Once they were safe in the privacy of his apartment he released her hand.

'I want to know why you pulled this stunt,' he said. 'And then we're going to have to renegotiate the contract or it's not going to work for me.'

CHAPTER EIGHT

WAS IT WRONG to notice how hot Dominic was when he was mad?

Ally tried to corral her wayward thoughts and stick to the problem at hand.

And it was a problem. She should have told him she'd decided not to accept the pay-off. That much was obvious. But she really hadn't thought it would be a deal breaker. And she had to wonder why it was.

But she was going to have to give him an answer first. An answer that would expose all her insecurities. Which was probably why she hadn't told him in the first place.

But the truth was, she'd already told him the reason; he just hadn't been listening. So now she would have to tell him again.

'I couldn't get past what happened to my mother with your father. Accepting your money felt like I was making the same mistake. She persuaded herself she loved him. But I'm not sure she ever really did. What she loved was the security his money provided. I don't want to sell myself short the way she did.'

'This deal, this marriage, hasn't got a damn thing to do with what happened all those years ago. We already established that.' The edge in his voice sharpened.

'Yes, it does. I won't compromise myself like that. I can't.'

'So you expect me to compromise my integrity instead,' he shot back.

'What?' she asked, because she was confused now as well as heartsore. She hadn't meant to cause an argument. And she certainly didn't want to infuriate him. But she couldn't budge on this. She'd tried and she just couldn't; her pride wouldn't allow her to accept the money. 'I don't... I don't understand.'

'Really?' he said, thrusting his fingers through his hair. 'Then let me explain. You don't want to be like your mother, but you're happy to make me into my father. To have me exploit you the way my father exploited her and hundreds of other women. The way he exploited my own mother. If you don't want to be like her, what makes you think I want to be like him?'

It didn't make any sense. This had nothing to do with his father. Far from it. But from his tortured expression it was obvious it mattered to him.

'But you're not exploiting me, Dominic,' she said, as patiently and gently as she could—she needed to defuse this situation and make him see sense. 'I want to be here. I signed that contract and went through with the ceremony earlier in full knowledge of the facts. I just don't want the money. It's too much. You're not responsible for what happened to my mother. They were the grown-ups, not you.'

'*Mon Dieu.* How do you know what I am responsible for when you don't even know what happened that night?'

The growled admission struck her like a blow. Bringing back the memories she had never really confronted. And the words her mother had whispered before dragging her out of bed in the middle of the night, her cheek bruised and her eyes wet with tears, returned.

'*Something terrible's happened, baby. Pierre's very angry with me and Dominic. We have to leave.*'

'What are you saying, Dominic?' A horrible thought curdled in the pit of her stomach. Had something happened between her mother and Dominic? The thought had never even occurred to her. Because it would be ludicrous and paranoid—but a stifling coating of jealousy joined the snakes writhing in her belly, regardless.

Which only disturbed her more. Imagine being jealous of a dead woman. A woman who was her own mother.

He swore and turned away from her, striding to the open-plan kitchen and pulling a beer out of the fridge. He snapped off the cap against the countertop and gulped down half the bottle.

She followed him, her insides churning. A part of her had always wondered what had happened to turn Pierre against her mother. But it couldn't be this, could it?

'Did Pierre catch you together?' she asked.

Had her mother seduced a sixteen-year-old boy? The thought was so appalling she knew she would never be able to get past it. She had clung to that last modicum of respect for her mother for so long—through the drug addiction, the endless affairs with increasingly inappropriate men. But this would destroy the last of it. And be worse than anything she'd been forced to witness her mother do in the years after that night.

'Is that why he hit her?' she asked. 'Why he kicked us out? Did you and my mother have a relationship?'

But as she steeled herself against hearing the worst, Dominic choked on the beer and the bottle slammed down on the countertop.

'What the…? Are you…? How do you say it in English?' he said, the frustration hitting boiling point. 'Are you insane?' he managed. 'Of course I didn't have a relationship with *Monique*.'

The stabbing pain in Ally's belly unlocked. *Oh, thank God.* Her mother hadn't done the unthinkable and seduced a child.

'I was only sixteen and your mother was in her thirties, stunningly beautiful and in love with my father. Even I was never that precocious,' he said, sounding so shocked she felt pretty foolish for even thinking it might have been a possibility, let alone actually asking him. But she was still glad she had. She never wanted that ugly picture in her head ever again. And now at least it was gone... But if that wasn't what had caused his father to hit her mother, what had? And why would Dominic feel responsible?

'But you were there, when Pierre hit her?' she asked. He must have been. Because her mother had mentioned him and he had just implied as much. 'Do you know why he hurt her? Why he turned on her?'

His gaze became shuttered, but not before she caught the flash of something that looked like regret.

He braced his hands against the countertop and dropped his head. She could see the tension in the rigid line of his shoulder blades, and hear the deep sigh as his chest released.

'There was no reason,' he said, but she could hear the bitterness that he couldn't disguise. 'My father never needed a reason. His temper was volatile and easily roused. I think your mother made some innocuous comment about their engagement. And he exploded.'

'I see.' Ally's chest deflated, his agonised words, the description of what he'd witnessed, having the hideous ring of truth. 'So he *had* offered her marriage?' she whispered.

Dominic's head lifted, and he nodded. 'Of course, it

was how my father liked to operate. Dangle the carrot and then apply the stick.'

Ally's heart shrank in her chest.

Dominic gulped down the last of the beer. And dumped the empty bottle in the trash. He looked exhausted. As exhausted as she felt. She noticed the scar bisecting his left eyebrow, the scar she'd wondered about often as a child.

He liked to dangle the carrot, then apply the stick.

His statement stirred the memories again, of all the altercations she'd witnessed between father and son that summer. The bullying, the insults, the constant, endless attempts by Pierre to let his son know he was a bastard, that he wasn't enough.

As a child she'd been in awe of Pierre, the way her mother had. Because he'd always been so charming to her, she'd never been able to figure out why he was so mean to Dominic. But now she could see, Pierre had treated her like a pet that summer, not a daughter. And a tool, his praise for her just one more stick to beat Dominic with, to let him know that even his mistress's child had a greater place in Pierre's affections than his illegitimate son.

'I'm sorry,' she said. 'For bringing it up, for making you relive that summer and those events.'

His eyes met hers, the confusion in them as compelling as the wariness. Dominic, she thought, was not a man comfortable with displays of emotion, or affection—no wonder this evening had exhausted him.

But even so she refused to hold back. Reaching across the breakfast bar, she placed her palm on his cheek, trying to soothe the bone-deep exhaustion she could see in his eyes.

'And I'm sorry for thinking, even for a moment, you were to blame for the horrid way my mother and I were treated at the end of that summer, when it was always, always him.'

* * *

Dominic tensed, and jerked his head back, away from the soft stroke of her fingers.

The compassion and understanding in her eyes horrified him almost as much as the desire to lean into the caress. To take whatever solace she offered.

She dropped her hand, and tensed, as if his rejection were a physical blow.

But he didn't deserve her sympathy, or her apology. She didn't know the full extent of what had happened that night—that his father wasn't the only one to blame.

But he had absolutely no intention of telling her.

It was ancient history now. And it had no bearing on who they were now. And on their marriage.

One thing was clear, though: despite everything that had happened to Alison, and however much she might think she was as cynical and pragmatic about this relationship as he was because of those struggles—she wasn't. Some of that hopeful, generous, open-hearted child still remained. Or she would never have believed his explanation about that night so easily, been so ready to absolve him. And she certainly would not have refused to take the one million pounds he'd offered her.

Walking round the breakfast bar, he cupped her chin, pulled her head up. 'I don't want to talk about the past again. It is dead and has been for a long time.'

It was a brutal thing to say, especially when he saw the humiliating colour fire into her cheeks. But he had to be cruel to be kind now, or she would invest too much of herself in this relationship.

'You must take the money,' he said again. 'For this arrangement to work.'

She tugged her chin out of his hand, looked down at her clasped hands, the knuckles white with strain.

He waited for her to accept the inevitable. She had to know he was giving her an ultimatum.

When she lifted her head all he could see in her eyes was an aching sadness—and even though he didn't feel particularly triumphant, he thought he had won.

But then she shook her head and to his astonishment she said, 'I can't, Dominic. I just can't. If that means we have to part, then I'll understand.'

He was so shocked, the riot of emotions flowing through him so strong and so new—panic, fear, regret, but most of all loss—he had no idea how to process them, let alone how to combat them.

'Non,' he said. Placing his hands on her cheeks, he drew her face towards his. Before he could think better of the impulse, he covered her mouth with his. He wasn't going to lose her; he couldn't.

She opened for him and he plunged his tongue into the recesses of her mouth. Taking, demanding, possessing her—refusing to accept her stubbornness, her intransigence.

The deal. The deal required she stay. That was the reason he felt so desperate. The reason the yearning was so intense. It had to be.

Her instant and unequivocal surrender was like a drug. Sex would fix this problem.

The blood rushed to his groin as he lifted her into his arms and carried her towards his old bedroom. The one she'd chosen the day before.

This is madness. She knows this is madness. We don't have to end this over something so foolish. As long as I can prove she still wants me too. That's all that really matters here.

He placed her on her feet, held her waist and looked into amber eyes, dark with arousal. 'We can fix this in the morning,' he said, his voice hoarse. He would figure out a way if it killed him. 'But for now I want to do what we do best.'

It wasn't really a question but she nodded anyway. And his heart leapt in his chest.

This isn't over. Not yet.

Yes, I want you. I want this. I don't want to leave.

The heat plunged low in Ally's abdomen, rebounding in her sex.

Just take me to bed and let's forget, for tonight at least.

She shuddered, her body alive with too much sensation, as his hands skimmed over her bottom and lifted her dress. He dragged her into his embrace, until the thick evidence of his desire rubbed against the soft, liquid warmth flooding between her thighs.

She didn't see how they could fix this. But for now all she wanted to do was feel, because it might be her last chance.

His thumbs edged under the legs of her panties. He cupped her bottom in hard hands.

'I can't go slowly. Is that okay?' he asked, his voice full of an urgency that only made her more desperate.

'Yes,' she said, her sex already clutching and releasing, desperate to feel that thick length inside her, one last time.

'Bien.' He found the hammering pulse in her neck with firm lips.

She clung to him, trying to dispel the fear, and the sadness.

She jumped at the sound of rending fabric as he ripped away her panties, and her senses soared. The turmoil of emotions forgotten, as giddy shock became giddy excitement.

He turned her round and bent her over the bed.

Her thighs quivered as she heard him release himself

from his pants. Large hands positioned her, skimming over her hips, brushing her bottom, then the huge head of his erection notched at the slick seam of her sex.

She jerked, shocked by the need coursing through her like wild fire as he impaled her in one slow thrust.

'Always so wet for me, Madame LeGrand,' he said, but the tone sounded rough, and raw.

She groaned as he filled her to the hilt, the penetration from this angle so deep what had been overwhelming before became devastating.

He began to rock, out and back, going deeper, taking more. She gripped the coverlet, trying to anchor herself for the heavy thrusts, trying to control the depth of penetration. Her muscles contracted, pushing her towards that high wide ledge, but his movements only became more frantic, the pleasure refusing to subside.

His thumb found her swollen clitoris, sending her soaring, shattering, flying again. Her shocked sobs matched his deep guttural groans.

One large callused palm found her breast, ripping away the silk of her dress, the confining lace of her bra, until hot skin found hot skin. Freed, the stiff peak engorged under his relentless caresses, driving her even higher as he sank deeper and deeper inside her.

The sound of sex, graphic and basic, the cries of pleasure and passion, filled the room, the sensations dazzling and disorientating.

She crashed over one final time and fell to earth. He grew even larger inside her, the hot seed pumping into her as he shouted out his fulfilment.

She collapsed onto the bed.

The shaking began as he eased out of her.

'Are you okay?' he said, his gruff voice rippling through her in the darkness.

'Yes,' she said, because she was, even though the thought of having to leave him tomorrow was crucifying her.

She rolled over and sat up, gathering the torn bodice of her dress, feeling suddenly defenceless. Scared to look at him. Scared not to.

'I damaged your beautiful gown,' he said. 'Can it be repaired?'

'It's okay,' she said. 'I can make another. I like to do it,' she added, because he looked a little dazed. She knew the feeling. How could the sex be so powerful, so overwhelming, so right, when everything else seemed so wrong?

He nodded. 'We will talk tomorrow morning. And work this disagreement out,' he said.

The sadness settled back over her body, dispelling the golden glow of the orgasms he'd given her. But she nodded. Prepared to pretend she believed it.

'I'll see you in the morning,' he said.

'Yes,' she said.

She wanted to snag his wrist, to ask him to stay, to sleep with her, to hold her, just this once, but she knew that indulgence would only make tomorrow harder.

So instead she watched him leave the room. Then dropped back on the bed and blinked furiously, to stop the tears she wanted to shed from falling.

Their marriage had been legal for approximately three hours. And already it felt so much more real than it should. Which was why she couldn't give in and accept the money.

She had to preserve her independence, and this was the only way she could think of to do it, because it would be far, far too easy to surrender everything to this man. Not just her body, but also her soul.

While all time knowing he would never be willing to surrender more than his body in return.

CHAPTER NINE

FEVERISH THOUGHTS CIRCLED Ally's brain as she showered and dressed the next morning. It was past nine o'clock when she stepped into the apartment's living room feeling as if she were about to step into the abyss.

Dominic sat at the breakfast bar eating a bagel and scrolling through what she suspected were market reports on his phone.

He put the bagel down and wiped his mouth when he spotted her.

'*Bonjour*, Alison.'

She drew in a breath and forced herself to walk towards him. Even dressed in jeans and a T-shirt, his feet bare and his damp hair slicked back from his forehead, he looked indomitable and unreachable.

Her heart sank. She'd gone over all the possible solutions she could think of to their problem and she couldn't see one. She couldn't take the money, and Dominic would not accept her refusal.

'Don't look so worried,' he murmured as he held out his hand. 'I have an idea that will satisfy me and I hope will also satisfy you.'

She placed her fingers in his palm, felt the familiar frisson of electricity as he grasped her hand and directed her to the stool next to him.

'I still can't accept the money,' she said, scared that his solution would involve going over the same ground as yesterday.

'And I cannot accept leaving you destitute when we part.'

She wouldn't be destitute, but it was pointless arguing about it once more.

'Then we're at an impasse.' She blinked furiously, pathetically close to tears, again. Why was she about to cry?

His intransigence, his unwillingness to bend on a point that was so important to her, surely proved this arrangement had always been doomed to failure.

'Not necessarily.' His lips curved in a persuasive smile. 'How about, rather than giving you a million pounds at the end of this marriage, I invest in your business instead?'

'What business?' she asked, completely nonplussed.

'Your fashion design business, of course,' he said.

'But I don't have a fashion design business.'

'This is exactly the point. You don't have one, but you should.' His gaze slid over the short dress she had put on, ready to return to London on the next plane. He touched the flounced neckline. 'This is one of your designs, is it not?'

She nodded, brutally aware of the approval in his eyes.

'You are extremely talented. Even I can see this and I know nothing about fashion. Megan De Rossi does and she agrees with me. She asked where your designs were retailing yesterday at the gallery, is this not so?'

'That was just a casual comment,' she said. 'She was being kind and friendly.'

'No, she wasn't, because I phoned her an hour ago and asked her if she would be willing to throw her support behind your brand.'

'You did...*what*?' Ally jumped off the stool. 'Dominic, how could you?' She covered her face with her hands, wishing the beautiful concrete floor of his apartment would crack open and swallow her whole.

His fingers curled around her wrists and he drew her hands away from her face. He peered at her, the smile so confident now it was verging on smug. 'Don't you want to hear what she said?'

'No! I don't.' She yanked her hands free, not sure whether she wanted to shout at him or simply curl up in a ball and weep. 'She's your friend, and you put her on the spot. I have no doubt she was polite.' She stepped away from him.

How would she ever survive the humiliation?

Megan De Rossi had been wonderful. And for that bright beautiful moment when the other woman had admired her design yesterday, Ally had felt as if she belonged, truly belonged. But it had all been an illusion. An illusion that Dominic had shattered with careless disregard for her feelings.

'You've exposed me to ridicule, Dominic. Can't you see that? I haven't even finished fashion college yet. I've got months of work left before my final year show. And then, if none of the fashion houses are interested, it could be years before I manage to get an internship. They're hugely competitive and I don't even know if I've got what it takes to—'

'Megan wants to invest,' he interrupted her, his smile not smug so much as sympathetic.

'What?' What on earth was he talking about now?

'Megan De Rossi wants to invest in your brand, *ma belle*,' he said again, chuckling as he grasped both her wrists again and tugged her struggling body back towards him, until she was positioned between his thighs. 'She loves your designs. She says you have huge potential. I told her I was considering bankrolling your collection. I asked her for her advice, whether she thought it would be a good investment. I didn't want to suggest something that would not succeed. She not only said it would be a fabulous investment, she said she wanted to invest, too.'

'She…she didn't.' Ally's body went limp, the shock making her knees tremble. Megan De Rossi had liked her designs enough to invest in them? It didn't even seem possible, let alone plausible. This was huge. It was beyond huge. It was… Everything.

'She did,' he said. Resting his hand on her neck, he rubbed his thumb across her collarbone where her pulse was pounding like a jackhammer. 'Why are you so surprised?'

'Because…' The tears that she had refused to shed yesterday made her throat raw, and her eyes sting. 'Because it's… It's like a dream come true.'

Dominic tucked a knuckle under her chin, the glitter of unshed tears destroying him. He'd wanted to find a solution to the problem of the money; it seemed he'd found much more than that.

How could he not have realised how insecure she was? Because she'd been so brave and bold and determined up to now—that was why. But underneath that was a woman who had had to fight for every chance, every opportunity, and drag herself through God only knew what to make her dream a reality. Well, she didn't have to drag herself any more. He was going to make sure she soared.

'So, if I said I was going to invest in your start-up, you would accept?'

He saw the dazed hope in her face fade a little. 'But I don't know anything about business. All I know is how to design and make clothes.'

He nodded. This much he could help her with. 'Luckily for you, I know a lot about business,' he said. 'The idea is we would be partners in this venture.' Like a real husband and wife, he thought, but didn't say; he didn't want to spook her, any more than he wanted to spook himself. 'I'll give you all the financial and business support you need. Rent premises in London for your workshop, pay for the salaries of your staff…'

'Staff?' Her eyes went so large he had to resist a laugh.

'Yes, staff. A business manager, a personal assistant, a publicist, and those are just the basics. I would assume a fledgling fashion brand would also need creative staff.'

'But… Isn't that going to be very expensive?' she said and he could already hear her insecurities putting the brakes on her dream.

But he wasn't going to allow it. This was the way he could give her something of value from their marriage. Something that would endure long after their liaison was over. Something that would ensure she would never be destitute again. And he would not have to feel responsible.

'You have to invest money to make money, Alison— that's the way business works.'

'But how will I pay you back?' she asked. And he had to bite his tongue.

He mustn't become frustrated with her, not again. Her insecurity—like his driving ambition—had stemmed from the scars inflicted on both of them that summer. *He* knew she could do this, but she did not, and until she did he would have to be her mentor, her supporter. Gently nudging her in the right direction until each new success showed her how much she could achieve. Confidence didn't happen overnight—confidence had to be built, brick by tortuous brick. He'd discovered that when building his own business, so now he could show her while she built hers.

'You won't pay me back,' he said, but before she could protest he held up his hand. 'Wait, let me explain. The money isn't a gift, or a pay-off, like the alimony payment I was proposing. I intend to get a handsome return on my money, eventually, once the brand is established. We'll make a formal agreement and, for my investment, I want a fifty per cent share of the profits.'

'But what will I be giving to the business that entitles *me* to fifty per cent?' she said, the frown on her face so adorable he wanted to kiss it. 'I haven't got any money to invest in it.'

She really was clueless about how business worked. Why did that make the thought of going into business with her all the more exciting?

'Your contribution is your time and your talent,' he said. 'I'm afraid I'm going to be far too busy with the Waterfront project here to be anything more than a silent partner. And I know absolutely nothing about fashion.'

'But what if I fail?' she said, and his heart cracked at the tremble of uncertainty.

He stifled the foolish feeling of empathy. This was business, just like their marriage, there was no place for sentiment—but even so he kept his voice gentle. 'If you fail, I write the investment off as an expense and reduce my tax burden. Either way, it is a win-win for me financially.'

But she wasn't going to fail. She had the talent, according to Megan, to be a success. The only thing holding her back would be lack of business expertise—which he could supply her with—and her own fear of failure.

And if there was one thing he could show her how to do, it was how to conquer that fear.

'So, what do you say? Do you want to go into business with me, Madame LeGrand?'

She pressed a hand over her breast, as if she were trying

to stop her heart jumping out of her chest. He knew how she felt, because he'd felt the same way when he'd signed his first deal with the precious stake he'd earned working round the clock as a cycle courier in Paris.

'I'm terrified,' she said, her honesty so captivating he struggled not to kiss her.

'Only terrified?' he asked.

'And also excited,' she admitted. Hope sparked in her eyes, and found an answering spark in his heart.

'So is that a yes?' he asked, needing the clarification.

'Yes—yes, it is!' she said.

'Magnifique!'

She laughed and grasped his shoulders as he wrapped his arms around her waist and spun her round in a circle.

'Congratulations, Madame LeGrand,' he said as he finally put her down, absorbing the delicious echo in his groin as her body pressed against his.

'Thank you. Thank you for suggesting this,' she said, her face alight with exhilaration. 'It's a brilliant solution.'

'Yes, I know,' he said, and she laughed again, the sound sweet and carefree.

He slanted his mouth across hers, his pulse pounding in his ears when her eager response turned the kiss from hungry to ravenous in a heartbeat.

He scooped her into his arms.

'Dominic, what are you doing?' she asked, breathlessly as he carried her back into the bedroom.

'Celebrating,' he said, although he thought that much was obvious.

It wasn't till much later though, as he headed down to his offices to get the legal team involved in setting up the new business, while Alison called Megan to talk about coming on board as an investor, that it occurred to him he wasn't even sure what made him smile the most.

The hum in his groin from the celebratory sex they'd just shared; the thought that the first stage of the Waterfront deal would be signed later today; the realisation he would be able to keep his fake wife, without any regrets; or the thought of the months ahead, when he would be able to help Alison blossom and grow into the woman she was always meant to be—both in bed and in business.

Now they had established trust and secure boundaries to their relationship—ensuring there would be no more messy heart-to-hearts about their feelings or about things that had happened so long ago they no longer mattered—their marriage could progress as originally planned.

They would live separate lives—with Alison busy working on her business in London, while he was engaged in the Waterfront deal in Manhattan.

As he bounded down the emergency stairs to his ninth-floor office, the thought was so enticing, he might even have been whistling.

CHAPTER TEN

'CAN YOU GET them to rethink, Muhammad? We need that Indian silk. It's a key component of the whole collection.' Ally spoke rapidly, her nerves fraying as she opened the gate to the London town house. The smattering of rain permeated the thin sweater she wore. Deciding to walk home this evening hadn't been the smartest idea, but she had wanted some fresh air after a week of eighteen hour days finishing off the designs. Panic constricted around her throat—and now the signature feature of every one might be missing.

She'd fallen in love with the stunning craftsmanship of the embroidered fabric offered by a charitable workshop in Mumbai. She'd been in negotiations with them for weeks— and everything had been going so well, they were due to sign the contracts an hour ago, when she'd got a call from her supplier, Muhammad Patel, with some very bad news.

'They're saying another buyer has promised them a better investment,' her supplier replied. 'I'm sorry, Ally, you've been great and I know they were really torn. Rohana was full of apologies when she told me,' he said, mentioning the workshop's owner who Ally had been dealing with. 'But the other buyer's got more clout in the marketplace.'

Which was code for another designer with an actual

name had stepped in and offered, if not more money, then more exposure.

'I understand,' she interrupted him, because she did. 'And please tell Rohana not to feel bad about this. They've got to make the right choice for their business.'

She shoved the phone into her bag, her anxiety threatening to choke her. What had she expected? She didn't have a pedigree, just a rich husband willing to invest in a pipe dream. It had been two months since her deal with Dominic, since she'd started playing businesswoman and pretending to be a fashion designer, and she didn't feel any more secure now than she had then.

Dominic had been wonderful, but he was busy, and she didn't want to bother him about the minutiae of her business problems on the few days a month when she got to see him. After the almost-end to their arrangement a day into the marriage, she'd been determined to stick to her end of the bargain—and to enjoy every second of time she had with him.

The sex had been awesome. The way he could make her body feel was a revelation—the familiar heat blasted through her at the memory of their last merry meeting in Paris a week ago, when he'd had to attend the opening of a rail project his company had financed and he'd wanted her there.

She had become addicted to his texts. Usually a curt two lines telling her where and when he needed her to be. She'd travelled all over the globe in the last two months. To Rio, to Cannes, to Paris and Hong Kong and even Niagara Falls. Whenever he'd summoned her, she'd gone. She'd become an expert at smiling for the cameras, and addicted to the stolen hours they had alone together, before and after the balls and galas, the charity banquets and high-profile sporting events he needed his wife to be seen at.

They spoke often about her growing business. His advice and encouragement had proved invaluable and he seemed genuinely interested in her progress.

But the wall he had erected after the almost-collapse of their marriage remained. It had cost her not to try to breach that wall again, to talk about more than just sex or business, because the yearning to know him better, to understand every little thing about him, remained too. He fascinated her, he always had and that would never change. But she'd forced herself to be content with the companionship—and the spectacular sex—and to remember the deal they'd made. That this relationship had a sell-by date—a sell-by date she'd agreed to.

Plus she adored being with him, and she didn't want to ruin their time together with pointless yearning for something more, when she already had so much.

Just as it was pointless to wish she could get his advice about this latest disaster. He always had a solution, and was willing to share his phenomenal expertise—but she didn't see how he could help her with this.

She was an upstart, a newbie, in this business. She'd wanted to succeed, not just for herself, but also to repay him for his confidence in her. But renting a studio in Holborn, hiring a business manager and a personal assistant and a brilliant seamstress, didn't suddenly make her a fashion designer. What it made her was a fraud—no wonder Rohana hadn't wanted her beautiful fabrics gracing the Allycat Collection.

Ally closed the back door and dumped her bag on the hall stand.

She rubbed her belly, the dull ache from the period that had started that morning just one more thing to drag her spirits down into her boots.

She slipped off the wet shoes, and took a moment to

knead her arches, which were sore after twelve hours spent on her feet directing traffic at the studio.

As she stood in the hallway where they'd first met again all those weeks ago, another wave of melancholy blindsided her.

Dominic had never returned to their London home… *Her* London home. Since that first night and the following morning.

She totally understood that. His life, his work, was in New York.

But as she stood staring into the empty hallway, she missed him. Terribly. Why not admit it? She missed him a little bit more every time she had to fly back to London without him.

How wonderful would it be to have him here tonight? To have that broad shoulder to lean on. That glorious body to explore, so she didn't have to think about how she was going to drag herself back up after this latest knock-down.

She tried to shake off the loneliness and longing, as she had so many times before, and headed towards the kitchen.

Get over yourself, Jones. You're just knackered. And scared.

As she approached the kitchen she picked up the muted hum of the TV playing a news channel.

She stopped. Hesitated.

Had Charlotte, the housekeeper, left the set on? Before she'd left for the evening?

Edging open the kitchen door, she gasped.

'Dominic?'

The wave of emotion almost floored her.

Was she having an out-of-body experience? Because she'd imagined him in her home, *their* home, so many times in the last couple of months? Had she somehow conjured him up because she needed him here?

He seemed real and solid enough though, as he turned from the countertop. Dressed in faded denim and a T-shirt, his feet bare and his hair mussed, he looked so different from how she usually saw him—which was either formally dressed or gloriously naked.

'At last you're home. Where have you been?' he said, in his usual direct way, the slight frown making her heart tick into her throat. 'It's past ten o'clock—you should have finished work hours ago.'

Yup, that was her husband: pushy and overprotective.

He stalked towards her, then cradled her cheek, his gaze gliding over her face, his expression intense and observant. *'Tu as l'air fatiguée.'*

You look exhausted.

She leaned into his callused palm despite the less than complimentary comment. Joy enveloped her as she breathed in his scent. Spicy cologne and clean pine soap. A scent she often dreamed about on the nights she spent alone.

She covered his hand. 'I didn't know you were coming to London,' she said, not making any effort to keep the pleasure out of her voice. 'It's so wonderful to see you.'

She smothered the tiny voice, warning her not to get sentimental, or over-invested. Just this once, she wanted to rejoice in the unexpected gift of spending an evening home alone with her husband.

'I've got a meeting in Mayfair tomorrow,' he said. 'And some news about the business that I wanted to deliver in person.'

News? About his business? She couldn't imagine what it could be, but it was so good to have him standing in front of her, warm and solid and frowning. And even more wonderful to know that when something happened in his working life, she was the one he wanted to tell about it.

It was comforting to know that even if their marriage had considerable limitations they had managed to become friends as well as lovers in the last two months.

'What's the news?' she said, then grimaced as a cramp tightened across her abdomen.

He swore softly, then clasped her shoulders. 'What's wrong? Are you ill?'

'No, I'm… I'm fine,' she said, stupidly pleased by his concern.

'Don't lie,' he said, lifting her chin. 'I can see the pain in your eyes.'

'It's nothing,' she said, but the cramp chose that precise moment to tighten like a vice and a small groan escaped her lips.

'That's it!' He tugged his smartphone out of his back pocket. 'I'm calling an ambulance.'

She laughed and grasped his wrist as he lifted the phone to his ear. 'Dominic, don't. Really, that's not necessary, it's just…' She hesitated, a flush heating her skin.

'It's just what?' he demanded, his frown deepening.

'It's period pain,' she said, realising how ridiculous it was to be embarrassed to talk to her husband about something so natural. 'It started this morning. It's always sore the first twelve hours or so.'

His arm dropped, as he tucked the phone back into his pocket, but the frown remained. She wondered if he was one of those men who freaked out about women's menstrual cycles. Weird she didn't even know that, when they'd been married for two months. But then being on the pill meant she'd been able to time her periods so they didn't fall on the nights they spent together.

'Have you taken any painkillers?' He slid a warm hand around her neck, his thumb stroking the pulse-point below her ear.

'Not yet,' she said.

He pressed a kiss to her forehead. 'Then let's fix that, first,' he said with his usual confidence.

No surprise there, then. Dominic *wasn't* one of those guys who was freaked out by periods. But then why would he be? He'd dated loads of women before her.

She stifled the ungenerous thought. And the prickle of envy that came with it. He was with *her* now, in *their* kitchen. That was what mattered.

Crossing to the kitchen counter, he opened and closed the drawers.

'They're in the drawer on the far right,' she said, realising she had moved things around some since he'd lived here.

He poured her a glass of water and watched while she took a pill. Then handed her another. 'Take two,' he said. 'I didn't like the sound of that groan.'

She dutifully obeyed then handed him back the glass.

'Is there anything else that will help?' he asked. 'A massage? A heat pack? Food? Wine? Sex?'

'*Sex?* You wish!' She smiled at the urgent, solicitous tone. 'That's the absolute last thing I want,' she said, protesting maybe a bit too much as a familiar heat flushed her skin.

Who knew? The thought of making love to her husband while she was having her period wasn't nearly as icky as she might once have assumed. But he didn't need to know that, she decided. It would be nice just to absorb him tonight and the novelty of having him in their home, and take some much-needed comfort from their friendship to bolster her flagging ego. Her period was the perfect excuse not to jump each other the first chance they got.

'Well, hey, it was worth a try,' he said, smiling sheepishly as he put the box of pills and the water glass on the countertop.

Nope, definitely not a guy freaked out by periods.

'So what's your news?' she said, trying to get comfortable on the kitchen stool as her belly tightened again. 'Is it the Waterfront deal?'

'Nope,' he said. 'But I'm not telling you until we've got you comfortable. I don't want you freaking out on me.'

Freaking out? Why would she freak out? Her tired mind shot straight to a worst-case scenario. Was he about to tell her he didn't need his fake wife any more?

'*Arrêtes*... Stop it.' His smile widened as he clasped her chin. 'I can see you're panicking already. Relax, it's good news, I swear. You're going to be pleased when you get used to the idea.'

Get used to the idea. Okay, that didn't sound that good either. How could something to do with his business affect her, other than their marriage? But then he kissed her on the nose, the gesture so sweet, her heart butted her tonsils so hard she had trouble breathing, let alone thinking.

Dominic forced himself to release her, aware of the emotion glittering in her eyes. And ignored the tight feeling in his chest.

He'd dealt with this feeling many times before. His heart felt too full, too big every time he gave her advice and her eyes lit up with understanding, every time he gave her a compliment and she blushed, every time they made love and he watched her respond without holding an ounce of herself back until she shattered. And every time he left her bed and the desire to keep her, to hold her, to stay with her just a little longer threatened to overwhelm him.

This time was no different from any of those. He

couldn't allow himself to get sentimental about what they had, or too attached.

It would only complicate this relationship more. And it was already complicated enough. But as she looked at him, the gratitude plain on her face, he couldn't seem to make himself regret his concern at the bruised smudges under her eyes. She needed a decent meal, and for the painkillers to kick in before he told her his news.

He knew it was going to freak her out, because according to Megan she'd already resisted this development, which was why he'd flown across an ocean to persuade her.

That was her insecurity talking. She needed a nudge now, and he intended to give it to her. But only once she'd stopped looking so fragile.

The sweet smile, and the explanation—that she was struggling with period pain—had been a relief. So much so that when her smile had disappeared, he'd felt the loss of it right down to his soul.

And he had a bad feeling he knew the cause. She had assumed he was going to suggest they end the marriage.

Which was insane. Why would he end an arrangement that was working so well?

He'd been in complete control of when and where and how often they met. And the sex had been phenomenal— hot, raw and wildly exciting. So much so that he'd got into the habit of accepting invitations to events he would never usually have bothered attending—simply so he would have an excuse to get his hands on her hot, sweet, responsive body again.

Which had to explain why each time they were together, each time he took her to his bed, he'd found it harder and harder not to demand she stay.

It was probably a good thing she was on her period

and not in the mood this evening. He needed to put a few brakes on his libido.

Too much of a good thing was turning him into a fool.

'Have you eaten?' he asked. 'It should get the painkillers working faster.'

'Not since breakfast.'

He swore under his breath. 'No wonder you look so pale.'

He returned to the counter where he'd begun to assemble a sandwich from the supplies he'd found in the fridge.

'What do you want on your sandwich?' he asked. 'There's three different types of ham, Emmental and provolone cheese, *de la salade*, *des avocats et des tomates*?'

'Anything and everything,' she said and he glanced over his shoulder. 'I'm starving.'

'What's so funny?' he asked, even though her spontaneous smile had tugged on the weight in his chest.

She propped herself back on the stool, the flush of pleasure on her cheeks only making her more captivating. 'I'm just looking forward to sitting here and watching the big bad billionaire make me a sandwich.'

He raised an eyebrow at the amused and incredulous tone. 'You think I don't know how to make a sandwich? I worked twelve-hour shifts making sandwiches in a bistro on the Ile de France for six weeks after busting my ankle on the bike the summer after I arrived in Paris.'

'You broke your ankle?' Her face fell comically. 'How? Were you badly hurt?'

The concern shadowing her eyes had the weight in his chest dropping down into his stomach. Not good. 'Long story,' he murmured.

She got the message and didn't press, and the moment passed. Thankfully.

They ate their sandwiches with a Cabernet he had found

in the cellar. And she asked him about four more times to tell her his news. He resisted, until he had her resting in the living room on the sofa. Sitting beside her, he picked up her feet and put them in his lap, because the urge to touch her never went away, period or no period.

She sighed, and a deep shudder went through her as he dug into the arch of her foot with his thumb.

'Good?' he asked, pleased as he felt the tight muscle release—even if her soft moan wasn't making him feel particularly relaxed.

'Spectacular,' she murmured, the flushed smile the only reward he needed.

'How is the pain?'

'Gone,' she said. 'Now will you tell me what your business news is?'

He assessed her to make sure she wasn't lying, but she looked comfortable and sated, and as relaxed as he was going to get her.

He worked the muscles in her feet a moment more. Realising he was a little nervous himself. He had been sure this was a good thing, that she needed this push, but he hoped he hadn't miscalculated.

'Dominic, please,' she said. 'What's happening with your business?'

'It's not my business, it's yours. Or rather ours.'

'What about it?' she said, her foot tensing right back up again.

'I've arranged for you to show the Allycat Collection at a Fashion Week prelim event for new designers in July in TriBeCa. Megan suggested it. It's basically a competition to win a spot at the week itself in September.'

'You did what?' She jerked her feet out of his lap, her face going so pale she looked as if she were about to pass out. 'You can't be serious? I'm not ready for this. The collection's not ready. July is only a few weeks away.'

'It's a month and a half away,' he said.

'Oh, God.' She swung her feet to the floor and bent over, clutching her stomach as if she were about to be sick. 'I haven't even made any of the prototypes yet,' she moaned.

'Megan told me the designs are incredible and the make-up and fitting stage shouldn't take more than a month. Plus you only need a small sample for this show.'

'You've been talking to Megan behind my back?' She was still clutching her stomach, the horrified expression making the weight in his abdomen swell.

He'd known she would be against the idea at first, which was precisely why he'd taken this step without consulting her. She was still letting her insecurities rule her decision-making process.

'Megan only brought the opportunity up in passing because she couldn't understand why you hadn't thought of entering. I contacted the organisers on my own.'

'You don't know what you've done.' She stood up, pressing a hand to her forehead. 'Maybe I could back out.'

He stood and placed his hands on her shoulders, turned her round to face him. 'We're not backing out,' he said. 'Whatever you need to make this happen, you have my full support.'

He hadn't meant to upset her and it made his stomach hurt too, to see her in this much distress; he hadn't realised she was still this insecure. Everything she'd told him about the business, and everything he'd gleaned from Megan, had been overwhelmingly positive. Apparently, she'd been holding out on him.

But that didn't alter the fact this was a great opportunity. Even if she didn't win the competition, it would give her visibility and experience. So far, she'd stayed in her comfort zone. You couldn't make things happen in business if you did that.

'I can't do it,' she said, the panic and devastation clear in her voice. 'I don't even have the proper materials any more. The fabric I had planned to use as the signature feature of my collection just got poached by another designer.'

He held her shoulders and pulled her into his arms. Damn, she was shaking. She wasn't just freaking out now, she was having a full-on panic attack.

He cradled her face in his hands, pulled her gaze to his. 'Can you get a replacement?'

'It took me two months to find this one. And I don't have that time. Not if I'm going to show a collection that doesn't even exist in six weeks.'

At least she was admitting the show would happen. He took that as a positive step.

Reaching into his back pocket, he pulled out his phone. 'Who's the supplier?'

'It's a Mumbai co-operative. They work with girls and women who have been abused or made homeless. Their workmanship is exquisite and the fabrics they make stunning. But they need exposure, exposure I can't give them. It was naïve of me to think I could when I'm…'

'This show will give them exposure, no?'

'Yes, but…' Flags of colour appeared on her pale cheeks, but her eyes remained dark with fear. 'Not the exposure they need, if it's a disaster.'

His frustration flared—why hadn't she told him about this problem when she'd arrived? But he banked it. She was scared. He understood scared. But he had her back. That was what he'd promised her two months ago. Now it was time to deliver.

'What's the name of the co-operative?' he asked.

'The Dharavi Collective.'

He keyed in Selene Hartley's number and lifted the phone to his ear. 'Selene, there is a fabric workshop in Mumbai called the Dharavi Collective. Allycat Designs would like to secure exclusive use of their fabrics for the next year. We will beat any price they have been offered by a rival brand and would also like to put the full weight of LN India behind them to get funding and exposure for their charitable work.'

After Selene had asked him a few further questions about the negotiation, he ended the call.

'If they have already signed with your rivals we can negotiate with them for a licence to use the material.'

Alison blinked, looking shell-shocked. 'I didn't know you had offices in India.'

'LeGrand Nationale is an international company,' he said. 'I've been to India many times. It's a fascinating, beautiful country, full of talent and initiative. And projects such as this collective. Why wouldn't I have offices there?'

'Yes, why wouldn't you?' she said. But her chin dropped to her chest and her shoulders slumped and he knew they were not out of the woods yet.

The fabric situation was only a symptom of a much bigger roadblock. Alison's fear of failure.

He tucked a knuckle under her chin. 'You must talk to me, Alison. I can't help, if you don't tell me what the problem is.'

'I just…' She sighed. 'I'm not sure I'm good enough. Everything's happening too fast. I'm scared to make a mistake, to let anyone down. If the show fails, the—'

'No, no, no.' He gripped her face, pressed a kiss to her forehead, to stop the rambling irrational fears. 'This is nonsense, Alison.' The heavy weight twisted into a knot. 'You won't fail, but, even if you did, it is not the end, it is just an opportunity. A beginning. There are many ways we can ensure the collective will be okay, but that's not the real fear that is holding you back, am I right?'

She sucked in a jerky breath, and he watched her step back from the cliff edge, but then she nodded. Because however panicked she was, she was not stupid.

'Yes, the real fear is that I'll fail. That I'll take everyone down with me. But I don't know how to stop worrying about it. How to get past it.'

'You never stop worrying, that's not how it works,' he said. 'I have over five thousand employees worldwide. People who depend on me to feed and clothe and house themselves and their families. And that responsibility weighs on me constantly. But every day I take new risks. Sometimes there is a reward, other times a punishment. And if the risk doesn't pay off, if I fail, I try to bear the brunt of the punishment, to protect the people who work for me. But without the risk and the reward, my business would die anyway, do you see?'

'But it's easier for you to take those risks,' she said, although he could see he was getting through, because the colour had come back into her cheeks. 'You're good at it. You know when a risk is worth taking and how to survive the punishment.'

'Precisely, so next time you must let me help. Not bottle up your fear.'

His phone buzzed. He pulled it out of his pocket and read the text from Selene. Then smiled.

Problem solved.

Clicking on the link Selene had sent through, he passed the phone to his wife. 'Your new fabric supplier Rohana has a message for you.'

He watched over Alison's shoulder as the message played. An excited woman, gesticulating madly at the screen, told Alison how pleased they were to be working with her on the collection and how they couldn't wait to send the first batch of materials.

Alison sniffed as she passed him back the phone. 'I don't believe it. You fixed a problem I've been wrestling with for weeks in a two-minute phone call.' Her grin was tentative but there, which was all he cared about. They had weathered this storm, just like the last one. She would do the show, despite her misgivings, and it would be a triumph, because just like the Dharavi Collective she was brilliant at what she did, even if she was the last one to believe it.

He nodded. 'Of course.'

She choked out a laugh. 'I guess being married to a twenty-eight-year-old billionaire has it uses,' she said. 'Even if I keep tripping over his enormous ego.'

He laughed. Slinging an arm around her shoulder, he placed a kiss on the top of her head, to resist the powerful urge to kiss the teasing smile off her lips. Because that would be bound to start something they would not be able to finish.

'Actually I'm not that precocious,' he murmured. 'I turned twenty-nine while we were in Paris.'

He only realised his mistake when she whipped round and stared at him, her eyes huge with shock.

'It was your birthday while we were in Paris? Why didn't you say something? We should have celebrated. I should have bought you a present. Baked you a cake. Something. Perhaps we could celebrate it now?'

The weight in his stomach twisted back into a knot as he noticed the sheen of hope and excitement.

'Forget I mentioned it,' he said. 'I don't celebrate it,' he added.

'Why not?' she said.

'Because I never have,' he replied.

'*Never?* Not even when you were a child?' She sounded horrified.

'My mother didn't consider my birth something to celebrate,' he said. 'Getting pregnant was what ended her affair with my father.'

He'd always tried not to let it bother him. Marking his birthday each year would have been painful for his mother. It had made him feel left out when other children had talked about their birthdays, but he'd forced himself not to care. They hadn't had money for gifts anyway, so what would have been the point? In truth, he'd only found out about his birth date by accident, after discovering his birth certificate—with his father's name on it—in one of his mother's drawers.

'But, Dominic, that's awful.'

'What you don't have, you don't miss,' he said, suddenly wanting to cut off the conversation. Why had he confided so much?

'Are you sure you don't want to start celebrating it?' Alison said. 'I make a mean chocolate cake.'

'Yes, I'm sure.'

He steeled himself against the shadow of hurt in her eyes. And the brutal pang of longing. What would be the point of celebrating his birthday this year, when there would be no one here to celebrate with him next year?

CHAPTER ELEVEN

Can you come to Rome tomorrow night? Selene will make all the arrangements if you can spare the time before the show. D

ALLY READ THE text that had popped up on her smartphone five minutes ago for the twentieth time. Or was it the thirtieth time? She was looking for hidden meaning, or additional information. Or some sign that things had changed in their relationship, if only a little bit, since their night together in London.

But Dominic's text was exactly the same as all the others she'd received over the past three months requesting her presence by his side—polite, pragmatic and distant.

The giddy jump in her pulse was familiar, but the strange feeling of disappointment not so much.

Why had she expected there to be something more this time? It had been three whole weeks since his visit to London—and they had both been extremely busy.

Three weeks since she'd woken up to find him gone again, and had been stupidly crestfallen.

They'd had a wonderful evening, after he'd given her a heart-to-heart about her business, persuaded her to do the runway show in TriBeCa and fixed her problem with the Dharavi Collection...

And confided in her why he didn't celebrate his birthday.

But as they'd sat on the couch together watching an old black and white movie on the large flat-screen TV she never used, a series of unanswered questions had tormented her. How had he survived as a child with so little love? How selfish was his mother, that she hadn't wanted to celebrate her son's birth? Had she made him feel guilty just for being born? It had made Ally feel desperately sad for him. But it had made her even sadder to know he didn't want to celebrate it with her.

He'd shut down as soon as he'd told her, closed himself off again and made it clear she couldn't go there. So she hadn't.

Still she'd hoped he might be there in the morning. So she could get up the guts to ask him a few of the questions that still burned inside her, but of course he hadn't been.

She clicked on the phone's reply bar but her fingers stalled as she tried to formulate a response to the businesslike text—a reply that didn't sound too needy, or too clingy, or too over-emotional.

This was an invitation she'd been waiting for and hoping to receive every day for the past three weeks, ever since that morning—she didn't want to spoil it with expectations that were unlikely to be fulfilled.

Eventually she settled on a simple reply.

Looking forward to it. I could do with a break from all the chaos here. A

But as soon as she'd sent the text, she added another line.

I've never been to Rome.

She didn't want him to know how much she was looking forward to seeing him.

What mattered wasn't what Dominic put in a text, but that he had asked her to be with him and she was going to see him again, tomorrow night.

Twenty-four hours later she was feeling considerably less positive as she stood in the empty penthouse suite of a five-star hotel overlooking the Palazzo Poli.

Decorated in glorious Baroque flourishes to match the building outside, with an imposing four-poster bed in the main bedchamber, the suite of rooms was spectacular. She'd been whisked by limousine from Fiumicino airport and then greeted in Dominic's suite two hours ago by one of his assistants and a small army of beauty professionals. Ally had brought her own gown for the evening—one of the early prototypes she and her seamstress had been working on for the past two weeks. But even after being prepped by the team of beauticians and a hair stylist for an hour, she didn't feel any more secure.

Why hadn't Dominic met her at the airport? It was nearly six o'clock and she'd been ready for over an hour; all she'd received so far was a text to say he would be late—but no explanation as to why.

Rome's nightlife buzzed with vitality a hundred feet below as she stood on the suite's ornate balcony. The scene was awe-inspiring—or should have been. The water tumbled over the iconic Roman stonework of the Trevi Fountain, given an enchanting glow by the nightlights. The fountain was the imposing centrepiece of a square choked with tourists and a few courting couples.

But, unlike the many other new sights and sounds she'd seen since marrying Dominic, the scene below her failed to inspire the usual excitement or exhilaration. Because, for the first time, he wasn't here to share it with her.

Her gaze landed on one of the couples in the square, fooling around on the side of the fountain. The girl stood with her back to the water and threw in a coin over her shoulder. Her boyfriend locked his arms round her waist and swung her in a circle. The noise of the crowd and the free-flowing water drowned out the sound but she was sure she could hear the girl's carefree giggle floating on the warm Roman evening.

The sight pierced her heart—reminding her of the time when Dominic had lifted her and spun her around in his arms when they'd agreed to become business partners. She'd felt so young and happy in that moment, convinced that, whatever the limitations of their marriage, she was doing the right thing, but now she wasn't so sure. Had she become too dependent on Dominic, on his strength and support? She'd tried so hard to remember that end-date, that this relationship was essentially a business arrangement with some spectacular benefits. But why didn't it feel like that any more? And where had this yearning come from to know more about him, to have him give her more?

She heard the suite door open and close behind her.

A low voice rippled down her spine. 'Alison, *bonsoir*— sorry I am late.'

Swinging round, she felt her heart leap into her throat. The swell of emotion so strong and elemental at the sight of him—strong and indomitable in the tailored tuxedo— it flooded through her body like a tsunami.

And suddenly she knew the answer to the question she had been so careful not to ask herself until now.

The reason she wanted more, she needed more, was that she had fallen hopelessly in love with her husband.

'Bonsoir,' she said, her voice coming out on a panicked

whisper as she pressed shaking palms into the red velvet of her gown.

Oh, Ally, what have you done?

'You look exquisite,' he murmured.

She forced a smile to her lips, despite her fear. 'So do you.'

In a tuxedo Dominic was completely devastating. But that wasn't the reason her heartrate was accelerating like a racing car on the starting grid at Brands Hatch.

He gripped her fingers and pulled her into his embrace. Something dark and dangerous flared in his rich chocolate eyes and he pressed his lips to her neck, making the sensitive skin sizzle and burn.

'I wish we didn't have to go to this damn event now,' he murmured as his hands stroked her bottom.

She felt the instinctive shudder of need—and wished they didn't have to attend it either. Her panties were already damp at the prospect of his lovemaking. She wanted the security of hard, sweaty sex, of feeling him deep inside her, to take the fear and panic away. At least for a little while. Until she knew what to do with this revelation. Because she instinctively knew Dominic was far from ready to hear it.

But surely he would be, given time. He'd already been like a real husband in so many respects, offering her support and encouragement, pushing her to be the best she could be in business. Giving her ecstasy and security in equal measure. And she hoped she'd given him the same. If only he would let her give him her love this could be a good marriage, a strong marriage, a lasting one.

'Do we have to go?' she asked.

He let out a strained chuckle and lifted his head. 'Unfortunately, yes. It is a charity event. If we do not show it will reflect very badly on our public image.' He smiled, the sensual smile that always drove her wild—full of a boy-ish charm she had come to adore. 'Especially as everyone will guess what we were doing instead.'

She blushed as his teasing ignited the hot spot between her thighs.

'Plus we don't want to waste an opportunity for you to get exposure for this dress.' His hand remained fastened to her side as he led her across the suite to pick up the stole she'd left on the chaise longue. 'Is it one of the designs for the show?'

He wrapped the stole around her bare shoulders and then lifted the tendrils of hair that hung down her neck.

'Yes,' she said, hearing the strained chuckle at her shiver of reaction.

'It is beautiful,' he said, the desire flaring in his eyes as he escorted her to the penthouse suite's private elevator.

She held onto him as they stepped into the gilded lift. The fear and panic coalescing in her stomach into a well-spring of hope as he murmured: 'You are going to be a sensation in three weeks' time.'

And for the first time, she believed it. If she could conquer that fear, surely she could conquer this one, too, and find a way to tell him, eventually, how much more she wanted from this marriage.

They arrived at the elegant forecourt of the Teatro dell'Opera di Roma less than fifteen minutes later for a production of Verdi's *Otello*.

Ally absorbed the stunning grandeur of the nineteenth-century auditorium as they were escorted into the royal box—red velvet upholstery and curtains added another layer of luxury to the intricate gold plasterwork. She dipped her head back, letting her gaze travel past the five tiers of viewing galleries at the other side of the stage until it reached the rotunda decorated with nymphs and cherubs cavorting across a heavenly sky.

While Dominic thanked the young usher who had brought them to their seats and gave him a generous tip, Ally scanned the programme. She didn't understand much of it because it was all written in Italian, until her gaze snagged on the name of the charity, which was in French. How odd. *Fondation pour les Garçons Perdus.*

'That's interesting,' she said as Dominic took the seat beside her. 'The charity this event is supporting is French.'

'Is it?' he said, undoing the button on his tuxedo, but tension had rippled across his jaw.

'I think so. The name is French. Doesn't that mean Foundation for Lost Boys?' She showed him the programme, pointing to the French wording.

'Yes, I guess so,' he said, but then he took the programme from her hand and placed it on the table in front of them. 'Come here,' he said, and gripped her hand as the lights dimmed.

'Dominic, what are you doing?' she gasped as he tugged her out of her seat.

As applause rained down from the different tiers, the opening bars of the opera rang around the auditorium— stark and dramatic—and the curtain lifted, she found herself pulled into Dominic's lap. His callused palm sent giddy arousal sinking into her sex as it stroked her thigh under her gown.

'I want you too much,' he growled as his hand sank into her hair, sending the pins holding the elaborate do flying.

Before she could protest, or even get her bearings, his mouth was on hers—firm, seeking, demanding. His tongue drove the hunger as he forced her to straddle him, her damp panties connecting with the thick ridge in his pants.

He was fully erect, hard and long. The feel of his need

was like a match lighting the fire inside her. As he sucked on her tongue, drawing her deeper into the erotic fog, his hand travelled to the juncture of her thighs and the heel of his palm pressed against the aching bundle of nerves.

She bucked, the contact too sweet, too brutal.

'Dominic?' She dragged her head back. 'We can't, we'll be arrested. People can see us.' She moaned against his ear as his hand continued to tantalise the swelling spot between her legs. The music and the deep male voices from the stage reached a crescendo, drowning out her ragged pants as the battle raged inside her.

'No one is watching,' he said, the urgency in his voice matching her own.

But even cocooned in darkness, she felt exposed, raw, her heart sinking into her abdomen, her need too visceral, too demanding.

'Stand up,' he commanded, then grasped her waist to lift her off his lap. He stood and dragged her to the side of the booth, giving them a semblance of privacy, hidden behind the heavy velvet curtain she'd been admiring only moments before.

'I want to be inside you,' he said.

She nodded, her heart ramming her throat at the urgency in his voice.

She could have sworn she could hear the sibilant hum of his zip releasing above the cacophony of sound coming from the stage. His hands stole under the layers of velvet and taffeta in her dress; her back butted the wall as he boosted her into his arms.

'Wrap your legs around my waist,' he urged, the thick head of his penis probing past the gusset of her panties and finding the slick folds of her yearning sex.

She did as he told her, disorientated. How could she survive this need? This desperation?

She clung to him as he thrust heavily inside her.

She groaned, the fullness immense. He paused, but only for a moment, to give her time to adjust to the brutal pleasure. Then he started to move. Slow at first, but then faster, harder, rocking out, thrusting deep. Her pants became sobs, his groans became grunts, until all she could hear, all she could feel was the devastating wave washing through her like a tsunami. She tumbled over, but he didn't stop, didn't even slow down, dragging her back into the maelstrom.

The dark need grew again, becoming huge, becoming overwhelming, the coil at her core twisting, as he dug ruthlessly at the spot inside her he knew would destroy her control... The pleasure became pain, so sharp, too sharp. She clung on, grasping his shoulders, and rode the whirlwind only he could create.

'*Encore.*'

The guttural French demand echoed in her head.

Again.

She plunged over the edge, her cry muffled against his shoulder as he plunged into her one last time and then followed.

Her galloping heartbeat slowed, but her wits remained scattered in the heady wave of afterglow. His fingers tensed on her hips, the ache immense as he eased out of her.

He held her arm as she tried to steady herself, her legs like limp noodles, as he placed her on her feet.

She must look a mess, her dress creased, her breathing uneven, her hair falling down on one side.

'*Pardon,*' he said, the word so rigid and filled with self-disgust she flinched. 'I don't know what happened to me.'

She lifted a hand to his cheek, caressed his stiff jaw, hearing the self-recriminations, the fury with himself, and wanted to weep. 'It's okay, Dominic, I was desperate, too. It's been a long three weeks.'

And I love you.

The declaration echoed in her mind, but she held onto the words. It was too soon, not the right moment, to burden him with more, when he already seemed to be burdened with so much she didn't understand.

His phone buzzed. He lifted it out of his pocket and she could see the screen.

A woman's face appeared by the call sign, next to the name 'Marlena'.

Who's Marlena?

'I must take this,' he said, then stepped away from her.

He spoke furiously into the phone in a stream of fluent Italian.

He spoke Italian?

Whoever Marlena was, she had his full attention as the call continued, none of which she understood.

It could only have lasted a few minutes, but it felt like hours as she watched the emotions cross his face in the shadows of the booth, for once unguarded and unrestrained. Concern, panic, desperation, was that what his love really looked like?

Desdemona's melodic soprano from the stage couldn't drown out the discordant beats of her heart as he ended the call.

'I must leave,' he said.

He lifted her fingers to buzz a kiss across the knuckles but his detachment, his distance, felt like a physical blow. He wasn't here with her any more, he was with Marlena.

'Wait, Dominic.' She held onto his hand, refusing to let him discard her so easily when her sex was still aching from his lovemaking.

She knew he'd kept things from her. She knew he had never wanted her to see past the barriers he put around his heart. And she'd respected that because she'd thought she had to, until he was ready. Until they were *both* ready to take the next step.

But she had never thought, not even for a moment, that this marriage had been a complete sham—a cover for something else.

All this time, while she had been convinced he wasn't ready to love, had he been giving what she yearned for to someone else?

'Who's Marlena?' she asked, her voice dull.

His scarred brow rose in surprise, but then she saw the guilt flicker across his face.

'She does not concern you,' he said. 'Stay and enjoy the rest of the show.' The suggestion came out as a command. Cold and final.

As he strode out of the box without a backward glance, her heart—which had been so full, so joyous, so hopeful only moments before—shattered.

Dominic was still shaking as he climbed into the SUV and barked an instruction at his driver.

A new message appeared on his phone in Italian from Marlena Romano.

Dominic, there is no need to leave the event. We have alerted the police to Enzo's disappearance and will inform you as soon as we have any news.

He typed a reply in Italian—not easy with his fingers still trembling from the feel of his wife, coming apart in his arms. And the look of devastation on her face afterwards.

Not a problem, Marlena. I am on my way.

He had caught Enzo, a ten-year-old street kid, trying to pick his pocket that afternoon, while he had been waiting outside the hotel for the car that was due to take him to the airport and Alison.

He'd been so preoccupied with thoughts of his wife and how much he wanted to see her again, to hold her, to find out how her show was progressing, that the nimble-fingered young thief had almost got away with his wallet.

But as soon as he'd grabbed the child's bony wrist, heard the boy's cry of distress and seen the angry defiance in his jaded eyes, it had been like looking into a mirror. And all the reasons why he shouldn't be quite so eager to see Alison again had come tumbling back to him.

Marlena was right, of course. It wasn't an efficient use of his celebrity to leave an event that had been planned for months to help fund the Lost Boys charity he had set up in Rome and a collection of other European cities, to help street kids like himself, both boys and girls—children who had no hope and no chance and no opportunities. To give them the support and encouragement they needed to succeed and tap all that wasted talent and potential before it was too late.

All he would be doing was getting in the way. Marlena and her staff were highly trained and extremely capable and once the police located Enzo, and returned him, the staff would be better placed to convince the boy to take the chance the home could offer him.

But when he had received Marlena's call he hadn't been thinking straight. The truth was he hadn't been thinking at all.

He'd needed a way out, an excuse to escape from the emotions threatening to choke him as he'd looked at his wife's dishevelled appearance, and the dazed shock in her eyes, and felt like an animal.

How could his hunger, his need, have got so spectacularly out of control that he'd taken her against a wall during a public event? When was it ever going to end? Because the more he had her, the more wild he became.

And the driving hunger for sex wasn't even the worst of how delusional he was.

He'd seen the way Alison had gazed at him when he strode into the hotel suite earlier that evening. Her eyes soft with longing.

They only had a few more months of their marriage left, and already he had let it get so far out of hand he couldn't even control his hunger for her, let alone the greed to have more of her than he could ever deserve.

That would have to end tonight. He would speak to Marlena, gauge the situation with Enzo, wait for word from the police and stay away from Alison until she had gone back to London. And he wouldn't contact her again, until he was finally back in control of his senses.

The car sped past the Coliseum on its way out of Rome towards the suburbs.

The arc lights illuminated the ancient building's broken façade and for the first time, instead of seeing the epic majesty of the place, and everything the people who had built it had achieved, all he saw was a ruin, the brutal bloodshed once celebrated within its walls a symbol of the hollow shame inside him.

CHAPTER TWELVE

ALLY WATCHED THE black SUV stop in front of a large mansion block in the outskirts of the city.

Dominic got out of the car and headed past the children's play equipment in the building's front garden, the bars of a climbing frame glinting in the moonlight. Confusion accelerated the hammer thuds of her heartbeat.

She wasn't even sure what had possessed her to follow him. She'd left the opera in a daze, the pain of his betrayal so huge it was almost choking her.

The questions running through her mind telling her what a fool she'd been.

Why had she assumed their marriage would be exclusive? After all, he'd never put that stipulation in any of the paperwork he'd made her sign. Why had it never even occurred to her to ask? Because she'd never asked him about anything? She'd never insisted or demanded a single thing. She'd trusted him implicitly, right from the first.

But as the young cab driver had sped through the streets of Rome following the SUV with the skill and precision of Jason Bourne in a chase scene—and telling her in broken English how much he'd always wanted a fare like this one—the open wound in her chest had made it brutally clear that stupidity and naiveté weren't her only flaws. She still loved him, despite her suspicions.

'*Scusa, signorina?* You go in?' the cab driver asked from the front of the car.

Did she want to go in? Indecision added to the trauma.

The building Dominic had disappeared into looked like a school. Or maybe a children's home.

Did his mistress work here? What if she'd made a terrible mistake and he wasn't seeing another woman? Perhaps she should return to the hotel as he'd requested, wait for him to come back?

But even as the desperate hope that she had been wrong, or misguided, that she'd jumped to the wrong conclusion, bubbled inside her, the voice in her head that had persuaded her to follow him in the first place refused to be silent.

Was this really about whether or not Dominic had been seeing another woman? Or was it much more fundamental than that?

He'd shut her out, from so much of his life, his past, his future, and yet he had become such an important part of hers. He'd refused to let her in. Hidden behind the business arrangement they'd made long after it had stopped being just about business and become so much more for her.

She'd fallen in love with him weeks ago, maybe even months ago, and she'd been in denial about that, too. But she wasn't in denial any more.

Whatever this place was, whoever Marlena was, they were significant in Dominic's life and yet she knew nothing about them. Good grief, she hadn't even known her husband spoke fluent Italian.

He'd talked about trust once before, when they'd consolidated their marriage bargain—but she'd always trusted him. It was him who had never trusted her...

Opening her purse with trembling fingers, she pulled out two twenty-euro notes and passed them to the driver. '*Grazie, mille.*'

'*Grazie, signorina.* You want I wait?' he asked as he took the money.

Yes. Just in case I don't get up the guts to follow him into that building.

She stifled the plea. She'd been enough of a coward already. Letting him set the boundaries of this relationship. She didn't want to be bound by that contract any more. She wanted a real marriage. Or no marriage at all. She couldn't live like this, or she would be exactly what she'd always strived to avoid. A shadow of who she could be, a woman like her mother, chasing dreams and not facing reality.

'No, *grazie*,' she said and forced herself to step out of the car.

She took a deep breath, which did nothing to calm her racing heartbeat, or close the hole that had opened up in her belly. And walked up the path to the building's main entrance as the cab drove away.

As she rang the bell she read the sign on the door: *Fondazione per Ragazzi Perduti.*

It was an Italian translation of the charity named in the opera programme—the charity Dominic had pretended to know nothing about.

The bitter truth stabbed at her stomach like a rusty blade. So he'd lied about that too.

The door opened, and a middle-aged woman in jeans and a jumper stood in front of her, her warm caramel eyes widening in surprise.

Marlena.

Ally recognised her immediately; she was striking, even though she looked considerably older than she had in the picture on Dominic's phone Ally had glimpsed a half-hour ago.

Ally almost smiled at the shock on the woman's face.

This situation would have been comical if it weren't so tragic.

'Signora LeGrand?' she said, and Ally realised she must have recognised her from the press photos, but as Ally nodded, unable to speak round the boulder of misery in her throat, the woman didn't look remotely guilty or abashed.

A tiny portion of the pain faded. So Marlena wasn't Dominic's lover. She had been wrong about that. But the relief she ought to have felt didn't come.

Why had Dominic deliberately let her assume the worst? Exactly how much contempt did he have for her and their marriage? And how much more pathetic could he make her feel? When she had chased him across Rome simply to have the truth confirmed.

'Buena sera,' the woman said, her expression changing from surprise to concern. 'Come,' she said, gesturing for Ally to step into the lobby of the building. 'Dominic is here—you are looking for him, yes?'

The lobby was warm and bright, modern and colourful. Framed children's paintings covered the walls. There was a chalkboard pinned with a series of flyers and messages in Italian. She could hear rap music playing and see what looked like a rec room through a glass partition, where a group of teenagers lounged, some watching a football game on a large flat-screen TV, others competing with each other on a computer console.

'I told him he did not need to come,' Marlena said from behind her, her English perfect. 'Enzo absconded earlier, but the police have found him. I am so sorry your evening has been interrupted.'

'Enzo? Who's Enzo?' she said, blankly.

'Enzo is the homeless boy Dominic caught trying to pick his pocket this afternoon.' The woman smiled, but her puzzled expression said it all; clearly she had expected Dominic to mention this boy to Ally.

'Dominic brought him to us earlier. He is one of the many children Dominic has helped with his patronage of *la fondazione*,' the woman added.

Her explanation was drowned out by the pounding in Ally's ears when Dominic appeared from a door at the back of the lobby, staring at his phone as he spoke in a stream of Italian. The only word she understood was *'polizia'*.

'Dominic?' Marlena interrupted him and his head jerked up. 'Your wife has arrived.'

His whole body stiffened, and Ally felt the rusty blade in her stomach twist.

'Alison, why are you here?' he said, the edge in his voice sharpening the knife. She wasn't wanted here, in this part of his life, that much was obvious.

'I… I came to find you,' she managed to get out as he marched towards her.

'Come.' His fingers closed over her bare arm like an iron band. 'We should leave.' He said his goodbyes to Marlena, but didn't give her a chance to do the same before he had escorted her out of the building.

'Get in the car,' he said as he opened the door to the large black SUV.

She slid into the seat, and stared out of the window as she heard him get in behind her. Her stomach felt as if it were a ship in a storm, being tossed on the undulating waves of her emotions. She couldn't speak, couldn't even think as the car pulled away from the kerb.

'I cannot believe you followed me here,' he said, sounding both angry and incredulous. 'When I asked you to stay at the opera.'

She ought to say something, in her own defence, but as she gazed into the night she decided for once she had nothing to apologise for. If he hadn't wanted her there, he shouldn't have left her with the impression he was running off to see another woman.

'I'd appreciate it if you didn't do that again.' He bit off the words in staccato bursts of temper. 'I prefer not to be humiliated in front of people who work for me.'

Wouldn't we all prefer that? she thought bitterly.

Silence descended over the dark interior of the car as they made their way back through the city. The tension became like a living breathing thing as she refused to look at him. But finally the one thing that had always failed her in the past began to burn in her gullet like a comet, choking off everything else—the heartache, the pain, the humiliation, the embarrassment, the confusion and panic—until all that was left was the rage.

The rage that she had learned to bury deep, during the years spent watching her mother die.

The car pulled up at the kerb, but, instead of waiting for Dominic to get out and walk around the car to open her door, Ally got out on her own and marched towards the hotel entrance.

She heard him shout something behind her, but she kept on going, the rage cleansing, empowering, enlightening. It flowed through her veins now, burning through everything in its wake like a fireball.

He caught up with her in the lobby, grasped her arm to swing her round to face him. 'Where the hell do you think you are going?' he said—looking wary now as well as angry.

Good.

'To our suite, to pack my bag and go home.' She yanked her elbow free.

Everything she could say, everything she wanted to say, everything she should have said weeks, maybe even months ago careered around her head like dodgem cars in a cheap arcade as she stormed into the elevator and stabbed the button. She'd left him standing in the lobby. He shook his head, as if he were dazed, and then charged after her, but he was too late, the doors closing before he could get his hand inside.

'*Arrêtes*, Alison, we must talk,' he shouted, obviously expecting her to hit the 'open door' button. She didn't.

Everything that needed to be said was still lodged in her solar plexus.

The elevator arrived at their floor. She scrambled in her purse to find the key card, desperate to get into the suite and lock him out.

He'd broken her heart deliberately. It was the only thing her tired brain could grasp hold of. He'd known how she was coming to feel about him, and he'd hurt her, crushed her because he could.

She found the card, but as the green light flashed on the door, the emergency exit slammed open. He must have run up the stairs rather than waiting for the elevator. His footsteps raced down the corridor.

She rushed inside, swung round to slam the door closed just as his palm slapped against the wood. He pushed it open and she scrambled back into the room.

'Get out. I don't want you in here,' she said, the tears streaking down her face.

'*Ma belle*, stop—don't cry…you mustn't cry.'

He reached out to cradle her cheek, his anger replaced by devastation.

But she slapped his hand away. 'Why mustn't I?' she said around the choking sobs now.

'Because I am not worth it,' he said.

Did he really believe that? It seemed that he did from the shame and regret burning in his eyes. But she didn't care, she wasn't going to let him off that easily.

'Why did you do it? Why did you let me believe Marlena was your mistress? Why won't you let me into your life? Why does everything have to be a secret?'

'Because you would hate me more, if you knew what was inside here.'

He pressed a hand to his heart, the need and desire in his eyes almost as painful as the shame.

She backed up until there was nowhere else to go.

'Let me love you. Let me take away the pain?' he said.

He was talking about sex, she understood that, when she wanted so much more, but she couldn't say no to him as he found the zip on the back of her dress and pulled it down. She pushed his jacket off his shoulders, yanked at the buttons on his shirt; the fight to get naked became a battle.

He kicked off his shoes, she unhooked her bra, he unzipped his trousers, shoved them down, the rampant erection bouncing up to tempt her, to mock her.

Within seconds they were naked, panting, the feral need to mate, to forget, gripping them both the way it had in the opera booth. He turned her to the wall, spread her legs and placed his palm above her head as he notched the thick head of penis at her entrance and thrust in from behind.

The visceral wave of pleasure as he ground into her stole her breath and her resistance and the whole of her heart.

Their frantic mating was over in seconds, the glorious peak slamming into her with the force and fury of a freight train as he emptied himself inside her for the second time that night.

They sank to the carpet together, their breathing ragged, the sweat drying on their skin. But as she turned in his arms, to hold his head, to look into his eyes—they hadn't settled anything, they'd only made it more complicated—her gaze snagged on the cheval mirror at the other side of the room. At first all she saw was the tangle of limbs, her pale skin starkly white against his tanned body. Then her heart seized.

A criss-cross of white scars marred the smooth skin of his back. The marks ranged from his shoulder blades right down to the lighter skin of his backside.

What had happened to him? Who could have done such a thing?

'Some people deserve to be hurt, ma petite.'

And suddenly she knew exactly who. And the words he had whispered before they'd fallen on each other—to try and erase the hurt with sex—came back, too.

'Because I am not worth it.'

Sharp pain dug into her stomach, her gasp of distress ringing off the room's luxury furnishings.

His body went rigid and he heaved himself off her. Their gazes locked.

Shame flickered across his face, making the knife in her gut plunge deeper.

All the questions, came tumbling back, but she had answers to them all now.

So this was why they'd always made love in the dark or the semi-darkness…why he always left her in the morning…why he hadn't shared a bedroom with her…why he locked the door so she couldn't join him in the bathroom. It was another secret he'd guarded for three months.

He reached behind him to drag on the shirt that had fallen off his shoulder. To cover the scars.

She grasped his wrist, felt the warm blood pulsing through him, and her heart broke inside for the boy he'd been. 'Don't hide them from me, Dominic, you don't need to,' she whispered, naked, vulnerable, but unafraid.

She'd had no idea his father had been such a monster,

but how could she not have known, when all the signs had always been there?

'Your back… The scars…' She choked the words out and saw the muscle in his cheek flex as he looked away. 'Did Pierre do that?'

His eyes darkened, his expression becoming strained and tense.

'I'm so sorry.' She allowed all the compassion she felt for that boy to show in her face.

'Why are you sorry? You didn't do it,' he said, his voice clipped and wary. 'It was a long time ago and I deserved it.'

'Dominic, how can you possibly believe that?'

Dominic pressed his thumb to her lips. He didn't want to talk about that time in his life, or that night. Why the heck did she think he'd gone to so much trouble to stop her seeing the scars? But he hated seeing the sheen of moisture in his eyes, the compassion he didn't deserve.

Somehow, she had sneaked under his skin. Made him care when he didn't want to care. Made him want more than he should. And more than he would ever be able to reciprocate.

She was so young and vulnerable, so honest and open, so brave and strong, but she had no idea who he really was. He had hoped to keep this from her, had clung to the delusion that if she never discovered the truth, they could end their marriage with dignity. But this relationship had never played out on the terms he'd tried to insist upon. He'd become captivated, enchanted by her and invested in a future he had no right to expect.

And by trying to protect her he'd only hurt her more.

'I'm not that screwed-up kid any more, and my father has been dead for a long time,' he said, determined to take that misty look out of her eyes.

'I know, but why did you hide…?'

'Shh, Alison.' He stroked his thumb across her lips—wishing he could kiss her into silence. But knowing he had to stop being a coward, and tell her the truth.

She blinked, those amber eyes glossy with tears. 'Did you get those scars that night? Because you were protecting my mother?'

'No.' If only that were true. 'She was protecting me, that's why he hit her, why he threw you both out. I snapped, sick of the insults. I thought I could best him, thought I could finally make him pay for what he'd done to my mother, by abandoning her and me. But I was wrong. I was a stupid child, hyped up on my own bitterness and resentment. She found him using his belt on me and she tried to stop him.'

'Oh, Dominic…' Her eyes widened, the compassion so fierce, he had to fist his fingers to stop from taking what he wanted from her. 'I'm so sorry…'

'You misunderstand me, Alison. I was young and foolish and full of bravado and I was spoiling for a fight with him. And you and your mother paid the price.'

'You can't blame yourself for your father's violence, surely you must see that,' she said. 'You didn't do anything wrong.'

Hadn't he? It certainly hadn't felt right when he had been crawling through the grounds, puking into the underbrush as he'd struggled to breathe through three broken ribs and stave off unconsciousness before he got to the road.

'Maybe.' He wanted to believe the faith in her eyes; he'd lived with the guilt of that night ever since he'd found out how destitute she and her mother had been. But that wasn't the biggest problem. 'The point is I'm not that boy any more. I look after number one now. Always. I can't give you what you need.'

He brushed her short curls back from her cheek, pressed his lips to the soft skin. She shuddered with reaction, her wide amber eyes darkening on cue.

He forced himself to drop his hand, the rough chuckle strained.

'Yes, you can. You already have. I love you, Dominic,' she said, with such yearning, such honesty. 'So much.'

The guilt gripped his insides.

This was his own fault. He'd stepped over a line three weeks ago in London, maybe even before that. Every time they made love, he wanted to absorb more of her kindness, her care, her tenderness—and Alison's romantic nature, her sweet, compassionate heart had done the rest.

'You can't love me,' he said, forcing his voice to remain firm, despite the riot of emotions churning in his stomach. 'You don't know me.'

He found his boxers and put them on. Then handed her his shirt and turned his back, waiting for her to cover herself. He threaded his fingers through his hair, his hand shaking. He couldn't look at her, couldn't see the pale skin, the marks he'd left on it from their lovemaking, and tell her the truth.

'You cannot love me, Allycat,' he said, his voice breaking on the words. 'No one can.'

'Why not?' Ally asked.

Dominic lifted his head, his chocolate eyes full of the secrets that he'd worked so hard to hide. And suddenly she understood, who he had been protecting all this time—with his insistence on them living separate lives, in separate countries. Why he had never wanted to stay overnight, why he had hidden the scars, denied their significance, even denied her feelings for him.

He hadn't been protecting himself, he had been protecting her.

'Why, Dominic?' she asked again. 'Why can't I love you?'

He shook his head, looked past her, but the light had left his eyes, becoming flat and wary. 'I am sorry I hurt you,' he said with a finality that chilled her. 'That was not my intention, even if it was inevitable. I will have my lawyers finalise the divorce.'

But as he turned to go, to walk out of her life, she rushed after him and grasped his arm.

'Dominic, stop.'

He glanced down at her fingers, but she refused to remove them. She curled her hand around his forearm instead and gathered every ounce of her courage to say the one thing she knew he would not want to hear. The one thing he had denied for so long, the thing that had been inculcated in him as a young boy by a woman who had never wanted to celebrate his birth and a man who had acknowledged him on a whim one summer and then discarded him in the cruellest way imaginable.

'You're not worthless,' she said.

He tugged his arm free, the amused frown a defence.

'I know I'm not. LN is worth upwards of five billion dollars on the open market,' he said.

'You're not worthless,' she said again.

'I know that,' he replied. But he backed up a step, and her heart broke for him all over again.

The arrogance, the control, the desperate need not to accept her love. Not to need it. It had all been a defence, all along. Because he'd loved his mother and tried to gain his father's respect and they had both thrown his need back in his face.

Of course he didn't trust her feelings, because he didn't trust his own.

This marriage *had* always been more than a business arrangement. His desire to cherish and protect her. His insistence that he invest in her business. His encouragement and concern. And she'd let her own insecurities blind her to that truth. She hadn't challenged him…she hadn't even put up a fight. But she was going to fight now.

'You're not worthless,' she said again. 'Whatever she made you think, whatever he told you. You're not.'

He shook his head, but she could see the arrogance falling away. She'd struck right at the heart of his insecurities but she couldn't let up now. However painful it was for him, however big a risk it was for her, she had to see this through.

'I *do* love you. And it's not because you're incredible in bed, or one of the richest guys on the planet. Or because you've supported my business, supported me.' She let out a weak laugh as the confused frown descended on his face.

No one had ever loved him for who he was. But she did. And she intended for him to know it and believe it. Then they would see.

'Why, then?' he asked, as if he genuinely didn't know. And she had the opening she needed.

'It's because you let me follow you around like a puppy that summer and you never once complained. It's because you blamed yourself for what happened to my mother, to me, when it was never your fault.'

'But you suffered so much,' he said.

'And so did you,' she said, realising so much of that valiant boy—who had wanted payback for his own mother and had taken on a monster to do it—still existed, even if he couldn't see it. 'It's because when I rang your bell all those months ago, you insisted on tending my leg.'

'I was planning to seduce you,' he qualified again. 'I needed a wife.'

She grinned. 'Do you hear me complaining?'

'You were innocent,' he said, his eyes dark with the heat and intensity she had come to adore. 'However much you enjoyed it,' he added, cupping her cheek.

She felt the sizzle of heat, and the connection that had always been there, ever since that summer, arc between them.

She covered his hand, leant into the caress. 'I loved that you were so scared of exploiting that innocence, even though it really wasn't a big deal to me,' she said, loving his concerned frown even more.

Honestly, men! What was the big deal with virginity?

'And because you fought to give me security and stability in this marriage,' she added, the swelling in her chest making her heart beat in hard, heavy thuds. 'Even though it was supposed to be fake.'

'It never felt fake, even when I wanted it to,' he murmured, cupping her other cheek, and touching her forehead with his.

At last, she'd broken through that shield he erected to protect himself from rejection. The shield that had made him believe he didn't deserve to be loved. That he didn't deserve her.

The connection was so sure, so solid, she could hear it in his ragged breathing. How ridiculous that they'd both denied the importance of that connection for so long.

'It's because you're the kind of man who wants to give children like Enzo the helping hand you never had,' she continued. 'And because you pulled out all the stops to help me achieve my dream, even when I was busy sabotaging it with self-doubt.' She sighed. 'And because you gave me a foot rub to try and ease my pain.'

'That's such a small thing,' he murmured, his voice barely a whisper as she held his waist and he caressed her neck, his fingers threading into her hair.

'Well, it was a really excellent foot rub,' she said, smiling at him. 'So not *that* small.' Then she sobered. 'It's the small things that matter, Dominic. As much as, if not more than, the big things.' She drew back, so she could look into his eyes. The small things they'd both been denied by living separate lives when they deserved to be together.

'Now do you believe I love you?' she asked quietly.

He nodded. 'But do you love me enough to stay with me?' he asked, the yearning, the longing that she'd thought was hers alone clear in his voice.

She sucked in a deep breath. Knowing it would be so easy to just say yes. She already had so much more than she'd thought she'd have. But she couldn't chicken out. Her cowardice—and his—had brought them to this point. Now they both needed to be brave. He'd been brave enough to admit how unsure he was about love. She needed to be brave enough to demand what she needed.

'I want to stay, but I have conditions.'

His eyebrow arched. 'Conditions? What kind of conditions? Are we going to have to renegotiate the contract again?'

She laughed, the breath releasing in a rush. Maybe this was going to be much easier than she had assumed. 'No, we're going to have to tear it up.'

'I see,' he said.

'I don't want a time limit on our marriage. I want… I want us to be a real couple in every sense of the word. I don't want to limit my feelings for you. And I want us to live together. Either in London or New York, or wherever works.'

He nodded. 'I'm sure we can work something out,' he said, and her heart leapt into her throat.

'I want to be able to tell you I love you. And know that it doesn't scare you, or threaten you or—'

'It doesn't,' he said, interrupting her. 'It humbles me.'

'Really?' she asked, letting the last of her insecurities show.

'*Dieu*, Alison. How could it not?' he said. He stroked her cheek. 'You're so tough and smart and sweet. How could I not fall in love with you?'

'You don't have to say that to make me stay, Dominic,' she said, wanting to take the words at face value, but knowing she couldn't. Hadn't her mother believed them for all the wrong reasons? At least she wasn't going to make that mistake. 'Love is a gift, not an obligation,' she said, because she suspected he had no idea what love was. Who had ever loved him, but her? 'It's enough that you want to give this relationship a chance. A real chance. You don't have to love me back. Not yet.'

'That's very generous of you,' he said, but his lips curved in a rueful smile and she felt the bubble of hope break open inside her chest, spreading warmth and light where only minutes ago there had been despair. 'Unfortunately, it's too late for that,' he whispered against her lips, the soft glow of happiness joined by the sharp pulse of heat. 'Because I already do.'

Dominic let his mouth take hers, claiming his wife in a kiss that touched his very soul. He was still scared, still terrified really. He wasn't convinced he was as worthy as she believed him to be. Was still sure he didn't deserve her.

But after almost losing her, he was damned if he would let that hold him back from claiming her ever again.

She was his wife now, in every sense of the word. Damn the contract, damn his father, damn the fear that had held him back from admitting how he really felt for so long.

Yes, it was a huge risk. But Alison Jones, his Cinderella bride, was worth every ounce of effort it was going to take for him to prove, to himself as much as her, that he deserved to be her husband.

EPILOGUE

Fifteen months later

'SOCIAL MEDIA IS going mad, Ally. And listen to that applause. It's another triumph for the Allycat brand.' Megan De Rossi gave Ally a high-five as the last model strutted onto the catwalk and the wave of noise hit the backstage area. 'Consider New York Fashion Week well and truly conquered,' Megan added, tears forming in her eyes. 'You did it—they adore you.'

'*We* did it,' Ally said, beaming back at her. 'They adore *us*.'

All the hard work, the long hours, the endless worries about everything from a model's sprained ankle yesterday to those first days over a year ago when Dominic had secured her partnership with the Dharavi Collective had paid off. It had been a long hard road to this point—and there would be more bumps along the way—but her brand was due to launch at the end of the month in Europe at Paris Fashion Week and she was already clothing A-list movie stars, Grammy-winning pop stars and a string of influential celebrity vloggers. And now this, another triumph in TriBeCa after that nail-biting baptism of fire a year ago now, when she'd done that first prelim show Dominic had pushed her into.

She could still remember the sweat and tears of that first shaky step onto the fashion industry's world stage. Her nerves had reached fever pitch that evening but she'd pushed through them, and Dominic had been beside her at every step. Offering not just support and encouragement, but also his strength and determination. And the rewards had been immense, not just in that first tentative triumph—although she hadn't won a spot at New York Fashion Week that year, the exposure had started a word-of-mouth buzz about her designs that had led to orders and other opportunities—but also inside herself. Because after that night, she'd discovered that Dominic was right, that risk in business was the same as the risk she'd taken in her private life on him, on them… That risk wasn't something to be afraid of, not if you embraced it and put your all into it, because with risk came rewards, rewards beyond her wildest dreams.

'Come on, you need to take a bow,' Rohana, who was here with some of the women from her collective, shouted above the applause as she and Megan linked arms with Ally to lead her onto the catwalk.

As her team roared their support from the wings, she walked down the narrow runway with the two women who had been an integral part of making her brand such a success.

The cheers reached epic proportions, camera phones flashing, the media spotlights trained on her as the crowd rose to their feet.

But as she waved, and smiled, and bowed, she scanned the crowd. She could see Dario, Megan's husband, standing in the front row with their daughter Issy—who had been given special dispensation to attend the show without her brothers—and Katie, Megan's sister, with her husband, Jared, who had their toddler daughter, Carmen, in his arms. But where was Dominic? She needed him here, because this was his triumph as much as hers.

'Be still my beating heart,' whispered Rohana. 'Your man is a fine sight to see.'

It was all the warning she had before Dominic leapt up on stage.

He strode towards her—the dark blue business suit doing nothing to disguise the ripple of muscle in his big body. The crowd went wild, beginning a chant of 'Kiss her' as he approached—which had become a feature of all her shows since that sidewalk kiss all those months ago in Nolita had made them an Internet sensation.

How far we've come, she thought as he reached her. Gripping her round the waist, he swung her round in a circle, then put her down and cradled her face in his palms.

'Congratulations, Allycat,' he said, then his lips were on hers. The kiss was driven, hungry, joyous, igniting all the needs that would never die.

Her hands found his waist as she clung to him and kissed him back, her tongue tangling with his, and let the love pour through her.

This man, this marriage, meant everything to her. Without it, without him, without love, even wowing New York Fashion Week wouldn't mean as much.

It was several hours later before they were finally alone together, in the limousine heading back to their Manhattan apartment. The apartment they rarely used since Dominic had made the decision to move permanently to London.

Ally clung to his hand, wishing she could just be beamed up now to their bedroom and they could finally celebrate the brand's latest success in style.

'Happy?' he murmured as he pressed her fingers to his lips.

'Ecstatic,' she said.

'*Bien*, because I have a suggestion,' he said.

'What is it?' she asked, loving the mischievous glint in his eyes. She certainly hoped his suggestion involved them both getting naked as soon as possible.

But then he surprised her.

'That we both take the next week off. It is way past time we had a honeymoon. Can you do it?' he asked.

'Absolutely,' she said without hesitation, because she couldn't think of anything more wonderful. It would mean rearranging her schedule, postponing the interviews she had lined up, getting her team to handle the European launch, but they'd already done a ton of advance publicity, and she trusted them.

'Where would you like to go?' he said. 'Name anywhere in the world and I will take you.'

'Honestly? I can choose anywhere?' she said, knowing there was only one place she wanted to go. And one person she wanted to be with.

Over the past year, her wanderlust had been sated a hundred times over. Ever since that night in Rome, when they had committed to making this a real marriage, life had been a roller coaster as she'd set up her business and his had continued to expand. They'd worked overtime to make this marriage work but it had meant shoehorning snippets of quality time in between all their other commitments. Each moment they'd spent alone together had been precious and wonderful and important...

But a whole week felt like a banquet, a banquet she didn't want to squander on sightseeing, or shopping, or elaborate meals in fancy hotels.

'Of course,' he said. 'Wherever you want to go, it is your choice.'

'Okay, then I want to go home to London, shut the

doors, turn off our phones and the Internet, tell everyone we've gone to Outer Mongolia and just stay there, with you, for a week. I want us to watch slushy movies together, cook all our favourite foods, have sex in every room and finally get around to celebrating all the birthdays of yours that we've missed.'

They'd celebrated his thirtieth birthday that summer and the memory of the particularly inventive way he'd found to devour the chocolate cake she'd baked him still made her blush.

Even so, she held her breath, wondering if he would object. Dominic was an active, driven over-achiever; getting him to sit still for long was never easy. But instead of objecting, he threw back his head and laughed. The sound was deep, and sexy and—was that relief she could hear?

Reaching across the seat to cup her cheek and pull her towards him, he whispered across her mouth. 'I like your thinking, Madame LeGrand. But I'm not sure we have enough bedrooms—there are twenty-nine birthdays to catch up on, after all.' Running a hand under her dress, he found the melting heart of her. 'But do not worry,' he added as his mouth descended to seal the deal. 'I can improvise.'

Happiness burst like a firework in her chest—not least because she knew exactly how good her husband was at improvising.

* * * * *

THE MAID'S
SPANISH SECRET

DANI COLLINS

For my editor, Laurie Johnson, and the wonderful team at Harlequin Mills & Boon in London.

Romance novels taught me to chase my dreams, and writing for Mills & Boon Modern Romance was a lifelong goal.

Thirty books in, I'm still astonished and eternally grateful that you've made this dream come true for me.

Thank you.

PROLOGUE

R ICO M ONTERO ARRIVED at his brother's villa, two hours up the coast from Valencia, in seventy-three minutes. He'd been feeling cooped up in his penthouse, hungry for air. He had pulled his GTA Spano out of storage and tried to escape his own dark mood, not realizing the direction he took until he was pulled over for speeding.

Recognizing where he was, he told the officer he was on his way to see his brother—a means of name-dropping the entire family. The ploy had gotten him out of having his license suspended, but he still had to pay a fine.

Since he was literally in the neighborhood, he decided not to compound his crimes by lying. He rolled his way through Cesar's vineyard to the modern home sprawled against a hillside.

He told himself he didn't miss the vineyard he had owned with pride for nearly a decade—long before his brother had decided he had an interest in grapes and winemaking. Rico's fascination with the process had dried up along with his interest in life in general. Selling that property had been a clean break from a time he loathed to dwell upon.

It's been eighteen months, his mother had said over lunch yesterday. *Time to turn our attention to the future.*

She had said something similar three months ago and he had dodged it. This time, he sat there and took the bullet. *Of course. Who did you have in mind?*

He had left thinking, *Go ahead and find me another scheming, adulterous bride.* But he hadn't said it aloud. He had promised to carry that secret to his grave.

For what?

He swore and jammed the car into Park, then threw himself out of it, grimly aware he had completely failed to escape his dour mood.

"Rico!" His sister-in-law Sorcha opened the door before he had climbed the wide steps. She smiled with what looked like genuine pleasure and maybe a hint of relief.

"Mateo, look. Tío Rico has come to see you." She spoke to the bawling toddler on her hip. "That's a nice surprise, isn't it?"

She wasn't the flawlessly elegant beauty he was used to seeing on Cesar's arm, more of a welcoming home-maker. Her jeans and peasant-style top were designer brands, but she wore minimal makeup and her blond hair was tied into a simple ponytail. Her frown at her unhappy son was tender and empathetic, not the least frazzled by his tantrum.

The deeply unhappy Mateo pointed toward the back of the house. "*Ve*, Papi."

"He's overdue for his nap." Sorcha waved Rico in. "But he knows *someone* took *someone else* into the V-I-N-E-Y-A-R-D."

"You're speaking English and you still have to spell it out?" Rico experienced a glimmer of amusement.

"He's picking it up *so* fast. Oh!" She caught Mateo as he reached out to Rico, nearly launching himself from her arms.

Rico caught him easily while Sorcha stammered, "I'm sorry."

If Rico briefly winced in dismay, it was because of the look in Sorcha's eyes. Far too close to pity, it contained sincere regret that her son was prevailing on him for something she thought too big and painful to ask.

It wasn't. The favor he was doing for his former in-laws was a greater imposition, spiking far more deeply into a more complex knot of nerves. What Sorcha thought she knew about his marriage was the furthest thing from reality.

And what she read as pain and anger at fate was contempt and fury with himself for being a fool. He was steeped in bitterness, playing a role that was barely a version of the truth. A version that made a sensitive soul like Sorcha wear a poignant smile as she gazed on him holding his young nephew.

Mateo stopped crying, tears still on his cheeks.

"*Ve*, Papi?" he tried.

The tyke had been born mere weeks before Rico's ill-fated marriage. Mateo was sturdy and stubborn and full of the drive that all the Montero males possessed. This was why he was giving his mother such a hard time. He knew what he wanted and a nap wouldn't mollify him.

"We'll discuss it," he told the boy and glanced at Sorcha. "You should change," he advised, unable to bear much more of that agonized happiness in her eyes.

"Why—? Ugh." She noticed the spot where Mateo had rubbed his streaming face against her shoulder. "You're okay?" she asked with concern.

"For God's sake, Sorcha," he muttered through clenched teeth.

He regretted his short temper immediately and quickly reined in his patience. His secret sat in him like a cancer, but he couldn't let it provoke him into lashing out, certainly not at the nicest person in his family.

"I didn't mean to speak so sharply," he managed to say, gathering his composure as he brought his nephew to his shoulder. "We're fine."

"It's okay, Rico." She squeezed his arm. "I understand."

No. She didn't. But thankfully she disappeared, leaving him to have a man-to-man chat with Mateo, who hadn't forgotten a damned thing. He gave it one more try, pointing and asking for Cesar, who had taken his older brother Enrique to speak to winemakers and pet cellar cats and generally have a barrel of a good time by anyone's standards.

Mateo's eyes were droopy, his cheeks red, very much worn out from his tantrum.

"I know what you're going through," he told the boy. "Better than you can imagine."

Like Mateo, Rico was the younger brother to the future *duque*. He, too, occupied the unlit space beneath the long shadow of greatness cast by the heir. He, too, was expected to live an unblemished life so as not to tarnish the title he would never hold. Then there was the simple, fraternal rivalry of a brother being that few years older and moving into the next life stage. Envy was natural, not that Monteros were allowed to feel such things. Emotions were too much like pets, requiring regular feeding and liable to leave a mess on the floor.

Rico climbed the grand staircase to the bedroom that had been converted to a playroom for the boys, not dwelling on Cesar's stellar fulfillment of his duty with two bright and healthy children, a beautiful home and a stunning, warmhearted wife.

"There are some realities that are not worth crying about," he informed Mateo as they entered the room. "Your father told me that." It was one of Rico's earliest memories.

Cry all you want. They won't care. Cesar had spoken with the voice of experience after Rico had been denied something he'd desperately wanted that he could no longer recollect.

Cesar had come to reason with him, perhaps because he was tired of having his playmate sent into solitary confinement. Reason was a family skill valued far more highly than passion. Reason was keeping him silent and carrying on today, maintaining order rather than allowing the chaos that would reign if the truth came out.

Doesn't it make you mad that they won't even listen? Rico had asked Cesar that long-ago day.

Yes. Cesar had been very mature for a boy of six or seven. *But getting mad won't change anything. You might as well accept it and think about something else.*

Words Rico had learned to live by.

He was capable of basic compassion, however.

"I'll always listen if you need to get something off your chest," he told his nephew as he lowered them both into an armchair. "But sometimes there's nothing to be done. It's a hard fact of life, young man."

Mateo wound down to sniffling whimpers. He decided to explore Rico's empty chest pocket.

"Should we read a book?" Rico picked up the first picture book within reach. It was bilingual, with trains and dogs and bananas labeled in English and Spanish.

As he worked through the pages, he deliberately pitched his voice to an uninflected drone. The boy's head on his chest grew heavier and heavier.

"Thank you," Sorcha whispered when she peeked in.

Rico nodded and carried the sleeping boy to his crib. The nanny came in with the baby monitor.

Rico followed Sorcha down the stairs saying, "I'll go find Cesar. If Mateo wakes, don't tell him what a traitor I am."

"Actually, I was going to invite you for dinner later this week. There's something I want to talk to you about. Can we go into Cesar's office?" Her brow pleated with concern.

Rico bit back a sigh, trying to hold on to the temper that immediately began to slip. "If this is about me remarrying, Mother has passed along your concerns."

Your sister-in-law thinks it's too soon, his mother had said yesterday, not asking him how *he* felt. She had merely implied that in Sorcha's view, he was in a weakened state. His choice had been to confirm it or go along with his mother's insistence on finding him a new wife.

"This is something else," Sorcha murmured, closing the door and waving toward the sofa. "And my imagination could be running wild. I haven't said anything to Cesar."

She poured two glasses of the Irish whiskey she had turned Cesar on to drinking and brought one to where Rico stood.

"Really?" he drawled, wondering what she could possibly impart that would need to be absorbed with a bracing shot. He left the whiskey on the end table as they both sat.

"Please don't be angry with me. I know I was over-stepping, suggesting your mother hold off on pressing you to remarry, but I care about all of you." She sat with her elbows on her thighs, leaning forward, hands clasped. "You may not be the most demonstrative family, but you *are* family. I will never stay silent if I think one of you needs…" Her mouth tightened.

"Sorcha." He meticulously gathered his forbearance. "I'm fine." And, before he had to suffer another swimming gaze of tormented sympathy, he added, "If I were in your shoes, I would understand why you think I'm not, but honestly, you have to stop worrying about me."

"That's never going to happen," she said primly, which would have been endearing if he didn't find it so frustratingly intrusive. "And there may be other factors to consider." She sipped her drink and eyed him over it. Then sighed. "I feel like such a hypocrite."

He lifted his brows. "Why? What's going on?"

She frowned, set down her drink and picked up her phone, stared at it without turning it on. "Elsa, our nanny, showed me something that came up in her news feed."

"Something compromising?" Sorcha would have taken up the concern with Cesar unless— Oh, hell. Had something gotten out from the coroner's report? "Is this about Faustina?" His molars ground together on reflex.

"No! No, it's not about her at all." She touched her brow. "Elsa always comes with us when we have dinner at your mother's. She's acquainted with the maids there and follows some of them online."

At the word *maid* a premonition danced in his periphery. He refused to reach for the drink, though. It would be a tell. Instinctively, he knew he had to maintain impassivity. He couldn't tip his hand. Not before he knew exactly what was coming next.

"To be honest, I rarely check my social media accounts," he said with a disinterested brush of non-existent lint from his knee. "Especially since Faustina passed. It's very maudlin."

"I suppose it would be." Her expression grew pinched. She looked at the phone she held pressed between her palms. "But one way or another, I think you should be aware of this particular post."

Biting her lips together, she touched her thumb to the sensor and the screen woke. She flicked to bring up a photo and held it out to him.

"On first glance, Elsa thought it was Mateo dressed up as a girl. That's the only reason she took notice and showed me. She thought it was funny that it had given her a double take. I had to agree this particular photo offers a certain resemblance."

Rico flicked a look at the toddler. He'd never seen Mateo in a pink sailor's bib and hat, but the baby girl's grin was very similar, minus a few teeth, to the one he had coaxed out of his nephew before the boy's head had drooped against his chest.

"I actually keep my privacy settings locked down tight," Sorcha said. "I've heard photos can be stolen and wind up in ads without permission. I thought that's what had happened. Elsa assured me she never shares images of the boys with anyone but me or Cesar."

The Montero fortune had been built on the development of chemicals and special alloys. Rico had learned early that certain substances, innocuous on their own, could become explosive when in proximity to one another.

Sorcha was pouring statements into beakers before him. A maid. A baby that looked like other children in the family.

He wouldn't let those two pieces of information touch. Not yet.

"It's said we all have a double." His lifetime of suppressing emotion served him well. "It would seem you've found Mateo's."

"This is the only photo where she looks so much like him," Sorcha murmured, taking back her phone. "I looked up the account. Her mother is a photographer."

Photographer. One beaker began to tip into another.

"This is part of her portfolio for her home business. Her name is Poppy Harris. The mother, I mean. The baby is Lily."

His abdomen tightened to brace for a kick. A sizzle resounded in his ears. Adrenaline made him want to reach for his drink, but he only lifted his hand to scratch his cheek—while his mind conjured the forest of lilies that had surrounded them in his mother's solarium as he and Poppy had made love so impulsively.

"Do you…remember her?" Sorcha asked tentatively.

Skin scented like nectarines, lush corkscrews of curly red hair filling his hands as he consumed her crimson lips. He remembered the exact pitch of her joyful cries of release, the culmination of madness like he'd never known before or since.

And he remembered vividly the ticking of the clock on the mantel as he had sat in his mother's parlor the next morning, an itchy fire in his blood driving him mad. He'd been on the verge of going to look for her because he couldn't stop thinking about her.

Then Faustina had arrived, striking like dry lightning with sheepishly delivered news. Family obligation had crashed upon him afresh, pinning him under the weight of a wedding that had been called off, but now was back on. They would pretend the gap in the parade had never happened.

"Rico?" Sorcha prompted gently, dragging him back to the present. "I know this must be a shock." And there was that infernal compassion again.

He swore, tired to his *bones* of people thinking he was mourning a baby he had already known wasn't his. He was sorry for the loss of a life before it had had the chance to start. Of course he was. But he wasn't grieving with the infinite heartbreak of a parent losing a child. It hadn't been *his*.

And given Faustina's trickery, he was damned cynical about whether he had conceived *this* one.

"Why did you jump straight to suspecting she's mine?" he asked baldly.

Sorcha was slightly taken aback. "Well, I'm not going to suspect my own husband, am I?" Her tone warned that he had better not, either. Her chin came up a notch. "You were living in your parents' villa at the time. Frankly, your father doesn't seem particularly passionate about any woman, young or old. You, however, were briefly unengaged."

Rico had long suspected the success of his parents' marriage could be attributed to both of them being fairly asexual and lacking in passion for anything beyond cool reason and the advancement of family interests.

Sorcha's eyes grew big and soft and filled with that excruciating pity. "I'm not judging, Rico. *I know how these things happen.*"

"I bet you do." He regretted it immediately. It wasn't him. At least, it wasn't the man he was beneath the layer of caustic fury he couldn't seem to shed. Sorcha certainly didn't deserve this ugly side of him. She was kind and sensitive and everything the rest of them didn't know how to be.

She recoiled, rightly shocked that he would deliver such a belly blow. But she hadn't risen above the scandal of secretly delivering his brother's baby while Cesar had been engaged to someone else without possessing truckloads of resilience.

"I meant because my mother was my father's maid when she conceived *me*." Her voice was tight and strong, but there was such a wounded shadow in her gaze, he had to look away and reach for the drink she'd poured him.

He drained it, burning away the words that hovered on his tongue. Words he couldn't speak because he was trying to spare Faustina's parents some humiliation when they were already destroyed by the loss of their only child.

"I'll assume if you're lashing out, you believe it's possible that little girl is yours. How she came about is your business, Rico, but don't you *ever* accuse me of trapping Cesar into this marriage. I *left*, if you recall." She stood, hot temper well lit, but honed by her marriage to a Montero into icy severity. "And so did Poppy. Maybe ask yourself why, if you're such a prize, she doesn't want anything to do with you. *I* have an idea, if you can't figure it out for yourself."

She stalked to the door and swung it open, inviting him to leave using nothing more than a head held high and an expression of frosty contempt that prickled his conscience through the thick shields of indifference he had been bricking into place since Faustina had been found.

"I shouldn't have said that," Rico ground out, mind reeling so badly as he stood, his head swam. "I was shooting the messenger." With a missile launcher loaded with nuclear waste. "Tell Cesar what you've told me. I'll let him punch me in the face for what I said to you." He meant it.

She didn't thaw. Not one iota. "Deal with the message. I have a stake in the outcome, as do my husband and sons."

"Oh, I will," he promised. *"Immediately."*

CHAPTER ONE

POPPY HARRIS FILLED the freshly washed sippy cup with water only to have Lily ignore it and keep pointing at the shelf.

"You want a real cup, don't you?"

Two weeks ago, Lily's no-spill cup had gone missing from daycare. Poppy's grandmother, being old-school, thought cups with closed lids and straws were silly. Back in *her* day, babies learned to drink from a proper cup.

Since she was pinching pennies, Poppy hadn't bought a new one. She had spent days mopping dribbles instead, and she'd been *so* happy when the cup had reappeared today.

Unfortunately, Lily was a big girl now. She wanted an open cup. *Thanks, Gran.*

Poppy considered whether a meltdown right before dinner was worth the battle. She compromised by easing Lily's grip off her pant leg and then sat her gently onto her bottom, unable to resist running affectionate fingertips through Lily's fine red-gold curls. She handed her both the leakproof cup and an empty plastic tumbler. Hopefully that would keep her busy for a few minutes.

"I'm putting the biscuits in the oven, Gran," Poppy called as she did it.

She scooped a small portion of leek-and-potato soup from the slow cooker into a shallow bowl. She had started the soup when she raced home on her lunch break to check on her grandmother. Every day felt like a flat-out run, but she didn't complain. Things could be worse.

She set the bowl on the table so it would be cool enough for Lily to eat when they sat down.

"The fanciest car has just pulled in, Poppy," her grandmother said in her quavering voice. Her evening game shows were on, but she preferred to watch the comings and goings beyond their front room window. "Is he one of your models needing a head shot? He's *very* handsome."

"What?" Poppy's stomach dropped. It was completely instinctive and she made herself take a mental step back. There was no reason to believe it would be *him*.

Even so, she struggled to swallow a jagged lump that lodged in her suddenly arid throat. "Who—?"

The doorbell rang.

Poppy couldn't move. She didn't want to see. If it wasn't Rico, she would be irrationally disappointed. If it *was* him…

She looked to her daughter, instantly petrified that he was here to claim her. What would he say? How could she stop him? She couldn't.

It wasn't him, she told herself. It was one of those prophets in a three-piece suit who hand-delivered pamphlets about the world being on the brink of annihilation.

Her world was fine, she reassured herself, still staring at the sprite who comprised the lion's share of all that was important to her. Lily tipped her head back in an effort to drain water from an empty cup.

The bell rang again.

"Poppy?" her grandmother prompted, glancing her direction. "Will you answer?"

Mentally, Gran was sharp as a tack. Her vision and hearing never failed her. Osteoporosis, however, had impacted her mobility. Her bones were so fragile, Poppy had to be ever vigilant that Lily and her toys weren't underfoot. Her gran would break a hip or worse if she ever stumbled.

There were a lot of things about this living arrangement that made it less than ideal, but both she and Gran were maintaining the status quo, kidding themselves that Gramps was only down at the hardware store and would be back any minute.

"Of course." Poppy snapped out of her stasis and glanced over to be sure the gates on both doorways into the kitchen were closed. All the drawers and cupboards had locks except the one where the plastic dishes were kept. The mixing bowls were a favorite for being dragged out and nested, filled with toys and measuring cups, then dumped without ceremony.

"Keep an eye this way, Gran?" Poppy murmured as she stepped over the gate into the front room, then moved past her seated grandmother to the front door.

Her glance out the side window struck a dark brown bomber jacket over black jeans, but she knew that head, that back with the broad shoulders, that butt and long legs.

His arrival struck like a bus. Like a train that derailed her composure and rattled on for miles, piling one broken thought onto another.

OhGodohGodohGod… *Breathe.* All the way in, all the way out, she reminded herself. But she had always imagined that if this much money showed up on her doorstep, it would be with an oversize check and a television crew. *Not him.*

Rico pivoted from surveying her neighbor's fence and the working grain elevator against the fading Saskatchewan sky. His profile was knife sharp, carved of titanium and godlike. A hint of shadow was coming in on his jaw, just enough to bend his angelic looks into the fallen kind.

He knocked.

"Poppy—?" her grandmother prompted, tone perplexed by the way she was acting. Or failing to.

How? *How* could he know? Poppy had no doubt that he did. There was absolutely no other reason for this man to be this far off the beaten track. He sure as hell wasn't here to see *her.*

Blood searing with fight or flight, heart pounding, she opened the door.

The full force of his impact slammed through her. The hard angle of his chin, the stern cast of his mouth, his wide shoulders and long legs, and hands held in tense, almost fists.

His jaw hardened as he took her in through mirrored aviators. Their chrome finish was cold and steely. If he'd had a fresh haircut, it had been ruffled by the wind. His boots were alligator, his cologne nothing but crisp, snow-scented air and fuming suspicion.

Poppy lifted her chin and pretended her heart wasn't whirling like a Prairie tornado in her chest.

"Can I help you?" she asked, exactly as she would if he had been a complete stranger.

His hand went to the doorframe. His nostrils twitched as he leaned into the space. "Really?" he asked in a tone of lethal warning.

"Who is it, Poppy?" her grandmother asked.

He stiffened slightly, as though surprised she wasn't alone. Then his mouth curled with disparagement, waiting to see if she would lie.

Poppy swallowed, her entire body buzzing, but she held his gaze through those inscrutable glasses while she said in a strong voice, "Rico, Gran. The man I told you about. From Spain."

There, she silently conveyed. *What do you think of that?*

It wasn't wise to defy him. She knew that by the roil of threat in the pit of her stomach, but she had had to grow up damned fast in the last two years. She was not some naive traveler succumbing to a charmer who turned out to be a thief, or even the starry-eyed maid who had encouraged a philandering playboy to seduce her.

She was a grown woman who had learned how to face her problems head-on.

"Oh?" Gran's tone gave the whole game away in one murmur. There was concern beneath her curiosity. Knowledge. It was less a blithe, *isn't that nice that your friend turned up*. More an alarmed, *Why is he here?*

There was no hiding. None. Poppy might not be able to read this man's eyes, but she read his body language. He wasn't here to ask questions. He was here to confront.

Because he knew she'd had his baby.

Her eyes grew wet with panic, but through her shock, she reacted to seeing her lover, her first and only lover twenty months after they had conceived their daughter. She had thought her brief hour with him a moment of madness. A rush of sex hormones born of dented self-esteem and grand self-delusion.

Since then, her body had been taken over by their daughter. Poppy had been sure her sex drive had dried up and blown away on the Prairie winds. Or at least was firmly in hibernation.

As it turned out, her libido was alive and well. Heat flooded into her with the distant tingles of intimate, erotic memories. Of the cold press of his belt buckle trapped against her thigh, the dampness of perspiration in the hollow of his spine when she ran her hands beneath his open shirt to clutch at him with encouragement. She recalled exactly the way he had kissed the whisker burn on her chin so tenderly, with a growl of apology in his throat. The way he had cupped her breast with restraint, then licked and sucked at her nipple until she was writhing beneath him.

She could feel anew the sharp sensation of him possessing her, so intimate and satisfying, both glorious and ruinous all at once.

She blushed. Hard. Which made the blistering moment feel like hours. She was overflowing at the edges with mortifying awkwardness, searching her mind for something to say, a way to dissemble so he wouldn't know how far he'd thrown her.

"Invite him in, Poppy," her grandmother chided. "You're going to melt the driveway."

She meant because she was letting the heat out, but her words made Poppy blush harder. "Of course," she muttered, flustered. "Come in."

Explanations crowded her tongue as she backed up a step, but stammering them out wouldn't make a difference to a man like him. He might have seemed human and reachable for that stolen hour in his mother's solarium, but she'd realized afterward exactly how ruthless and single-minded he truly was. The passion she'd convinced herself was mutual and startlingly sweet had been a casual, effortless, promptly forgotten seduction on his part.

He'd mended fences with his fiancée the next morning—a woman Poppy knew for a fact he hadn't loved. He'd told Poppy that he'd only agreed to the marriage to gain the presidency of a company and hadn't seemed distressed in the least that the wedding had been called off.

Embarrassment at being such an easy conquest had her staring at his feet as she closed the door behind him. "Will you take off your boots, please?"

Her request gave him pause. In his mother's house, everyone wore shoes, especially guests. A single pair of their usual footwear cost more than Poppy had made in her four months of working in that house.

Rico toed off his boots and set them against the wall. Then he tucked his sunglasses into his chest pocket. His eyes were slate-gray with no spark of blue or flecks of hot green that had surrounded his huge pupils that day in the solarium.

After setting his cold, granite gaze against her until she was chilled through, he glanced past her, into the front room of the tiny bungalow her grandfather had built for his wife while working as a linesman for the hydro company. It was the home where Gramps had brought his bride the day they married. It was where they had brought home their only son and where they had raised their only grandchild.

Seeing him in it made Poppy both humble and defensive. It didn't compare to the grandiose villa he'd been raised in, but it was her home. Poppy wasn't ashamed of it, only struck by how he could so easily jeopardize all of this with a snap of his fingers. This house wasn't even hers. If he had come here to claim Lily, she had very few resources at her disposal. Maybe it would even be held against her that she didn't have much and he could offer so much more.

"Hello," he greeted her grandmother as she muted the television and set the remote aside.

"This is Rico Montero, Gran. My grandmother, Eleanor Harris."

"*The* Rico?"

"Yes."

Rico's brows went up a fraction, making Poppy squirm.

"It's nice to meet you. Finally." Gran started to rise.

Poppy stepped forward to help her, but Rico was quick to touch her grandmother's arm and say, "Please. There's no need to stand. It's a pleasure to meet you."

Oh, he knew how to use the warmth of his accented voice to slay a woman, young or old. Poppy almost fell for it herself, thinking he sounded reassuring when he was actually here to destroy their small, simple world.

Yet she had to go through the motions of civility. Pretend he was simply a guest who had dropped by.

Gran smiled up at him with glimmers of adoration. "I was getting up to give you privacy to talk. I imagine you'll want that."

"In that case, yes please. Allow me to help you." Rico moved to her side and supported her with gentle care.

Don't leave me alone with him, Poppy wanted to cry, but she slid Gran's walker in front of her. "Thank you, Gran."

"I'll listen to the radio in my room until you come for me." Her grandmother nodded and shuffled her way into the hall. "Remember the biscuits."

The biscuits. The least of her worries. Poppy couldn't smell them yet, but the timer would go off any second. She moved her body into the path toward the kitchen door, driven by mother-bear instincts.

"Why are you here?" Her voice quavered with the volume of emotions rocketing through her—shock and protectiveness and fear. Culpability and anger and other deeper yearnings she didn't want to acknowledge.

"I want to see her." He set his shoulders in a way that told her he wasn't going anywhere until he did.

Behind her, the sound of bowls coming out of the cupboard and being knocked around reassured her that Lily was perfectly fine without eyes on her.

A suffocating feeling sat on her chest and kept a vise around her throat. She wanted him to answer the rest of her question. What was he going to do about this discovery? She wasn't ready to face the answer.

Playing for time, she strangled out, "How did you find out?"

If they hadn't been standing so close, she might have missed the way his pupils dilated and his breath seemed to catch as though taking a blow. In the next second, the impression of shock was gone. A fierce, angry light of satisfaction gleamed in his eyes.

"Sorcha saw a photo you posted of a baby who looks like Mateo. I investigated."

Odd details from the last two weeks fell into place. She dropped her chin in outrage. "That new dad at the day care! I thought he was hitting on me, asking all those questions."

Rico's dark brows slammed together. "He came on to you?"

"He said he took Lily's cup by mistake, but it was an excuse to talk to me." Poppy was obviously still batting a thousand where her poor judgement of men was concerned.

"He took it for a DNA sample."

"That is just plain *wrong*," she said indignantly.

"I agree that I shouldn't have to resort to such measures to learn I have a child. *Why didn't you tell me?*" he asked through clenched teeth.

He had some right to the anger he poured over ice. She acknowledged that. But she wasn't a villain. Just a stupid girl who'd gotten herself in trouble by the wrong man and had made the best of a difficult situation.

"I didn't realize I was pregnant until you were married. By then, it was all over the gossip sites that Faustina was also expecting."

It shouldn't have been such a blow when she'd read

that. His wedding had been called off for a *day*. Loads of people had a moment of cold feet before they went through with the ceremony. She accepted she was collateral damage to that.

She had been feeling very down on herself by then, though. She ought to have known better than to let herself get carried away. She hadn't taken any precautions. She had been careless and foolish, believing him when he had told her that he and his fiancée hadn't been sleeping together.

The whole thing had made her feel so humiliatingly stupid. She had hoped never to have to face him or her gullibility ever again.

So much for that.

And facing him was so *hard*. *He* was so hard. A muscle was pulsing in his jaw, but the rest of him was like concrete. Pitiless and unmoved.

"Faustina died a year ago last September," he said in that gritty tone. "You've had ample opportunity to come forward."

As she recalled the terrible headlines she'd read with morbid anguish, her heart turned inside out with agony for him. She had nursed thoughts every day of telling him he had a child after all, but...

"I'm sorry for your loss." She truly was. No matter what he'd felt for his wife, losing his child must have been devastating.

His expression stiffened and he recoiled slightly at her words of condolence.

"My grandfather was quite ill," she continued huskily. "If you recall, that's why I came home. He passed just before Christmas. Gran needed me. There hasn't been a right time to shake things up."

His expression altered slightly as he absorbed that.

She imagined his sorrow to be so much more acute than hers. She mourned a man who had lived a full life and who had passed without pain or regret. They'd held a service that had been a true celebration of his long life.

While Rico's baby had been cheated of even starting its own.

Rico nodded acceptance of her excuse with only a pained flicker as acknowledgment of what must have been his very personal and intensely painful loss.

Had grief driven him here? Was he trying to replace his lost child with his living one? *No.* The thought of it agonized her. Lily wasn't some placeholder for another child. It cracked her heart in half that he might think she could be.

Before she could find words to address that fear, the timer beeped in the kitchen.

Lily had become very quiet, too, which was a sure sign of trouble. Poppy turned to glance around the doorframe. Lily sat with one finger poking at the tiny hole on a bowl's rim, where the bowl was meant to be hung on a nail.

Firm hands settled on her shoulders. Rico's untamed scent and the heat of his body surrounded her. He looked past her into the kitchen. At his daughter.

Poppy told herself not to look, but she couldn't help it. She was afraid he would be resentful that Lily had lived when his other baby hadn't. Even as she feared he was planning to steal her, she perversely would be more agonized if he rejected her. He had come all this way. That meant he felt something toward her, didn't it? On some level, he wanted her?

His expression was unreadable, face so closed and tense, her heart dropped into her shoes.

Love her, she wanted to beg. *Please*.

His breath sucked in with an audible hiss. He took in so much air, his chest swelled to brush against her back. His hands tightened on her shoulders.

At the subtle noise, Lily lifted her gorgeous gray eyes, so like her father's. A huge smile broke across her face.

"Mama." The bowls were forgotten and she crawled toward them, pulling herself up on the gate.

Lily's smile propelled Poppy through all her hard days. She was Poppy's world. Poppy's parents were distant, her grandfather gone, her grandmother... Well, Poppy didn't want to think about losing her even though she knew it was inevitable.

But she had this wee girl and she was everything.

"Hello, button." Poppy scooped up her daughter and kissed her cheek, never able to resist that soft, plump bite of sweet-smelling warmth. Then she brushed at Lily's hands because it didn't matter how many times she swept or vacuumed, Lily found the specks and dust bunnies in her eager exploration of her world.

This time when Poppy looked to Rico, she saw his reaction more clearly. He was trying to mask it with stoicism, but the intensity in his gaze ate up Lily's snowy skin and cupid's-bow mouth.

Her emotions seesawed again. She had needed this. Her heart had needed to see him accept his daughter, but he was a threat, too.

"This is Lily." Her name was tellingly sentimental, not the sort of romantic notion Poppy should have given in to, but since her own name was a flower, it had seemed right.

Poppy faltered, not ready to tell Lily this was Daddy.

Lily brought her fingers to her mouth and said, "Ee."

"Eat?" Poppy asked and slid her hand down from her throat. "You're hungry?"

Lily nodded.

"Sign language?" Rico asked, voice sharpening with concern. "Is she hearing impaired?"

"It's sign language for babies. They teach it at day care. She's trying to say words, but this works for now." Poppy stepped over the gate into the kitchen and snapped off the oven. "Do you, um…" She couldn't believe this was happening, but she wanted to put off the hard conversations as long as possible. "Will you join us for dinner?"

A brief pause, then, "You don't have to cook. I can order something in."

"From where?" Poppy chuckled dryly as she set Lily in her chair. "We have Chinese takeout and a pizza palace." *Not* his usual standard. "The soup is already made."

She tied on Lily's bib and set the bowl of cooled soup and a small flat spoon in front of her.

Lily grabbed the spoon and batted it into the thick soup.

"Renting the car was a challenge for my staff," he mentioned absently, frowning as Lily missed her mouth and smeared soup across her own cheek.

"Gran said you're driving something fancy," Poppy

recalled. She had forgotten to look, unable to see past the man to anything else.

"An Alfa Romeo, but it's a sedan."

With a car seat? Poppy almost bobbled the sheet of biscuits as she took them from the oven. "Are you, um, staying at the motel?"

He snorted. "No. My staff have taken a cottage an hour from here so I have a bed if I decide to stay."

Poppy tried to read his expression, but he was watching Lily, frowning with exasperation as Lily turned her head, open mouth looking for the end of the spoon.

In a decisive move, he removed his jacket and draped it over the back of a chair. Then he picked up the teaspoon beside Poppy's setting and turned the chair to face Lily. He sat and began helping her eat.

Poppy caught her breath, arrested by the sight of this dynamic man feeding their daughter. His strapping muscles strained the seams in his shirt, telling of his tension, but he calmly waited for Lily to try before he gently touched the tip of his teaspoon to her bottom lip. He let Lily lean into eating it before they both went after the next spoonful in the bowl.

Had she dreamed of this? *Was* she dreaming? It was such a sweet sight her ovaries locked fresh eggs into their chambers, preparing to launch and create another Lily or five. All she needed was one glance from him that contained something other than accusation or animosity.

"You said the timing was wrong."

It took her a moment to realize he was harking back to the day they'd conceived her. She could only stand there in chagrined silence while a coal of uncomfortable heat burned in her middle, spreading a blush upward, into her throat and cheeks and ending in a pressure behind her eyes.

He glanced at her. "When we—"

"I know what you mean," she cut him off, turning away to stack hot biscuits onto a plate, suffused in virginal discomfiture all over again. He'd noticed blood and asked if she had started her cycle. She'd been too embarrassed to tell him it was her first time. She was too embarrassed to say it now.

"I should have taken something after." She didn't tell him she had hung around in Spain an extra day, hoping he would come find her only to hear the wedding was back on.

That news had propelled her from the scene, consuming her with thoughts of what a pushover she'd been for a man on a brief furlough from his engagement. Contraception should have been top of mind, but...

"I was traveling, trying to make my flight." Poppy hugged herself, trying to keep the fissure in her chest from widening. She felt *so* exposed right now and couldn't meet his penetrating stare. "I honestly did think the timing was wrong. I didn't even realize I was pregnant until I was starting to show. I had next to no symptoms." There'd even been a bit of spotting. "I thought the few signs I did have were stress related. Gramps's health was deteriorating. By the time it was confirmed, you were married." She finally looked at him and let one hand come out, palm up, beseeching for understanding.

There was no softening in his starkly unforgiving expression.

"I didn't think you would—" She couldn't say aloud

that she had worried he wouldn't want his daughter. Not when he was feeding Lily with such care.

Helpless tears pressed behind her eyes.

He knew what she had almost said and sent her another flat stare of muted fury. "I want her, Poppy. That's why I'm here."

Her heart swerved in her chest. The pressure behind her eyes increased.

"Don't look so terrified." He returned his attention to Lily, who was waiting with an open mouth like a baby bird. "I'm not here to kidnap her."

"What, then?" She clung tight to her elbows, needing something to anchor her. Needing to know what was going to happen.

"Am I supposed to ignore her?"

"No." His question poked agonizing pins into the most sensitive spots on her soul. "But I was afraid you might," she admitted. "I thought it would be easier on both of us if you didn't know, rather than if you did, but didn't care."

Another wall-of-concrete stare, then a clearly pronounced, "I care." He scraped the spoon through the thick soup. "And not only because the maids in my mother's house are bound to recognize the resemblance the way Sorcha's nanny did and begin to talk. She's a Montero. She's entitled to the benefits that brings."

Now he stood directly on Poppy's pride.

"We don't *need* help, Rico. That's another reason I never told you. I didn't want you to think I was looking for a handout. We're fine."

"The day care with the nonexistent security is 'fine'? What happens when it's known her father is wealthy?

We take basic precautions, Poppy. You don't even have an alarm system. I didn't hear you click a lock when you opened the front door."

They lived in rural Canada. People worried about squirrels in the attic, not burglars in the bedroom.

"No one knows you're rich. Gran is the only person who even knows your name and I wasn't entirely forthcoming about…who you really are." Poppy gave a tendril of hair a distracted brush so it tucked behind her ear for all of five seconds. "Do you mind if I get her? She takes medication on a schedule and needs to eat beforehand. We try to stick to a routine."

"Of course." He lifted two fingers off the bowl he still held steady for Lily's jabs of her own spoon. "We'll discuss how we'll proceed after Lily is in bed."

CHAPTER TWO

POPPY OPENED THE GATE and set it aside, leaving Rico to continue feeding his daughter.

He had watched Sorcha and Cesar do this countless times with their sons. He'd always thought it a messy process best left to nannies, but discovered it was oddly satisfying. His older nephew, Enrique, had reached an age where he held conversations—some that were inadvertently amusing—but babies had always struck Rico as something that required a lot of intensive care without offering much in return.

Sorcha had pressed her sons onto him over the years, which had achieved her goal of provoking feelings of affection in him, but, like his parents, he viewed children as something between a duty and a social experiment. Even when he had briefly believed Faustina had been carrying his heir, the idea of being a father had only been that—an idea. Not a concept he had fully internalized or a role he understood how to fulfill effectively. Fatherhood hadn't been something he had viewed with anticipation the way other creative projects had inspired him.

But here he sat, watching eyes the same color as

his own track to the doorway where Poppy had disappeared. A wet finger pointed. "Mama."

"She'll be right back." He imagined Poppy would actually spend a few minutes talking to her grandmother in private.

Lily smiled before she leaned forward, mouth open.

Damn, she was beautiful. It wasn't bias, either. Or his fondness for the nephews she resembled. She had her mother's fresh snowy skin and red-gold lashes, healthy round cheeks and a chin that suggested she had his stubbornness along with his eyes.

A ridiculous swell of pride went through him even as he reminded himself that he didn't know conclusively that she was his. The DNA test off the cup had been a long shot and hadn't proved paternity either way.

Nevertheless, he'd been propelled as much by the absence of truth as he would have been by the presence of it. From the time Sorcha had revealed her suspicion, a ferocious fire had begun to burn in him, one stoked by yet another female keeping secrets from him. Huge, life-altering secrets.

He hadn't wanted to wait for more tests, or hire lawyers, or even pick up the phone and *ask*. He had needed to see for himself.

Who? a voice asked in the back of his head.

Both, he acknowledged darkly. He had needed to set eyes on the baby, whom he recognized on a deeply biological level, and on the woman who haunted his memories.

Poppy had seemed so guileless. So refreshingly honest and real.

He thought back to that day, searching for the moment where he'd been tricked into making a baby with a woman who had then kept her pregnancy a secret.

He remembered thinking his mother wouldn't appreciate him popping a bottle of the wedding champagne—even though she'd procured a hundred cases that had been superfluous because the wedding had been called off.

Rico had helped himself to his father's scotch in the billiards room instead. He had taken it through to the solarium, planning to bum a cigarette from the gardener. It was a weakness he had kicked years ago, but the craving still hit sometimes, when his life went sideways.

It was the end of the day, though. The sun-warmed room was packed to the gills with lilies brought in to replace the ones damaged by a late frost. The solarium was deserted and the worktable in the back held a dirty ashtray and a cigarette pack that was empty.

"Oh! I'm so sorry."

The woman spoke in English, sounding American, maybe. He turned to see the redheaded maid who'd been on the stairs an hour earlier, when Faustina had been throwing a tantrum that had included one of his mother's Wedgwoods, punctuating the end of their engagement. He would come to understand much later what sort of pressure Faustina had been under, but at the time, she'd been an unreasonable, clichéd diva of a bride by whom he'd been relieved to have been jilted.

And the interruption by the fresh-faced maid had been a welcome distraction.

Her name was Poppy. He knew that without looking at the embroidered tag on her uniform. She stared with wide doe eyes, the proverbial deer in headlights, startled to come upon him pilfering smokes as though he was thirteen again.

"I mean…um…*perdón*." She pivoted to go back the way she'd come.

"Wait. Do you have a cigarette?" he asked in English.

"Me? No." She swung back around. "Do I look like a smoker?"

Her horror at resembling such a thing amused him.

"Do I?" he drawled. "What do we look like? The patriarchy?"

"I don't know." She chuckled and blushed slightly, her clear skin glowing pink beneath the gold of filtered sunlight, like late afternoon on untouched ski slopes. "I, um, didn't know you smoked." She swallowed and linked her hands shyly before her.

Ah. She'd been watching him, too, had she?

His mother's staff had been off-limits since his brother's first kiss with a maid before Rico had even had a shot at one. He didn't usually notice one from another, but Poppy had snagged his attention with her vibrant red hair. Curls were springing free of the bundle she'd scraped it into, teasing him with fantasies of releasing the rest and digging his hands into the kinky mass.

The rest of her was cute as hell, too, if a bit skinny and young. Maybe it was her lack of makeup. That mouth, unpainted, but with a plump bottom lip and a playful top was all woman. Her brows were so light, they were almost blond, her chin pert, her eyes a gentle yet very direct dark ale-brown.

No, he reminded himself. He was engaged.

Actually, he absorbed with a profound sense of liberation, he wasn't. Faustina had firmly and unequivocally ended their engagement, despite his mother's best efforts to talk her back on board.

His mother had retired with a wet compress and a migraine tablet. He had come in here because he couldn't go home. His house was being renovated for the bride who was now refusing to share her life with him. Driving all the way to his brother's house to get blind drunk had felt like an unnecessary delay.

"I don't smoke." He dropped the empty pack and picked up his drink. "I rebelled for a year or so when I was a teen, but it seemed like a good excuse to talk with Ernesto about football and other inconsequential topics." He was sick to death of jabbering about weddings and duty and the expected impact on the family fortune.

Her shoulders softened and her red-gold brows angled with sympathy. "I'm really sorry." She sounded adorably sincere. "I'll, um, give you privacy to…"

"Wallow in heartbreak? Unnecessary." Faustina's outburst had been the sum total of passion their marriage was likely to have borne. "I don't want to chase you away if you're on your break."

"No, I'm done. I know we're not supposed to cut through here to get to the change rooms over the garage, but I was hoping to catch Ernesto myself. He gives me a lift sometimes."

"Are you American?" he asked.

Her strawberry blond lashes flickered in surprise, her expression growing shy. Aware.

An answering awareness teased through him, waking the wolf inside him. That starved beast had been locked inside a cave the last six months, but unexpectedly found himself free of the heavy chain he'd placed around his own neck. The sun was in his eyes, the wind was ruffling his fur and he was picking up the scent of a willing female. He was itching to romp and tumble and mate.

"Canada." She cleared her throat. "Saskatchewan. A little town with nothing but canola fields and clouds." She shook her head. "You wouldn't have heard of it."

"How did you wind up here?"

"I'd tell you, but I'd bore you to death." Despite her words, a pretty smile played around her mouth and a soft blush of pleasure glowed under her skin.

"I came out here to smoke. Clearly I have a death wish."

After a small chuckle, she cautioned, "Okay, but stop me if you feel light-headed."

Definitely not bored, he thought with a private smile. She wasn't merely a first cigarette years after quitting, either. To be sure he was drawing in this lighthearted flirting with avid greed, but he found himself enjoying her wit. He was genuinely intrigued by her.

"I saved up to trek around Europe with a friend, but she broke her ankle on the second day and flew home." She folded her arms, protective or defensive, maybe. "I tagged along with some students from a hostel coming here, but a few days after we arrived, one of them stole everything I had." She slapped a what-can-you-do? smile on it, but the tension around her eyes and mouth told him she was still upset.

He frowned. "Did you go to the police?"

"It was my fault." She flinched with self-recrimination. "I gave him my card to get some cash for me one morning. He must have made a copy or something.

Three days later he'd syphoned all of my savings and was gone. I had my passport, a bag of raisins and my hairbrush. Losing my camera gutted me the most. It was a gift and my memory card was still in it, not that I'd had the chance to fill it. It was a huge bummer." She summed up with philosophical lightness.

"You're a photographer?"

"Not anymore," she asserted with disgust, then shrugged it off. "At least I had prepaid for a week at the hostel. I asked around and got on with a temp agency. I was brought in to help clean the pool house and guest cottage. Darna liked my work and asked me to stay on full-time in the big house. I've been saving for a ticket home ever since."

"How much do you need?" He reached into his pocket.

"Oh, no!" She halted him, horrified. "I have enough. I just worked it out with Darna that today was my last day. She thought she would need me through the rest of June for—" She halted, wincing as she realized who she was talking to.

Rico let the awkwardness hang in the air, not to punish, but because he was finding her candor so refreshing.

"It seemed like the wedding was going to be really beautiful." She sounded apologetic. "I'm sorry it didn't work out."

He wasn't. That was the naked truth, but he deflected by saying, "I've heard that Canadians apologize a lot. I didn't believe it."

"We do. Sorry." She winked on that one.

Was she sorry?

Rico came back to the tap of a dirty spoon against the back of his knuckles.

Poppy had been twenty-two, disillusioned after being shortchanged on chasing her dreams, yet willing to come home to fulfill family obligations. He had understood that pressure and had confided his own reasons for going along with family expectations.

That affinity had led to a kiss and his feet had somehow carried her to the sheet-draped furniture hidden amongst the jungle of fragrant lilies.

Since learning about Lily, he'd been convinced Poppy had somehow tricked him the way Faustina had, for her own nefarious ends.

That suspicion wasn't playing as strongly now that he was here. Her home was unpretentious, dated and showing signs of age, but neat and well cared for. Her bond with her grandmother and daughter seemed genuine and from the reports he'd commissioned, she was this side of financially solvent. She didn't even have a speeding ticket on her record.

He'd picked up two on his way here, but that was beside the point.

In the past, he had seen what he wanted to see. He couldn't allow himself to be so credulous again.

He made himself take a cool moment to watch Lily's concentrated effort to touch the end of her spoon into the soup and bring the taste to her mouth. She grinned as she succeeded, spoon caught between her tiny white teeth.

He had no proof, but he was convinced she was his. He *had* to claim her.

As for Poppy, he was still absorbing the impact she

continued to have on him. He still reacted physically to her. One look at her in jeans and a loose pullover and his mouth had started to water. No makeup, hair gathered into a messy knot of kinks on her head, wariness like a halo around her, yet he'd had to restrain himself from reaching for her. Not to grab or take possession, but simply to *touch*. Fill his hands with the textures of her.

Was her skin as smooth and soft as his erotic dreams replayed? Would her nipples tighten if he licked then blew lightly again? Did her voice still break in orgasm and would that sound once again send pleasurable shivers down his back?

That chemistry was a weakness, one that warned him to keep his guard up, but it didn't deter him from his plan one iota.

In fact, it stoked a fire of anticipation deep in the pit of his belly.

Poppy's tension remained through dinner, even though Rico went on a charm offensive against her grandmother, breaking out levels even Poppy hadn't realized he possessed, asking after her health and offering condolences over Gramps.

"I'm very sorry to hear you lost him. I remember Poppy saying he wasn't well, just before she left Spain."

Poppy released a subtle snort, suspecting he only recalled that detail because she had reminded him of it an hour ago.

He frowned with affront. "I asked you why you weren't using the money you'd saved to see more of Europe. You said your grandparents needed help moving into a care facility."

For one second, she saw glints of blue and green in his irises, telling her he remembered *everything* about that day.

A spike of tingling heat drove sharp as a lance through her. She crossed her legs, bumping her foot against his shin in the process and sending a reverberation of deeper awareness through her whole body.

"We were talking about moving," Gran said, forcing Rico to break their eye contact. "I couldn't look after Bill myself, but having Poppy here bought us an extra year in our home." Gran squeezed her hand over Poppy's, the strength in her grip heart-wrenchingly faint. "He would have faded all the faster if we'd been forced to leave this house. I'll always be grateful to her for giving us that. I don't know what I would have done if she hadn't been here in the months since he's been gone, either. She's been our special blessing her whole life."

"Gran." Poppy teared up. She knew darned well she'd been more of a burden.

"And Lily is ever so precious, too." Gran smiled at the baby. "But it's time."

"Time?" Poppy repeated with muted alarm.

"I'll call your aunt Sheila in the morning," she said of her sister, patting Poppy's hand before she removed her touch. "I'm on the top of the list at that facility near her apartment. I'm sure I can stay with her until a room opens up."

"Gran, *no*."

"Poppy. We both know I shouldn't have been here this winter, making more work for you on top of looking after the baby. You were shoveling the drive on your one day off to get me to the doctor's office. I have no business near that ice by the front steps, either. You're penning up Lily, worrying I'll trip over her. *I'm* worried. No, I don't want to hold you back from the life you ought to be leading."

"This *is* the life I want to lead." Poppy's chin began to crinkle the way Lily's did when she was coming down with a cold and Poppy had to leave her at day care.

"Oh, is your fancy man moving in with us, then?" Gran asked.

"I see where Poppy gets her spark." A faint smile touched Rico's lips. "Poppy and I have details to work out, but you're right that my life is in Spain. I'm here to marry her and take Poppy and Lily home with me."

After a brief, illogical spike of elation, Poppy's heart fell with that bombshell news. Her mind exploded. He wasn't wrenching their daughter from her arms, but she wasn't relieved in the least. She immediately knew this wasn't about her. He'd married for coldly practical reasons the first time. He might dazzle her grandmother with kindness and charisma, but it was a dispassionate move to get what he wanted by the quickest, most efficient means. She shouldn't be shocked at all by his goal or his methods.

"*My* life is here with Gran," Poppy insisted shakily. "She needs me nearby, even if she moves into assisted care."

"Poppy." The fragility of her grandmother's hand draped over hers again. "What I need is to know that when I'm gone, you're settled with someone who will take care of you and Lily. That person ought to be her father." She patted lightly, saying with quiet power, "I know what this would have meant to you."

If her own father had shown up to take her home, Gran meant. The hot pressure behind her eyes increased.

Even so, there was a part of Poppy that simply heard it as her grandmother wishing Poppy would cease to be a burden upon her.

A spiked ball lodged behind Poppy's breastbone, one she couldn't swallow away. It was so sharp it made tears sting her eyes.

"It's obvious Poppy won't be comfortable unless you're comfortable, Eleanor. Give us a chance to finish our talk. Then you and I will discuss your options. I'm sure we can find solutions that satisfy all of us."

Poppy wanted to shout a giant, scoffing, *Ha!* She rose to clear the table.

CHAPTER THREE

POPPY BATHED LILY and put her to bed, not giving her daughter the attention she deserved because her mind was still whirling with Rico showing up and demanding more than his daughter. *Marriage.*

Had she spun that fantasy in her girlish mind? Yes. Even before she slept with him. She had been fascinated by him for weeks, acutely aware of him whether he was making a dry comment or sipping a glass of orange juice. He'd seemed aloof, but in a laid-back way. When she had overheard Faustina going full Bridezilla, shattering a vase and screaming that their wedding was off, Rico had only said in a calm voice, "Let me have the bottom of that. I'll have to replace it."

Deep down, she'd been thrilled that Faustina had ended things. Happy for him.

In the solarium, he'd been that charming man she'd seen tonight at dinner, the one who expressed so much interest in others, it was easy to miss that he gave away very little about himself.

He had told her enough that day, however. Enough that she had been fooled into thinking he liked her. That there was a spark of...*something.*

She'd been wrong. This was the real man. He was severe and intimidating, not raising his voice because he didn't have to. His wishes, delivered in that implacable tone, were sheer power. She instinctively knew there was no shifting him on the course he had decided.

He didn't want her, though. She was merely an obstacle he was overcoming as expediently as possible. Her grandmother would see this marriage as a move toward security, but Poppy refused to trust his offer so easily. What if he got her over there and promptly divorced her? Took her to court for custody? There was no way she could survive without Lily.

Lily settled and Poppy went to the front room. Rico had finished the calls he'd been making and was chatting with her grandmother.

Having him in her home made her squirm. It was her private space where she revealed her true self in faded, toothless photos on the wall next to some of her earliest photography efforts. She and Gran had been working their way through a box of paperback romances that Poppy had picked up at a garage sale and Poppy's latest passionate cover was splayed open on the coffee table.

On the mantel stood Poppy's framed employee of the month certificate. Her boss at the bus depot had given it to her as a joke. Aside from him, she was the only employee and she was part-time. Gran had had her first good laugh in ages when Poppy had brought it home. Then they'd wept because Gramps would have enjoyed it, too.

Beside the certificate stood a generic birthday card from last month signed, *Love, Mom*. It was the only message besides the preprinted poem.

Rico was seeing far too much of *her* in this space. Maybe gathering ammunition for why his daughter couldn't stay here. A man so low on sentiment wouldn't recognize the comfort in the worn furniture and the value of memory-infused walls.

"The weatherman said it's a good night for stargazing," Gran was telling Rico while nodding at the television. "You might even see the northern lights."

"It's freezing outside," Poppy protested. "Literally." Spring might be a few days away on the calendar, but there was still thick frost on her windshield every morning.

"Bundle up." Gran dismissed Poppy's argument with the hardy practicality of a woman who'd lived on the prairies her whole life. "Your grandfather and I always came to agreement walking around Fisher's Pond. I have the phone right here." She touched the table where the cordless phone lived. "I'll call if Lily wakes and fusses."

Poppy glanced at Rico, hoping he would say it was late and he would come back tomorrow.

"I left my gloves in the car. I'll collect them on my way."

She bit back a huff and layered up, pulling on boots, mittens and a toque before tramping into what was actually a fairly mild night, considering the sky was clear and there was still snow on the ground.

The moon turned the world a bluish daylight and her footsteps crunched after Rico as they started away from the car. He wound a red scarf around his neck as they walked.

"Before today, I had only flown over prairies, never driven through them." His breath clouded as he spoke.

"Were you fighting to stay awake?"

"No, but it's very relaxing. Gives you time and space to think."

She didn't ask him what he'd been thinking about, just took him past the last house on their street, then along the path in the snow toward the depression that was Fisher's Pond.

It was a busy place midwinter. Neighborhood children played hockey every chance they got, but signs were posted now that the ice was thinning and no longer safe. The makeshift benches and lights were gone leaving only the trampled ring around the pond that was popular with dog walkers in summer. Tonight, they had the place to themselves.

"I haven't seen the Milky Way like that, either," he said, nodding at the seam of stars ripped open across the sky. "Not clear and massive like that."

"Rico, I can't go to Spain with you."

"I can hire a live-in care aid." His tone became very businesslike. "Or support her in any facility she chooses. You can be back here within a day if concerns arise. Do not use your grandmother as an excuse to keep my daughter from me."

Wow. She rubbed her mitten against her cold nose, trying to keep the tip of it from growing numb.

"She's not an excuse. She's my family."

He absorbed that, then asked, "Where are your parents? Why has it fallen on you to look after your grandparents?"

"I wanted to." She hugged herself. "They've always been good to me. Even when I came home pregnant."

Especially then. Buying the assisted-living unit

would have required selling the house, leaving Poppy without anywhere to live. It had been everyone's wish that they stay together in that house while Gramps was so sick, but Gran was right. They couldn't sustain this. Poppy had been mentally preparing herself for spending the summer clearing out the house. That didn't mean she was ready to move with her daughter around the globe, though.

"Did your parents pass away? Have you always lived with them?"

"I have, but my parents are alive. Divorced. Dad works in the oil patch." She tried not to sound as forlorn as she had always felt when talking about her parents. "He shows up every few months for a week or so, sleeps on the couch and does some repairs. He used to give Gran money sometimes, for taking care of me. I think he gambles most of what he makes. It's one of those things no one in the family talks about, but money has always been an issue with him."

"Thus the divorce?"

"I'm sure that was part of it. Mom had her own issues." She turned from the cleared patch that faced the pond and started on the path around it.

She hated that she had to reveal her deepest shame, but he ought to know it, so he would understand her reasons for refusing to marry him.

"They were really young when they had me. Mom was only nineteen. Not ready for the responsibility of being a parent. My dad brought her here to live with his parents then left to work far away. Mom stuck around until I was two, then she started moving around, living the life she thought she was entitled to, I guess."

"Partying? Drugs?"

"Freedom, mostly." Poppy understood now how overwhelming parenting was, but *she* hadn't dropped her daughter like a hot potato just because it was hard. "She didn't want to be a mom. She wanted to 'explore her potential.'" Poppy air-quoted the phrase. "She tried modeling in Toronto and worked as a flight attendant out of Montreal. She was a music promoter in Halifax, went to Vancouver to work on a cruise ship. Followed a man to India for a year then came back and opened a yoga studio in California. That's how she met her current husband, teaching one of his ex-wives to downward dog. He's a movie producer. They have two kids."

Two sulky, spoiled children who complained about the meals Poppy's mother cooked for them and the music lessons and soccer practices she drove them to.

Poppy tried not to hate them. They were family, but they were also entitled little brats.

"You never lived with her?" Rico asked behind her.

"By the time she was settled, I was starting high school. Bringing me across the border even for a visit was more bureaucracy than she wanted to face. She still hasn't seen Lily except over the tablet. I think she wishes I had never been born. Not in a spiteful way, but she would rather pretend her youthful mistake had never happened."

The path became streaked by the shadows of a copse of trees. She plodded into it, trying not to be depressed by her parents' neglect when they'd left her with such amazing grandparents.

"What I'm hearing is that you wish both of your parents had taken steps to bring you to live with them."

"Is that what you're hearing?" She stopped and turned, thinking her grandparents had been onto something because there was safety in the darkness, where her vulnerability wasn't painted in neon letters across her face. "Because I've come to realize they did me a favor, leaving me with people who tucked me in and told me they loved me every night."

She had surprised him by turning to confront him. He had pulled up, but stood really close. His face was striped by ivory and cobalt.

"Have you told them? Your parents?" she asked.

"I told them she was likely mine, even though the DNA results were inconclusive. I said—"

"What?" Poppy's elbows went stiff as she punched the air by her thighs. "Why did you even *come* here if you didn't *know*?"

"Because I had to know," he said tightly, "Your guilty expression when you opened the door was all the proof I needed."

She was such a dope, confirming his suspicions before he even *knew*. How did he disarm her so easily again and again?

"What was their reaction?" she asked, focusing on her deeper concerns. The *duque* and *duquesa* had struck Poppy as being aliens in human skin, assimilating on earth well enough not to be detected, but incapable of relating to normal people or showing genuine emotion.

"They asked to be kept informed."

"I see. And is your mother still on the hunt for the next Señora Montero?"

"How the hell do you know that?"

"I'm capable of reading a headline."

"Elevate your browsing choices. Gossip sites are garbage. If you wanted to know what I was doing with my life, you should have called *me*."

"I'm more interested in how your mother is going to react to Lily."

"She'll accept a fait accompli. She's done it before."

When Cesar's indiscretion with Sorcha had resulted in Enrique. But as far as Poppy could tell, Rico's father had barely noticed he had a grandson while his mother had given Enrique tight smiles and offered unsolicited suggestions on how he could be improved. *He looks due for a haircut, Sorcha.*

So Poppy snorted her disbelief. "I've seen what her type of 'acceptance' looks like and it's colder than an arctic vortex."

"Be careful, Poppy."

"That wasn't a cheap shot. I'm saying Lily is far too important to me to set her up to be the subject of criticism and disapproval for the rest of her life. If they're going to treat her like a stain on the family name, I won't take her anywhere near them."

He probably thought she should be grateful he was planning to let her accompany him and her daughter, but he only said, "They're not demonstrative people. There will be no welcome embrace from either of them. Reconcile yourself to that right now. They do, however, bring other strengths to the table. We Monteros look after our own."

"My stepfather can put her in movies if she decides she wants wealth and fame."

"Wealth is not fortune, fame is not standing," he stated pithily. "What sort of future are you planning for her? You'll date, perhaps introduce her to a few contenders and, one day, when you're convinced you're in love, you'll allow another man to raise *my* child without any of the genuine advantages to which she's entitled? In ignorance of her family and the attached opportunities overseas? No. I won't let you deny her what's rightfully hers."

"It's not up to you. And don't say it like that! 'When I'm *convinced* I'm in love.' *I love Lily.* Try to tell me that feeling is a figment of my imagination." She would knock him through the ice. "Do *you* plan to love her? Because, given what I saw of your upbringing, you were never shown how."

A profound silence crashed over them.

"Just as you were never taught to hold your temper in favor of a civil conversation?" Oh, he sounded lethal. The cold in the air began to penetrate her clothes.

"Answer the question," she insisted. "My love for Lily took root the day I learned I was pregnant." It had grown so expansive her body couldn't contain the force of it. It quivered in her voice as she continued. "I won't set her up to yearn for something from you that will never happen. I've been there and it is far too painful a thing to wish onto my child. *You know it is.*"

She had pushed herself right out onto the ledge of getting way too personal. She knew she had, but that was how much her daughter meant to her.

The umbrage radiating off him should have flash-melted the snow and razed the trees, illuminating the skies in an explosion of light.

Even so, she nudged even further by warning through her teeth, "Don't shove your way into her life unless you intend to be there every single moment, in every possible way she might need you to be."

His hands jammed into his pockets and his profile was slashed with shadows.

"You—" Something made him bite off whatever he had been about to say. He made a sucking noise through clenched teeth, as though enduring the removal of a bullet or something equally wounding. "My brother's sons are not unhappy. He had my same upbringing. He's managed to become quite attached. I would expect to form that sort of connection with my own child."

She was glad for the dark then, because sudden, pitying tears froze to her lashes. His words were such a careful admission that he was fine with not being loved as a child, but would find a way to extend his heart to his daughter.

For that reason alone, for the opportunity to gift him with his child's unconditional love, she knew she would have to allow him into Lily's life.

"Even so…" She folded her arms and squished handfuls of her quilted sleeves with her woolen mittens. She had had a front-row seat to the way his parents' marriage worked and it was…*sad*. They spoke without warmth to each other, as if they were inquiring about a telephone bill minus the anxiety that they might struggle to pay. "What kind of marriage would that be as an example for her?"

"A calm and rational one?" he suggested.

"I don't want rational! I want what my grandparents had." She waved wildly in the direction of the house where she had witnessed deep, abiding love, every single day. "I want pet names for each other and a love that endures through a lifetime."

"You want me to call you red?"

"Don't make fun of me. Or them," she warned. "Gran stayed in that drafty house an extra year for Gramps, because she knew it would break his heart to leave it. Now she can't stand to sleep in it without him there beside her."

"And you want that?" He sounded askance.

"It beats being married to a stranger. Occupying a mausoleum of a house while pursuing separate lives."

"My parents' marriage is an alliance based on shared values. That's not a bad thing if you agree on those values beforehand."

"Speaking from experience, are you?"

Another harsh silence descended. This time she regretted her words. His pregnant wife had died. He might not have loved Faustina, but it must be a very raw wound.

Recalling that, her suspicions of his motives arose again. Maybe he would come to care for Lily, but why was he here now? What did he *really* want?

"Rico… You understand that one baby cannot replace another, don't you?" She knew she had to tread softly on that one, but couldn't hold that apprehension inside her. "If that's why you're here, then no." It broke her heart to deny Lily her father, but, "I won't let you do that to Lily."

He stiffened and she braced herself for his scathing reaction, but it wasn't at all what she expected.

"Faustina's baby wasn't *mine*."

CHAPTER FOUR

THE WORDS WERE supposed to stay inside his head, but they resounded across the crisp air. Through the trees and off the sky. They made icicles drop like knives and stab into the frozen snow.

From a long way away, he heard Poppy say a hollow and breathless, "What?" Her thin, strained voice was no louder than his own had been, but rang like a gong in his ears.

He pinched the bridge of his nose, the leather of his gloves cold. All of him was encased in the dry ice of Canadian winter while his blood pumped in thick lumps through his arteries. His chest tightened and his shoulders ached.

"I shouldn't have said that. We should get back." He glanced the way they'd come, but it was shorter if she would only keep moving ahead on the path.

Thankfully, he couldn't see a soul. They were the only pair of fools out here stumbling through the dark. He waved for her to proceed.

"Rico." Her mitted hand came onto his forearm. "Is that true?"

The quaver in her voice matched the conscience

still wobbling like a dropped coin in the pit of his stomach.

"Forget I said it. I mean it, Poppy."

"I can't." She didn't let him brush away her grip on his sleeve. "*It matters.* Tell me."

"If I tell you…" He shifted so he cupped her elbow, holding her before him. "It stays between us. *Forever.* Do you understand?"

He had already said too much, but she was the mother of his child. His *actual* child. He had only tentatively absorbed that knowledge, only enough to know that one way or another he would bring them both back to Spain with him. Marriage was the quickest, most practical means of doing that. Therefore, she deserved to know the truth about his first marriage. As his wife, he expected her to protect his secrets as closely as he would guard hers.

And, damn it, he felt as though he'd been holding his breath for a thousand years. He couldn't contain it one minute longer.

"Her parents found her," he said, overcome with pity for them, despite his bitterness at Faustina's lies. The colossal waste of life couldn't be denied. The unborn baby might not have been his, but he was a decent enough human being to feel sadness and regret that it had been as much a victim as its parents.

"Where?" Poppy asked with dread.

"The garage. It wasn't deliberate. They'd packed bags, had train tickets. She was with her parents' chauffeur, naked in the back seat. They must have made love, perhaps started the car to warm it, then fallen asleep. They never woke up. Carbon monoxide poisoning."

"Oh, my God." She covered her mouth. "That's *horrible*."

"Yes. Her parents were devastated. Still are. They didn't know about the affair. They begged me to keep it under wraps."

"So you've been letting everyone think— How do you know the baby wasn't yours?"

"I had the coroner run tests."

"You told me that day you two weren't sleeping together." She twitched in his grip.

He released her. His palm felt cold, even inside his glove. He was solid ice, all the way to his core, still playing what-ifs in his head.

"Do you think *she* knew it wasn't yours?" she asked tentatively.

"Of course she knew," he spat with the contempt he felt for himself as much as for Faustina. "I had already begun to suspect. As soon as they found her, I knew what she had done. We *weren't* sleeping together. We made love *once* during our engagement. Faustina insisted. Said she wanted to be sure we'd be a good fit. After that, there were excuses. Headaches. Finally she said we should wait until the ceremony, to make our wedding night more exciting."

He hadn't argued. The first experience had barely moved him, certainly hadn't rocked his world the way another very memorable experience had. He skimmed his gaze over Poppy's face, so ghostly in the moonlight.

He'd told himself things would improve with Faustina once they got to know one another. He hadn't realized yet that it was possible to fall into immersive pleasure so profound he could be transported from the world around him. So much so that he made love with a woman he barely knew in the near-public solarium and had thought about her every day since.

He ran his gloved hand over his face. The seam in his palm scraped his skin, allowing him to focus on the rest of the ugly story.

"I believe she learned she was pregnant and slept with me so she could pass the baby off as mine."

"When?"

He knew what she was asking. "A few weeks before she broke things off with me on the day you and I were together."

Poppy rubbed her arm where he'd held her elbow.

"I've since learned that when she left my parents' house, she went straight to her own and told them she had called off the wedding. Her father threatened to disinherit her. They're very faithful and strict, demanded she abide by the agreement. They would have fired the driver if they'd had any inkling of her reason. Maybe even sued him for damages or destroyed him in some other way. Faustina's choice was to live destitute with her lover or crawl back to me."

It was the only explanation for how a stable, well-bred, otherwise honest woman could have behaved in such an underhanded way.

"A week before they died, she used her settlement from our marriage to close on a small house in the north of Spain, near his relatives. That's where they were headed."

"That's so…sad."

"Sad and sordid and I torture myself every day wondering if she would be alive if I'd refused to marry her that next morning."

"Why did you agree? The presidency?" Her voice panged in a way that grated against his conscience. The opportunity to run Faustina's father's company, proving himself in his own arena away from Cesar's shadow, had been the carrot that drew him into the engagement, but it wouldn't have enticed him to go through with the wedding the second time.

"She said she'd just found out she was pregnant, that it was the reason she'd been so emotional the day before. She said the baby was from that *one time*—when I used a condom, by the way. I should have suspected she was lying, but..." Here were the what-ifs. What if he had asked more questions, balked, told her he'd slept with the maid? That he'd *liked* it.

He hadn't done any of that. He'd done his duty by his family. He had done what was expected because, "I thought the baby was *mine*."

"When did you start to suspect it wasn't?"

"The wedding night. She didn't want to have sex. Said the pregnancy was turning her off." Rico had been nursing his own regrets and hadn't pressed her. "She was very moody. Conflicted, obviously. And putting her ducks in a row to leave me. We never did sleep together again. Things grew strained as I realized she was keeping something from me. I put off a confrontation, but it was coming. Then I got the call from her father."

"I'm so sorry, Rico. It's truly awful that you've had to carry this."

"I don't want your pity, Poppy." He curled his hands

into fists, straining the seams in his gloves. "I want your silence. I expect it. Not even Cesar knows and we don't keep much from one another. But I swore to her parents I'd keep it quiet."

"What about the company?"

"Her father asked me to stay on as President. He's sickened that she tricked me. I could weather the scandal if the truth came out, but it would destroy them. Despite Faustina's behavior, they're good people. I don't want to hurt them any more than they have been."

"I'll never say a word," she promised.

He nodded, believing her because they were in this together now.

"You understand why I told you? If she had been honest and up front about her situation, I would have helped her, maybe even raised that baby if she had asked me to. I wouldn't have punished the child for her failings." His anger returned, making his nostrils sting. "But I don't appreciate that you have also kept secrets from me, Poppy."

He heard her breath catch as though he'd struck her.

"I will *not* ignore my actual blood. I want *my* daughter."

She took a step back, but he caught her arm, keeping her close and tilting his head to peer through the shadows straight into her eyes.

"You *will* come to Spain. You *will* marry me and we will make this work."

Poppy might have knocked his hand away if she hadn't needed his touch to steady her; his words were that impactful.

"That's a big leap," she managed shakily. "I won't keep you from knowing her, Rico. I see why Lily being yours has extra significance for you." Her heart was aching under the weight of what he'd revealed and she had only just heard it. It had been festering in him for nearly two years. "But you and I barely know each other."

"We know each other," he scoffed gently. "I just told you something I haven't told *anyone*."

And she had shared her heartache over her parents' neglect.

A similar thing had happened that day in the solarium. Their conversation had somehow become deeply personal. Her crush on him had been instant and she'd never meant it to become obvious to him, but for weeks she had longed to talk to him in a meaningful way. She had wanted to find out who he was beneath his shell of gorgeous looks, easy manners and unsmudged armor.

She recalled telling him about that liar of a backpacker who had stolen everything she had, then asked why he had agreed to an arranged marriage.

Why compete with a business rival if a marriage can turn them into a partner? Faustina's very upstanding family would never connect themselves so intimately to any but the most exemplary politician, which polishes my father's already stellar reputation in the upper house of Parliament. Faustina gains the social standing of marrying into a titled family. My mother gets the heiress and the wedding event she envisioned for my brother.

It had seemed so laughably factual. She had asked him what he stood to gain and he'd mentioned running a company he would control, allowing him to pursue ambitions away from working for his brother.

A rational part of her brain had warned her that she deserved someone better than a man bouncing off a broken engagement, but her pride had needed the focused attention of someone so much grander than she was. She had thought the camera thief had genuinely liked her, but he'd been flattering her to blind her. Rico hadn't wanted anything from her except *her*. If he was rebounding after his own rejection, that was okay. It was one more detail that made them equals.

And when their kisses had escalated with passion, she hadn't wanted to stop. His lovemaking had been exactly what she had needed in that moment. Much as she believed she would only marry for love, she had known a soul-mate connection was an elusive thing. Expecting the full package of love and pleasure and a lifelong commitment for her first time wasn't realistic.

It had been enough to have infatuation and a man who ought to be firmly out of her reach, but who brought her entire body to life by simply watching the release of a button on her dress, then lifting his gaze to check in with her as his finger traced a caress against her skin.

She put a halt to recalling the rest or she'd succumb to him all over again without so much as a single protest.

"This is the second time we've spoken," she pointed out, inwardly shaking at how profound their encounters had been. "We made love *once*."

"With spectacular results." His gloved hand took hold of her chin. "I'm not just talking about Lily."

She was so glad he couldn't see her blush, but her helplessness was on full display in her strained voice. "That was… You were relieved you weren't marrying," she accused. "Coming off a dry spell with the first woman you happened across."

"I noticed you before that."

They were close enough that the fog of their breath was mingling.

"I wouldn't have kissed you if you hadn't made a point of telling me you'd finished your last shift and were no longer an employee," he reminded. "The attraction was mutual."

"I didn't make a *point* of it." Maybe she had. He had asked if she wanted to leave and had moved aside, giving her plenty of space to walk past him to the change rooms where she'd been headed when she had bumped into him. She had stayed, eager to keep talking to him. Basking in the glory of being noticed by him.

"Do you ever think about that day?" he asked.

Constantly. She wouldn't admit it, though.

"Hmm?" he prompted, lowering his head. He stopped before he kissed her.

She let her eyes flutter closed and parted her lips in invitation.

He only grazed his mouth against hers, provoking a buzzing sensation in her lips.

She put out a hand, but the knit of her mitten only found the smooth leather of his jacket, too slippery to hold on to.

While he kept up that frustratingly light tickle. His hand shifted to cup the side of her neck, the rough seam on his thumb grazing the tender skin in her throat.

"Do you?" He refused to give her what she wanted until she answered.

Her skin grew too tight for the anticipation that swelled within her. Beneath the layers of her thick jacket, her breasts grew heavy. Her thighs ceased to feel the cold through the denim of her jeans.

"Yes," she admitting on a throb of longing.

He made a noise of satisfaction and stepped so his feet were outside her own. His hot mouth sealed across her lips.

A sob of delight broke in her throat as his hard lips raked across hers, making real all the erotic fantasies she'd replayed in the long nights since leaving Spain. Her arms went up around his neck and he swept her closer still. So close she could hardly breathe.

She didn't care. The thick layers of their coats were a frustration, one that seemed to hold them off from one another. She wanted them *gone*. Wanted passion to take her over the way it had that day, blanking out the world around her with levels of excitement and pleasure she hadn't known existed.

His kiss deepened with greed, as though he couldn't get enough of her, either. She opened fully to him, licked into his mouth and felt his arms tighten around her in response. She ran her hand up past his scarf, pressed the back of his head, urging him to kiss her harder and harder still. She wanted him to mark her. Savage her.

Because he already had.

This passion between them was as destructive as it was glorious. She needed to remember that. Otherwise, she would succumb and wind up far out of her depth again.

As though he recognized the risk as well, he dragged his head up and sucked in a breath, but he didn't let her go.

Panting, she blinked her eyes open. His face was in darkness with a kaleidoscope of colors haloed behind him.

"Look." She seized the distraction to pull herself out of his arms. She wasn't even sure if what she was seeing was real or the leftover fireworks he had so easily set off behind her eyelids.

She staggered slightly as she led him out of the trees. The expanse of sky was bigger than a thousand movie screens above them and the stars had faded behind glowing swirls. Shimmering bands of pink and purple and red danced within the curtains of green. Every few seconds a spear of color shot toward the earth in knife-like streaks. The jabs of color felt so tangible and close, she expected to be struck by one.

"This is beautiful." Rico drew her back against his chest and folded his arms across her collarbone and stomach.

She was still weak from their kiss. She leaned into the wall he made, wondering if he could feel the thump of her still unsteady heart through their winter layers.

"One of my first memories is coming out here with my grandfather," she confided softly. "I asked when my mother was coming back and he brought me out here. I thought he was going to tell me she had died. He said he didn't know if she was coming back, but then he pointed to the sky. I asked what it was and he said he didn't know that, either. That there would always be things in this world we're left to wonder about."

"Gas particles from the sun collide with the earth's atmosphere," Rico informed her.

"Don't ruin it." She nudged her elbow back into his ribs. "It's *magic*. I've taken a million photographs of them, but none capture how amazing this really is. How small it makes you feel."

"I've never seen it like this." His chin touched the top of her head.

"Me, neither." This was the most glorious display she'd ever witnessed and she didn't care that she didn't have her camera. She would never forget sharing this with him: the timbre of his voice vibrating through her jacket, the heat of his breath against her earlobe where it poked from beneath her toque, the weight of his arm across her and the way all those colors glowed inside her even as they danced before her unblinking eyes.

She hesitated then confessed softly, "Gramps brought me out here when I was pregnant, too. I wanted to keep Lily, but I didn't know how I would manage it. It felt too much of an imposition to stay with them. He was upset that he wouldn't be around to look after me and Gran. We had a little cry then saw these lights. He said it was a reminder that even dark nights offer beautiful moments and said that's what Lily would be for all of us if I stayed with them."

Rico's arm tightened across her chest. His voice was low and sincere. "I'm sorry I didn't meet him."

Her chest ached. "I think that's him right now."

A startled pause, then, "I don't believe in things like that, Poppy."

"It's okay." She touched the arm that continued to hold her close. "I do."

"If I did—" His lips pressed to her ear through the knit of her toque. "I think we both know what he's saying."

Her throat grew tight. *Marry Rico.*

He drew back slightly so he could reach into his jacket. When he brought his hand around in front of her, he held a small box. He stayed behind her as he pried up the lid so she stood in the circle of his arms as he offered her the ring.

The band could have been silver or yellow or rose. The diamond caught glints of colored light, blinding her.

Had he really come all this way, not knowing for sure if Lily was his, but brought a ring just in case?

She let him pick up her left hand and tug at the mitten. She took the discarded mitt with her free hand. As though under a spell, she turned to face him.

She tried to think of reasons to persuade him this was wrong or stupid or doomed to fail. Marrying him was all of those things.

But she wanted to marry him. Her compulsion to know him remained. Beneath the anger and armor of indifference was a man who wanted to know his daughter. That meant everything to her.

As the aurora borealis continued to crash silently over them, full of mystical power and spirit voices, she told herself that Gramps wouldn't steer her wrong. He wouldn't tell her to marry Rico if this would ruin her life. He was telling her to say goodbye to her home and family and begin building her new one.

The cool ring caught slightly on her knuckle, then it was on her finger, heavy as the promise it symbolized.

Rico's mouth came down to hers again with magnificent heat, burning away her bleak doubts and fears, filling her with hope and possibility.

CHAPTER FIVE

You should have told me sooner. I would have made arrangements. Someone from the family should have been there.

RICO READ THE TEXT from Pia and swore, then dropped the phone onto the custom recliner beside the one he occupied.

Across from him, buckled into her own, Poppy looked up from distracting Lily with a book. Lily was making noises of dismay at being strapped into her car seat while the view beyond the windows turned to clouds.

"What's wrong?" Poppy asked him.

"A text from my sister, scolding me about the wedding."

"She's upset?" Poppy's expression dimmed.

"That I didn't invite her. I pointed out there hasn't been time."

It hadn't occurred to him Pia would want to come. His parents had urged him to wait for the DNA results and expressed consternation that he hadn't. Cesar's reaction to his impending nuptials had been a curt text.

Sorcha told me. Congratulations.

Rico had given up at that point and focused on the tasks at hand.

Poppy's gran had been moved to her sister's apartment, where she would occupy a guest room for a few days. Rico had had to push to make it happen, but he had arranged to have her personal items moved into a nearby, private seniors' complex that was so well-appointed, Eleanor had asked him if he'd won a lottery.

Poppy had been anxious about the entire process until she'd spoken with the extremely personable, on-staff doctor who had already been in touch with her grandmother's specialist. A nutritionist had made note of her grandmother's dislike of cumin. Her sensitivity to certain detergents had been conveyed to the housekeeping staff. Eleanor had looked in on the pool where physical therapy sessions were held and checked out the lively games room, approving the entire complex with a delighted nod.

Poppy's father had pointed out that the location in Regina would be easier for him to visit, too. He typically spent half a day driving after his flight landed. Rico had even hired a caretaker to look after the house until decisions had been made on whether to keep it in the family.

The last task had been a brief civil service at the courthouse. Poppy's father had given her away and her grandmother had wept happy tears. They had eaten brunch at an upscale café then climbed aboard his private jet.

Another text rang through, but he ignored it.

"Tell her I didn't even have my mother there," Poppy said.

"I explained why I was keeping it private."

"That wasn't a complaint," she said stiffly, making him aware of how tersely he'd spoken. "I didn't *want* my mother there." She picked up the book Lily dropped, mouth pinched.

Poppy had said she would inform her mother after Rico issued the press release. He'd had enough to juggle in the moment that he hadn't questioned her. Now he did.

"Why not?" Had she been afraid she wouldn't show up? Her mother sounded even less emotionally accessible than his own. At least La Reina Montero maintained appearances.

"I was afraid she wouldn't keep her mouth shut," Poppy muttered crossly. "I agree with you that it's kinder to let your parents inform Faustina's parents and give them a few days to prepare their own statement."

Loathe as he was to bring Faustina into this marriage on any level, he appreciated Poppy's understanding. Having a child Lily's age wouldn't reflect well on his fidelity, narrow window of a called-off wedding notwithstanding. This news would come as a shock to many, including Faustina's parents.

"I didn't mean to speak sharply. I don't usually make mistakes and they've been piling up lately."

For the most part, Rico was a meticulous planner. He had always been taught success was a matter of research and preparation. That lesson had played out as true more often than not and he had heeded its wisdom—right up until he had impulsively made love with his mother's maid.

He had promptly fallen back in line with the precisely orchestrated pageant his first wedding had been, only to discover his wife's betrayal. As resentful as he still was of that, he had to face the fact that if he had refused to marry Faustina when she had come back that next morning, she might be alive and happily ensconced with her lover and child. He wouldn't have the presidency that had seemed like such a delectable consolation prize, but he would have had the first year of Lily's life. Poppy bore some responsibility for his missing that, but so did he.

He had believed his tryst with Poppy was all the bucking of expectations he had needed before settling into the life laid out for him. Even after Sorcha had dropped this earth-shattering news on him, he had attempted to defuse it with surgical care, ordering an investigation and telling no one.

Then the test had come back inconclusive and he had come out of his skin. Mere days later, he had a wife and child. His parents thought he was behaving recklessly and a rational part of him wondered if they were right. He was relying on instinct without concrete evidence or other facts to back it up.

He caught Poppy's affronted glare and heard his own words.

"I wasn't suggesting this marriage is a mistake. But it will cause a tragic death to be splashed across the gossip sites again. *You* will be cast as the Other Woman."

She would be labeled an opportunist and a gold digger. Given her shock at his arrival, he couldn't accuse her of that, but others would.

"I'll look like a faithless husband and a deadbeat father. I'm not proud of any of that. Scandals are not my MO. I'm disgusted with myself for creating this situation."

"And what about Lily? Are you sorry you created her?" The fiery challenge in her expression was quickly schooled as the flight attendant approached to ask after their comfort.

Lily lifted her arms at the woman and pitifully begged, "Oof?"

"She thinks that means up," Poppy explained with a stiff smile. "I guess I was making that noise whenever I lifted her and didn't notice. Button, you have to stay in your seat. I'll apologize now for how miserable she's going to become."

Rico preferred a happy baby over one who was screaming, same as anyone. The baby in question, however, was his. He hadn't fully unpacked that knowledge and very tentatively felt around in the dank spaces within him, looking for the regret Poppy had accused him of feeling toward Lily.

"Our flight should be very smooth until we're over the Atlantic," the attendant said. "She could walk around if you want to let her work out some energy."

"She doesn't walk yet."

"There isn't much she can get into," Rico pointed out, still searching through the bitterness that encased him for resentment that was wrongly aimed at an innocent child. "All the drawers have catches so they won't open midflight."

Poppy peered at the floors. They were as spotless as they ought to be, given the salaries he paid his flight crews.

"You really wouldn't mind?" Poppy asked the attendant.

"Of course not." The attendant was bemused by the question and disappeared to fetch the coffee he requested.

Poppy heard his snort and shot him a frown as she unstrapped Lily. "Why am I funny?"

"This is my plane. If my daughter wants to pilot it through loop-de-loops, it's the crew's job to make it happen." That much he *was* sure of.

Poppy released a small oof of exertion as she pulled Lily out of her seat and stood her on the floor, next to her knee. Then she reached into the toy bag and handed Lily a giraffe. She tossed the half-dozen other toys onto the empty seat next to Rico.

Lily reached for the bag, needing to peek inside to see if more would appear.

"It's empty. They're all there," Poppy told her, pointing.

Lily dropped the giraffe, let go of Poppy's knee and took three toddling steps, completely unassisted.

Poppy gasped and reached out to catch her, but Lily slapped her dimpled hand onto Rico's knee. Her fingers closed like kitten claws into the fabric of his trousers as she steadied herself. Then she cruised around his leg and began examining the array of toys.

Poppy clapped her hand over her open mouth. Her eyes brimmed with excited tears. "Did you see that?" She dropped her hand, but emotion husked her voice.

"Those weren't her *first* steps." It couldn't be. There'd been no fanfare. No announcement over the PA that it was about to happen. It had occurred naturally, as if she'd been doing it all along.

Poppy nodded like a bobblehead doll on the dash of a derby car.

"They were. Just like that. Baby is gone and she's a toddler." She wiped her damp eyes. "I shouldn't be so silly about it. Gran kept saying it would happen any day."

Lily had found his phone amid the stuffed toys and plastic keys. He started to take it from her, but a fierce swell of pride moved his hand to her hair. He faltered briefly then grazed his palm lightly over her fine red hair, downy as a duckling.

She was such a tiny, perfect little human. Recognizing how vulnerable she was made his heart clench in a strange panic. An urge to protect rose in him, but he already knew he wouldn't be sufficient to the task. Not forever. Things would happen beyond his control. Then what? He had instinctively shied from this depth of responsibility, but here it was, thrust upon him, heavy and unavoidable, yet oddly welcome.

How could he not want to shield such a precious young life? How could he ever blame her for existing?

"You don't have to impress me, you know," he told Lily, rueful that he was so button-bursting proud of three little steps.

Lily grinned and held up his phone.

"Thank you," he said politely and pocketed the item, offering a teething ring in exchange. He shifted his attention to Poppy.

"We both could have handled many things better," he told her, clearing his voice to steady it while he mentally allowed the cloak of fatherhood to settle more comfortably over his shoulders. "But I will never, ever regard Lily as a mistake."

Rico gently transferred Lily into a blue crib that likely belonged to Mateo. Rico had said this darkened penthouse in Madrid was used by any member of the family who happened to have business in the capital.

Poppy carefully tucked blankets around her overtired little girl. The first half of the flight had gone well. Everyone had caught a few hours of sleep, but Lily had begun fussing when turbulence forced her to be strapped back into her seat. By the time she had cried herself out and begun to nod off, they were descending and her ears were popping, upsetting her all over again.

"I think she's down for the count," Poppy said with relief as they stepped out of the room.

Rico clicked on the baby monitor and brought it with them into the lounge where he turned on a few lamps. He moved with casual confidence, hardly a wrinkle in his clothes, his eyes heavy-lidded and inscrutable.

"Are you hungry?"

"No. I feel like all I did was eat on the flight." She crossed her arms and hunched her shoulders, hyperaware that they were alone for the first time since they'd stood under the stars that first night.

They were also married.

She had heard him tell the driver to leave their luggage in *his* room, but there was a conversation they needed to have before they shared it. She hadn't figured out yet how to broach it. She wished she could be blasé and sophisticated, but she felt callow and fearful of his reaction. Would he laugh? Look at her with disappointment?

"I…um…wouldn't mind a shower," she murmured, more for a chance to be alone and clear her head.

"Do you want company?" His voice lowered, growing thick with sensual invitation.

Her stomach took a rollercoaster dip and swirl while a wave of heat pushed out from her center, leaving her fingers and toes, nipples and scalp all tingling.

She wanted to laugh at how easily he segued into addressing the elephant, but some of her trepidation must have shown. His expression tightened.

"We don't have to if you're tired."

"It's not that," she murmured, more wired than tired, still trying to come to terms with everything that had happened in such a whirlwind. Drawing a breath of courage, she said, "I'm not sure what you expect."

A brief pulse of surprise, then he said stiffly, "I expect this marriage to include a sexual relationship. I'll never force it, though. And I would normally say a woman doesn't need an excuse for turning me down, but given Faustina's reasons, I'd like to understand yours."

"I'm not turning you down," she said with a small, nervous smile that wouldn't stick. "I expected we'd have sex. When I took Lily for her blood test the other day, I left her with the nurse so I could get an IUD." Sometimes her hair gifted her with the clichéd fiery blushes and now was one of those times. The entire room should have turned bordello red, she glowed so hotly with the admission that she had premeditated having sex with him.

He frowned. "You don't want more children?"

"Not right away." Her cheeks hurt, they were scorched so deeply. "This is a lot to get used to, don't you think? Without bringing a newborn into the mix?"

He tipped his head slightly, acknowledging the point, but a hint of suspicion glinted in his narrowed eyes. Perhaps he saw the rest of the logic that had propelled her decision—a new baby would make it more difficult for her to leave if she had to.

"I want this marriage to work," she assured him. "But there are things…" Her voice failed her. She cleared her throat. "Things we should discuss before…"

"Health concerns?"

"You mean disease? No! I'm perfectly fine. Are you—?"

"Completely fine," he clipped out. "I was asking if there were complications with delivering Lily that affected you?"

"No. Just the usual leftover imperfections of stretch marks and… Well, you can see I'm still carrying a bit of baby weight. Lily weaned herself three months ago and apparently these aren't going away." She waved at the chest that remained a cup size bigger than prepregnancy.

"I assure you I don't consider any of those things 'imperfections.' Particularly the added curves. Is that the source of your hesitation? You're self-conscious? We can keep the lights off if it will make you more comfortable. I'd prefer it, too. Otherwise my scar from my appendix surgery might turn you off."

"Why would— Oh. All right, I get your point." She rolled her eyes.

He paced closer, which made her freeze in place, skin growing tight with anticipation while nervous butterflies filled her torso, swirling around in every direction.

He touched her chin, coaxing her to meet his gaze with her own. "We've done this before," he reminded her.

"About that…" She clasped his flat wrist and squeezed her eyes shut. "That's the only time I've had sex. Ever."

She felt the flex in his wrist and the slight increase of pressure in his grip on her chin.

"Open your eyes," he commanded, voice seeming to resonate from the depths of his chest.

She did, meeting his gaze with chagrin. She wasn't ashamed of being a virgin so much as feeling guilty for having misled him that day.

All she could see were his eyes, iridescent almost. Like granite that revealed flecks of precious gems when wet, glints of blue and green in the gray surrounding a giant black pool. His pupils were huge. Atavistic.

Yet skeptical.

"*Ever*," she reiterated helplessly.

Rico couldn't think of another time he'd been utterly speechless. Not that his mind had the capacity to filter any moments other than the one she was referring to. The shyness of her hands squeezing him through his pants and fumbling with his belt.

Enthusiasm counted for more than expertise when it came to lovemaking. If he'd given any thought to her

lack of finesse, he had likely imagined she was as overcome as he was. He couldn't say his own performance
had been particularly adept, given the stolen nature of
their tryst.

He remembered clearly that moment afterward,
though, when his lingering pleasure had dimmed because he had feared he had hurt her.

Is your cycle starting?

I guess. Sorry. She'd been mortified.

Don't apologize. At least we're safe from—

He'd been appalled at forgetting the condom. He
never forgot.

"I don't like lies," he warned her now, lips numb.
This news was melting his face off his skull.

"I'm being honest." She winced as though she was
squirming inside. "I want to sleep with you, but I don't
want you to be…" She swallowed. Her voice remained
strained. "Disappointed. *I* don't want to be disappointed."

The word wafted over him, so far from what he
might be feeling as to be incomprehensible. Then his
ego absorbed the hit.

"Were *you* disappointed that day?"

"No." She withdrew from him a few steps and
crossed her arms.

But she had nothing to compare it to. Her lack of experience began to penetrate. Belated concern struck.
They'd been quite passionate. "Did I hurt you?"

"No. I mean, a little, but not…" She looked to the
ceiling as though seeking deliverance. "I was fine with
the discomfort. There were compensations," she added
with a small groan of embarrassed irony.

"You felt pleasure?" He had to know. "You weren't faking your enjoyment, were you? Did you climax? Because I thought you did, but—"

"Are we really doing a forensic audit on it?" she cried, face so red it should have been accompanied by five alarms.

"I need to know, Poppy." It was imperative.

"I didn't fake anything! Okay? Quit asking such personal questions."

"How is this too personal? We were both there and I'm making sure we were both *there*. My pride is every bit as delicate as any man's. When it comes to the bedroom, if you're not satisfied, I'm not satisfied. I will make you that promise right now."

She ducked her eyes into her hand. "Thanks. And I'd love to make the same promise, but *I don't know what I'm doing.*"

"You don't have to be defensive about it. I'm glad you told me. And your number of past lovers is far less important to me than how many you have *now*." Obviously. "Shall we agree we'll keep it to one?"

She peered at him over her hand, admonishing, but also earnest as she promised, "Of course I'll be monogamous."

"Thank you. So will I." But he was still having trouble believing she had shelved all her passion once she'd discovered it. "There really hasn't been anyone since me?"

"Who would I sleep with, pregnant out to here?" She set her hand in the air beyond her navel. "I was looking after my grandparents and a newborn. Babies make you want to have a date with your pillow and no one else, trust me."

She looked too uncomfortable to be telling him anything but the truth.

It was starting to impact him that the most profound sexual experience of his life had been with a virgin. He wasn't sentimental, but there was something endearing in knowing he was her only lover.

"Why me?" he asked gently. "Why that day?"

"Because I was feeling like my whole trip had been a bust and I wanted one decent memory to take home with me."

"I was a *souvenir*?"

"I was just a notch on your belt, wasn't I?" she shot back.

His heart lurched and he had to look away, thinking of the way he had obsessed about her ever since. He had tried to relegate her to a notch. Instead, she'd been another persistent what-if.

"It's fine that you were only taking what I offered," she said, hugging herself. "I didn't care that you had all the experience and seduced me. I wanted you to. But now you're only having sex with me because we're married and you're stuck with me. That would be fine if I felt like I was bringing something to the table, but I don't have any sexual confidence because I've only done it *one time*." Her brow furrowed.

Aside from the chaste kiss after the ceremony, he hadn't touched her since their kiss under the stars, but he'd been acutely aware of her every minute since she had opened her door to him. His ears were attuned to each inflection in her voice—the chuckling remarks she exchanged with her grandmother, the loving tone she used when speaking to Lily. He had studied the fit of her jeans, drunk in the scent of her hair, enjoyed the smooth warmth of her hand if their fingers happened to touch. He had noted the way her lips closed over a fork and the little frown that appeared between her brows if she was growing stubborn.

He had spent every night lying awake, recalling their passionate union until he was so filled with ardor, he ached.

He couldn't believe she didn't know that.

But he had taken pains to keep his reaction hidden so as not to let her undermine him with what he perceived as a weakness. He hadn't wanted to admit that he had obsessed about her from the first moment he'd seen her dusting his mother's furniture.

"You have a lot to compare to and I don't want to start our marriage by falling short of your expectations." She offered a dejected smile. "That's why we're standing here instead of in the shower."

CHAPTER SIX

POPPY FELT LIKE a head case and was trying not to apologize for it. Women were allowed to have reservations. To feel conflicted. She might want sex, but she didn't want empty sex. Not this time. Not when she had tried that the first time and discovered she wasn't capable of keeping her emotions out of the experience.

But Rico was her husband and the father of her child and their kisses had reassured her that their lovemaking would be as pleasurable as it had been the first time.

Maybe she was expecting too much.

Was that what he was thinking behind that enigmatic expression? A muscle was pulsing in his jaw as though he was trying to crack nuts with his teeth.

"I haven't been with anyone else, either," he finally said.

"Oh, please." Disappointment in him descended like a curtain while her heart latched a little too hard on to that outrageous statement. "It's been nearly two years!" He could have his pick of supermodels. He'd gotten the maid with a wink and a smile, hadn't he?

"I already told you that I slept with Faustina *once*. Weeks before you." He opened his eyes to scowl with affront at her distrust. "I didn't cheat on her, and given the way my marriage ended, I haven't been feeling very amorous."

She found that believable, actually.

"Until very recently," he added pointedly, pretty much flinging sexual awareness at her and leaving her coated in it. "All of which could impact *my* performance. You're not the only one with high stakes here."

"Oh, I'm sure we're on exactly the same level of nerves," she muttered sarcastically.

He relaxed slightly, eyeing her. "Do you think about it?"

"What? Sex?" The whole world tilted like a magnifying glass. One moment certain things had loomed large, now all of that went out of focus while a bright ray of heat singed into her bones. "With you, or…?"

"Anyone. But sure, me."

She was *not* going to admit that she thought about him *all the time*. "I can't believe you're asking me these things."

"This is exactly the sort of conversation a husband and wife should be able to have."

"Do *you*?" she challenged.

"Think about you? Of course. I've often recalled our lovemaking and imagined doing things with you that we didn't have time to enjoy."

He was admitting to fantasizing about her. And he wasn't flinching in the least. He was staring right into her eyes and making *her* think of things she wished they'd done.

His brow went up in a light challenge.

She swallowed, hot all over.

"I imagine you're in the shower with me. For instance," he provided in a drawl that somehow pulled all her nerve endings tight. "If you're looking for a seductive move, I guarantee you an invitation to join you will always pique my interest."

She narrowed her eyes. "I don't appreciate you making fun of me."

"I'm not joking," he assured her, but amusement lurked around his mouth.

"Fine," she said with annoyance. "Let's move this to the shower, then."

"Poppy."

His voice caught like a hook in her heart, pulling her around without even touching her before she could hurry down the hall.

She caught her breath. If he said he didn't want to, she might lose her nerve and never find it again.

"What?" she demanded when he waited until she quit spinning her gaze around the room in avoidance and made herself look at him.

"This isn't a test." His voice grew grave. Tense. "If you're not ready, say so."

"I said I want to!" She waved in the direction she'd been headed.

He came toward her, brows raised in a mild scold. "You're nervous. Maybe instead of barreling into the shower, we should slow down."

"I want the awkwardness over with," she admitted, bordering on petulant.

He gently peeled her hands off her elbows and held them in a loose grip. "But if I'd been in less of a hurry last time, I might have noticed you were new to this. *I* want to be sure you're with me every step. Why don't we start with a kiss?"

"Really?" She rolled her eyes toward the ceiling. "Fine. If that's what you want."

"Humor me." He stepped in and stole a single kiss, one of those deliberately light ones that made desire soak through her like gasoline.

She shifted lightly on her feet, instantly restless, but not in a hurry to go anywhere. "You could try that again."

He did, lingering. Taking his time finding the right fit, playing with levels of pressure.

While she shyly returned his kiss, her whole body became sensitized to everything around them. The lamplight chasing them toward the hall, the scent of faint cologne against his cheek and the slight rustle of their clothing as they stopped holding hands and reached to touch. Her hand came to rest on the fabric of his shirt, curling into a fist that crushed the fine linen while her mouth moved with tremulous passion beneath his, encouraging him.

That bashful invitation seemed to test his control. He growled and deepened the kiss. His hands found her waist and drew her fully against him.

All the memories she had convinced herself were fantasy were becoming real. He was here. She was in his arms, in his home. This was her new life. It was too much. A small cry sounded in her throat.

He lifted his head. Both of them tried to steady their breath.

She suddenly remembered him saying, *You deserve better than the lowlife who took your camera.*

She had known she did, but she hadn't believed she deserved him. Not for more than a brief hour. At the time, she had countered, *She didn't deserve you, either. I hope you find someone better.* She had wanted him to see *her* as an option. To *want* her.

Did he? She could tell he was affected by their kiss, but he was pulling himself back under control as she watched.

This was the true source of her apprehension. That she would lose herself to his touch again and whatever grip or autonomy she had over her life would slip away. After their first time, even before she had learned she was pregnant, she had known her life would never be the same. Every other man would be compared to him and fall short.

After tonight, he would know he could do this to her. He could break down her barriers without effort, own her body and soul. Her eyes began to sting at her defenselessness.

His hands moved soothingly across her lower back. His eyes had gone more blue than gray and were shot with sparks of green, hot as the center of a flame. As he slowly drew her in again, he made a noise that was a question.

She settled gladly against him. Melted into him.

If she had had the strength of mind, of willpower, she might have balked. But she wanted this. She craved his touch like she'd been sucked into quicksand and suddenly found the vine that would pull her free.

He lowered his head and took another thorough

taste of her, long and lazy and luscious. The stab of his tongue acted like alcohol, shooting pleasurable trickles of heat through her veins. She grew loose of limb and warm and weak. She moaned softly and curled her arms around his neck, encouraging him.

He settled into a passionate kiss, not aggressive, but full of confidence. Unhurried and possessive. Seductive.

She quit thinking about whether she was being reckless or not skilled enough. She let herself sink into the play of his mouth across hers and simply feel. Feel the hardness of him with her whole body as she rose on her tiptoes. Feel the silk of his hair with her fingers and the faint abrasion of chin stubble as he twisted his head and swept his tongue across hers.

She immersed herself in the feel of *him*. The sweep of his hands across her back and down to her hips, the iron thighs holding steady as she leaned into him. The erotic hardness of his erection pressing into her abdomen, telling her she was affecting him.

The knowledge he was aroused sent arrows of answering lust deep into her belly. Lower. Each bolt was tipped with flame, burning her hotter as their kisses went on until she was melting and dripping with anticipation. Making pleading noises without conscious awareness of it.

The scoop of his hands under her backside surprised her, but her legs locked around his waist as he lifted her. She found herself nose to nose with him.

"Hold on." He looked as though he commanded armies, his face a mask of sharp angles as he carried her down the hall.

She clung across his shoulders, and buried her face

in the masculine scents against his neck. She nuzzled his throat and lightly bit his earlobe, smiling when she made all the muscles in his body flex in reaction.

His hands tightened against her backside and she chuckled with feminine power, thrilling, then falling—

She gasped and let go to put out her hands, but he caught her with strong arms across her back, bending with her, coming with her and covering her as she landed gently on the mattress.

Barely any light had followed them into the room. They'd forgotten the baby monitor, but Lily was across the hall. Poppy would hear her—but dearly hoped she wouldn't.

She glanced toward the en suite.

"We'll get there," he murmured of the shower, propping himself over her on one elbow. "This is nice for now." His legs were tangled with hers, his hips heavy on hers. With his free hand, he popped the first button on her top. *"Sí?"*

She smiled shyly, not sure what she was supposed to agree to. He could undress her if he wanted to, but this was the furthest thing from "nice." It was exhilarating and dangerous and consuming. It was everything she wanted.

And there was something awfully sweet about a man who wanted to seduce her when she was already there.

"You have to answer, *cariño.*" His fingers came up to comb tendrils of hair away from her face.

"Sí," she whispered.

"Perfecto." He stroked the backs of two fingers down her throat and finished opening her shirt, revealing her breasts in her demicups.

She tried to open his shirt, but, like the first time, had none of his skill. His buttons were small and tight. Impossible. He brought his hand up and brushed hers away then swept his hand in a sharp yank that tore off buttons and ripped holes.

She gasped. "You didn't have to do that!"

"I did," he assured her, catching her hand and bringing it to his hot chest. "I've waited a long time for your touch."

His words sent her heart into a spin. She greedily brushed aside the gaping edges of his shirt and claimed his taut skin. The texture of his chest hair played against her palms and his breath sucked in when she skimmed the heels of her hands across the tight points of his nipples.

He said something in Spanish that she didn't have the wherewithal to translate, but his hand slid across her waist, making her realize he had finished releasing her buttons and now took his time exploring all the flesh he had bared. He made a circle against her quivering belly, stroked his thumb across the bumps of her ribcage, then traced the zigzag stitching on the bottom of her bra.

She should have bought something better. Her underclothes were boring beige, purchased from a big box store. He didn't seem to mind. He drew circles on the soft cups. There was no padding. She felt his touch almost as if she was naked. Her nipples stood up against the thin fabric, waiting for more. Begging for it.

Time stood still. His smile of pleasure was almost cruel as he teased her. She didn't realize she was furtively raking her thumbs across his nipples until his fierce gaze came up to hers and he said in a low growl, "Two can play that game, *preciosa*."

With a casual flick of the front closure, her bra released and he brushed the cup aside. His nostrils flared as he took a moment to admire her blush-pink areoles and the turgid nipples atop them. Then he dipped his head, catching her nipple in his hot, damp mouth, devouring her.

She bit back a cry and arched, barely able to withstand the burn and rush of blood that made the tips unbearably tight and sensitive before he began to pull and tease and scrape with his teeth.

She bit her lip and thrust her fingers into his hair, but he didn't let up. He continued his delicious torture until she writhed against him, hips lifting in ancient signals of willingness.

He rose to kiss her mouth, drowning her in pure sensuality before he moved to her other breast, keeping his hand on the first, circling his thumb on the wet, taut button in a way that sent currents of desire straight through her. She grew wet with yearning. She was both embarrassed and becoming desperate, alternately trying to squeeze her thighs together and open them with invitation.

His legs were pinning hers, though, keeping her beneath him in a sensual vice where she couldn't escape the pleasure he was bestowing on her. She finally clasped the sides of his head and dragged his mouth up to hers again. She pushed her tongue between his lips, flagrant and uninhibited.

Take me, she begged with her kiss.

He groaned, shifted. Got his hand between them and

released her jeans. He made another sound of deep satisfaction as he pushed his hand into her open fly, covering heat and damp cotton. His touch was wickedly skilled, rocking as he eased his touch deeper into the notch of her thighs, until she was lifting into the pressure of his palm, streaks of glorious pleasure arcing through her back. Only then did he slide a finger beneath the placket to brush her skin, leave her pulsing, then returning to soothe. Incite.

"I thought it was my imagination, the way you reacted like this," he said against her throat, deepening his caress in a way that was exquisitely satisfying, yet a profound tease.

"Rico." Growing mindless, she ran her hands over his chest and sides beneath his open shirt and across his back, arching to feel more of his naked skin with her bare breasts.

"Show me you weren't faking. Show me I can make it happen for you."

His trapped hand was making her wild. She moved with his touch, unable to resist the lure of the pleasure he offered. His mouth went back to her breasts and that was it. Seconds later she fell off the edge of the earth, but went soaring into the ether.

As cries of culmination escaped her parted lips, he lifted his head and covered her mouth, kissing her with rapacious hunger that she returned with greed.

She gave up trying to open his belt and tried to worm her hands under it.

He was speaking Spanish again, swearing maybe. His hand caught her chin and he licked into her mouth as if he couldn't get enough of her. Then he made a pained noise as he lifted enough to jerk his own belt open and release his pants.

They moved in unison, pulling away to yank and divest and kick their pants off their legs. Naked, they rolled back into one another, near frantic.

This was how it had been that other time. There was no stopping this force. It was stronger than both of them.

And knowing he was as helpless to it as she was made it okay.

As he settled himself over her, however, she felt his tension. The care he took as he settled his hips low between her thighs and braced his weight on his elbows. She could feel his exertion of will over himself and by extension, her.

His whole body shook with the effort, but there was clarity behind the passion that glazed his eyes.

"Rico." She closed her eyes against that betrayal, wanting him to fall back into the miasma with her. She slid her touch between them, seeking the shape of him. So taut and smooth, damp on the tip, tight at the base.

His breathing grew ragged, telling her she was lacerating his control.

"Poppy." His voice reverberated from somewhere in his chest, ringing inside hers. "Open your eyes."

She didn't want him to read how anguished she was. How her soul was right there, seeking his as her body yearned for the impalement of his flesh. It was too much.

"Let me see you."

She opened her eyes and time slowed.

"Take me into you," he commanded, biting at her chin, using his powerful thighs to spread hers apart.

She guided the tip of him against her folds, parting, distantly thinking she ought to be more self-conscious, but she was only joyful. She was *aching*. She needed this slick motion of him against her sensitive button of nerves. She hummed with pleasure, growing wetter. Needier. She gloried in the pressure as he slowly forged into her, so hot as to burn her slick, welcoming flesh.

And sweet. Oh, the sweet, sweet easing of the ache as he invaded. The breadth of him was exactly as she remembered it. There was even a moment of distress when she thought he was more than her body could accept. Her fear eased within the next heartbeat as he settled and pulsed within her.

They were both quaking.

She thought he might have asked her if she was all right, but she only pulled him into a kiss. This moment was utterly perfect. She never wanted it to end.

But after a few drugging kisses, he began to move and she remembered now that pleasure was music on a scale, some notes sharper than others, but every single one a necessary part of the beautiful whole.

There was the smoothness of his skin across his shoulders, the power in them so delicious against the stroke of her palms. There was the friction of his waist against her inner thighs as her legs instinctively rose to hug him. The stretch of tendons at her inner thighs somehow added to the sweet tension that gripped her.

There was his mouth, dragging new, glorious sensations against her throat and jaw, then sucking her earlobe and making her scalp tighten before he kissed her, letting her taste the blatant sexuality in him. There was the silk of his hair grazing her cheek when he sucked a love bite against her neck. The moans they released were the chorus to their dance and the colors behind her closed eyes were matched only by the erotic sensations streaking through her whole body as he thrust and withdrew.

The sensations where they joined were particularly acute. No friction or tenderness, just shivering waves of joy that began lapping closer together, coiling tension within her until the intensity became unbearable.

"Rico." She writhed beneath him, fingernails digging into his buttocks, aching for more of him. Harder. *Deeper.*

"Only me." He held her face between his hands. Possessive, no question, but she thought she tasted wonder in the graze of his lips across hers. A strange reverence that sent quivers of joy through her whole being.

"Only you," she agreed. But she didn't think she could stand this level of tension. Trembles of arousal shivered over her, alarming in their intensity. "It's too much."

"Bear it," he said with a savage flash of his teeth. "Feel what we do to each other."

He moved in heavier strokes, her slippery heat gripping him instinctually, making the friction all the more acute and glorious. She gasped in breathless need as the universe opened with infinite possibility. Her hips rose to meet his and his shoulders shuddered with tension as he held back. Waited for her. Waited.

His eyes were black, his cheeks flushed. They were both coated in perspiration. She wanted to tear the flesh from his bones, she was at such a screaming pitch of arousal.

Then she tightened convulsively in the first notes of release. His control cracked. He moved faster, the bed squeaking beneath them. She didn't care about anything but the purposeful thrusting that was driving her so close to the edge she was ready to scream with agony. Anticipation. Craven demand for satisfaction. Her thighs clamped around his waist and her arms clung to his shoulders. She was ready to beg.

He made a feral noise and pushed his hand under her tailbone, tilted her hips and struck a fresh spear of sensation through her, throwing her soaring off the cliff, her climax so profound she opened her mouth in a soundless scream, gripped in the paroxysm of complete ecstasy.

While his own body clenched and shuddered over her. Within her. His eruption became an intimate complement to her own, extending her pulses of pleasure so they simply held each other tight, letting the convulsions, the clenches and twitches and fading pulses of aftershock wash over them again and again.

CHAPTER SEVEN

POPPY WOKE DAZED and tender and alone. She sat up, looking for the baby monitor without finding it. It was daylight. The clock said 9:10 a.m.

She looked at the pillow, but even though both of their suitcases were still standing near the foot of the bed, his pillow was undented.

After making love, they had dozed, caught their breath, then made love again. She had a vague recollection of him leaving after that. She hadn't been able to move or even ask where he was going, but apparently he hadn't come back.

Which put a hollow ache in her chest.

Waking alone felt like a terrible start to their marriage. She had thought his passion meant he wanted her. After soaring through the heavens most of the night, she was juddering back to earth, landing hard as she realized he might want her physically, but that was all.

She put on yesterday's clothes and scowled at her pale face in the mirror. Her hair stuck out like shocks of lightning and she couldn't even get a brush through it. She wanted to check on Lily before she showered, though. She grabbed the mass together in a fat ponytail and walked out in search.

A glance into the room where Lily had slept showed the single bed had also been slept in. Her heart panged at the evidence he hadn't had insomnia. He'd preferred to sleep apart from her. Were they to have a marriage like his parents? One based on "shared values"?

They shared two things—a child and passion. It might be enough to build on, but relationships were a two-way street. If he was going to put literal walls between them, they didn't stand a chance.

Telling herself this was only Day One and she needed to give this time, she continued to the lounge.

She found Rico on the sofa, reading his tablet and nursing a coffee. Lily was on a blanket nearby, working her way through a box of unfamiliar toys. She gave a scolding cry when Poppy appeared and held up her arms, demanding a cuddle where she rested her head on Poppy's shoulder while Poppy rubbed her back. Lily was a resilient little thing, but they both needed the reassurance of a hug after facing all these recent changes.

"Why didn't you wake me when she got up?" She hid behind their daughter, mouth muffled against Lily's hair while she kept her lashes lowered, too nervous of what she might see in his eyes to meet his gaze.

"I wanted to let you sleep." His voice rasped across her nerve endings, waking her to sensual memory without any effort at all. Maybe it was the words, the suggestion that he had worn her out—which he had.

"She's had toast and banana," he added. "The housekeeper is making us a proper breakfast. It should be ready shortly."

"I could have cooked."

"We pay her to do it."

Lily pointed at the toys and Poppy set her down to continue playing.

"Thank you." Poppy hugged herself. "I'm not used to anyone getting up with her. Gran could keep an eye on her if my back was turned, but Lily was getting too heavy and fast for her to do much else."

"A potential nanny is meeting us in Valencia. You can look forward to sleeping in every day, if you want to."

"I can look after my own daughter." Especially if she wasn't working. That part was bothering her. Her income had been piecemeal with a small, but reliable paycheck from working part-time at the bus depot and occasional top-ups with school portraits and the odd headshot or boudoir shoot. Now she was reliant on Rico. It was way too much like being a burden. Again.

"There will be many occasions when you'll have to be at my side without her. You'll want the consistency of a regular caregiver."

"What do you mean, 'many'?" She finally looked at him, but he only raised his brows in mild surprise.

"Do you need a paper bag to breathe into? Why are you looking so shocked?"

"Because I thought you would go to work and maybe I'd find a job around your hours and we would eat dinner together, watch TV and go to bed like normal people."

He sipped his coffee. As he set it aside, he revealed a mouth curled into a mocking smile.

"This is my normal. Whether you work is entirely

your choice. I know many power couples in which both spouses hold down high-profile positions."

Maybe not the bus depot, then.

"I also know many women, including my mother and Sorcha, who make a career of running a household, planning charity fund-raisers and attending events in support of their husbands."

"How charmingly old-fashioned." She meant antiquated and patriarchal.

The deepening of his smirk told her he knew perfectly what she was saying.

"As I say, my normal. If you do intend to work, we'll definitely need a nanny. At least that much is settled."

Poppy wanted to stamp her foot in frustration. She couldn't go after him about doing his share on the child-care front, though. Not when he'd gotten up with Lily on his first morning with her, letting Poppy sleep in.

"I've booked a stylist to come by in an hour or so." His gaze went to her bare, unpolished toes and came back to her electrocuted hair.

Her hand went to the seam in her distressed jeans. "Why?"

"I'm introducing you and Lily to my parents this evening."

"I've met them," she reminded with an urge to laugh, because it was such a gross overstatement. She had stood behind Darna on three occasions without garnering even a glance as Darna had nodded understanding of the duquesa's orders. Rico's father had once held out a dirty glass as she walked by, not even looking at her, let alone thanking her for taking it.

"The press release will go out while we're there. I

expect a few photographers will gather at the gate. You need to look the part."

"Paparazzi are going to want photos of *me*? Really?" She crossed one foot over the other and hugged herself. "How are your parents going to react to that?"

"By presenting a united front. That's why we're having dinner there."

"*Presenting* a united front," she repeated. "That tells me how sincerely they'll welcome me at their dining table, doesn't it? And then what?" She thought of all the gossip sites where she'd seen pictures of him with Faustina, then snapshots of his grim expression as he put her in the ground. "Rico, I can't do this," she realized with sudden panic. "I'm not prepared. You know I'm not."

"That's why I've called a stylist. You'll be fine."

To her horror, tears of frustration and yes, fear, pressed into her eyes, but the housekeeper came in and invited them to sit down to the breakfast she had prepared.

Poppy had to suck up her misgivings and let her new life unfold.

"You look beautiful," Rico said sincerely. "If you could drop the wide-eyed terror, you'd be flawless."

His attempt to lighten Poppy's mood fell flat.

Her stylist had understood perfectly the effect Rico wanted and had spent a good portion of the day achieving it.

Poppy wore a bronze slip with a lace overlay embroidered with copper roses. It was simple and feminine, sophisticated yet held a decidedly innocent flair. Her hair had been meticulously coaxed into tamer waves then gathered into a "casual" chignon suitable for a low-key dinner with family. Her makeup was all natural tones and her heels were a conservative height.

By the time he'd offered the jewelry he'd bought her, she'd looked like a dog that had been at the groomers so long she'd lost her will to live.

Now the fresh-faced nanny, who couldn't be more than a year over Poppy's age, suggested carrying Lily into the villa so their daughter wouldn't stain or snag Poppy's dress.

Rico agreed and Poppy shot him a glance of betrayal then fell into step beside him, mouth pouted.

Her angry dismay plucked at his conscience like a sour note on a string. He kept telling himself that she had already seen the workings of his family from an insider's perspective. None of this should be a surprise to her. And this was how it *was*. He couldn't pretend their life would be anything different. That would be a lie.

Even so, he sensed she'd put up a wall between them and it rankled. Which was hypocritical on his part because he'd taken steps to withdraw from her last night, after their lovemaking had left him in ruins.

What should have been a sensual celebration of a convenient marriage had become a conflagration that had turned him inside out. He had been right back to that interminable family dinner after his encounter with Poppy two years ago. Cesar and Sorcha had turned up— an engagement Rico had completely failed to recall had been scheduled. They'd eaten in polite silence while his mother had stiffly come to terms with Rico's wedding being off. She had already been floating the names of alternatives and a timeline for courtship.

Rico had sat on the pin of a land mine, wanting to rise from the table and go after Poppy. He hadn't seen a way in which he could even sustain an affair with her, though. As he'd eaten what might have been sawdust, facts had been reiterated about his father's prospects in the next election. The importance of certain alliances had been regurgitated.

Rico wasn't so shallow as to value money and appearances and power over all other things, but he understood how possessing those things allowed him and his family to live as comfortably as they did. All the actions he took were about them, never only himself.

So, even though his engagement had been broken, even though he was sexually infatuated with his mother's maid, another bride would be slotted into place very quickly. The show must go on.

There had been some relief in living up to those expectations, too. As earth-shattering as his encounter with Poppy had been, he had instinctively recognized how dangerous that sort of passion was. How easily exposure to a woman who provoked such a deep response within him could dismantle him. Turn him against the best interests of his family and even impact him at a deeper level. A place even more vulnerable than the injuries of bruised ego and broken trust that his first wife had inflicted on him.

That premonition was playing out. His daughter had been the excuse, but the lure of Poppy had drawn him halfway around the world. He hadn't waited for tests to prove they should marry. He had accomplished it with haste and dragged her back here as quickly as he could.

Last night had proved to him they were still a volatile combination. Afterward, he'd felt so disarmed, so *satisfied* with having blown up his own life, he had had to leave her to put himself back together.

If Lily hadn't awakened a few hours later, he might very well have succumbed to temptation and crawled into bed with Poppy again.

He couldn't let her have that kind of power over him. That was what he kept telling himself. He had to keep control of himself or there would only be more scandal and disruption.

But he loathed that stiff look on her face.

It was too much like the ones on his parents' faces as they entered the small parlor where Faustina had once thrown down a vase like a gauntlet.

He ground his teeth, wishing at least Pia was here, chronically shy and uncomfortable as she might be. His sister was off studying snails or some other mollusk in the Galápagos Islands, however. Cesar had taken Sorcha and the boys to visit Sorcha's family in Ireland. There was nothing to soften this hard, flat evening for Poppy.

"My father, Javiero Montero y Salazar, Excelentísimo Senor Grandeza de España, and my mother, La Reina, the Duque and Duquesa of Castellón. You both remember Poppy." He wasn't trying to be facetious, but it came out that way.

His mother smiled faintly. "Welcome back."

Poppy was so pale he reached for her hand. It was ice-cold.

She delicately removed it from his hold and gave Lily's dress a small tug and drew the girl's finger from her mouth, smiling with tender pride. "This is Lily."

His parents both took a brief look at their granddaughter and nodded as if to say, *Yes, that is a baby.*

"A room has been prepared upstairs," Rico's mother said to the nanny, dismissing her and Lily in a blink.

The light in Poppy's eyes dimmed. It struck Rico like a kick in the gut.

This is who they *are*, he wanted to tell her. There was no use wishing for anything different, but he could still hear the thread of hurt and rejection in her tone as she had told him about her parents never coming back for her.

He wanted to take her hand again, reassure her, but at his mother's invitation, she lowered to perch on an antique wing chair, hands folded demurely in her lap.

Champagne was brought in; congratulations were offered. Poppy's hand shook and he neatly slid a coaster under her glass before she set it on the end table.

His mother very tellingly said, "I imagine you're still settling in. We'll move into the dining room right away so the baby can have an early night."

This evening would *not* be a drawn-out affair. The rush was a slight, but Rico didn't want to subject Poppy to their company any longer than necessary so he didn't take issue with it.

The first course arrived and Poppy tried offering a friendly smile at the butler. It was countered with an impassive look that made her cheerful expression fall away. She blinked a few times.

The staff would talk to her when his parents weren't around, he wanted to tell her. This was how they were expected to act with guests and she shouldn't take it as a rejection.

His father cleared his throat.

Poppy glanced at him with apprehension. Rico briefly held his own breath, but his father only asked Rico about the progress he'd made on some alloy research.

Annoyed, Rico was forced to turn his attention to answering him, which left his mother to make conversation with Poppy.

"I'm told you enjoy photography, Poppy. How did your interest come about?"

Poppy shot him a look, but he hadn't provided that tidbit. This was also who his mother was. She would ferret out any item suitable for small talk that would avoid addressing more sensitive horrors like the fact Rico had messed with the maid, had an illegitimate child and brought them into the villa as "family."

Poppy spoke with nervous brevity. "When I was ten, my grandfather asked me to help him clean the basement. We came across his father's equipment. My great-grandfather was a freelance photographer for newspapers."

"What type of newspapers?" his mother asked sharply.

"Mother." Rico quit listening to his father and gave the women his full attention.

"The national ones," Poppy replied warily, sensing disapproval. "Sports, mostly. The odd royal visit or other big event. I was intrigued so my grandfather closed in a space and showed me how the development process worked."

"You should have shown me." Rico was ridiculously pleased to hear she shared the same spark of curiosity that had drawn him into chemical engineering.

"I haven't used it in years. We quickly realized the cost of chemicals and paper wasn't sustainable. I switched to digital photography."

"Metol or hydroquinone," Rico's father said in one of his stark interjections, as though he'd retrieved a file from the dusty basement of his own mind. "Sodium carbonate and sodium sulfite for proper pH and delay of oxidation. Thiosulfate to fix it. None are particularly expensive, but there's no market for the premixed solutions. We got out of it years ago."

"Only niche artists are using them, I imagine," Poppy murmured.

"Speaking of art," his mother said with an adept pivot from boring science. "I'm attending an opening in Paris next month. I imagine you'll be decorating a house very soon. What sort of pieces might you be looking for?"

Poppy looked as though a bus was bearing down on her.

"It's early days, Mother," Rico cut in. "We'll talk more about that another time."

At this point he was only looking as far as getting through this evening.

The meal passed in a blur of racking her brains for the names of Canadian politicians who might have said something brilliant or stupid lately and trying to look as if she knew how to eat quail in gazpacho. Poppy was infinitely relieved when they left and went to Rico's Valencian penthouse.

This wasn't a family property. It was his own home, purchased after Faustina had died. It was luxurious and in a prime location with a pool and a view, but it was a surprisingly generic space, tastefully decorated in masculine tones yet completely without any stamp of his personality.

She dismissed the nanny, put Lily to bed herself, then moved into the bedroom to kick off her heels and sigh with exhaustion.

Rico came in with a nightcap for each of them.

She immediately grew nervous. It had been a long, trying day, one that had started out with a rebuff when she'd woken alone. That sense of foreboding had grown worse as his stylist had spent hours turning her into some kind of show pony.

She suspected she had disappointed anyway. As he set down his own drink and loosened his tie, she had a sick, about-to-be-fired feeling in her stomach, much like the one she'd had when she'd lost her first babysitting job after accidentally letting the hamster out of its cage.

"Well?" she prompted, trying to face the coming judgment head-on.

"I thought it went well."

She strangled on a laugh. "Are you kidding? I've never spent a more horrendous two hours and twenty-three minutes in my life."

"You were there, then." He shrugged out of his jacket.

"Don't make jokes, Rico." She stared at him, but he wasn't laughing. Uncertain, she asked, "Was that really a normal dinner for you? The way it's been your whole life?" She had thought her own mother awful for calling in lame efforts at nurturing with insincere apologies from afar. His parents had displayed zero remorse as they had openly dismissed his newfound daughter.

"Don't be ridiculous," he said with scathing sarcasm. "I didn't sit at that table until I was twelve. Children are invited to the dining room when they know how to eat quietly and speak only when spoken to."

She thought of the way Lily squealed and slapped her tray and wore more food than she ate. But even Gran with her old-fashioned ideals about child-rearing had always insisted that dinner was a time for the whole family to come together.

"Why are they *like* that?"

He stripped his tie and threw it away with a sigh. "My father is a scientific genius. He only speaks logic and rational debate. Emotion has no effect on him. It's one of the reasons he makes a genuinely good politician. He reads and considers policy on its own merit, not worrying about his popularity or future prospects. Mother was born with a title, but no money. She had to marry it and prove she was worth the investment. Having brought herself up this far, she refuses to backslide. And, after thirty-five years of my father's lack of sentiment, she's abandoned any herself."

"That sounds so empty. Is she happy?"

"They set out with specific goals and achieved them. They are content, which is the standard to which we've been taught to aspire."

She searched his expression. "And you're *content* with that?"

"Why wouldn't I be? My life is extremely comfortable." He peeled off his shirt, revealing his gorgeous chest and tight abs.

She swallowed and turned away, annoyed with herself for reacting so promptly to the sight of him.

"Is that why you agreed to an arranged marriage the first time? To maintain the status quo?"

"Yes. I was expected to do my part in preserving the life we all enjoy." His voice was suddenly right behind her, surprising her into lifting her gaze to the mirror.

He lightly smoothed his hand across her shoulders, grazing an absent caress against her nape as he ensured no tendrils of hair would catch as he unzipped her.

"How angry are they that Lily and I ruined everything?" She braced herself as she held his gaze. "Be honest. I need to know."

"They don't get angry." He sounded mild, but she thought she caught a flicker of something in his stoic expression.

"What about you? You were angry when you showed up at my door."

"And I wound up telling you something I had sworn to take to my grave. Heightened emotions don't help any situation."

"What does that mean?" With a niggling premonition, she began unpinning her hair, not wanting to remove the gaping dress and be naked when she was beginning to feel defenseless. "I want to fit in, Rico. I want to be a team player and know what to say about decor and houses and all those different people she was talking about. But along with not being prepared to live at this level of wealth, I'm wired for emotion. Don't expect me never to get angry. Or to stop feeling."

His cheek ticked and she could hear the thoughts behind that stiff mask. *Don't expect me to start.*

Which made her angry. Furious that she'd spent every minute since he'd shown up on her doorstep having her emotions bombarded until they were right there, under the thin surface of her skin, tender and raw, while he had somehow used tonight's endurance event of a dinner to shore up his shields so he was more withdrawn than ever.

"That's what you want, though, isn't it?" she realized, appalled to see her shimmering nascent hopes for deeper intimacy disappearing faster than she could conjure them. "You want me to learn not to care. To feel nothing. Certainly I shouldn't aspire to happiness, should I?"

"Happiness is achieved by keeping your expectations realistic. That's a proven fact."

It was such a cynical thing to say, it physically hurt her to hear it.

"What about desire?" In a small stab at getting through to him, she let the dress fall off her arms. She stepped out of it before tossing it onto the foot of the bed. "Do you want me to quit feeling *that*?"

"That's physical." He let his gaze rake slowly down her pale form from shoulder to thighs, jaw hardening along with his voice. "And you're starting a fight for no reason."

"I'm sorry you feel that way," she said facetiously. "I'm going to shower. Would you like to join me? Yesterday it was one of your many fantasies, but maybe you *feel* different today."

His eye ticked and she knew he was sorry he had ever told her that. Did she feel guilty for using it? Not one bit.

She slid her panties down and left them on the floor.

It was a bold move, one far beyond her experience level. If he left her to shower alone, she would probably drown herself in there, but she desperately wanted to prove to both of them that she had some kind of effect on him. Some means of reaching through that armor of his.

She moved into the bathroom and stepped into the marble-tiled stall, bigger than the porch on Gran's bungalow.

He came into the bathroom as the steam began to gather around her. He dimmed the light so the gilded space became golden and moody and he stripped off his pants.

She watched him, reacting with an internal clench when she saw he was aroused.

When he came into the shower, she lost some of her moxie and turned her face into the rain of warm water from the sunflower head above her.

His cool hands settled on her hips and his thumbs dug lightly into the tops of her butt cheeks. "You have a gorgeous ass."

"Even with the dimples?" Her heartbeat was unsteady.

"Especially with." He took hold of the wet mass of her hair, holding her head tipped back while he scraped his teeth against the side of her neck. "I will always accept this invitation, Poppy. But you had better know what you're inviting."

She gasped. The sensations he was causing were cataclysmic. All her senses came alive. He settled his cool body against her back, his chest hair lightly brushing before the warm water sealed them together. His hard shaft pressed into the small of her back and her buttocks tightened in excited reaction. Her breasts grew heavy, her loins tingled. The humid air became too heavy to breathe and her bones melted like wax in the sun.

Blindly she shot a hand out to the slick wall and wound up leaning both hands there while her hips instinctively tipped with invitation.

"What are you trying to prove?" he growled, slapping one hand beside her own on the wall.

Nothing. She was reacting, pure and simple.

He briefly covered her like any male mounting his mate and his teeth sank lightly against her nape again. His free hand splayed across her abdomen, then roamed her wet skin to cup her breast.

In a sudden move, he pulled her upright and spun her so the world tilted around her. She found the hard tiles against her shoulders. His knees nudged between hers and his thighs pinned hers. He bracketed her head between his forearms and touched his nose to hers before he claimed the kiss she was starving for.

He held nothing back, wet mouth sliding across hers with carnal greed, slaking her thirst after this arid day. She flowered. She opened and ran with dewy nectar. She unfurled her arms around him and twined them across his back, lifted her knee up to his hip and invited him into her center. Rocked and tried to make him lose control the way she continued to abandon hers.

"Let's talk about your fantasies, hmm?" His hands caught her wrists and pinned them beside her head while his tongue slithered down her neck and licked into the hollow at the base of her throat. "What do you want?"

He drew back slightly and gazed down on her with unabashed hunger.

"Rico." She turned her wrist in his grasp and shifted with self-consciousness. Her nipples stood up with blatant, stinging arousal. She brought her foot back down to the floor, but his feet were still between hers.

"Did you ever touch yourself and imagine it was me?" He dropped one hand and drew his fingertip through her swollen folds, looking down again as he languidly caressed her. "Did you want to *feel* my hand here?"

She was immediately disoriented, glad for the hard wall at her back as she rose into his touch and draped her arm across his shoulders, seeking balance.

"Tell me," he commanded between kisses. "Tell me or I'll stop."

"Yes," she gasped.

He rewarded her by bending to suck one nipple, then the other, driving further spikes of pleasure into that place he continued to tease. A keening noise sounded and she realized it was her, unable to express her agonizing climb of desire in any other way.

Now he was on his knees, licking at her. Splaying her and gently probing and circling and driving her to the brink of madness. She realized distantly that she had her hands fisted in his wet hair, that she had completely abandoned herself to him. To the exquisite pleasure he relentlessly inflicted upon her. Within moments, cries of ecstasy tore from her throat, filling the steamy, hollow chamber.

He ran his mouth all over her thighs and stomach, soft bites that claimed his right to do so as she stood there weakly, heart palpitating, breath still splintered.

He stood and snapped the water off, staring at her while she leaned helpless and overwhelmed. Outdone.

Meeting his gaze was like looking into the sun, painful in its intensity. Painful in how blind and exposed she felt, but she couldn't look away. Couldn't pretend he hadn't peeled her down to her core until she was utterly at his mercy.

While he remained visibly aroused, but in complete control.

"The way we make each other feel is a hell of a lot more than many couples have. Recognize that. Be satisfied with it."

She wasn't and never would be.

But when he held out a hand, she let him balance her as she stepped out onto the mat. He dried her off and took her to his bed, where he satisfied her again and again and again.

CHAPTER EIGHT

Rico woke in the guest bed he'd been using all week and listened, thinking Lily must be stirring. He ought to be sleeping more heavily considering the quantity and quality of sex he was enjoying, but his radar remained alert to the other occupants of his penthouse.

He listened, thought he must be imagining things, started to drift off then heard the burble of a video chat being connected. The volume lowered.

He rose, already wearing boxers in case he had to go to Lily. His door was cracked and it swung open silently, allowing him to hear Poppy's hushed voice reassuring her grandmother.

"No, everything's fine. I couldn't sleep and thought this would be a good chance to chat without a baby crawling all over me. How are you settling in?"

"Same as I told you yesterday," her grandmother said wryly. "You're the one with the gadabout life. What have you been up to?"

He stood and listened to Poppy relay that the nanny had taken Lily for a walk today while she had pored over properties with a real estate agent. He'd been going in to work each day, but taking her out at night. She mentioned this evening's cocktail party where he had introduced her to some of his top executives and their wives.

She made it sound as though she had had the time of her life when she'd actually been petrified and miserable, not that she'd been obvious about it. He knew how she behaved when she was comfortable, though. She laughed with Lily and traded wry remarks with her grandmother.

That woman was making fewer and fewer appearances when she was with him, however, which was beginning to niggle at him. He glimpsed her when they made love. She held nothing back in bed, but tonight she had disappeared quickly after they had wrung untold pleasure from each other. She had rolled away and her voice had pulled him from his postcoital doze.

"Will you check on Lily as you go?"

"Of course." He had told himself he was glad she'd kept him from falling asleep beside her. His will to leave her each night grew fainter and fainter, but staying seemed the even weaker action. He wasn't Lily, needing his cuddle bear clutched in his arm in order to drift off.

He wasn't sure what he had expected from this marriage. When contemplating his first to Faustina, he had anticipated following his parents' example. Like his siblings, he had been raised to keep his emotions firmly within a four-point-five and a four-point-seven. Not a sociopath, but only a few scant notches above one. He had never been a man of grand passions anyway and had been comfortable with the idea of a businesslike partnership with his spouse.

That certainly hadn't worked out. Given the betrayal

and drama he'd suffered at Faustina's hands, he had wanted this marriage to conform to that original ideal.

It didn't. Poppy didn't. He kept telling himself she would get used to this life, but seeing her natural exuberance dim by the day was eating at him. He didn't know what to do about it, though. This was their reality.

"Dinner will be served soon. I have to start making my way or it will be cold by the time I arrive," Eleanor said with a papery chuckle.

"Okay. I love you. I miss you." She ended the call, but didn't rise.

He was growing cold standing there, but didn't go back to bed. He could see her shoulders over the back of the sofa. They rose slightly as she sighed deeply. Her breath caught with a jag. She sniffed.

A terrible swoop of alarm unbalanced him. The embarrassed moment of walking in on something personal struck, yet he couldn't turn away and leave her to it.

As her shoulders began to shake and she ducked her head into her hands, beginning to weep in earnest, a rush of something indefinable came over him. A sharp, shimmering, deeply uncomfortable *ache* gripped him. It was so excruciating, it made him want to close himself in the guest room and wait for it to pass.

But he couldn't turn his back on her while she was like that. A far stronger compulsion pushed him down the hall toward her.

"Poppy." Her name scratched behind his breastbone. At some level he understood he was responsible for this misery she was exhibiting. He had some scattered thoughts of all that he was providing her, but he knew she didn't care about those things. She was a complex, emotional creature and it struck him how completely ill-equipped he was to handle that.

She lifted a face tracked with silver and made an anguished noise, clearly mortified that he was seeing her this way. Again he thought to give her privacy, but he couldn't let her suffer alone. This was his fault. That much he understood and it weighed very heavily on him.

"Come." He gathered her up, the silk of her pajamas cool against his naked chest.

"I don't want to make love, Rico. I want to go *h-home*." The break in her voice rent another hole in him.

"Shh." He carried her to the bed where he'd left her a few hours before and crawled in with her to warm both of them. He told himself that was what this was, even though the feel of her against him had the effect of pressing a cut together. It didn't fix it, but it eased some of the pain. Slowed the bleeding and calmed the distress. "It's okay," he murmured.

"No, it's not." Her words were angry, despairing sobs. "I'm so homesick I hurt all the time. At least the last time I was stuck here, I made friends, but no one will talk to me."

"Who's refusing to speak to you?" he asked with sharp concern.

"*Everyone.* The staff. They only ask me if I want something, never joke or make me feel like they like me. They're only being polite because you pay them to be."

"That's not true." He suddenly glimpsed how isolated she must be in her new position and cursed himself for not recognizing it would be so acute.

"I have nothing in common with *your* friends. They

talk too fast for me to even understand them. You're Lily's father and I want her to know you, Rico. I know I have to stay here for her sake, but why does the nanny get to take her for a walk while I have to go to stupid parties? I hate it here. I hate it so much."

"Shh," he soothed, closing his hand around the tight fist on his chest and kissing her hard knuckles. "This is going to be an adjustment for all of us."

"How is this an adjustment for *you*? You're completely unaffected! I can't do this, Rico. I *can't*."

His neck was wet and her hair stuck to the tear tracks, keeping that fissure in him stinging. He rubbed her back, trying to calm her while her desolation shredded his ability to remain detached.

There are some realities that are not worth crying about, he had told Mateo a few weeks ago. He'd been taught to believe no one would care, but he *did* care. Not the generic regard of one human for another, but a deeper, more frightening feeling he didn't know how to process.

Everything in him warned that he should distance himself, but he couldn't ignore her pain.

He knew what he had to do. It would cost him, but he would do it. This anguish of hers was more than he could bear.

Poppy woke from the dense fog of a deep sleep to hear Rico's morning voice rasping on the baby monitor.

"We'll let Mama sleep this morning."

The transmission clicked off, but as Poppy rolled onto her back and straightened her limbs, she discovered the warm patch beside her on the bed.

He had stayed the night? She was chagrined that he'd caught her in the middle of a pity party, but she hadn't been able to hold it in any longer. She had tried, honestly tried not to care about all of those things.

She did care, though. She was lonely and out of her depth. Her only friend was the daughter she had to share with a nanny who adored her, but whom Poppy was growing to resent by the day.

She threw her arm over her eyes, trying not to spiral back into melancholy. They had appointments to view properties today, she recalled. She could hardly wait to have a bigger house to get lost in, and more staff to treat her like some kind of visiting foreign official.

A few hours later, she was beside Rico as he drove a shiny new SUV up the coast. Poppy had understood the property agent would be driving them to view potential homes, but she didn't complain. It felt nice to be just the three of them for a change.

"You should have told me to bring my camera," she murmured, quite sure she would have a kink in her neck from swiveling her attention between the sunny coastal beaches and the craggy hillocks interspersed with picturesque ancient villages. "I'm used to staring at wheat and sunflower fields on long drives."

"Think about what sort of space you want for your studio as we look at potential homes. I'm sure a darkroom could be built into just about any corner of a house, but give some thought to how that will fit with our day-to-day living."

"A darkroom! I told you, that's expensive." She wouldn't mind a studio, though.

"As it turns out, I happen to have money. If that's

where your interest lies, pursue it." He turned into a private road that lacked a for sale sign and wound through a vineyard.

"There's no money in photography." Not the sort his level of society expected a woman to make if she was going to pursue a career over homemaking.

"I don't expect you to make money. Do it for yourself. Be an artist."

"You're going to be my patron? Don't pander to me just because I acted like Lily last night." She spoke to the window to hide her embarrassment.

"I'm not. I want you to be happy."

That swung her around because no, he didn't. He had specifically told her to settle.

He might have recalled that conversation, too. His expression grew stiff as he braked and threw the vehicle into Park.

Poppy glanced around. "I don't see the agent."

"It's not for sale. This is Cesar and Sorcha's home."

"Why didn't you tell me we were meeting them today?" She glanced down at the pantsuit she'd put on hoping to look the part of a rich man's wife viewing villas as if she knew what such a man needed.

"You look perfect." He stepped out. "They don't know we're coming so they'll be equally casual."

"Why don't they know we're coming?" she asked as he came around while she was opening the back door to get Lily.

"You're supposed to wait for me to come around and open your door for you," he chided.

"I know how to open my own car door. I also know how to look after my own daughter." She brushed him away from trying to reach in, then grunted as she released Lily and took her weight, dragging her out. "What I don't know is how I'm supposed to behave when you drop me on relatives who don't know I'm coming."

Lily squinted as Poppy drew her from the car and buried her face in Poppy's neck.

"I'll keep her," Poppy murmured as Rico tried to take her. It was pathetic to hide behind her daughter, but she needed Lily's sturdy warmth to bolster her.

A maid let them in and the view took her breath as they moved from the foyer to a front room where huge picture windows overlooked the Mediterranean.

"Tío!" A young boy of about four ran in wearing red trunks and nothing else.

Rico picked him up. "You remember Enrique? Cesar's eldest?" he asked Poppy.

"You've grown," she murmured. *"Bon dia,"* she added in the small amount of Valencian dialect she knew the family used among themselves.

"Say hello to Poppy and Lily," Rico prompted him.

"Hola. ¿Cómo estás?" Enrique asked with a confidence beyond his years.

Rico gave Enrique's backside a pat. "You're wet. How are you swimming? It's too early in the year."

"I got in to here." Enrique touched his belly button.

"And now you're eating your lunch," Cesar said, strolling in wearing crisp linen pants and a shirt he was buttoning. He nodded to send Enrique back outside.

This was the most relaxed Poppy had ever seen Cesar, but he still projected a chilly formality not unlike

the duque and duquesa. In fact, he greeted his brother
with a look that bordered on hostile.

"You've lost your drop-in privileges with my family." It was a very civil, *Get the hell out.*

Because of her and Lily? Because they were a stain
on the family name?

With a muted noise of distress, Poppy closed her
arms protectively around Lily and looked to the door.

Rico glanced at her with concern then scowled at his
brother. "Now you've gone and hurt *my* wife's feelings."

Cesar frowned at her. His gaze dropped to Lily and
his frown eased.

"Whose feelings?" Sorcha came up behind her husband. She was blond and effortlessly beautiful in a
summer dress with a forget-me-not print. Daywear di-
amonds sparkled in her ears.

"Poppy." Her surprise warmed into a welcoming
smile that sent the first trickles of relief through Poppy's defensively stiff limbs. "And here's Lily." Sorcha
came right up to them and gave Lily's elbow a tickle.
She tilted her head to meet the gaze Lily shyly kept
tucked into Poppy's neck.

"Will you come see me? Let me introduce you to
your cousins?" Sorcha held out her hands. "They'll
share their lunch with you. Are you hungry?"

Lily went to her. Who could resist the promise of
food and the warm lilt of an Irish accent?

"Thank you, darling. That's quite a compliment."
Sorcha cuddled her close, then glanced at Rico. Her
tone dropped to permafrost. "*You* can wait in the car."

"I deserve that," Rico said with tense sincerity. "I
regret the hurt I caused you. I wouldn't interrupt your

weekend, but Poppy needs you, Sorcha. Will you help her? If not for me, then for her sake and Lily's? Please? I know how you feel about family."

"That's below the belt!" Sorcha tucked her chin, looked as though she wanted to punish him further, then gave a little sigh. "Since you've brought me this *very* precious gift—" She snuggled Lily more securely onto her hip. "I will forgive you. *This one time.*" She smiled at Poppy without reserve. "And of course I'll help you any way I can. I would have called you later this week." Another dark look toward Rico. "I didn't want to wait until our gala next month. I'm so glad you're here. Come join us."

"What did you do?" Poppy hissed at Rico as he fell into step beside her.

"Said something that doesn't bear repeating." To her surprise, he took her hand and wove their fingers together, giving her a little squeeze. "But Sorcha knows what you're up against. Let her be your guide."

It struck her that this had been hard for him. She doubted it was in his nature to ask for help any more than it was in hers. He and Cesar were obviously on rocky ground, but he had invaded their family time for her sake.

"Please tell Chef we're four adults and three children for lunch now," Sorcha said easily to the hovering butler.

"Champagne," Cesar added, holding Sorcha's chair as she lowered with Lily and kept her in her lap. "Boys, this is your cousin, Lily. Can you say hello and welcome her and Auntie Poppy to the family?"

Enrique began to giggle. He pointed his fork at Cesar. "That's Papi."

Poppy smiled. "Maybe you'll have to call this one Tío Mama now." She thumbed toward Rico as he helped her with her own chair.

Enrique nearly tumbled out of his, laughing at the absurdity as he repeated, "Tío Mama."

Poppy bit her lip with remorse, suspecting she'd released a genie that wouldn't go easily back into its bottle. She called on one of Gramps's favorite tricks for getting through to a child who had a case of the sillies. She leaned over and spoke very softly so Enrique would have to quiet to hear her.

"My grandfather used to tell me it was okay to tease your family with a funny name when you were alone, but you have to remember to be respectful when you're with others. Will you be able to do that?"

Enrique nodded and clamped his smile over his fork, eyes full of mischief as he looked at Rico.

"Sorry," Poppy mouthed as she caught Sorcha's amused glance. "You have a very beautiful home," she added, glancing at the placid pool and the profusion of spring blooms surrounding it.

"Thank you. We're extremely happy here." Sorcha looked to her husband for confirmation, but her smile reflected more than happiness. Even two years ago it had been obvious to Poppy these two were deeply in love.

While Rico wore his customarily circumspect expression.

"I want one of those," Cesar informed Sorcha with smoky warning, nodding at Lily where she sat contentedly in Sorcha's lap, fist clenched around a spear of juicy peach.

"Let's keep this one." Sorcha pressed her smile to the top of Lily's head. "She's exactly what we've been thinking of."

"We should probably try making our own before we resort to stealing."

"Picky, picky. But if you insist, I'll have my people talk to your people. Schedule a one-on-one for further discussion."

"Really?" Rico drawled of the flirty banter. "In front of the children?"

"They've walked in on worse," Cesar muttered, rising as the butler arrived with the champagne. "Learn to lock doors," he advised while Sorcha looked to the sky.

The lunch passed with easy chatter and the wiping of sticky fingers.

"I'm so glad Rico brought you today," Sorcha said later, after a travel cot had been found for Lily and she'd been put down for her afternoon nap while the men took the boys into the vineyard. Sorcha sobered. "I'm very glad he went looking for you. Are you angry with me?"

"For telling him? No." Poppy crossed her arms. "I'd been thinking about doing it. Things were complicated at home so I put it off, but it's all worked out." For Gran and Lily. Her? Not so much.

"I'm sorry for interfering. I know how hard that decision can be, but I couldn't let him miss out on Lily. He shut right down after Faustina. My heart broke clean in half for him. I'm so happy to see the way he's taken to her."

Poppy nodded dumbly, shielding her gaze with a glance toward the floor so Sorcha couldn't read the bigger story in her eyes.

"He wants to be a good father. I was afraid of... Well, nothing, I guess," Poppy admitted ruefully. When it came to Rico's feelings for Lily, she had every confidence their bond would only continue to grow.

"But?" Sorcha prompted.

"It's hard." Her throat thickened and she felt tears pressing behind her eyes. "This is all really hard. Rico and I don't have what you and Cesar did. The years of familiarity and caring."

Sorcha choked on a laugh. "Do I make it look like it was easy for us to get where we are? That is quite a compliment and good on me for selling that image, but no. I assure you that what we have was achieved through blood, sweat and tears. Years of loving my boss, if you want the truth. Which is how and why Enrique came about," she added dryly. "But like the rest of his family, Cesar had kicked his heart under the sofa and forgotten about it. So there will definitely be some heavy lifting required to find Rico's. I'm sorry to tell you that." Sorcha sobered. "But I think it's understandable, given what he's been through."

Sorcha thought she knew what Rico had been through, but he wasn't nursing a broken heart over a lost baby. That was what made this so hard. This wasn't a matter of mending his heart. Or finding it. It was a matter of him wanting to give it to her. And he didn't.

But she only nodded again, protecting the secret Rico had entrusted to her.

"It will all be worth it, Poppy. I promise you," Sorcha said with a squeeze of her arm. "In the meantime, you have me. I'm happy to help you navigate this new world. When I was in your position, I needed help, too.

One of these days we'll go shopping with my friend Octavia. She really does know how to make all of this look easy. For now, let's go to my closet. I'll show you what is absolutely essential. Try not to faint."

Poppy could feel Rico's heart slowing to lazy slams beneath her breast. Her sweating body was splayed bonelessly across him. She knew she ought to move, but he stroked his hand down her spine and traced a circle on her lower back, making her shiver. She clenched around him in a final aftershock of ecstasy.

He turned his head, brushing his lips against her temple in what she took as a signal to move. As she started to pry herself off him, however, his arms closed more firmly around her.

"You can stay right here all night," he murmured lazily.

"Don't you want to go to the guest room?"

His arms dropped way from her. She rolled off him.

"Do you want me to?" All the indolent warmth disappeared from his tone.

"No." Her voice was barely audible. "But why are you staying? Because you feel sorry for me?"

"No. Why would you think that?"

"You slept with me last night because I was crying."

"I came to bed with you because you were crying. I stayed because I wanted to."

"You didn't want to those other nights?"

A sigh.

"Rico, I keep telling you I've never done this before. This might be how you normally conduct a sexual relationship, but it's not the way I thought marriage was supposed to be."

He bit off a laugh. "This isn't normal. That is the problem, Poppy." He sighed and repeated more somberly, "That is the problem."

Even she, with her limited experience, understood that their passion was exceptional. She had climaxed three times before he'd clasped hard hands to her hips and bucked beneath her, releasing with a jagged cry. She imagined she would have fingerprint bruises under her skin and perversely enjoyed having such an erotic reminder linger for days.

Sex was the easy part. Talking to him, catching him alone and digging up the courage to speak her mind and face difficult answers was the hard part. But she made herself do it.

"Is that why you haven't wanted to sleep with me? Too much sex? Am I being too demanding?"

He blew out a breath that was amused yet exasperated. "No. Although I fear for our lives on a nightly basis."

"Please don't make jokes, Rico. I need to understand. You're the one who said I should keep my expectations realistic. Tell me what realistic looks like because I don't *know*."

"I don't know, either," he admitted after a moment. "That's why I'm not processing this any better than you are. I thought our first time was an anomaly. It wasn't. It's shocking to me how powerfully we affect each other. It doesn't matter that you just spent an hour wringing me out. I want you again. *This isn't normal.*"

"I don't like it, either! I hate that you can snap your fingers and I fall onto my back."

He threw his arm over his eyes and released a ragged, self-deprecating laugh. "I'm the one who was on his back tonight, *corazón*. In case you hadn't noticed."

"It's not very comforting to hear that when you're clearly annoyed by it. Why does it bother you so much that we react this strongly?"

Another silence where she thought he might ignore her question. Finally he admitted, "Passion is dangerous. You know that Cesar was in a car crash some years ago?"

"I only know what's online about it."

"Mmm. Well, it happened after he slept with Sorcha. Directly after. I'd always been aware he had a physical infatuation with her. He didn't give in to base urges any more than I ever thought I would, but that day he did. And he decided the passion they shared was worth blowing up his life for. Mother was pushing him toward an arranged marriage. He went to Diega and told her he wouldn't be asking her to marry him. We don't know if he was overwrought or what, but he skidded off the road after he left her and nearly died."

Part of her panged with empathy. For all his habitual detachment and his recent disagreement with Cesar, Rico was as close to his brother as he was capable of being with anyone. It must have been a terribly worrisome time for him.

But what she also heard was that he really did think the passion between them posed a mortal danger—which equally told her he would hold her at arm's length because of it.

"It's not like I'm doing this on purpose, you know." She rolled away. "I'm a victim, too."

"I know." He followed her, dragging her into the spoon of his body. His voice tickled hotly through her hair. "I'm realizing that uncontrollable passion isn't only a crazed act in a quiet solarium. It's a hunger that refuses to be ignored. I'm not a dependent person, Poppy. I don't like being unable to suppress a craving that isn't a *need*. But I don't see the sense in hurting you, making your assimilation here more difficult because I'm displeased with myself."

It was hardly a declaration of love, but he didn't want to hurt her. It was something. She relaxed deeper into the bend of his body.

"You *are* trying to kill me," he accused, aroused flesh pressed to her backside.

She rolled to face him, stretching against him in a full-body caress.

"Maybe this is our normal."

"Maybe it is. Let's hope we survive it."

Over the next few weeks, Poppy tried to think of this new life as something she could do, rather than something that was being done *to* her. It helped to take the wheel, even if she wasn't sure where she was going. She began reviewing the week's menu with the housekeeper and making additions to the shopping list. She toured several properties and told Rico why she felt some of them wouldn't suit—one had a distinct perfume in the air from the fertilized fields next door, another had rooms that were very closed off from one another.

Rico was dead set on getting a vineyard again and

wanted a pool. Poppy mentioned she'd prefer to be close to Sorcha and Lily's new cousins, to which he said, "Of course. That's the area I'd prefer as well."

She even sat down with the nanny and cleared the air. Poppy admitted this was all new to her and she sometimes felt threatened. Ingrid confessed to feeling she wasn't working hard enough and that's why she kept stepping up, trying to take Lily off her hands. By the time they finished their coffee and cake, they'd worked out the fine points of a long-term contract, both of them relaxed and smiling.

Rico continued dragging her to dinners and networking events, but they went more smoothly after she began taking Sorcha's advice and asking the other wives for recommendations on things like shoe boutiques and hair stylists. Their responses went in one ear and out the other, but at least they seemed to warm to her.

"Let me know when you need an interior designer," one said at one point.

"We have to find a house first. That's proving a challenge," Poppy admitted with genuine frustration.

Twenty minutes of sharing her wish list later, the woman offered a lead on a property that was farther up the coast from Cesar's villa. It wasn't officially on the market, but rumor had it the family needed the money and would accept the right offer.

Rico made a few discreet inquiries and they viewed it the next day.

"I asked Mother if she knew anything about it. She said to be careful when we open the closets," Rico told her as they stepped from the car.

"Skeletons?" Poppy asked, but her smile wasn't only

amusement. Despite the clear signs of age and neglect, a covetous joy rang through her as she took in the stone house, instantly falling in love with the tiled roof and cobbled walkway and darling gated courtyard where she imagined Lily safely playing for hours.

Arches down the side formed a breezeway that wrapped around both levels then overlooked the pool— which needed repair and filling—but it offered a view of the Med that rivaled Cesar and Sorcha's.

Inside, the rooms were desperate for updating. Rico went a step further and said, "This floor plan should be completely reconfigured."

"When are they moving out?" she asked, looking at the furniture draped in sheets.

"They've already taken what they want. We would buy it as is. Mother will know which collectors to call to get rid of most of this."

The scope of the project was enormous, but Poppy was strangely undaunted. In fact, as she discovered a spiral staircase, she excitedly scooted up it. The small rooftop patio looked in every direction for miles and doubled as a sheltered place for intimate dining, utterly charming her.

"We could build out this direction," Rico said, firmly holding on to Lily as he leaned to see off the side. "Perhaps put a guest cottage at the edge of the orange grove."

There were other fruit trees along with a flower garden and a plot off the kitchen for a small vegetable garden, something Poppy's grandparents had always had when she'd been young. It became too much for all of them in later years, but the idea of Lily eating fresh strawberries gave Poppy such a sense of nostalgia and homecoming, she had to swallow a cry of excitement.

"Everything is pollinated by the bee hives in the lower corner," Rico informed her, referring to some notes on his phone. "Apparently we would have our own honey."

Poppy blinked. "Why do I love the idea of keeping bees?"

"I don't know, but I'm intrigued, too."

As they walked out a lower door to view the hives, Rico nodded meaningfully at an exterior door. "Wine cellar."

She knew what he was driving at and shook her head, not wanting to get her hopes up. It was too perfect already. "You'd need it for wine, wouldn't you?"

They entered a big, dim room filled with nearly empty racks. While he glanced at the labels on the handful of bottles left behind, she explored the rear of the cellar, discovering a narrow, windowless room with a low ceiling. A few shelves held empty glass canning jars, suggesting it was a root cellar. A bare bulb was the only light.

Poppy was overwhelmed by what seemed like her birthday, Christmas and every other wish-making day come true. She began arranging her future darkroom. The tubs would go there, the enlarger there. She might cry, she wanted this so badly.

"Am I wrong or is this everything we want?" Rico was carrying Lily and followed Poppy into the narrow room.

This was everything she could ever wish for herself

and her daughter. The only thing she could want after this was her husband's heart.

Her own took an unsteady tumble as she realized how deeply she was yearning for that when every other part of their marriage was slotting into place.

Then he slid his free arm around Poppy and scooped her in for a quick kiss, sending her emotions spinning in another direction.

"Well done."

"We haven't seen the bees yet," she pointed out, wobbling between delirious happiness and intense longing. She worried often that his feelings toward her were still very superficial, but if he was willing to give her this—not just the castle above it, but the space to explore the creativity inside her—surely that meant he cared for her on a deeper level?

"By all means, let's go see the bees," Rico said magnanimously, oblivious to her conflict. "If there are birds to go with them, I'm sold."

"Your daddy thinks he's funny," she told Lily, trying to hide her insecurities.

"Da." Lily poked him in the cheek.

"Dada, yes." He caught her hand in his big one and kissed the point of her tiny finger. "You're as smart as your mama, aren't you?" He kissed Poppy again. "Yes?"

She shakily nodded.

Rico called to make an offer before they left. A week later, Poppy added meetings with interior designers and landscape contractors to her already busy weeks.

Even with those small successes, she was hideously nervous when she finished dressing for the Montero gala. It was an annual event, one that Sorcha and Rico's mother hosted on alternate years. Sorcha had told her what she had spent on her own gown and said, "Match it. This is your debut as a Montero." Then she had sent her favorite designer to the penthouse to consult with Poppy.

Poppy turned in the mirror, feeling like the biggest fraud in the world. Who was that woman? Had she gone too demure? The gown had a high neck and cap sleeves, but the fitted bodice accentuated her curves. The top was a very dramatic gold satin with a floral pattern in carmine and saffron and chestnut. The skirt was an A-line in crimson silk that moved like pouring paint, graceful and luxurious, following her in a small train even after she put on five-inch heels.

Her final touch was an art deco bracelet the stylist had recommended. Poppy, neophyte that she was, hadn't realized the stones were genuine sapphires and topaz and the gold twenty-four karat until the woman had looked up from her phone with excitement.

"Your husband signed off on it. He *does* want to make a statement, doesn't he?"

Poppy had smiled wanly, head swimming at what she'd accidentally bought.

She felt light-headed now as she walked out to the lounge, wondering what he would make of all of this, especially her hair. It had been straightened to within an inch of its life, then a slip of gold ribbon woven through a waterfall braid around her crown.

Rico paused with his drink halfway to his mouth.

She wrinkled her nose and took a slow turn, corkscrewing the skirt around her. *Super sophisticated,*

Poppy. Don't try that again. She gave it a small ruffle to straighten it then stood tall, facing him again.

He hadn't moved.

"What's wrong?" She started searching for the flaw.

"Absolutely nothing." He set aside his drink and came to her, lifted the hand with the bracelet. "You look stunning."

"Really? Thank you. You look really nice, too." A tuxedo, for heaven's sake. She covered her racing heart. "Are we solving an international crime this evening?"

Someone was definitely targeting his heart. Rico almost said it, but it was too close to the truth.

She looked up at him and he read the sensual awareness that was always there between them, ready to be stoked into flame. There was a glow from deeper within her, too. One that was wide and bright and hot, like the sun about to rise behind the mountains and pierce through him.

It was beautiful, making him catch his breath in a strange anticipation, but he made himself break eye contact and move them out the door.

He was still trying to find the middle ground between providing Poppy the supportive attention she craved and maintaining some sort of governance over himself. He recalled chiding his brother once for having affection for Sorcha. *You don't want to admit you have a weakness where she's concerned.*

It was a weakness. Not only of character. It was a vulnerability that could be exploited so he steeled himself against allowing his affections to run too deep.

Even so, he found himself eager to show her off.

He'd never been one of those men who wore a woman like a badge of virility, but apparently, he was capable of being that guy.

The pride swelling his chest and straining the buttons of his pleated shirt wasn't really about how Poppy made *him* look, though. Hell yes, he stood taller when he escorted her into the marquise behind Cesar's villa. But he stuck close to her not to be seen with her, or even to protect her—which he would in a heartbeat if anyone stepped out of line.

No, he was enjoying watching the way her confidence was blossoming. He couldn't change his world to make it easier for her to fit into it, but seeing her grow more comfortable with these trappings pleased him. *Eased* him.

She smiled and greeted couples she had already met and calmly ignored the occasional sideways glance from people still digesting the gossip that Rico Montero had married the mother of his love child.

She even showed less anxiety when they caught up with his parents, exchanging air kisses with his mother and speaking with genuine enthusiasm about the new house. She had clearly been studying at Sorcha's knee because she then asked his mother, "Would you have time next week to review the floor plan with me? Sorcha assures me I'll need the space for entertaining, but I don't want the front room to feel like a barn."

"Email my assistant. I'm sure she can find an hour for you."

It sounded like a slight, but the fact his mother was willing to make time for her was a glowing compliment.

"You're building a darkroom," Rico's father said.

"Yes." Poppy faltered briefly with surprise, then tried her newfound strategy on him. "I wondered if you could advise me on where best to source the chemicals?"

"Your husband can do that."

Rico bit back a sigh. He held Poppy's elbow cradled in his palm and lightly caressed her inner arm while saying, "It's not always clear whether my father is genuinely interested or merely being polite." *Be polite*, he transmitted with a hard look into his father's profile.

"Rico," his mother murmured, her own stern expression reminding him they were all aware of his father's limitations. And they were in *public*.

"I am interested." Rico's father frowned, being misinterpreted. "Keep me apprised of your progress," he ordered Poppy. "I'd like to observe the process when you're up to full function. La Reina, I've seen people we ought to speak to."

"Of course." They melted into the crowd.

"Wow," Poppy said as they moved away. She slapped a bright smile on her face, but he saw through to the woman who felt ground into the dust.

"This is why the house you found us is so perfect." He stroked her bare arms. "It's even farther away from them than this one."

Her hurt faded and her mouth twitched. "That's not nice."

"No. And you don't realize it, but he was being as nice as he gets. His asking to observe you is quite the commendation."

"Really?" She dipped her chin, skeptical.

"Mmm-hmm. If I cared about scoring points with my parents, I would be high-fiving you right now."

"We could dance instead," Poppy suggested. "What's wrong?"

"Nothing." Except he'd just recalled the steps he was taking that, as far as scoring points with his parents went, would wipe him to below zero in their books. He would owe future favors. *That* was the cost of giving in to base feelings like passion and infatuation.

So he wouldn't.

"Let's dance," he murmured and drew her onto the floor.

CHAPTER NINE

POPPY WAS FALLING for Rico. Really falling. This wasn't the secret crush of a maid for a man who hadn't even noticed her. It wasn't the sexual infatuation of a woman whose husband left her weak with satisfaction every night. It wasn't even the tender affinity of shared love for their daughter, although what she was feeling had its roots in all of those things.

This was the kind of regard her grandparents had felt for each other. She knew because she began doing the sorts of little things for Rico that they used to do for one another. If he tried a particular brandy while they were out, and liked it, she asked the housekeeper to order some in. When discussing the decor of his home office in the new house, she had the designer track down a signed print of his favorite racecar driver, now retired but still revered.

And when she had an appointment to spend the morning looking at photography equipment, she impulsively called Rico's assistant and asked if her husband had plans for lunch. He was pronounced available so she booked herself as his date and made a reservation, dropping in to surprise him.

His PA, a handsome man about her age whom she was meeting in person for the first time, rose to greet her. He looked startled. Alarmed. Maybe even appalled.

"Senora Montero. You're early." He smoothed his expression to a warm and welcoming smile. "I'm Anton. So good to meet you. Why don't I show you around while Senor Montero finishes his meeting?"

Poppy might be a country girl at heart, but she knew a slick city hustle when she was the victim of one. She balked, heart going into free fall. All her optimistic belief that she and Rico were making progress in their marriage disintegrated. One dread-filled question escaped her.

"Who is he with?"

Before Anton could spit out a suitable prevarication, the door to Rico's office cracked. He came out with an older couple. Everyone wore somber expressions.

Rico's face tightened with regret when he saw her. Anton offered a pinched smile of apology. He moved quickly to the closet where the older woman's light coat had been hung.

The older couple both stiffened, clearly recognizing her while Poppy's brain scrambled and somehow made the connection that they must be Faustina's parents.

The brief anguish she had suffered mildewed into horror. Rico wasn't meeting some Other Woman. *She* was that reviled creature.

How did one act in such a profoundly uncomfortable moment? What should she say? All she could conjure was the truth.

"I wanted to surprise you," she admitted to Rico,

voice thick with apology. "I didn't realize you would be tied up." She thought she might be sick.

Rico introduced her to the Cabreras. Neither put out their hand to shake so Poppy kept her own clutched over her purse, nodding and managing a small smile that wasn't returned.

"The woman you 'dated very briefly when your engagement was interrupted,'" Faustina's mother said with a dead look in her eye.

"I'm very sorry," Poppy choked, reminding herself that they had lost their only child and would hurt forever because of it.

"I'm sure you are," Senora Cabrera said bitterly. "Despite gaining all the prestige and wealth my daughter brought to this marriage. What do *you* bring except cheap notoriety and a bastard conceived in adultery?"

Poppy gasped and stumbled slightly as Rico scooped her close, pressing her to stand more behind him than beside him.

"The hypocrisy is mine. Don't take your anger out on Poppy." His tone was so dark and dangerous, she curled a fist into the fabric of his jacket in a useless effort to restrain him, fearing he would physically attack them. "Leave innocent babies out of this altogether."

A profound silence, then Senora Cabrera sniffed with affront. Her husband clenched his teeth so hard, Poppy could have sworn she heard them crunching like hard candy behind the flat line of his lips.

"I've given you some options," Rico continued in a marginally more civilized voice. "Let me know how you'd like to proceed."

"Options," Senor Cabrera spat. "None that are worth

accepting. This is hell," he told Rico forcefully. "You have sent us to hell, Rico. I hope you're happy."

The older man whirled and jerked his head at his wife. She hurried after him. Anton trotted to catch up and escort them to the elevator while Rico swore quietly and viciously as he strode back into his office.

Poppy followed on apprehensive feet, quietly closing the door and pressing her back against it. She watched him pour a drink.

"I am *so* sorry. Anton didn't tell me they would be here or I wouldn't have come. I asked him not to tell you I was dropping in. This is all my fault."

"I knew you were coming." He threw back a full shot. "I thought we would be finished an hour ago. It went long—you were early. Bad timing." He poured a second. "Do you want one?"

"It was that bad?" She wondered how many he'd had before talking to the older couple. Maybe she ought to make some espresso with that machine behind the bar.

"It was difficult." He poured two glasses and brought them to the low table where melting ice water and full cups of coffee sat next to untouched plates of biscotti. He set the fresh glasses into the mix and threw himself into an armchair.

She lowered herself to the sofa, briefly taking in the classic decor of the office with its bookshelves and antique desk. A younger version of Senor Cabrera looked down in judgment from a frame on the wall. She felt utterly helpless. Deserving of blame, yet Rico wasn't casting any, just slouching there, brooding.

"What sort of options did you give them?" She hated

to ask, sensing by their animosity his suggestions hadn't been well received.

"I told them I was stepping down."

"From being president?" A jolt went through her. It was the last thing she had expected. "Why?"

"I have to." He frowned as if it was obvious. "I had my parents prepare them for it when they informed them about you and Lily. I've stayed to keep things on an even keel, but today I gave them the alternatives for transitioning me out of the chair."

She could only blink, remembering what he had told her in the solarium the day Faustina had broken his engagement. Poppy hadn't meant to pry, but she had admitted to not understanding the appeal of an arranged marriage. She had been compelled to ask what he would have gained.

I was to become president of Faustina's father's chemical research firm. Cesar and I work very well together, but this would have given me a playground for my personal projects and ambitions. My chance to shine in my own spotlight.

He'd been self-deprecating, but she had sensed a real desire in him to prove something, if only to himself. She completely understood that. It was akin to what drove her interest in photography.

"What will you do?" she asked now.

"Go back to working under Cesar. There's always room for me there."

But it wasn't what he wanted. "You married Faustina so you could move out from his shadow. You have your own ambitions."

"I'll find another way to pursue them." He flicked his hand, dismissing that desire.

"But—" She frowned. "What happens with this company? Do they become your competitors again?"

"One option is to leave this enterprise under Cesar's direction. Another would be for us to sell this back to them at a discounted price. They'd be gaining a much more lucrative business than when I took over." He muttered into his glass. "So I think that's what they'll choose."

"How much would it impact you if they do? Financially, I mean?" Her blood was congealing in her veins. They'd just bought a house. Not a cute bungalow in a small prairie town that a union wage could pay off in twenty years, but a mansion with acres of grapes and the sort of view that cost more than the house. Her palms were sweating. "Why didn't you tell me this was happening?"

"Because it doesn't affect you. The sting in the pocketbook will be short-lived, some legal fees and a return of some stocks and other holdings. I'll have to restructure my personal portfolio, but our family has weathered worse. Things will balance out."

She could only sit there with a knot of culpability in her middle.

"Rico, I hate that I brought nothing to this marriage. I didn't know I was going to *cost* you. Not like this." Her eyes grew hot and she braced her elbows on her knees to cover her eyes with her palms. "I've been spending like a drunken sailor. I just ordered equipment for— I'll call them. Cancel it." She looked for her purse.

"Poppy." He leaned forward and caught her wrist.

"Don't take this the wrong way, but a few thousand euros on photography equipment isn't going to make a dent in what's about to change hands. Cesar and I have discussed how to finance this. You and I are perfectly fine."

"But this is my fault! Now he's going to hate me, too. Sorcha will stop being my friend. I'm sorry, Rico. I'm so sorry I slept with you and ruined everything."

Her words hit his ears in a crash, like the avalanche of rocks off a cliff that continued roaring and tumbling long after the first crack of thunder, leaving a whiff of acrid dust in the air.

They came on top of words spoken by Señora Cabrera that had made him see red. *A bastard conceived in adultery.*

That was not what Lily was. Their attack against Poppy had been equally blood boiling and now *Poppy* was expressing regret over their daughter's conception?

"Don't you *dare* say that."

Maybe it was the alcohol hitting his system, maybe it was the pent-up tension from his meeting releasing in a snap. Maybe it was simply that he was confronted with Poppy's emotions so often, he was beginning to tap into his own, but rather than suppress his anger, he let himself feel it. It raged through him because her words *hurt*.

"I told you I will never regard Lily as a mistake and don't you ever do it, either." He threw himself to his feet, trying to pace away from the burn of scorn that chased him. "I would give up every last penny I possess so long as I can have her in my life."

Damn, that admission made him uncomfortable. He

shot her a look and saw her sit back, hand over her chest, tears in her eyes. She was biting her lips together, chin crinkling.

Was he scaring her? He swore and pushed a hand into his hair, clenching hard enough to feel the pain of it, trying to grapple himself back under control.

"Thank you, Rico," she said in a voice that scraped. "I hope you know that's all I've ever wanted for her. Parents who love her. Not all of this." She flicked a hand around the room.

"I do know that." He swallowed a lump from his throat, but it remained lodged sideways in his chest. He felt pried open and stood there fighting the sensation.

"But I'm starting to see that you and your family support a lot more people than just me and Lily. It shouldn't be such a revelation to me. When I needed a job, your mother gave me one and I was grateful. Now I can see that this lifestyle you're protecting has value to more people than just you. That's why it's upsetting to me that I'm undermining it. I think I'd feel better about it if you'd at least yell at me."

"I'm not going to yell at you." Was he angry? Yes. About many things, but none that mattered as much as his daughter. "My career ambitions and the bearing our marriage has had on them are insignificant next to what I've gained through this marriage. *You brought our child.* There's nothing else you could have brought that comes close to how important she is to me."

There was a flash of something like yearning in her eyes before she screened them with her lashes. She reached to pluck a tissue from the box and pressed it under each eye.

"It means a lot that you would say that. I struggle with exactly what they said. Every day." Her mouth pulled down at the corners. "Feeling like I snuck in through a side door, using my daughter as a ticket. I feel like such an imposter." She sniffed.

"Stop feeling that way," he ordered, coming over to sit beside her, facing her. "It's a terrible thing to say, but I can't imagine Faustina showing our baby the same sort of love that you show Lily. I'm lucky my child has you as her mother."

Her eyes grew even bigger and swam with even more tears. Her mouth trembled in earnest.

"Please don't cry. You're making me feel like a jerk."

"You're being the opposite of a jerk. That's why I'm crying."

She had worn her hair in a low ponytail today and half of it was coming loose around her face. He wound a tendril around his finger, thinking of how often he saw her wince and pry Lily's fist from the mass, never scolding her for it.

How could anyone resist this mass, though? He dipped his head to rub the ribbon of silk against his lips. Watched her gaze drop to his mouth and tried not to get distracted.

"There's something I've been wanting to ask you," Rico began.

Her gaze flashed upward, brimming with inquisitive light. "Yes?"

Unnatural, fearful hope filled him even as he second-guessed what was on his tongue. He couldn't believe these words were forming inside him. Not as the next strategic move in the building of the Montero empire, either. Not in reaction to what outsiders said about their marriage. No, this was something that had been bubbling in him from the earliest days of their marriage, something he didn't want to examine too closely because it occupied such a deep cavern inside him.

"Rico?" she prompted.

"With the house almost ready, I keep thinking we should talk about filling more of those rooms."

Her pupils threatened to swallow her face. "Another baby?"

"I know you wanted to wait." He let go of her hair and covered the hand that went limp against his thigh. He pressed his lips together, bracing himself for rebuff. "If you're not ready, we can table it, but I wanted to mention it. My relationship with Pia and Cesar—we're not as close as some, but I value them. I realize many things contribute to the distance between you and your half-siblings, but the age gap is a factor. That's why I thought sooner than later would benefit Lily."

He heard his upbringing in the logic of his argument and recognized it as the defense tactic it was. If he kept his feelings firmly out of the discussion, there was no chance they would get trampled on.

Poppy blinked and a fresh tear hit her cheek, diamond bright. "Are you being serious? You want to make a baby with me *on purpose*?"

The magnitude wasn't lost on him. Marriages could be undone. Property could be split. The entanglement of a child—*children*, if he had any say in it—was a far bigger and more permanent commitment.

"I do."

* * *

"You didn't tell me there's such a thing as a babymoon,"
Rico said a month later as they toured the empty rooms
of their villa, inspecting freshly painted walls, window
treatments and light fixtures. Furniture delivery would
start next week.

"You'd have seen one by now if you had ever changed
a diaper," she teased. "Instead of handing Lily off to
the nanny."

Rico's mouth twitched, but he only drew her onto
the private balcony off their master bedroom. It made
her feel like the queen of the world to stand there looking so far out on the Mediterranean she was sure she
glimpsed the cowboy boot of Italy.

"Besides, we're not there yet."

After a visit to the doctor a couple of weeks ago,
they were officially "trying." Today, Rico had asked
the designer about setting up a nursery *when the time
comes*. The woman had cheerfully promised a quick
turnaround on redecorating the room of their choice.
"Most couples take a babymoon for a few weeks so we
aren't disrupting their daily life," the woman had added,
then had to explain to Rico what it was.

"We never even had a honeymoon," he pointed out
now.

"There's been a lot going on. A lot for Lily to adjust
to. I wouldn't want to leave her even now, when we're
about to move into this house and change everything
again."

"We could take her with us."

"I think that's called a family vacation, not a honeymoon."

"You're full of cheek today, aren't you?" He gave one of her lower ones a friendly squeeze. "We could take the nanny so we get our alone time. Really put our back into the honeymoon effort. See if we can't earn ourselves a babymoon."

She chuckled. "So romantic." But she kissed him under his chin, ridiculously in love when he was playful like this—

Oh. There it was. The acknowledgment she'd been avoiding. Because if she admitted to herself that she was fully head over heels, she had to face that he wasn't.

"Romance is not my strong point, but sound logic is."

He gathered her so her arms were folded against his chest, fingertips grazing his open collar, but his words echoed through the hollow spaces growing wider in her chest.

"The transition is almost finished with the Cabreras," he continued. "Cesar has some projects he wants me to take the lead on in a couple of months. I won't have much downtime once I'm knee-deep. This is our window for a getaway. Let's take it."

"If you want to," she murmured, thinking she ought to feel happy. Excited. But she only felt sad. She felt the way she had as a child, wishing her mother and father wanted her. It shouldn't have mattered. She'd been loved by her grandparents.

But she'd still felt the absence of it from people she thought *should* love her.

And she felt it again now.

"What's wrong?"

"Nothing," she lied, conjuring a smile. "Where…? Um…where would you want to go?"

"I don't know. Somewhere that Lily would enjoy and you could play with your new camera. Maybe we could tie in a visit to your grandmother at the end. I know you're missing her."

"You wouldn't mind?"

"Of course not. I wish she would agree to come live with us here. You know you can visit her anytime. I'll come with you as often as I can."

"Thank you." A tiny spark of hope returned. Whenever he doted on her, she thought maybe he *was* coming to love her. Tentative light crept through her. "Okay. Let's do it."

Two weeks later, they were riding elephants through the rainforests of Thailand.

"This is not camping," she told him when they arrived at the hidden grotto where sleep pods were suspended in the trees. "Camping is digging a trench around your tent in a downpour at midnight so you don't drown in your sleep."

"I think this is 'glamping,'" the nanny murmured in an aside as the pod she would share with Lily was pointed out to her. "And *thank you*."

They dined on rare mushrooms and wild boar, coconut curry soup and tropical fruit with cashews. When they fell asleep, replete from lovemaking, the wind rocked their pod and the frogs crooned a lullaby. They woke to strange birdcalls and the excited trumpet of a baby elephant as it trampled into a mud pool.

Poppy caught some of the elephant's antics with her new toy, a Leica M6. She switched out to her new digital camera to catch some shots of Lily to send to Gran then held her as she fed the baby elephant, chuckling as Lily squealed in delight.

A click made her look up and she found Rico capturing them on his phone.

"New screen saver," he said as he tucked it away.

Poppy flushed with pleasure, in absolute heaven. She began to think she really was living happily-ever-after, cherished by her husband, making a family with him. Her life couldn't be more ideal.

Then, as they came off their last day in the forest to stay a few days at a luxury beach resort on the coast, she discovered that, for all their success the first time, they weren't so lucky this time. She wasn't one-and-done pregnant.

It wasn't even the light spotting that had fooled her with Lily. She had a backache and a heavier than normal case of the blues.

Plenty of women didn't conceive right away. There was no reason she should take it this hard. She knew that in her head, but her heart was lying there in two jagged pieces anyway.

Rico came into the bedroom of their suite as she was coming out of the bathroom.

"I sent the nanny to the beach with Lily. We—" He took off his sunglasses and frowned. "What's wrong?"

He wore a T-shirt and shorts better than any man she'd ever met. The shirt clung to his sculpted shoulders and chest and his legs were tanned and muscled. One of her favorite things in the world was the scrape of his fine hair when she ran the inside of her thigh against his iron-hard ones.

Everything about him was perfect.

And she wasn't. She hadn't even gotten this right.

"It's not working. I'm not pregnant."

"Oh." He was visibly taken aback. "You're sure?"

She bit back a tense, *Of course I'm sure*, and only said, "Yes." She turned her back and threw sunscreen and a few other things into a beach bag.

"But it only took once last time."

"I know that." She drew a patience-gathering breath. "I don't know why it didn't happen." She blinked, fighting tears. "But it didn't and there's nothing I can do about it."

"Poppy." He touched her arm. "It's fine. We're having fun trying, right? Next time."

She didn't want him to be disappointed. That would make her feel worse. But it didn't help to hear him brush it off, either. She dug through her bag, unable to remember if she'd thrown her book in there.

"You go. I'll catch up."

"Poppy. Come on. Don't be upset. This isn't a test that we have to pass or fail."

"Not for you it isn't. For me? Yes it is. Every single day! Either I bring value to this marriage or I'm just a hanger-on."

"I have *never* meant to make you feel like that."

"I feel like that because that's what I *am*." The rope handle of her bag began to cut into her shoulder. She threw the whole works onto the floor, standing outside herself and knowing this was toddler-level behavior, but there was poison sitting deep inside her. The kind that had to come out before it turned her completely septic. "At least when I was looking after my grandparents, I was *contributing*. You don't need me to look after Lily. The nanny does most of the work."

"You *love* Lily. I told you that's all—"

"Yes! I love her. That's what I bring. The ability to give you babies and love them. Except now there's no baby." She flung out a hand.

"We've just started trying! Look." He attempted to take her by the shoulders, but she brushed him off and backed away. "Poppy. I don't know much about this process, but I do know it takes some couples a while. There is no need to be this upset."

"I *want* to be upset!" She hated how backed into a corner she felt. She pushed past him and strode to the middle of the room only to spin around and confront. "But I'm not allowed to be upset, am I? There's no such thing as emotion in your world, is there? I'm supposed to fit into a tiny little box labeled Wife and Mother." She made a square with her hands. "And uphold the family image, except I'll never be able to do that because I'm forever going to be a blotch."

"Calm down," he ordered.

She flung out a hand in a silent, *There it is*.

He heard it, too, and sighed. He gave her a stern look. "You're not a blotch. We've been over all of this. You contribute. I don't know why you struggle to believe that."

"Because I've been a burden my entire life, Rico. My grandparents were planning to do things in their retirement. Take bus tours and travel and *see* things. Instead, they were stuck raising me."

"It didn't sound to me like that was how your grandmother felt."

"That's still how it *was*. That's how I wound up working in your mother's house. I couldn't bear the thought of asking them for money when they'd supported me all those years. Then I came home and bam. Pregnant. Back to being a parasite. Gramps didn't want to sell that house because he was afraid I would go broke paying day care and rent. I was supposed to pay Gran back after all those years she took care of me, but now you're supporting her. *And* me. That feels *great*."

"You are not a parasite. Eleanor is my daughter's great-grandmother. I *want* to look after her. And you."

"See, that's it." She lifted a helpless hand. "Right there. You don't want to look after *me*." She pressed her hand to the fissure in her chest where all her emotions were bleeding out and making a mess on the floor. "You want to look after Lily's mother. Exactly the way they took in their son's daughter for his sake. You don't want *me*, Rico."

"You're upset. Taking things to heart that don't require this much angst."

Her heart was the problem. That much he had right. It felt like her heart was beating outside her chest.

"Do you love me?" she asked, already knowing the answer. "Do you think you're ever going to love me?"

Her question gave him pause. The fact a watchful expression came across his face as he searched for a response that was kind yet truthful was all the answer she needed.

"Because I love you," she admitted, feeling no sense of relief as the words left barbs in her throat. Her lips were so wobbly, her speech was almost slurred. "I love you so much I ache inside, all the time. I want so badly to be enough for you—"

"You are," he cut in gruffly.

"Well, you're not enough for me!" The statement burst out of her, breaking something open in her. Between them. All the delicate filaments that had connected them turned to dust, leaving him pallid. Leaving her throat arid and the rest of her blistered with self-hatred as she threw herself on the pyre, adding, "This isn't enough."

His breath hissed in.

"At least my grandparents loved me, despite the fact I'd been dumped on them. But I waited my whole childhood for my parents to want me. To love me. I can't live like that again, Rico. I can't take up space in your home because your children need a mother. I need more. And what breaks my heart is knowing that you're capable of it. You love Lily. I know you do. But you don't love me and you won't and *that's not fair*."

He let her go.

He shouldn't have let her walk out, but he didn't know what to say. He knew what she wanted to hear him say, but those words had never passed his lips.

From his earliest recollection of hearing the phrase, when he realized other children said those words to their parents, he had instinctively understood it wasn't a sentiment his own parents would want to hear from him. They weren't a family who said such a thing. They weren't supposed to feel it. Or *want* to feel it.

So he let her walk out and close the door with a polite click that sounded like the slam of a vault, locking him out of something precious he had only glimpsed for a second.

Which seemed to empty him of his very soul.

He looked around, recalling dimly that he'd thought to enjoy an afternoon delight before joining their daughter on the beach for sand castles and splashing in the waves.

Not pregnant. He had to admit that had struck harder than he would have expected. It left a hole in his chest that he couldn't identify well enough to plug. He knew how to manage his expectations. He'd spent his entire life keeping his low, so as not to suffer disappointment or loss. Despite that, he was capable of both. He wanted to go after Poppy and ask again, *Are you sure?*

She was sure. The bleak look in her eyes had kicked him in the gut. He wasn't ready to face that again. That despair had nearly had him telling her they didn't have to try again ever, not if a lack of conception was going to hit her so hard it broke something in her.

He wanted a baby, though. The compulsion to build on what they had was beyond voracious. How could Poppy not realize she was an integral part of this new sense of family he was only beginning to understand?

Family wasn't what he'd been taught—loyalty and rising to responsibility, sharing a common history and acting for the good of the whole. That was part of it, but family was also a smiling kiss greeting him when he walked in the door. It was a trusting head on his shoulder and decisions made together. It was a sense that he could relax. That he would be judged less harshly by those closest to him. His mistakes would be forgiven.

Forgive me, he thought despairingly.

And heard her say again, *You're not enough for me.*

He was still trying to find his breath after that one. He knew how it felt to be accepted on condition, better than she realized. The gold standard for approval in his childhood had been a mastery over his emotions. Tears were weakness, passion vulgar. He should only go after things that made sense, that benefited the family, not what he *wanted*.

Do you love me?

He didn't know how. That was the bitter truth.

He would give Poppy nearly anything she asked for, but he refused to say words to her that weren't sincere. How the hell would he know one way or the other if what he felt was love, though? He hadn't had any exposure to that elusive emotion, not until his brother had gone off the rails with Sorcha, causing his parents to shrink in horror, further reinforcing to Rico that deep emotions prompted destructive madness.

Love had *killed* Faustina, for God's sake.

He hated himself for hurting Poppy, though. For failing her. The sick ache sat inside him as he went out and looked for her. She wasn't on a lounger under the cabana with the nanny, watching Lily play in a shaded pocket of sand.

He moved to stand near them, scanning for Poppy, figuring she would turn up here eventually.

It took him a moment to locate her, walking in the wet sand where waves washed ashore and retreated. Was she crying? She looked so desolate on that empty stretch so far from the cheerful crowd of the resort beach.

She wasn't a burden. It killed him that her parents had

let her grow up feeling anything less than precious. She brought light into darkness, laughter into sober rooms.

She had brought him Lily—literally life. He glanced at his daughter. She was batting down each of the castles the nanny made for her. The most enormous well-being filled him whenever he was anywhere near this little sprite. Poppy shone like the sun when she was with Lily, clearly the happiest she could possibly be.

That was why he wanted another baby. He didn't know how to express what he felt for Poppy except to physically make another of these joy factories. With her. He wanted her to have more love. The best of himself, packaged new and flawless, without the jagged edges and rusted wheels. Clean, perfect, unconditional love.

From him.

He swallowed, hands in fists as he absorbed that he may not know how to love, how to express it, but it was inside him. He would die for Lily and if Poppy was hurting, he was hurting.

He couldn't bear that. Not for one more minute.

He looked for her again, intent on going after her.

She had wandered even farther down the beach, past the flags and signage that warned of—

He began jogging after her, to call her back.

Long before he got there, the sea reached with frothy arms that gathered around her legs and dragged her in. One second she was there, the next she was gone.

"Poppy!" he hollered at the top of his lungs and sprinted down the beach.

One moment she was wading along, waves breaking on her shins. Without warning, the water swirled higher.

It dragged with incredible strength against her thighs, eroding the sand from beneath her feet at the same time. The dual force knocked her off-balance and she fell, splooshing under.

It shocked her out of her morose tears, but she knew how to swim. She mostly felt like an idiot, tumbling like a drunk into the surf. As she sputtered to the surface, she glanced around, hoping no one had witnessed her clumsiness.

As she tried to get her feet under her, however, she couldn't find the bottom. She was in far deeper water than she ought to be. As she gave a little dog paddle to get back toward the beach, she realized she was being sucked away from it. Fast.

Panic struck in a rush of adrenaline. She willed herself not to give in to it. This was a rip current. She only knew one thing about them and that was to swim sideways out of it.

She tried, but the beach was disappearing quickly, making her heart beat even quicker. Her swimsuit wrap was dragging and tangling on her arms. When she tried to call out for help, she caught a mouthful of salt water and was so far away, no one would hear her anyway.

Terrified, she flipped onto her back, floating and kicking, trying to get her bearings while she wrestled herself free of the wrap and caught her breath.

Think, think, think.

Oh, dear God. She popped straight and the people were just the size of ants. Had anyone even noticed she'd been swept out? She looked for a boat. Were there sharks? *Don't panic.*

She was beyond where the waves were breaking.

This was where surfers would usually gather, sitting on their boards as they watched the hump of waves, picking and choosing which to ride into shore.

She didn't know how to bodysurf, though. It was all she could do to keep her head up as the waves picked her up and rolled toward the beach without her.

Treading water, she saw nothing, only what looked like a very long swim to shore. She thought she might be on the far side of the current that had carried her out. A crosscurrent was drifting her farther toward the headland, away from where she'd left Lily on the beach.

Lily. She tried not to cry. Lily was safe, she reminded herself.

This was such a stupid mess to be in. She had picked a fight with Rico then walked away to sulk. Why? What did she have to complain about? He treated her like a queen. No one she knew took tropical vacations and rode elephants and slept in five-star oceanfront villas with butler service to the beach.

I'm sorry, baby, she said silently as she began to crawl her arms over her head, aiming for the headland that was a lot farther than she'd ever swum in her life. A few laps in a pool were her limit. Just enough to get her safety badge when she was ten. *I'm sorry, Rico. Please, Gramps, if you can hear me, I need help.*

Rico absconded with a Jet Ski, scaring an adolescent boy into giving it up with whatever expression was on his face. The only words he'd had in him had been a grated, "My wife."

Her coral wrap had been his beacon as he raced to the family with the Jet Skis. Now it was gone.

He ran the Jet Ski along the edge of the riptide, gaze trying to penetrate the cloudy water, searching for a glint of color, of red hair, terrified he'd find her in it and terrified he wouldn't.

He sped out to where the head of the current mushroomed beyond the surf zone, dissipating in a final cloud of sand pulled from the beach. Still nothing.

Dimly he noted two surfers and a lifeguard from the resort joining his search, zigzagging through the surf.

He had to find her. *Had to.*

In a burst of speed, he started down the far side of the rip and had to fight the Jet Ski to get back toward the current. Another one, not as strong, ran parallel to the beach. He realized she might have been drawn toward the headland. It was a huge stretch of water to get there.

Despair began to sink its claws into him.

Bill, help us out, he silently begged her grandfather's spirit.

A glint above the water caught his attention. A drone?

He looked toward the beach and saw the operator waving him toward the headland.

Using the drone as a beacon, he gunned the Jet Ski that direction, searched the chop of waves. *Please, please, please.*

A slender arm slowly came out of the water. It windmilled in a tired backstroke, slapping wearily on re-entry.

Swearing, he raced toward her. The resignation in her eyes as she spotted him told him how close she'd been to giving up. He got near enough she put a hand on the machine, but he had to turn it off and get in the water with her to get her onto it, she was that weak.

She sat in front of him, trembling and coughing, breaths panting and heart hammering through her back into his own slamming in his chest. She hunched weakly while he reached to start the Jet Ski again. He shifted her slightly so he could hold on to her and steered it back to shore.

He was shaking. Barely processing anything other than that he had to get them to dry land.

"I'm sorry," she said when he got to the small dock where the startled family had gathered with damned near every living soul in Thailand.

The crowd gave them a round of applause. The nanny stood with Lily on her hip, eyes wide with horror at the barely averted catastrophe.

"Oh, Lily," Poppy sobbed, and hugged her daughter, but Lily squirmed at her mother's wet embrace.

A lifeguard came to check on Poppy.

"Have a hot shower. You'll be in shock. Lie down and stay warm. Drink lots of water to flush the seawater you drank."

Rico nodded and took her into their villa, bringing her straight into the shower and starting it, peeling off their wet clothes as they stood under the spray.

"I'm so sorry," she said, feeling like she was drowning all over again as the fresh water poured like rain upon them.

He dragged at the tie on her bikini top only to tighten the knot. He turned her and she felt his fingers between her shoulder blades, picking impatiently at the knot.

"I wasn't paying attention. It was stupid. I'm really sorry. Please don't think I did that on purpose. I was upset, but I wouldn't leave Lily. I know she needs me."

"I need you!" he shouted, making her jump.

She turned around and backed into the tiles, catching the loosened top so she clutched the soggy, hanging cups against her cold breasts.

"You scared the hell out of me. I thought—" His face spasmed and she saw drops on his cheeks that might have been from the shower, but might have been something else. "What would I do without you, Poppy?"

He cupped her face and the incendiary light in his eyes was both fury and something else. Something that made her hold her breath as he tenderly pressed his thumbs to the corners of her mouth.

"I wanted to go looking for you the day after the solarium. Do you know that? I didn't know where to start. Ask the staff? It was too revealing. Try to catch you at the hostel? The airport? You hadn't told me the name of the town where you lived, but I imagined I could find out. I didn't want to wait that long or travel that far, though. Not if I could catch you before you left."

He was talking in a voice so thick and heavy with anguish it made her ache.

"It was an irrational impulse, Poppy. We don't have those in this family. I couldn't admit to *myself* how attracted I was. I couldn't let anyone else see it, not even you. I had to live up to my responsibilities. After Cesar, *I* had to show some sense. It was better to let you go. *But I didn't want to.*"

Her mouth trembled. "Then Faustina took away any choice you might have."

"Yes." He moved his hands to lift the bathing suit cups off her chest and high enough to pull the tie free from behind her neck.

Her hair fell in wet tendrils onto her shoulders. He drew her back under the spray, took a squirt of fragrant body wash in his palm and turned her to rub the warm lather over her back and shoulders, working heat into her tired, still trembling muscles.

"Everything in my world went gray. Through the wedding, into my marriage and after she was gone. I didn't care about anything. I had achieved maximum indifference." His hands dug their soapy massage into her muscles, strong and reassuring. "Then Sorcha told me you might have had my baby. I tried to approach the situation rationally. I did. But the test came back inconclusive and I got on the plane. I had to see you. I had to know."

"What if Lily hadn't been yours?"

He turned her. A faint smile touched his mouth. "Can you imagine? There I was spitting fire and fury and you might have said she was Ernesto's."

"The seventy-year-old gardener? Yes, he's always been my type."

He turned her to settle her back against his chest. He ran his firm palms across her upper chest and down her arms, not trying to arouse, but the warmth tingling through her held flickers of the desire that always kindled when they were close.

"I have a feeling it wouldn't have mattered if she wasn't mine." His voice was a grave rumble in his chest. A somber vow against her ear. "I can't see myself turning around and going home just because I happened to be wrong. One way or another, you were meant to be here in my life. I was meant to be Lily's father."

She swallowed, astonished. Shaken. Questioning whether this man of logic really believed in fate.

"You're talking like your bohemian wife who thinks her grandfather can talk to her through the stars."

His hand slowed and his chin rested against her hair. "You think I didn't ask him for help? Did you see the drone above you?"

"No. But that would be a tourist, not Gramps."

"It was in the sky, Poppy. I was begging him for some sign of you."

He turned her to face him.

Her arms twined themselves around his neck because they knew that was where they belonged. Lather lingered to provide a sensual friction between their torsos.

"I love you." He stared deeply into her eyes as he spoke, allowing her to see all the way to the depths of his soul. To the truth of his statement. "I'm sorry it took something like this for me to say it. To *feel* it. In my defense, it was there—I just didn't know what it was."

She tried to hold it together, but her emotions were still all over the place. Her mouth trembled and tears leaked to join the water hitting her cheeks. "I love you, too." Her voice quavered. "I shouldn't have said you weren't enough. I was upset."

"I know." His gaze grew pained. "Maybe instead of 'trying,' we'll just see. Hmm? I don't want you to think our marriage hinges on whether we have another baby. I love *you*."

"Okay. But I really do want your baby." The yearning and disappointment was still there, but as she let her head rest on his shoulder, the hollowness eased. The darkness was dispelled by the light of his love.

"Me, too." He pressed his wet lips to her crown. "And when the time is right, I'm sure we'll have one."

Weeks later, Rico crowded her to scan the strips of negatives with her.

"I want the one I took of you in front of the waterfall," he said.

Poppy never minded the touch of his body against hers, but, "You're here to tell me how your father will behave. Act like him and pick something he might like."

His parents were coming for an early dinner, their first visit to the finished house. Sorcha and Cesar had plans elsewhere so it would be only the four of them. They would show them the beehives and the wine cellar and, at the explicit request of the duque, Poppy would demonstrate her darkroom.

"The waterfall is a good shot," Rico said, not backing off one hairbreadth. "The ripples in your hair mirrored the path of the water. I've wanted to see it since I took it."

It was poorly framed and crooked, but she could fix that.

Actually, it was a decent shot, she decided, once the negative was in the enlarger. It was perfectly focused and the light was quite pretty, dappling through the jungle leaves. It was taken from behind her. She sat up to her waist in the water, looking toward the waterfall. She had been wearing her bikini and the strings were hidden by the fall of her hair so she looked like a naked nymph spied in her natural habitat.

"I am not showing this one to your father."

She had already run test strips from this batch so she set her timer and switched the overhead light to red. Then she set the paper for exposure.

"How long do we have?" His hands settled on her waist.

"Not long enough." The timer went off and she chuckled at the noise of disappointment that escaped him.

She moved the paper into the developer bath and gently rocked until the second timer pinged. She moved the paper to the fixing bath, explaining as she went.

"This last one is water, to wash off the chemicals." She left the image in the final bath.

"See? It's great," he said.

"It is," she agreed, washing her hands and drying them. "*Now* ask me how much time we have."

"Enough?"

"It shouldn't stay in there more than thirty minutes." She closed one eye and wrinkled her nose. "But we shouldn't stay in *here* more than thirty minutes or we won't have time to get ready for our guests."

"I can work with that."

"I know you can," she purred throatily and held up her arms.

He ambled close, crowded her against the counter beside the sink then lifted her to sit upon it. "Have I told you lately how much I love you?"

Every day. She cradled his hard jaw in soft hands, grazing her lips against the stubble coming in because he hadn't yet shaved. "Have I told you lately that you make all of my dreams come true?"

Maybe not all. They were still "seeing," not "trying," but their love was tender and new. They were protecting it with gentle words and putting no pressure on it with expectations they couldn't control.

"I want to," he said, hands slowing as he ran them over her back and up to pull the thick elastic from her hair. "I want you to be happy."

"I am. So happy I don't know how to contain it all." She skimmed her fingers down to his shirt buttons, good at this now. She smiled as she spread the white shirt. It glowed pink in the red light. She slid light fingers across the pattern of hair flat against thick muscle and drew a circle around his dark nipples.

"Me, too," he said, skimming the strap of her sundress down her shoulder and setting kisses along the tendon at the base of her neck. "I didn't know happiness like this was possible. That it was as simple as opening my heart, loving and allowing myself to be loved. You humble me, being brave enough to teach me that."

This was supposed to be a playful quickie, but his words and the tenderness in his touch were turning it into something far more profound.

"This is what I wanted the day we made love the first time. I wanted to know the man you didn't show to anyone else. Thank you for trusting yourself to me." She held his head in her hands, gazed on the handsome face that she read so easily these days. She pressed her mouth to his.

He took over, gently ravaging in a way that was hungry and passionate and reverent. She responded the way she always did, helplessly and without reserve. She trusted herself to him, too, and it was worth that risk.

Their intimacy went beyond the right to open his belt or slide a hand beneath her skirt. His touch was possessive and greedy, but caring and knowing. Hers wasn't hesitant or daring, but confident and welcomed with a growl of appreciation.

He slowed and gazed into her eyes, not because he sensed she needed it, but because, like her, he sensed the magnitude of the moment wrapping around them. Their love would grow over time, but it was real and fixed and imprinted into their souls now. Irrevocable. Unshakable.

They moved in concert, sliding free of the rest of their clothes, losing her panties to a dark corner, drawing close again and *there*. He filled her in a smooth joining that set hot tears of joy to dampen her lashes.

"I love you," she whispered, clinging her arms and legs around him. "I love when we're like this. This is everything."

"Mi amor," he murmured. "You're my heart. My life. Be mine, always."

They moved in the muted struggle of soul mates trying to break the limits of the physical world and become one. For a time, as they moved with synchronicity, mouths sealed and hands chasing shivers across each other's skin, they were nearly there. The rapture held them in a world where only the other existed, where the culmination was a small death to be eluded before the ecstasy of heaven swallowed them whole. Golden light bathed them as they held that delicious shudder of simultaneous orgasm.

Slowly it faded and they drifted back to the earthly world. Poppy came back to awareness of the hard surface where her backside was balanced, the leather of Rico's belt chafing her inner thigh. One bared breast was pressed to his damp chest, his heart still knocking against the swell. His breathing was as unsteady as hers, his arms folded tightly across her back, securing her in her precarious position. She nuzzled her nose in his neck and licked lightly at the salty taste near his Adam's apple.

Within her, he pulsed a final time. She clenched in response.

"I may have a small fetish for the scent of vinegar and sulfur for the rest of my life," he teased, nuzzling her hair. "That was incredible."

She suspected they might have a small something else after this, but she didn't say it. It was only a feeling. An instinct. A premonition she didn't want to jinx.

It proved true a few weeks later.

"Really?" Rico demanded with cautious joy. "It's absolutely confirmed? Because—"

"I know," she assured him, understanding why he was being so careful about getting attached to the idea. She had been wary to believe it, too, despite missing a cycle and having a home test show positive. "But the doctor said yes. I'm pregnant."

He said something under his breath that might have been a curse or a murmur of thanks to a higher power. When he drew her into his embrace, she discovered he was shaking. She felt his chest swell as he consciously took a slow, regulated breath and let it out.

"You're happy?" she guessed, grinning ear to ear, eyes wet as she twined her arms around his waist.

"I want to tell the whole world."

"Most people don't tell anyone until after twelve weeks."

"Can I tell Lily?"

That cracked her up. "Sure. Go ahead."

After a frown of concentration, Lily grabbed a doll by the hair and offered it to Poppy. "Baby."

"Pretty much how I expect my mother to react," Rico drawled. "But at least you and I know what an important occasion this is. Where should we go on our babymoon?"

"I was thinking exotic Saskatchewan?"

"To see your Gran? Excellent idea. But first, come here." He drew her into his lap and kissed her. "I love you."

"I love you, too."

They kissed again and might have let it get a lot steamier, but Lily stuck an arm into the cuddle and said, "Me."

"Yes, I love you, too. Come on." Rico scooped her onto Poppy's lap and kissed the top of his daughter's head. "I don't know where we'll put the new baby, but we'll find room."

EPILOGUE

One year later...

POPPY WATCHED RICO carefully set their infant son in her grandmother's welcoming arms while Poppy's heart swelled so big, she thought it would burst.

"Sé gentil," Lily cautioned her great-grandmother with wide eyes.

"English, button," Rico reminded her, skimming his hand over the rippling red-gold waves. He called Lily button and angel and he called Poppy flash and treasure and keeper of my heart.

"Be gentle," Lily repeated in the near whisper they'd been coaching her to use when her little brother was sleeping. She was two and a half and talking a blue streak in two different languages, sneaking in a little Valencian and the Swiss nanny's French here and there.

"I will be very gentle, my darling," Gran said with a beaming smile and damp eyes. "Will you stand here beside my chair while your mama takes our picture?"

Rico stepped out of the frame, waited while Poppy snapped, then took the camera so she would have a few of her with her grandmother and the children. She didn't let herself wonder how many more chances she would get for photos like this, only embraced that she still had the opportunity today.

"He's beautiful," Gran said, tracing her aged fingertip across the sleep-clenched fist of Guillermo, named for her husband, William. "And heavy," she added ruefully.

"He is," Poppy agreed, gathering up Memo, as Lily was already calling him. Poppy kissed his warm, plump cheek. "Two kilos more than Brenna—that's Sorcha and Cesar's little girl. She's only a couple of weeks younger."

"Brenna is, is, is—" Lily hurried to interject with important information, but hit a wall with her vocabulary.

"Your cousin, sweetheart."

"My cousin," she informed Gran.

"You're very lucky, aren't you? To have a little brother and cousins, too."

"Mateo is bossy."

"Mateo might express similar opinions about his cousin," Rico said with dry amusement, waving Poppy to sit on one end of Gran's small sofa. He took the other and patted his knee for Lily to come into his lap.

Lily relaxed into his chest, head tilted to blink adoringly at her daddy. "Can I see Mateo?"

"In a few days. We're visiting Gran and then we're going camping. Remember?" Poppy said.

"And buy Mateo a toy," Lily recalled.

"That's right. Before we go home, we'll buy toys for him and Enrique."

"And Brenna?"

"And Brenna," Poppy agreed.

"You were so homesick when you first went to Spain. Now look how happy you are." Eleanor reached out her hand to Rico. He took it in his own. "Thank you for making her smile like this."

"Thank *you*." He secured Lily on his lap as he leaned across to kiss Gran's pale knuckles. "We still have a room in Spain for you," he told her for the millionth time. "It's very warm there."

"I'm too old for migrating around the world like a sea turtle," she dismissed with a wave of her hand. "I have my sister and my friends here. But you're sweet to keep asking."

They stayed through the dinner hour so Gran could show off her great-grandchildren and handsome grandson-in-law.

"Poppy is becoming famous for her photography," Gran made a point of announcing over dessert. "There was a bidding war at the auction."

"It was for charity," Poppy said, blushing and downplaying it. "Rico's brother was being nice, topping each bid."

"Don't be modest. That's not what happened at all," Rico chided. "Cesar was incensed that people kept trying to outbid him. My sister-in-law wanted it and he wanted her to have it."

"It was so silly," Poppy said, still blushing. "I could have printed her another."

"They wanted the only one and now they have it," Rico said. The negative had been signed and mounted into the frame. "Poppy has an agent and is filling out her portfolio. We expect she'll have her first show next year. We're heading north in the morning, hoping to catch the aurora borealis."

The whole table said, "Ooh."

The next night, they were ensconced in a resort that billed itself as one of the best places for viewing the northern lights. Their children were abed, the nanny reading a book by the fire and Poppy and Rico were tramping through the trees to a lake that reflected the stars and the sky.

The world was still and monochromatic under the moonlight, the air crisp with the coming fall. They stood holding hands a long moment, absorbing the silence.

"Well, Gramps," Poppy murmured. "We haven't heard from you in ages. Care to say hello?"

Nothing.

"I vote we pass the time by necking," Rico said.

"I always have time for that," Poppy agreed, going into his arms.

His lips were almost touching hers when she sensed something and opened her eyes. She began to laugh.

"There he is."

Rico looked above them and couldn't dismiss the appearance with science. Like love, it was inexplicable, beautiful magic.

* * * * *

COMING SOON!

We really hope you enjoyed reading this book. If you're looking for more romance, be sure to head to the shops when new books are available on

Thursday 22ⁿᵈ August

To see which titles are coming soon, please visit

millsandboon.co.uk/nextmonth